The Best
AMERICAN
ESSAYS
2013

The Best AMERICAN ESSAYS® 2013

Edited and with an Introduction
by CHERYL STRAYED

Robert Atwan, Series Editor

A Mariner Original

HOUGHTON MIFFLIN HARCOURT

BOSTON · NEW YORK 2013

ISSN 0888-3742
ISBN 978-0-544-10388-7

Printed in the United States of America
DOC 10 9 8 7 6 5 4 3 2 1

"The Art of Being Born" by Marcia Aldrich. First published in *Hotel Amerika*, Spring 2012. Copyright © 2013 by Marcia Aldrich. Reprinted by permission of Marcia Aldrich.

"Free Rent at the Totalitarian Hotel" by Poe Ballantine. First published in *The Sun*, June 2012. Copyright © 2012 by Poe Ballantine. Reprinted by permission of Poe Ballantine.

"What Happens in Hell" by Charles Baxter. First published in *Ploughshares*, Fall 2012. Copyright © 2012 by Charles Baxter. Reprinted by permission of Darhansoff & Verrill Literary Agents.

"Letter from Majorca" by J. D. Daniels. First published in *The Paris Review*, Summer 2012. Copyright © 2012 by J. D. Daniels. Reprinted by permission of J. D. Daniels.

"His Last Game" by Brian Doyle. First published in *Notre Dame Magazine*, Autumn 2012. Copyright © 2012 by Brian Doyle. Reprinted by permission of Brian Doyle.

"A Little Bit of Fun Before He Died" by Dagoberto Gilb. First published in *ZYZZYVA*, Fall 2012. Copyright © 2012 by Dagoberto Gilb. Reprinted by permission of Dagoberto Gilb. "Fun" by Wyn Cooper originally appeared in *The Country of Here Below*, Ahsahta Press, 1987. Reprinted by permission of the author.

"When They Let Them Bleed" by Tod Goldberg. First published in *Hobart*, Winter/Spring 2012. Copyright © 2012 by Tod Goldberg. Reprinted by permission of Tod Goldberg.

"The Book of Knowledge" by Steven Harvey. First published in *River Teeth*,

Contents

Foreword

WHEN I BEGAN STUDYING literature as a graduate student in the early 1960s, I approached the subject in ways so many of my generation did, as the study of poetry, fiction, and drama. My bible at the time was a critical volume published in the late 1940s by René Wellek and Austin Warren called *Theory of Literature*, which clearly privileged fictive works over nonfiction, though literary works then were so exclusively identified with poems, novels, and plays that the privileging barely went noticed. When in the mid-sixties I took a seminar on Ralph Waldo Emerson with the brilliant critic and quintessential Emersonian Richard Poirier, we concentrated on Emerson as a thinker and prose stylist, as the central figure of American literature, but I don't recall a single bit of discussion that regarded Emerson as an essayist, as a writer wholly engaged with a particular literary genre.

Essays were a minor genre, at best, and at worst one of the many forms of subliterature. They didn't reward critical study except in the growing discipline of freshman composition, where students were exposed to the work of George Orwell, Virginia Woolf, James Baldwin, E. B. White, Loren Eiseley, Joan Didion, and many other essayists past and present, though in an academic setting that generally prioritized rhetoric over literature. As someone serving in the trenches of freshman composition, I also grew familiar with these writers, often through college essay anthologies designed to assist young instructors in teaching first-year students how to write effectively. My reading was thus divided between two opposing curricula—the main graduate school curriculum, which favored fiction, poetry, and drama, and the freshman writing curriculum, which permitted essays and literary nonfiction, such as that of Gay Talese, Gloria Steinem, Terry Southern, George Plimpton, Nora Ephron, and Norman Mailer, all of whose work I eagerly read and taught. It wasn't exactly schizoid, but it was always clear which works fell into the realm of serious literature and which didn't.

I will always recall one course that violated those literary boundaries. In 1965 I was fortunate to be admitted into a seminar taught by William Phillips, the prominent editor of *The Partisan Review.* We met once a week in the offices of that illustrious literary journal to read and discuss contemporary criticism—Lionel Trilling, Philip Rahv, Dwight Macdonald, Alfred Kazin, Mary McCarthy, Leslie Fiedler. Since a number of these writers and critics would visit periodically I also had the pleasure of meeting them at readings and receptions. Hanging out at the *Partisan Review* offices, sharing the excitement of current literary gossip, hearing a glamorous Susan Sontag read "Notes on Camp" upon its publication in the magazine, or having an impromptu lunch with Philip Rahv— these experiences put me in touch with essays in a way I had never been before. It made so much academic discourse appear dull, and it also made the reading I did for my freshman writing courses seem far more engaging and relevant than the reading required for the graduate school curriculum. It was exciting to move from *PMLA* (the publication of the Modern Language Association) to *The Partisan Review,* and I realized I was far more interested in the world of public intellectuals than in literary scholarship. I began to see essays as provocative, sexy, a way of being in the world that could be both satisfyingly aesthetic and socially active. For that *Partisan Review* seminar on contemporary criticism I wrote a paper on Norman Mailer as an essayist, focusing on his rough-and-tumble collection *Advertisements for Myself.*

Years later, through the 1970s and 1980s, I continued to immerse myself in essays, inspired by the connection I had formed with the genre while studying with Mr. Phillips (we were not to call him "Professor") at *The Partisan Review.* For me, essays could be every bit as "literary" as poems, novels, and plays, and by the mid-eighties I began to think that they deserved an annual volume that showcased the year's best. When I began gathering essays in 1985 for the first volume in the series, I discovered that one of the unanticipated pleasures of the project was being in touch with the editors of literary periodicals. I blithely assumed I knew what these would be but very quickly came across journals I had no idea existed, and that too was a large part of the enjoyment I took in compiling the collection.

In that first year, for example, a new magazine with the zany name *ZYZZYVA* (see Dagoberto Gilb, "A Little Bit of Fun Before He Died," p. 254) was launched by Howard Junker in San Francisco. Taking its title from the last word in the dictionary (at least it is in my *American Heritage Dictionary of the English Language*), *ZYZZYVA*, now under the editorial direction of Laura Cogan, has remained one of the leading West Coast literary journals, consistently and attractively publishing many of the nation's outstanding writers.

It's easy to overlook the fact that this series features both writers and the periodicals that publish them. You may not notice at first glance, but this collection is almost completely dependent upon the existence of literary magazines. If you glance down the table of contents you'll see, aside from prominent periodicals such as *The New Yorker, The New Republic, The New York Times Magazine,* and *Harper's Magazine,* some magazines you may never have heard of — *Hotel Amerika, Hobart, River Teeth, The Normal School, South Loop Review.* If you look at the list of notable essays in the back, you'll see perhaps even more unfamiliar journals: *n + 1, Ninth Letter, Gulf Coast, Lake Effect, Fifth Wednesday, Zone 3.* Some periodicals, of course, like *Ploughshares, The Paris Review,* and *Prairie Schooner,* are preeminent among literary periodicals and are well known to writers who submit their work regularly and to editors and agents who are always scouting for new work and looking to discover new voices and emerging writers. But for the most part, I think it's safe to say that the average American reader is unfamiliar with many of the literary magazines featured or listed in this collection.

The vitality of American literature has long depended on the almost heroic efforts of literary magazines, which manage to survive today despite budget reductions, rising costs, and an unstable publishing environment. It's true that every year I see magazines fold — *The Partisan Review,* for example, unfortunately stopped publishing in 2003 — but new magazines keep appearing. Some seem to rise out of the ashes of their predecessors. When the excellent *Ohio Review* came to an end in 1999, one of its associate editors, David Lazar, created *Hotel Amerika* (see Marcia Aldrich, "The Art of Being Born," p. 132), which he took with him to Columbia College in Chicago when he moved there in 2006. Featuring a generous sampling of cutting-edge writing in all genres, traditional and hybrid, *Hotel Amerika* has maintained an eye-catching and creative literary identity for over a decade. It is always a pleasure to read.

Another impressive magazine coming out of Chicago's Columbia College is *South Loop Review* (see Vicki Weiqi Yang's "Field Notes on Hair," p. 217). Published annually and edited by ReLynn Hansen, *South Loop Review* concentrates on creative nonfiction and art, describing itself as designed "for audiences who look for strong, compelling resonant voices that give insight into contemporary experience and cultural phenomena." With an artistic focus, the editors "give greater emphasis to non-linear narratives and blended genres" and "welcome montage and illustrated essays, as well as narrative photography." Readers interested in the creative process will appreciate the journal's dedication to the craft of nonfiction and its interviews with some of the nation's most innovative writers; a recent issue, for example, featured David Shields on the always challenging topic of truth and nonfiction.

Other relatively new magazines also focus exclusively on nonfiction. One of the most highly respected is *River Teeth,* a "Journal of Nonfiction Narrative" founded by Joe Mackall and Dan Lehman in 1999 on the campus of Ashland University in Ohio. Although the general reading public may not be familiar with the journal, it is well known to nonfiction writers for its exacting standards and wide-ranging topics (the two essays reprinted here—Steven Harvey, "The Book of Knowledge, p. 274, and Jon Kerstetter, "Triage," p. 123—come from the same issue). *River Teeth* also sponsors a premier annual nonfiction writing conference.

Another recent addition to the literary magazine scene is *The Normal School* (see Ander Monson, "The Exhibit Will Be So Marked," p. 153), which takes its name from the old term for a teachers college. Now in its sixth year of print publication, the magazine was founded by Sophie Beck, Steven Church, and Matt Roberts and is supported by CSU Fresno, where Steven Church (whose own work has appeared in *The Best American Essays*) teaches creative writing. According to Sophie Beck, the magazine was originally conceived as a home for "homeless writing—things that were too long, too short, too experimental, or unclassifiable that could be nestled in with classically crafted pieces." A large-size, typographically inviting magazine that publishes all genres, *The Normal School* is indispensable for anyone interested in discovering new directions in the contemporary essay.

Lately a number of literary journals have abandoned print for online formats. Yet *Hobart* (see Tod Goldberg, "When They Let Them Bleed," p. 205) began life online in 2001 but then launched into print a few years later. Edited by Aaron Burch, *Hobart* (not affiliated with the New York State men's college of that name), though published irregularly, still maintains an active online presence. Though it modestly calls itself "another literary journal," *Hobart* is far from typical, especially in some of its theme issues, which, like the one on "Luck" published in 2012 to commemorate the magazine's thirteenth issue, feature a captivating range of writing and some remarkably quirky items.

These are just a few of the literary journals I read regularly. Years ago, when I taught courses on magazine writing I'd begin by asking students which magazines they would submit work to. It should probably not have come as a surprise, but I was nevertheless surprised to see that nearly all of them said *The New Yorker*. I assume this response had less to do with their talents and ambition than with the fact that it was the only magazine of a literary nature they'd heard of. *The New Yorker* is without doubt a great magazine, one that publishes memorable work issue after issue, forty-seven issues a year. Yet it's interesting to note that in this collection *The New Yorker* appears only once. This volume is indeed a tribute to the astonishing amount of great writing that is consistently published year after year in what we used to call the "little magazines."

The Best American Essays features a selection of the year's outstanding essays, essays of literary achievement that show an awareness of craft and forcefulness of thought. Hundreds of essays are gathered annually from a wide assortment of national and regional publications. These essays are then screened, and approximately one hundred are turned over to a distinguished guest editor, who may add a few personal discoveries and who makes the final selections. The list of notable essays appearing in the back of the book is drawn from a final comprehensive list that includes not only all the essays submitted to the guest editor but also many that were not submitted.

To qualify for the volume, the essay must be a work of respectable literary quality, intended as a fully developed, independent essay on a subject of general interest (not specialized scholarship), originally written in English (or translated by the author) for publication in an American periodical during the calendar year. Today's essay is a highly flexible and shifting form, however, so these criteria are not carved in stone.

Magazine editors who want to be sure that their contributors will be considered each year should submit issues or subscriptions to The Best American Essays, Houghton Mifflin Harcourt, 222 Berkeley Street, Boston, MA 02116. Writers and editors are welcome to submit published essays from any American periodical for consideration; unpublished work does not qualify for the series and cannot be reviewed or evaluated. Please note: all submissions must be directly from the publication and not in manuscript or printout format. Editors of online magazines and literary bloggers should not assume that appropriate work will be seen; they are invited to submit printed copies of the essays (with full citations) to the address above.

As always, I appreciate all the assistance I regularly receive from my editors, Deanne Urmy and Nicole Angeloro. Liz Duvall once again expertly handled production. I remember the excitement of reading the first essay I'd seen by Cheryl Strayed, then a graduate student in creative writing at Syracuse University. "Heroin/e" appeared in what was one of my favorite magazines at the time, *Doubletake,* in 1999 and was selected by Alan Lightman for *The Best American Essays 2000.* Since that early appearance, Cheryl Strayed has emerged as one of the country's outstanding nonfiction authors. It is a pleasure to have her return to the series, this time as an editor. Her keen sense of prose narrative is evident throughout this collection, as is her receptivity to a diversity of voices and periodicals. So get ready to experience an abundance of exciting essays.

R.A.

Introduction

WHEN I TEACH WRITING I tell my students that the invisible, unwritten last line of every essay should be *and nothing was ever the same again.* By which I mean the reader should feel the ground shift, if even only a bit, when he or she comes to the end of the essay. Also there should be something at stake in the writing of it. Or, better yet, everything.

The stakes of my own first essay couldn't have been higher, beginning as it did at dawn in Taos, New Mexico, on the Fourth of July in 1997, when I woke abruptly and tearfully, as if from a nightmare, and sat straight up in my bed with the icy realization that I was forgetting my mother. It was a strange thing to realize, given the fact that in the six years she'd been dead I'd written about little else, my nascent body of work a mosaic of her too-short life. My mother the horse-crazy army brat. My mother the pregnant nineteen-year-old bride. My mother the battered wife. My mother the scrounging-to-get-by single mom. My mother the bread-baking, back-to-the-land animal lover. My mother the intellectually avid optimist. My mother the forty-five-year-old cancer-riddled corpse.

You could fairly well say she was my subject, though *obsession* might be a more accurate word. Both before and after her young death she was at the heart of every short story I wrote, and she was also at the center of the novel I was writing then—on that Fourth of July in Taos, where I was a resident at the Wurlitzer Foundation. Teresa Wood, the character I'd based on her, was my mother condensed and expanded, magnified and muted, twisted and reformed—my attempt to create the purest expression of who she was. But on that morning when I woke with a sense of urgency and regret, I understood in a flash that I'd done the opposite. All of that conflating and distilling and mishmashing hadn't made my mother more pure. It hadn't conjured her back to the world. It had only taken her from me in yet another way. Fiction had ruined her. *I* had ruined her. It was an unbearable thing to realize all at once. And so I did the only thing I could do. I went immediately to my computer and began writing with one simple mission: to remember my mother.

I wasn't trying to write anything that would be anything. The word *essay* didn't even come into my mind. I wanted only to transfer my version of the actual truth from my head to the page so a document of my mother's life and death would exist as a buffer against the other, fictional version I felt so deeply compelled to write. I began with a description of her naked dead body. How strange that moment was—when she was so profoundly there while also being so profoundly not there. From that first line onward, the words came raw and reckless and ravaging all day long. The hours passed without my noticing as I wrote and rewrote each sentence. I didn't eat. Or think. In my memory, I didn't even rise from my desk, though I must have. Out of a feeling of emotional necessity rather than artistic intention, I wrote the true story of my mother's cancer diagnosis and the ugly death that followed only seven weeks later; of the way my enormous grief turned into a self-destructive sorrow that manifested itself in heroin use (among other things); and of the brokenhearted acceptance I finally had to bear. By the time I stopped writing it was dark outside. Night. I paced the room as the pages I'd written printed out, and then I read them out loud to myself, understanding only then what I'd done. Written an essay.

The word *essay* means "to try," "to attempt," "to test." It's what I was doing that day when I woke and sobbed in my bed and ended up hours later with an essay in my hands. Trying, attempting, and testing are what writers do in every form, of course—the making of literature is always an experiment—but I think those words convey something essential and particular about the art of the essay. Behind every good essay there's an author with a savage desire to know more about what is already known. A good essay isn't a report of what happened. It's a reach for the stuff beyond and beneath. Essayists begin with an objective truth and attempt to find a greater, grander truth by testing fact against subjective interpretations of experiences and ideas, memories and theories. They try to make meaning of actual life, even if an awful lot has yet to be figured out. They grapple and reflect with seriousness and humor. They philosophize and confess with intellect and emotion. They recollect and reimagine private and public history with a combination of clarity and conjecture. They venture into what happened and why with a complicated collision of documented proof and impossible-to-pin-down remembrances. And they follow the answers to the questions that arise in the course of writing about what happened wherever they go. The essay's engine is curiosity; its territory is the open road.

This is what makes them so damn fun to read. Their vibrancy and intimacy, their mystery and nerve, their relentlessly searching quality is simultaneously like a punch in the nose and a kiss on the lips. A *pow* and a *wow*. An *ouch* and a *yes*. A stop and a go.

Or at least the essays I love most are like that. And that's what this collection is—the twenty-six essays among the hundred and some listed at the back of this book (many of which I also loved) that made me feel, for the brief time I spent reading them, as if the rest of the world had fallen away. The essay might be about a man's relationship to Mormonism or a woman's search for a serial killer she may or may not have encountered decades ago. It might be about the way one hears the music of Joni Mitchell differently over time or endures the death of a child or triages injured soldiers or survives five months at sea or gives birth to a daughter. It matters not. Though they display a range of styles and cover a diversity of subjects, the essays I deemed "best" this year share a powerful drive toward emotional and intellectual inquiry that deepens into a dazzling unfolding. Each of these essays left me saying *Ah* at the end, with joy or sorrow or recognition, with delight or dread or awe or all of those things mixed together. As if nothing would ever be the same again.

CHERYL STRAYED

The Best
AMERICAN
ESSAYS
2013

POE BALLANTINE

Free Rent at the Totalitarian Hotel

FROM *The Sun*

ON MONDAY MORNINGS I modeled for the painters at an old cannery converted into art studios in Eureka, California. Laughable as it was for a thirty-two-year-old man to strike nude poses on a wooden platform, I preferred it to what I usually did for a living: short-order cooking or unloading trucks. I stood up there on this particular Monday in 1987 trying not to move for two hours, suffering muscle cramps and loss of circulation, and, as always, faintly worried about getting an erection but somehow even more uneasy about the possibility of strangers seeing me through the windows—as if a roomful of strangers weren't ogling me already. Meanwhile down the hall my painter friend Jim Dalgee raved so violently that one of the artists suggested calling the police.

After I dressed and picked up my $60, I went down the hall and knocked on Jim's door. The ranting stopped for a moment, and there was a clatter, followed by the door jerking open and Jim sticking his head out. He did not let many people into his studio, but he liked me because we had both wasted our youth, had gotten off to terribly late starts, held similarly outdated and sentimental views on art, and showed no signs of ever becoming successful. A short man in his late forties with a brushed-up shock of black hair like the crest of a blue jay, Jim wore his standard paint-spattered work shirt, jeans, and tennis shoes. The room behind him was full of dense blue cigarette smoke that curled in the sunlight from the southern windows. He smelled strongly of turpentine and beer.

"Jim," I said, "we could hear you shouting all the way down the hall."

"Was I shouting?"

"Yes. At the top of your lungs."

"Come in, man. I've got coffee."

Jim's eight-by-ten, brick-walled studio was furnished with a small fridge and a card table with a coffeepot and a boom box on it. Nine years earlier he had fled his previous life as an L.A. salesman and migrated six hundred miles north to Eureka to start over as a painter at the age of thirty-eight. Stacked against and hanging from every wall were hundreds of his acrylic paintings, all of which he refused to sell or show. Jim's style was postimpressionism: Matisse, Pissarro, Cézanne. He admired foremost those who had started late, such as the stockbroker-salesman Paul Gauguin and the wretched lunatic Vincent van Gogh. Though I was not qualified to judge Jim's work, I would've liked to own his *Black Cattle Against Orange Moon at Dusk* or *Portrait of Camille Benoit Desmoulin's Head in a Basket.*

Though I had quit drinking and doing drugs the year before, I allowed myself the occasional consolation of a few cigarettes with Jim in his studio. I also planned one day to write a story about a fictional Jim jumping from the window to his posthumous fame. I poured myself a cup of coffee while he raged at the people on the street below, calling them "philistines" and "slobs." It was unusual to find him in such a state so early.

"Is everything all right?" I asked.

"The sleepwalkers!" he bellowed like an animal in pain.

"They're going to call the police," I said.

"They'll only be doing me a *favor!*" he shouted, sweeping his arm across the room, as if to indicate all the canvases he'd stretched that morning, the color-blobbed cardboard boxes he used for palettes, and the rows upon rows of acrylic paints in plastic squeeze bottles along the floor.

There was no point in talking to him when he was this far gone. The shouting would soon run its course and be replaced by a desperate apprehension that he didn't have long to live. I drank some coffee, shook a cigarette from Jim's pack, and fell into one of two yellow velveteen swivel chairs, a smoldering pedestal ashtray between them, like a giant clam with indigestion.

"I'm going to buy an albacore today," I said, applying a flame to the tip of my cigarette.

"The sycophants!" he snarled and then whirled from the window. "A what?"

"An albacore tuna, down on the docks. They're only a buck a pound. Do you want one?"

"No, nah." He waved in disdain and began to hunt for the cigarette he had just lit, his brow furrowed. "We need to get some more cigarettes."

Around one that afternoon Tarn McVie rapped lightly on Jim's door and stepped into the room. In his mid-twenties, Tarn already had paintings in galleries across the country and routinely sold single works for sums that could've sustained me for an entire year. His gigantic oil canvases awed me, and one sticks in my mind to this day: an orange nude coming at you through the water, flash of white at the knee. In spite of his conventional training, European-museum background, postmodern leanings, and early success without apparent struggle, McVie was the sort of natural, congenial artist that Jim and I both longed to be. He was also one of the few painters who refused to sign the petition presently going around to remove Jim from the building.

"Hello, men," he said. "Hear the news?"

"What news?" Jim said, teeth clamped down on his cigarette, another burning in the colossal ashtray between us.

"Market crashed."

"What market?" I asked.

"Stock market. Dow Jones fell over five hundred points," he said. "Highest point drop in history. There's nothing on TV except talk about it. You can't even watch *General Hospital*. Everyone says we're headed for the next Great Depression." His eyes sparkled as if we were all about to go on a field trip to paint tulips and the bus were waiting downstairs. "They're already calling it 'Black Monday.'"

I had never paid much attention to the Ferris-wheel vicissitudes of the New York Stock Exchange, but when $500 billion in stock value simply evaporates, when nearly 25 percent of the market ceases to exist, when the president of the United States preempts soap operas and game shows to urge everyone not to panic and numerous respected experts explain that the country has seen no comparable financial event since 1929, even the poor take heed. I had also been observing the wastrel, arrogant, and bellicose habits of my country for years, and my sensitive, aesthetic side tended toward portent and hyperbole. So I trusted the news media's Henny Penny proclamations that our Day of Reckoning had finally come.

Heading down the alley away from the artists' studios an hour later, I thought I would remember forever this day of ruin, October 19, 1987, the same way I remembered the assassination of John F. Kennedy. A man in a white shirt and blue tie staggered toward me with a dazed expression, and from the sky above I expected to see falling stockbrokers. I pictured myself on a freight train full of hobos. From every corner came the dire chatter of radios and TVs. Like all the gloomy broadcasters, I was convinced that the next Great Depression was upon us.

The fishing boats were in from their morning runs, and it now seemed imperative that I buy that albacore. Food would soon be in short supply, and there would be mobs in the streets, breaking windows and overturning cars.

The rheumy-eyed fisherman shrugged when I told him the news. "They can't break you if you're already broke," he said.

My fish, cleaned and bled, weighed fourteen pounds, and because albacore spoils rapidly, it was frozen as hard as a chunk of iron. Incongruous as it might seem to walk away from a fishing boat with a frozen fish, you couldn't beat the price, and albacore were much easier to cut into steaks this way. I carried it by the tail with a newspaper so it didn't freeze my hand.

I lived downtown in an apartment complex that, for its Second Empire façade, transient tenantry, and despotic manager, I had dubbed the Totalitarian Hotel. The manager, Mrs. Vollstanger, was a gouty old Prussian and always wore pearls and thick, embroidered white sweaters. She met me at the top of the grand staircase, arms folded, chin trembling, and glowered down at my fish.

"It's an albacore," I explained.

"Yes," she said. "I saw you coming." Mrs. Vollstanger had a telescope in the window of her third-floor apartment and kept track of all the goings-on below. "I have an eviction notice for you to serve."

I considered asking if she was aware of the stock market plunge but thought better of it, since bad news seemed only to cheer her. "Who's it for?"

"Hot Pants," she said, meaning my common-wall neighbor, a young woman named Annabelle Taft.

It didn't take Mrs. Vollstanger long to find derogatory nicknames for all her tenants. There was Moon Child and Clydesdale Maria and Porky Pete. I suppose behind my back I was Machine-Gun Typist.

"Annabelle?" I said. "Why?"

"I'm not running a brothel here," she retorted, one of her fondest declarations, along with "I'm not running a crack house/ animal shelter/home for unwed mothers here."

"Just let me get this fish in the freezer, and I'll be right up," I said, resisting the urge to salute. "Would you like a couple of tuna steaks?"

"No, thank you," she said.

My apartment was a single room with a set of high, arched, greenish windows, an electric stove, a fridge, a sink, and a very long entryway. Sometimes when someone knocked it took me so long to get to the door that my caller would be gone by the time I arrived. My place was full of moths, whose origin I could not determine. They were the small, rolled-up type, like pencil shavings. I had liked them at first for their silence and the intricate designs on their delicate wings, but now, with their growing numbers and regular obtrusion into my books, blankets, and bathtub, I considered them a nuisance.

My room was sparsely furnished with items left by the previous tenants, who had vacated abruptly. There was a vinyl-covered recliner and a dining room table, upon which sat my typewriter, and two chairs that went with the table. There was a television on a stand that I did not often use since it received only two channels, though occasionally I watched *I Love Lucy*—a program I had disliked as a child for all its yelling—and a PBS show hosted by theological psychologist John Bradshaw, who asserted that all my addiction problems could be traced back to my "wounded inner child." (Maybe I was hurt by early exposure to episodes of *I Love Lucy*.)

There were four boxes of *Paris Review*s that Jim had lent me, which I studied at night, especially the interviews with famous authors. Throughout the building the floors were covered with cheap carpet that with all its gold, green, and red filigree might've been called "gala," but it was so thin that it wrinkled, and there was no padding underneath, so that if you didn't have a mattress—I didn't—you had to build up a nest of blankets on the floor. The heat was regulated by Mrs. Vollstanger, so it was always cold, and it was best not to sleep by the windows, which had bubbles trapped in their glass and made me feel as if I were a specimen in some intergalactic aquarium.

I set my fish across the sink and promptly began to divide it into two-inch crosscut planks with a handsaw I used only for this purpose. While I worked, I thought about the coming of the next Great Depression and wondered how America would fall apart: Slowly or quickly? From the coasts inward or the middle out? With great fanfare or in a puff of smoke? And in which direction would everyone run this time? I also wondered if it had been wise to quit my job and sell my car.

Sawing up a frozen albacore is not much different from sawing up a green tree trunk. I got about twelve steaks, which I wrapped and stacked in the freezer beside all the wild game that Mrs. Vollstanger had cleaned out of her recently deceased husband's stand-up freezer and donated to me. A big-game hunter, he had labeled all his Cryovacked packages in permanent black marker: ELK, ELEPHANT, BLACK BEAR, ZEBRA, GAZELLE. So far I had been reluctant to try any of it for fear that Mrs. Vollstanger had actually killed, dressed, and Cryovacked her husband.

I also had a twenty-five-pound bag of pink beans, a twenty-five-pound bag of black-eyed peas, a twenty-five-pound bag of brown rice, ten pounds of white flour, four pounds of oats, and two pounds of buckwheat—a proper head start, I thought, on the anarchy and economic despair to come.

The door to Mrs. Vollstanger's apartment was open, and before I could knock, she invited me in. Mrs. Vollstanger had a big, well-lit, orderly apartment on the southwest corner, with a panoramic view of the bay and the Samoa pulp mill. You could predict with fair accuracy what the weather would be like by which way the smoke blew from the mill. Usually it was blowing in from the ocean, which meant fog and rain, but today the smoke flowed north, indicating fair weather.

"You've heard that the market slipped?" she said, handing me the envelope with the eviction notice for Annabelle Taft inside.

"'Slipped'?"

"Everything will be fine. We have a good man in office," she said, referring to then-president Ronald Reagan.

Mrs. Vollstanger rarely left the premises. Her groceries were delivered. She did not own a car. The tenants who curried her favor did her bidding, policed the unit, swept the lobby floors, ran errands, and maintained the laundry room. She spoke often in praise of the building's owner and of her responsibilities to his property, which, judging by its low rents and the number of liberties she was allowed with tenants, I could only imagine was some sort of tax shelter. Mrs. Vollstanger had raised four children, but I never saw any of them, and given the way she shook with rage without warning and preyed like a trapdoor spider on the weaknesses of those in her confidence, I didn't wonder why.

From my own experience with tyrants, I had identified her tendencies early on and managed to stay in her good graces by paying my rent on time, keeping my distance, and doing her dirty work when called. Mrs. Vollstanger would've enjoyed serving the notices herself, I believe, but she had been attacked on one occasion and threatened on another, so the mission had been passed on to someone more expendable.

I doubted the legal soundness of most of these notices, which usually contained only a thin basis for the eviction, such as suspected pets or, in the case of Annabelle, noise after 10 P.M. But the job of a henchman is execution, not judgment, and I needed the money. Even when eviction was justified, I always felt bad about ousting people from their homes. I felt especially rotten in this case, since the market had just crashed and I was, for flimsy reasons, turning a young woman out on the street. I don't think Annabelle was any more than nineteen. She worked at my favorite bakery (the chewy chocolate–macadamia nut cookies had no rival), and I knew from my few conversations with her in the hall that this was the first time she had ever lived on her own.

I knocked and thought I heard a noise inside, but there was no response. I figured she had spied me through the peephole and decided not to answer. Then I looked left and saw Annabelle coming down the hall with two stacked baskets of laundry. She wore shorts, and her lean swimmer's body was pale. Annabelle was from Montana, and by the drawings of surf and sun on the many letters that I saw posted downstairs for her friends and family back home, I'd deduced that she was proud of having landed on the mythological golden shore of California, even if it was cloudy, rainy, or foggy here in Eureka three hundred days out of the year.

I helped her with her baskets, then presented her with the envelope.

She squinted at it. "What is this?"

"It's, ah, an eviction notice."

"Why am I being evicted?"

"It's written there at the bottom. Noise after ten. It's in the lease . . . You never bothered me," I hastened to add. In fact, with no social life to speak of, I'd enjoyed the sounds of festivity that had come through her wall: giggling, clinking glasses, lovemaking. I knew it was the men who stayed overnight that had rankled Mrs. Vollstanger. My only complaint about Annabelle would've been that I was not one of the men.

She studied the paper without reading it, then shook it at me, her dark eyes so perplexed and hurt I felt like a villain in a Victorian novel. "Where am I supposed to go?"

"You have five days. There are a lot of vacancies downtown."

"You're a terrible person," she said, blowing a strand of hair out of her face.

"It's nothing personal. I'll help you move. I'm sorry about all of this."

"Get lost, and tell your—" Her voice broke, and she wiped at her eyes. "I thought you were nice."

Well, I was at one time, I thought, but by then she had slammed the door.

I hiked back up to Mrs. Vollstanger's and collected my $15 fee. After Annabelle was gone, I would paint her apartment in exchange for a free month's rent.

Normally in the evenings I worked on my great Rabelaisian satirical novel about greed and voluptuous social dependence in an allegorical lunatic asylum inhabited by evil clowns (which seemed even more appropriate now that we were all going down the tubes), but I was distracted by Annabelle's distress, the dirtiness of the $15 in my pocket, and the fact that soon millions would be out of work and rioting in the streets.

I picked up a *Paris Review* and thumbed through it. All good art, according to my 1951 Greenwich Village Artist's Code, came out of tumult, revolution, and hardship. The moths fluttered about as if I were some magnificent symbol of decay. Hungry, I rummaged in my freezer, brought out a chunk of black bear, stared at it for a minute, then unwrapped it and set it in a pan on low heat with onions. The sun set behind the buildings. The bear was tough and greasy, but I finished it, imagining that through some pantheistic hoodoo I might incorporate the bear's spirit, at the same time pushing out of my mind the possibility that it was Mr. Vollstanger's liver.

In the morning I rose cautiously from my nest of blankets and peeked out the window to note that the world had not visibly changed. The smoke from the mill was still scurrying north. I made coffee and oatmeal with apples and then walked four blocks to the headquarters of the *North Coast View*, where six months earlier I had answered an incredible ad that had read, "Writers Wanted," and despite never having published a thing in my life, I'd been hired to write book reviews at $25 apiece.

Two Irish-surnamed journalists in their late twenties owned and ran the *North Coast View*, a free, local, ad-heavy arts-and-culture monthly on newsprint that I had once heard referred to as an "innocuous street rag." I strolled into their office. Though I think it had helped me win the job, they regarded my 1951 Greenwich Village Artist's Code as quaint. Among writers the career path of quitting your job, selling your car, hustling like an old hooker with a toothache, and then eventually dying of syphilis or tuberculosis or shooting yourself in the stomach in a wheat field after you'd created a number of unrecognized masterpieces had been replaced by taking out a student loan and enrolling in the nearby university.

The joke was on them, however, for the Dark Ages were at hand, and only those who could ride the rails, roll their own cigarettes, and live on hand-sawn fish and black bear would survive.

"Are we still in business?" I asked point-blank as I came round the corner in my Goodwill Pendleton shirt, patched jeans, and wool watch cap.

"Until further notice" was the editor's complacent reply.

"You're not worried about the market crash?"

"We're not listed on the Dow Jones Industrial, last time I checked."

It was disconcerting to see everyone—Jim, Tarn McVie, Mrs. Vollstanger, the albacore fisherman, my two editors—take so mildly the greatest single-day point decline in Wall Street history.

"I'll get a book," I said.

"Take all you want."

In the back were hundreds of books publishers had sent hoping for reviews, the mass of them the sort of dreck that encouraged me about my own prospects of one day getting my novel published.

I selected a book about a group of oppressed women workers who cracked walnuts with their fists after their hammers had been taken away from them (at which point I personally would have quit cracking walnuts and headed home). As I strolled back to my apartment, the headlines in the newsstands trumpeted ominous declarations—"Bedlam on Wall Street"—though it was reassuring to see that they were still organized enough to turn a profit on calamity. I also noticed that the bakery I liked so much— the one where Annabelle Taft worked and which I would therefore have to avoid from now on—was busier than usual. Since Eureka was so far from the financial centers, I thought, the crash simply had not caught up to us yet, or it had somehow stimulated appetites for *krapfen* pastries and chewy chocolate–macadamia nut cookies.

When I got home, I read the book about women cracking walnuts without hammers, took notes, drank so much cinnamon tea I fogged the windows, got the hiccups, had a sneezing fit so violent I felt like Hitler at the rostrum, passed back and forth through the clouds of moths, longed for a chewy chocolate–macadamia nut cookie, and found that zebra, no matter how it is prepared, is best left on the zebra. My room grew dark, and, lit only by the street-light, I lay in my nest of blankets and listened to the soft moaning of Annabelle Taft next door.

Annabelle moved out three days later with the help of a dozen friends in army jackets, ripped jeans, and fingerless gloves, who scowled and sniffed at me in the hall whenever possible. She did not collect her security deposit or clean her apartment. She left behind a nasty note, a broken umbrella, a tube of green lipstick, a one-piece bathing suit emblazoned *Bozeman Barracudas* (still wet in the bathtub), and a trash can full of *North Coast View*s.

Annabelle's apartment looked out over the rooftop, and I remembered how cute she'd been lying out there on her towel, trying to get a tan on rare and usually cool days of sun. I confess that *cute* does not accurately describe the many ways I had thought about her, none of which, because of my overdiscipline and fear of intimacy, would ever amount to more than a fantasy. I also recalled how much fun it had been to talk to her about her California adventure, which brought to mind my first time out on my own: the exhilaration of shopping for groceries, acquiring furniture, preparing your own meals, having friends over, and staying up as late as you liked.

Normally I painted an apartment the size of Annabelle's in about four hours. The color, without exception, was oyster white, no trim. The apartments were painted so often that usually only one coat was needed. While I painted and moved my ladder about, I thought about women cracking walnuts with their fists and America coming down. I also thought about God, whom I had never believed in before, but now that I was trying to create flesh-and-blood characters so that my reader would feel something when I killed them off, I had begun to imagine that a higher being might have been doing this very thing on a much larger scale all along.

When I was done, I cleaned my brushes and rollers and put away the ladder, paint, and drop cloths. Tomorrow I would give Annabelle's keys back to Mrs. Vollstanger and get my receipt for one month's rent. I returned to my room and stood in the darkness for a while, looking out at the lights of ships on the bay. And I caught myself listening for the voice of Annabelle.

The next morning Jim was standing down the hall beside the open door of 214, an apartment I had painted six days before that had belonged to a woman who'd been evicted for having cats. Jim's wife, Hye, a school secretary, stood next to him, looking like someone who spent all her waking hours defusing bombs.

Jim called my name and strode over with a smile to shake my hand. He had a tremendous handshake, his forearm bulging.

"Howdy, neighbor," he said. "Guess you heard they voted me out." He explained that without his studio, he needed an apartment with better light so he could paint at home. This place had great light, he said. "And it's half the price of our place down on the waterfront. Hye likes it too," he added.

Hye was gone. The door downstairs was propped open, and she came trudging back up the steps with a boxful of books. In the dozens of times I had seen Hye with Jim, she had spoken a total of six words to me—cultural diffidence, I thought (she was Korean), or, more likely, she associated me with her husband's self-destruction.

Jim took a deep breath. "I've quit drinking."

Hye passed us, head down, as if we were strangers. I wondered how many times she'd heard Jim say this.

"Great news, Jim," I said. "Do you need any help moving?"

"Got most everything up," he said. "Now I need to lay some tarps. Come by later and check out my new studio."

"I'll bring you a pound of black-eyed peas for luck," I said.

Mrs. Vollstanger leaned over the rail above, pearls dangling, and smiled down at us in that chilly, maternal way of hers. "Do you have everything you need, Jim?" she asked sweetly.

On afternoons when the weather was tolerable, I liked to hang out in the park across the street from my apartment among the winos, unemployed lumberjacks, and a bearded man who sat cross-legged by the statue and offered to let you touch the "real Jesus" for only a quarter. Mrs. Vollstanger would be up there on the third floor doing telescope surveillance, and a few windows over and down Jim would be crouched before his easel, wool beret dipped over one eye, furiously trying to catch up on lost time.

I was trying to catch up on lost time too. My brain, floating in its amniotic chamber of inebriation for all those years, had gone to sludge. It was an effort to perceive things as they actually were and harder yet to render them clearly, which likely was the reason I clung to ready-made theories of art instead of developing my own. Following the example of my painter friends, I made daily "sketches" in my notebook: descriptions of my surroundings and the people as they passed, trying to retrain my eye in the hope that one day I would find my way to the book reviewers' pile, preferably in hardcover.

One afternoon the broad-shouldered Annabelle came along and sat down just a few feet from me. She wore pinstriped pants, knee-high rubber boots, and a windbreaker. A white band on her wrist read, "Love is time." She opened her notebook and began to write.

Before I'd handed Annabelle her eviction notice, I had seen her outside the building no more than seven or eight times, but now I ran into her everywhere: in the galleries (where I could too often be found depicted in various unflattering attitudes), at the library and the co-op, coming out of that restaurant that sold spinach pies, or gabbing in the coffee shop with her friends. At each encounter, if she did not ignore me altogether, she pretended to have stumbled upon some large species of cockroach. It pickled my stomach to be so loathed (for I didn't need an artist's vision to see my role as a jerk in all of this), and it made me want to quit serving evictions, even if that meant the end of my free rent at the Totalitarian Hotel. Apology seemed a thin gesture, and so I fantasized about asking her out instead: I'd walk her through my situation so that she could understand the sacrifices one had to make for art, and then maybe we'd go to her place afterward, where a pastel nude of me with darts in my ass would hang from her wall.

"Hey, how are you?" I called out.

"Busy," she replied, nose in her book.

"Writing a letter?"

"A story."

"I have your bathing suit and green lipstick."

"You can keep them," she said.

"I wouldn't know what to do with them," I replied with a chuckle that stuck in my throat.

"I have a suggestion," she said, ripping the page from her notebook, tearing it to bits, and stalking away.

The stock market sputtered and bumped along. Black Monday merged into Black November and on without chromatic variation into December. The financial experts, like a pack of gloomy cheerleaders, kept up the rah-rah of the apocalypse even as the fishing boats continued sailing in and out, the bakery kept baking, new books and fresh newspapers kept arriving, and the street sweepers moved up and down the pavement undeterred by the mist and rain.

One night while typing, the windows sweating with the humidity of my inspiration, my cinnamon tea, and a pot of simmering pink beans and elephant, I heard Jim railing at the philistines below. I hurried over and knocked on his door. Hye let me in as if I were a country doctor making a midnight call.

Jim staggered from the open window, arms outstretched, cigarette in one hand and can of beer in the other. "I'm back, my boy!" he cried.

There were moths in the apartment, a situation I thought endemic to the building (since they were the exact same moths as mine) or possibly an affliction of artists who'd started too late.

"Jim," I said, "you can't shout. Mrs. Vollstanger will evict you."

"The *rentier!*" he shouted gallantly, waving an arm through a squadron of eye-winged moths. "The harridan! Have a drink, old friend. Hye, get him a drink. Come look at my painting. Come look at what I've done."

In the coming days Jim painted with his door open, jazz and cigarette smoke pouring into the hallway. Around four every afternoon, just before Hye got home from work, he'd knock off and make his sacred trek to the liquor store. In the evenings, well oiled, he'd come to visit me, bringing a paper sack full of beer, old *Esquire* magazines, Henry Miller novels, and perhaps half a buttered baguette from the bakery or a plate of creamed cauliflower that Hye had made. We'd laugh about the moths, which I'd discovered had hatched from my weevil-infested bag of black-eyed peas, since discarded. He'd show me his latest painting, and I'd read him passages from my evil-clown novel, to which he'd listen intently, all the while nodding and huffing and afterward announcing without fail how much he admired the rhythm.

At night, whenever Jim began to rave, I'd tense for the eviction summons of Mrs. Vollstanger, then go over and tell him to keep it down. Twice I overheard him and Hye arguing. Hye did most of the talking: Did Jim realize that he was spending more on paints, canvases, cigarettes, and booze than she was making? They no longer had enough to put a down payment on a house. He denied fiercely her charge that art for him was nothing more than an excuse to drink. Why, then, she wanted to know, did he not try to sell his paintings or at least show them in the local galleries?

"Because I can't *sell* things anymore," he said. "Goddamnit, Hye, no one is going to remember a *sales*man."

Hye began to cry.

"The market will come back, babe," he told her. "And when it does, we'll buy a house. The one you like in Trinidad with all the redwood trees in the backyard."

Each day I waited for America to snap from its strings and fall on its face like a broken marionette, but by January not only had the stock market recovered, it had begun to make gains. Many who, like Jim and Hye, had not sold off their investments were better off financially than before the soon-to-be-forgotten crash. The experts, reversing themselves like a school of parrotfish, predicted that the Dow might soar as high as four thousand points by the end of the year. Black Monday had had no real effect on anything but my imagination.

It rained most of January, and I slaved over my book about evil clowns. Each day, as its shortcomings became more evident, I approached the typewriter with less enthusiasm. Finally I sat on the floor and read my satirical harlequin folly front to back as if it were someone else's work. It was the sort of effort I would've panned as a reviewer: "With its too-easy targets, total absence of sympathetic characters, and overall lack of message, I see little reason to bother with such a cynical assessment of American society. It is perhaps harsh but also fair to say that at an age when most novelists are producing their best work, this one is many years away from offering anything of value to a reader, much less revealing himself outside of posing naked on a wooden platform."

I banded and boxed the manuscript, lethargically paced the room, chuckled feebly to myself a few times, and thought about getting drunk. Finally I went to bed and slept for three days, getting up now and again for a slice of bloody red elk or a glass of water or to listen for Jim raging down the hall or Mrs. Vollstanger's unmistakable Gestapo knock on my door. I slept roughly, like a tree with all its bark burned off or a man buried in wet sand, but the dreams at least were good. In one I could paint with my mind, and in another everyone had a *u* in their last name.

When at last I got up to face the world again, the room was full of sunlight, and I had a strong craving for chewy chocolate–macadamia nut cookies.

"You're the writer, aren't you?" asked the young woman behind the glass case at the bakery.

"How did you know?" I asked.

"We used to listen to you type. You know Annabelle moved back to Montana. She really loved your book reviews." Her hand dropped to her hip. "She's going to be an author someday too. You should write her."

Later that evening Jim stopped by and drove me nine miles north into the redwood forest to the rustic cabin he and Hye had just bought in Trinidad, a town with a population of only a few hundred. We stood on the balcony in the cool shadows of the massive trees. "Do you believe it?" he said. "Look at the light! Smell the air! You can hear the ocean!"

Two days later Mrs. Vollstanger lost her temper with me because I'd moved an electric stove to the wrong side of a room. We argued. I said some regrettable things, all of them true, and was relieved that my days at the Totalitarian Hotel were finally over. More depressed and confused than I would admit, I packed what I could carry, leaving behind my security deposit, a clean room, a succinct note, and a freezer full of wild meat.

I sneaked down the grand staircase and walked to the bus depot a few blocks away. There were only three other passengers on the bus, so I racked my bags and nestled in with two seats to myself. Before I dozed off somewhere around Petaluma, I watched the darkness roll past the windows and wondered how long I would have to go on knowing nothing about art, or women, or my country.

ALICE MUNRO

Night

FROM *Granta*

WHEN I WAS YOUNG, there seemed to be never a childbirth, or a burst appendix, or any other drastic physical event that did not occur simultaneously with a snowstorm. The roads would be closed, there was no question of digging out a car anyway, and some horses had to be hitched up to make their way into town to the hospital. It was just lucky that there were horses still around —in the normal course of events they would have been given up, but the war and gas rationing had changed all that, at least for the time being.

When the pain in my side struck, therefore, it had to do so at about eleven o'clock at night, and a blizzard had to be blowing, and since we were not stabling any horses at the moment, the neighbors' team had to be brought into action to take me to the hospital. A trip of no more than a mile and a half but an adventure all the same. The doctor was waiting, and to nobody's surprise he prepared to take out my appendix.

Did more appendixes have to be taken out then? I know it still happens, and it is necessary—I even know of somebody who died because it did not happen soon enough—but as I remember it was a kind of rite that quite a few people my age had to undergo, not in large numbers by any means but not all that unexpectedly, and perhaps not all that unhappily, because it meant a holiday from school and it gave you some kind of status—set you apart, briefly, as one touched by the wing of mortality, all at a time in your life when that could be gratifying.

So I lay, minus my appendix, for some days, looking out a hos-

pital window at the snow sifting in a somber way through some
evergreens. I don't suppose it ever crossed my head to wonder
how my father was going to pay for this distinction. (I think he
sold a woodlot that he had kept when he disposed of his father's
farm, hoping to use it for trapping or sugaring or perhaps out of
unmentionable nostalgia.)

Then I went back to school, and enjoyed being excused from
physical training for longer than necessary, and one Saturday
morning when my mother and I were alone in the kitchen she
told me that my appendix had been taken out in the hospital, just
as I thought, but it was not the only thing removed. The doctor
had seen fit to take it out while he was at it, but the main thing that
concerned him was a growth. A growth, my mother said, the size
of a turkey's egg.

But don't worry, she said, it was all over now.

The thought of cancer never entered my head and she never
mentioned it. I don't think there could be such a revelation today
without some kind of question, some probing about whether it
was or it wasn't. Cancerous or benign—we would want to know
at once. The only way I can explain our failure to speak of it was
that there must have been a cloud around that word like the
cloud around the mention of sex. Worse, even. Sex was disgusting but there must be some gratification there—indeed we knew
there was, though our mothers were not aware of it—while even
the word *cancer* made you think of some dark, rotting, ill-smelling
creature that you would not look at even when you kicked it out of
the way.

So I did not ask and wasn't told and can only suppose it was
benign or was most skillfully got rid of, for here I am today. And so
little do I think of it that all through my life when called upon to
list my surgeries, I automatically say or write only "Appendix."

This conversation with my mother would probably have taken
place in the Easter holidays, when all the snowstorms, the snow
mountains, had vanished and the creeks were in flood, laying hold
of anything they could get at, and the brazen summer just looming ahead. Our climate had no dallying, no mercies.

In the heat of early June I got out of school, having made good
enough marks to free me from the final examinations. I looked
well, I did chores around the house, I read books as usual, nobody
knew there was a thing the matter with me.

Now I have to describe the sleeping arrangements in the bedroom occupied by my sister and me. It was a small room that could not accommodate two single beds, side by side, so the solution was a bunk bed, with a ladder in place to help whoever slept in the top bunk climb into bed. That was me. When I had been younger and prone to teasing, I would lift up the corner of my thin mattress and threaten to spit on my little sister lying helpless in the bunk below. Of course my sister—her name was Catherine—was not really helpless. She could hide under her covers, but my game was to watch until suffocation or curiosity drove her out, and at that moment to spit or successfully pretend to spit on her bared face, enraging her.

I was too old for such fooling, certainly too old now. My sister was nine when I was fourteen. The relationship between us was always unsettled. When I wasn't tormenting her, teasing her in some asinine way, I would take on the role of sophisticated counselor or hair-raising storyteller. I would dress her up in some of the old clothes that had been put away in my mother's hope chest, being too fine to be cut up for quilts and too worn and precious for anybody to wear. I would put my mother's old caked rouge and powder on her face and tell her how pretty she looked. She was pretty, without a doubt, though the face I put on her gave her the look of a freakish foreign doll.

I don't mean to say that I was entirely in control of her, or even that our lives were constantly intertwined. She had her own friends, her own games. These tended toward domesticity rather than glamour. Dolls were taken for walks in their baby carriages, or sometimes kittens were dressed up and walked in the dolls' stead, always frantic to get out. Also there were play sessions where somebody got to be the teacher and could slap the others over the wrists and make them pretend to cry, for various infractions and stupidities.

In the month of June, as I have said, I was free of school and left on my own, as I don't remember being in quite the same way at any other time of my growing up. I did some chores in the house, but my mother must have been well enough, as yet, to handle most of that work. Or perhaps we had just enough money at the time to hire what she—my mother—would call a maid, though everybody else said hired girl. I don't remember, at any rate, having to tackle any of those jobs that piled up for me in later summers, when I fought quite willingly to maintain the decency of our house. It seems that the mysterious turkey egg must have given me some invalid status, so that I could spend part of the time wandering about like a visitor.

Though not trailing any special clouds. Nobody in our family would have got away with that. It was all inward—this uselessness and strangeness I felt. And not continual uselessness either. I remember squatting down to thin the baby carrots, as you had to do every spring. So the root would grow to a decent size to be eaten.

It must have been just that every moment of the day was not filled up with jobs, as it was in summers before and after.

So maybe that was the reason that I had begun to have trouble getting to sleep. At first, I think, that meant lying awake maybe till around midnight and wondering at how wide awake I was, with the rest of the household asleep. I would have read, and got tired in the usual way, and turned out my light and waited. Nobody would have called out to me earlier, telling me to put out my light and get to sleep. For the first time ever (and this too must have marked a special status) I was left to make up my own mind about such a thing.

It took a while for the house to change, from the light of day and then of the household lights turned on late in the evening, from the general clatter of things to be done, hung up, finished with, to a stranger place in which people and the work that dictated their lives fell away, their uses for everything around them fell away, all the furniture retreated into itself without wanting or needing any attention from you.

You might think this was liberation. At first, perhaps it was. The freedom. The strangeness. But as my failure to fall asleep prolonged itself and as it finally took hold altogether until it changed into the dawn, I became more and more disturbed. I started saying rhymes, then real poetry, first to make myself go under but then hardly of my own volition. But the activity seemed to mock me. I was mocking myself, as the words turned into absurdity, into the silliest random speech.

I was not myself.

I had been hearing that said of people now and then, all my life, without thinking what it could mean.

So who do you think you are, then?

I'd been hearing that too, without attaching to it any real menace, just taking it as a sort of routine jeering.

Think again.

By this time it wasn't sleep I was after. I knew mere sleep wasn't likely. Maybe not even desirable. Something was taking hold of me, and it was my business, my hope, to fight it off. I had the sense to do that, but only barely, as it seemed. It was trying to tell me to do things, not exactly for any reason but just to see if such acts were possible. It was informing me that motives were not necessary.

It was only necessary to give in. How strange. Not out of revenge, or even cruelty, but just because you had thought of something.

And I did think of it. The more I chased the thought away, the more it came back. No vengeance, no hatred—as I've said, no reason, except that something like an utterly cold deep thought that was hardly an urging, more of a contemplation, could take possession of me. I must not even think of it, but I did think of it.

The thought was there and hanging on to my mind. The thought that I could strangle my little sister, who was asleep in the bunk below me and whom I loved more than anybody in the world.

I might do it not for any jealousy, viciousness, or anger but because of madness, which could be lying right beside me there in the night. Not a savage madness either, but something that could be almost teasing. A lazy, teasing, half-sluggish suggestion that seemed to have been waiting a long time.

It might be saying, Why not? Why not try the worst?

The worst. Here in the most familiar place, the room where we had lain for all of our lives and thought ourselves most safe. I might do it for no reason I or anybody could understand, except that I could not help it.

The thing to do was to get up, to get myself out of that room and out of the house. I went down the rungs of the ladder and never cast a single look at my sister where she slept. Then quietly down the stairs, nobody stirring, into the kitchen, where everything was so familiar to me that I could make my way without a light. The kitchen door was not really locked—I am not even sure that we possessed a key. A chair was pushed under the doorknob, so that anybody trying to get in would make a great clatter. A slow, careful removal of the chair could be managed without making any noise at all.

After the first night I was able to make my moves without a break, so as to be outside within a couple of smooth seconds.

There. At first everything was black, because I would have lain wakeful for a long time, and the moon had already gone down. I kept on staying in bed as long as I thought I could for several nights, as if it was a defeat to have to give up trying to sleep, but after some time I got out of bed as a regular habit, as soon as the house seemed to be dreaming. And the moon of course had its own habits, so sometimes I stepped into a pool of silver.

Of course there were no streetlights—we were too far from town.

Everything was larger. The trees around the house were always called by their names—the beech tree, the elm tree, the oak tree, the maples always spoken of in the plural and not differentiated, because they clung together. The white lilac tree and the purple lilac tree never referred to as bushes because they had grown too big. The front and back and side lawns were easy to negotiate because mowed by myself with the idea of giving us some townlike respectability. My mother had once had that idea too. She had planted a semicircular lawn past the lilac trees, and edged to it with spirea bushes and delphinium plants. That was all gone now.

The east side of our house and the west side looked on two different worlds, or so it seemed to me. The east side was the town side, even though you could not see any town. Not more than two miles away there were houses in rows, with streetlights and running water, and though, as I have said, you could not see any of that, I am really not sure that you couldn't get a faint glow if you stared long enough. To the west, the long curve of the river and the fields and the trees and the sunsets had nothing to interrupt them ever.

Back and forth I walked, first close to the house and then venturing here and there as I got to rely on my eyesight and could count on not bumping into the pump handle or the platform that supported the clothesline. The birds began to stir, and then to sing —as if each of them had thought of it separately, up there in the trees. They woke far earlier than I would have thought possible. But soon, soon after those earliest starting songs, there got to be a little whitening to the sky. And suddenly I was overwhelmed with sleepiness. I went back into the house, where there was suddenly darkness everywhere, and I very properly, carefully, silently, set the tilted chair under its knob and went upstairs without a sound, managing doors and steps with the caution necessary although I

seemed already half asleep. I fell into my pillow. And I woke late
—late in our house being around nine o'clock.

I would remember everything then, but it was so absurd—the
bad part of it indeed was so absurd—that I could hardly bother
about it. My brother and sister had gone off to school—being still
in public school, they were not getting time off for good exam
performances, as I was. When they got home in the afternoon, my
sister was somebody who could never have passed through such a
danger. It was absurd. We swung together in the hammock, one of
us at either end.

It was in that hammock that I spent much of the days, and that
may have been the simple reason for my not getting to sleep at
night. And since I did not speak of my night difficulties, nobody
came up with the simple information that I'd be better to get
more action during the daytime.

My troubles returned with the night, of course. The demons
grabbed hold of me again. And in fact it got worse. I knew enough
to get up and out of my bunk without any pretending that things
would get better and I would go to sleep if I just tried hard enough.
I made my way as carefully out of the house as I had done before.
I became able to find my way around more easily; even the inside
of those rooms became more visible to me and yet more strange. I
could make out the tongue-and-groove kitchen ceiling put in when
the house was built maybe a hundred years ago, and the northern
window frame partly chewed away by a dog that had been shut in
the house one night long before I was born. I remembered what
I had completely forgotten—that I used to have a sandbox there,
placed where my mother could watch me out the north window.
A great bunch of golden glow was flowering in its place now; you
could hardly see out of that window at all.

The east wall of the kitchen had no windows in it, but it had a
door opening on a stoop where we stood to hang out the heavy
wet washing and haul it in when it was dry and smelling fresh and
triumphant, from white sheets to dark heavy overalls.

At that stoop I sometimes halted in my night walks. I never sat
down, but it eased me to look toward town, maybe just to inhale
the sanity of it. All the people getting up before long, having their
shops to go to, their doors to unlock and window arrangements to
see to, their busyness.

One night—I can't say whether it was the twentieth or the

twelfth or only the eighth or the ninth that I had got up and walked—I got a sense, too late for me to change my pace, that there was somebody around the corner. There was somebody waiting there and I could do nothing but walk right on. I would be caught if I turned back.

Who was it? Nobody but my father. He too was looking toward town and that improbably faint light. He was dressed in his day clothes—dark work pants, the next thing to overalls but not quite, and dark shirt and boots. He was smoking a cigarette. A roll-your-own, of course. Maybe the cigarette smoke had alerted me to another presence, though it's possible that in those days the smell of tobacco smoke was everywhere, inside and out.

He said good morning, in what might have seemed a natural way except that there was nothing natural about it. We weren't accustomed to giving such greetings in our family. There was nothing hostile about this—it was just thought unnecessary, I suppose, to give a greeting to somebody you would be seeing off and on all day long.

I said good morning back. And it must have really been getting toward morning or my father would not have been dressed for a day's work in that way. The sky may have been whitening but hidden still between the heavy trees. The birds singing too. I had taken to staying away from my bunk till later and later, even though I didn't get comfort from doing that as I had at first. The possibilities that had once inhabited only the bedroom, the bunk beds, were taking up the corners everywhere.

Now that I come to think of it, why wasn't my father in his overalls? He was dressed as if he had to go into town for something, first thing in the morning.

I could not continue walking, the whole rhythm of it had been broken.

"Having trouble sleeping?" he said.

My impulse was to say no, but then I thought of the difficulties of explaining that I was just walking around, so I said yes.

He said that was often the case on summer nights.

"You go to bed tired out and then just as you think you're falling asleep you're wide awake. Isn't that the way?"

I said yes.

I knew now that he had not heard me getting up and walking around on just this one night. The person whose livestock was on the premises, whose earnings such as they were lay all close by, who kept a handgun in his desk drawer, was certainly going to stir at the slightest creeping on the stairs and the easiest turning of a knob.

I am not sure what conversation he meant to follow then, as regards my being awake. He had declared such wakefulness to be a nuisance. Was that to be all? I certainly did not intend to tell him more. If he had given the slightest intimation that he knew there was more, if he'd even hinted that he had come here intending to hear it, I don't think he'd have got anything out of me at all. I had to break the silence out of my own will, saying that I could not sleep. I had to get out of bed and walk.

Why was that?

I had dreams.

I don't know if he asked me, were those bad dreams?

We could take that for granted, I think.

He let me wait to go on, he didn't ask anything. I meant to back off but I kept talking. The truth was told with only the slightest modification.

When I spoke of my little sister, I said that I was afraid I would hurt her. I believed that he would know what I meant. Kill. Not hurt. Kill, and for no reason. None at all. A possession.

There was no satisfaction, really, once I had got that out. I had to say it then. Kill her.

Now I could not unsay it, I could not go back to the person I had been before.

My father had heard it. He had heard that I thought myself capable—for no reason, capable—of strangling my little sister in her sleep. He said, "Well."

Then he said not to worry. He said, "People have those kinds of thoughts sometimes."

He said this quite seriously but without any sort of alarm or jumpy surprise. People have these kinds of thoughts or fears if you like, but there's no real worry about it, no more than a dream. Probably to do with the ether.

He did not say, specifically, that I was in no danger of doing any such thing. He seemed more to be taking it for granted that such a thing could not happen. An effect of the ether, he said. No more sense than a dream. It could not happen, in the way that a meteor could not hit our house (of course it could, but the likelihood of it doing so put it in the category of couldn't).

He did not blame me, though, for thinking of it.

There were other things he could have said. He could have questioned me further about my attitude to my little sister or my dissatisfactions with my life in general. If this were happening today, he might have made an appointment for me to see a psychiatrist. (I think that is what I might have done, a generation and an income further on.)

The fact is that what he did worked as well. It set me down, but without either mockery or alarm, in the world we were living in.

If you live long enough as a parent, you discover that you have made mistakes you didn't bother to know about as well as the ones you do know about, all too well. You are somewhat humbled at heart, sometimes disgusted with yourself. I don't think my father felt anything like this. I do know that if I had ever taxed him, he might have said something about liking or lumping it. The encounters I had as a child with his belt or the razor strop. (Why do I say encounters? It's to show I'm not a howling sissy anymore, I can make light.) Those strappings, then, would have stayed in his mind, if they stayed at all, as no more than quite adequate curbing of a mouthy child's imagining that she could rule the roost.

"You thought you were too smart" was what he might have given as his reason, and indeed one heard that often in those times. Not always referring to myself. But a number of times, it did.

However, on that breaking morning he gave me just what I needed to hear and what I was to forget about, soon enough.

I have thought that he was maybe in his better work clothes because he had a morning appointment to go to the bank, and to learn there, not to his surprise, that there was no extension to his loan, he had worked as hard as he could but the market was not going to turn around and he had to find a new way of supporting us and paying off what we owed at the same time. Or he may have found out that there was a name for my mother's shakiness and that it was not going to stop. Or that he was in love with an impossible woman.

Never mind. From then on I could sleep.

RICHARD SCHMITT

Sometimes a Romantic Notion

FROM *The Gettysburg Review*

AT SCHOOL TODAY an esteemed member of my department said his grandfather, at age eighteen, "ran off" to join a circus. I thought, *Why do people say it like that? Anyone who ever joined a circus seems to have run away to do it.* My colleague is a poet, a wordsmith, a teacher of language, trained to be precise and accurate. I asked him why he said "ran off." "Was your grandfather a runaway? A fugitive of some kind?"

"Well, no," he said. He didn't know why he said "ran off." "The romantic exotica we associate with circuses, I guess."

We don't say that about other institutions. No one says that they ran off to join a university, or a sports franchise, or a Fortune 500 company, but circus employees are deemed runaways. Even the word *employee* doesn't jibe with public perception of circus workers. Circus people are not considered employed in the way one works for AT&T or Walmart. In a recent PBS documentary about New York's Big Apple Circus, the initial segment was called "Run Away." I can say for sure, because I know people on that show; very few of them, if any, are dyed-in-the-wool runaways. A few directionless young people? Sure. A middle-age crisis or two? Maybe. As *Washington Post* reviewer Hank Stuever said, "Though the dream may be very much intact as a metaphor for escaping life's monotony, people don't run away and join the circus much anymore."

Did they ever? I have not mentioned to my colleagues that by the time I was seventeen, I had run away from home three times. It was not romantic. I lied about my age, worked shit jobs, paid rent on squalid apartments with degenerate roommates. No car, no girlfriend. One morning in 1970, riding in the back of a flatbed truck on the way to a job site, I saw the Ringling Bros. and Barnum & Bailey Circus train parked under an I-95 overpass in Providence, Rhode Island. The train was white. The train yard black. I was a brick washer then. I spent my days at a construction site with a hose and a wire brush, scrubbing dried cement off red bricks. Before that I had a job pulling bent nails from boards and pounding them straight with a hammer. Minimum wage was $1.60 an hour. My roommate was huddled in the back of the truck, a junkie, hugging himself and shivering, the wind roaring and whipping. I pointed down at the train yard. "A white train," I yelled. The kid stared at me. He was drooling. All he heard was the word *white*.

After eight hours of brick scrubbing, blue jeans covered with red dust, I walked under the I-95 overpass, the steel stanchions droning with rush-hour traffic, and into the train yard. The white train was long, split in two sections, and lined up on parallel tracks. I walked between the cars on a concrete walkway receding to a common vanishing point. I looked in the windows and open vestibules. I saw a tanned woman in a gold thong lying on her stomach on a plastic chaise lounge, the folding kind you take to the beach; it was August, and she was gleaming in the late-afternoon sun. Beside her on the concrete was a can of Pepsi in a Styrofoam cooler, and next to that were the shining steel wheels of the train. I walked by in my brick-dust sneakers. She didn't budge. I passed a small cast-iron barbecue grill and ducked under a makeshift clothesline with laundry drying in the sun. Regular laundry, no spangles or sparkles. Further on a guy stood on a stepladder washing windows. He didn't look at me. It was very quiet. At some point I climbed three steps into one of the vestibules between cars and looked down the narrow hallways, carpeted, shoes outside doors. I hopped out the other side. There was nothing to see but this brilliant white train in the grimy Providence train yard.

So the picture is clear; I was a directionless youth seduced by what my colleague referred to as romantic exotica. Fair enough. But I was already a runaway. I thought I might find a job here as a practical endeavor, to get away from brick washing and junkies. And though the train was ethereal in context, it seemed more military than magical, functional over fantastic. Bleached underwear hanging over a barbecue grill, a woman sunbathing, a guy washing windows. There were no skirt-swishing, heel-slapping, tambourine-shaking gypsies doing folk dances. No one played an accordion. I headed back to the civic center.

People say "run away to join *the* circus" as if there is only one, and as if there is no doubt about joining it. As if the option resides solely with the runaway. One is fed up; the need to escape strikes; you find this entity called *circus* and presto, you are embraced. I found this was not true.

When I got back to the civic center, I saw piles of animal excrement steaming in the road, steel cargo wagons, elephants chained in a line, large cats in cages, men in blue work shirts with nifty patches: *The Greatest Show on Earth.* You think *circus* and expect this, but it was disorienting in dismal downtown Providence. The potpourri of people, animals, and apparatuses squelched the mundane stench of diesel exhaust and roaring gears from the nearby Greyhound bus station. Workers, people, hustled through massive doors on the backside of the civic center; it seemed anyone could cruise on in. But when I tried, I was halted abruptly by a stick across my chest, a cane wielded by an elderly white-haired gentleman with one leg about six inches longer than the other. "Where do you think you're going?"

"I was hoping to apply for a job," I said.

"A job, huh? What can you do?"

"I can do anything."

He scoffed.

What was I going to say? *I'm a brick washer? A nail puller?* Among the few things circuses do not have are bricks and nails.

"You gotta see Schwartzy, and you can't come in here until you do."

"Where might this Schwartzy be?"

"How the hell do I know?" His cane swept menacingly overhead. "What do I look like?" He was stout, with his spinal cord warped like a bow, his longer leg thrusting out to one side to accommodate its extra length, and he had a thick orthopedic shoe on the short leg. Later I found out this was Backdoor Jack. An integral part of a system designed to make running away with the circus not as simple as people romantically believe.

I retreated. People scurrying about were unapproachable; they moved with purpose, function, with no intention of stopping to talk to a town punk. That was another thing I learned later: I was a town punk. A condition glaringly obvious to circus people. I approached

a longhaired fellow. "Excuse me." He shouldered on, uttering gut-
tural sounds. *Of course,* I thought, *circus people are foreigners.*

Among the array of wagons scattered behind the civic center
was a diner on wheels: burgers sizzled, a line of people stood at a
serving window, a woman with a beehive hairdo took money and
handed out food and soft drinks. I got in line. I had seventy-five
cents. When it was my turn, the woman looked me in the eye.
"Cup of coffee, please," I said.

She set down a Styrofoam cup. "Fifty," she said, holding out her
palm.

I fumbled with my coins, making sure I had her attention.
"Where's Schwartzy?" I said, as if I knew him.

"Train, probably," she said. "Where else would he be?"

I took my coffee and got out of the way.

Train, probably. That was a long walk the first time. I headed back.
Maybe I could be a window washer. I was qualified for that. I walked
and spilled coffee as hot as molten lava over my hand. At the train,
the window washer was gone; his stepladder was there, his bucket
and squeegee. The tanning woman sunbathed; talking to her was
out of the question. I walked between cars, had to be a mile of them.
After a while the class of cars deteriorated, the spit polish and flash
of the first few cars gave way to peeled paint and sooty squalor. There
were garbage bags. The windows weren't washed. It was like walking from the good neighborhood to the bad, from wide lawns and
barbered bushes, to saltbox suburbs, to tenement walkups, to actual
animal habitat. Stockcars, pervasive zoo odors, heavy wooden ramps
soiled with various types of dried animal crap. Then from the un-
derpinnings of the train, a nest of gray hair atop stooped shoulders
emerged, a hunched, troll-like figure crawling from the black belly
of the train, dragging a fat rubber hose, the type used for pumping
septic tanks. An old man covered in soot and rail cinders. His face
resembled a tire tread in dried mud. He chewed something.

"Schwartzy," I said. "I'm looking for Schwartzy."

"Pie car," the old man said, his gums working.

"What's a pie car?"

The old man considered this. "Pie car," he said, pointing back
the way I'd come. "152."

I hadn't noticed the painted numbers next to the vestibules.
The car we stood at was 101. I looked back down the line. The
next one was 102. I turned and walked. Only fifty-one cars to go.

The sunbather was at 137, the window washer at 148. Car 152 was in the good neighborhood. It was a dining car. Of course, circus people eat. Red vinyl booths, center aisle, Formica counter. A cook in a chef's hat scrubbed a grill. "Closed," he said.

"Schwartzy here?"

The cook looked down to the end of the car where a baldheaded man squinted from behind bars. I walked toward the barred window. I saw the sign: PAYMASTER. "Hi," I said. Schwartzy was unusually short, with one wayward eyeball, maybe made of glass.

Circus people don't meet and greet. No one says hello, or goodbye, or what's up. They tend to stare at you until you state your business, and if you don't, or if your business isn't particularly intriguing, they walk away. And many of the administrative circus people, like Schwartzy and Backdoor Jack, had physical afflictions: missing limbs, clubfeet, harelips, purple splotches on their faces, and they all limped. This guy Schwartzy watched me through the bars. I tried to get a fix on which eye was doing the seeing, to which I should be directing my request.

"I was wondering," I said, "if you had any job openings."

"Are you a diesel mechanic?"

"Ah, no."

"I need a diesel mechanic."

"I was once a dishwasher." I was in a dining car, after all.

He shook his head. "Try concessions."

"Concessions?"

"At the building, see Bobby Johnson, he may have something for you."

"The building?"

He turned his back on the window.

I headed back to the civic center — *the building*.

Concessionaires were young and hung out front by the ticket windows, a bunch of them wearing candy-cane-striped smocks and setting up souvenir stands. They were hawkers, vendors, watching for anyone with money. "Hey you, come 'ere, how much money you got?"

"I'm looking for work," I said. "Do you know Bobby Johnson?"

"Do I know Bobby Johnson?" The kid was about my age, sitting on a box with his back to a wagon; he looked over at a tall black guy with a goatee who was piecing together a program display. "Hey, Pierre, do we know Bobby Johnson?"

It was clear that they did. "Do you know where he is?" I said.

"Do we know where he is?" He turned his face toward the open door of the wagon; inside I saw a desk, a swivel chair, a bunch of cardboard boxes. "Does anyone know Bobby Johnson?" It was clear too, he was messing with me.

Bobby Johnson, head of concessions, was inside the wagon, and, incredibly, he wore a black eye patch. He was tall, thin, and soft-spoken. He shook his head sadly. "I got nothing now," he said. "Why don't you head over to the red show? They're right down the road in Philadelphia." Ringling had two traveling units back then, red and blue; now they have a third, gold show, traveling different routes simultaneously. I had never been out of New England; Philadelphia, right down the road to this guy, might as well have been in Greece.

Not ten feet away the black guy, Pierre, suddenly bellowed, "Pro-grams! Get your programs!" There were absolutely no ticket buy-ers; the show didn't start for three hours. The front of the building overlooked a plaza facing downtown Providence. Men and women in business suits slogged out of office buildings and headed for parking garages. Pierre kept roaring, "Programs!" It was baffling and earsplitting. People two blocks away turned their heads.

At one point his boss, Bobby Johnson, poked his head out the door of the wagon and said, "Pierre, shut up, please." But the guy kept hollering. Johnson was a quiet man; I bent to hear what he said, which was, "Sorry, no jobs." At that point I gave up. In spite of romantic notions to the contrary, it seemed clear that one didn't simply decide to join the circus and have them issue you a ban-danna and a tambourine. I was doomed to my squalid apartment, junkie roommate, and brick washing.

But when I turned to go, Pierre stopped shouting and said, "Half these guys will quit when we go west."

"What?"

"What do you mean, 'what'? You want a job, don't you? All the guys you see here will quit when we go west." He raised his voice, shouting into the wagon, "Won't they, Bobby? Won't they quit when we go west?" Then to me, "Happens every year. You come to Albu-querque, he'll put you on." He gave me a reassuring nod. "Won't you, Bobby? Won't you put him on if he comes to Albuquerque?"

The boss poked his head out the door again. I watched his one good eye. Was he nodding? He was nodding. "Yeah," he said. "We always need help in Albuquerque."

"See, told you, come to Albuquerque you'll have a job. Programs!"

Upon further questioning, it became clear that this show was about to make one of their longest jumps of the season, a three-day run from the next town, Boston, across the country to Albuquerque, New Mexico. They rarely had runs that long, and when they did they always lost a lot of help. "Most of these guys are easterners," Pierre said. "They don't want to go out west. Happens when we come back too, the westerners all quit."

If Philadelphia was Greece, Albuquerque was another planet. I was raised in Rhode Island; my travel experience was limited to six-hour traffic jams each summer when my parents tried to get us to Cape Cod in July. I had twenty-five cents to my name. All I knew about Albuquerque was I would need a plane to get there, and I knew plane tickets cost more than a quarter. Walking back to my apartment, I reasoned it out. The circus was in Boston two weeks; two brick-washer paychecks at sixty bucks each; if I held out on the rent, paid weekly, I would have $120. I stopped at a phone and invested ten of my twenty-five cents to discover that one-way to Albuquerque was $80. Eureka! If I could dodge my landlord and roommates for a couple weeks, I would run away to join the circus.

I know you are thinking, *What an idiot. What a ridiculous plan.* But I had nothing in Providence. Is it possible to run away from nothing to something? Is that a romantic notion? Or a rational decision for a teenage brick washer earning $1.60 per hour and living with junkies? I wasn't a junkie myself, though I tried heroin a couple times when it was free. You can see why I shy from revealing this information to my esteemed colleagues. Why I leave the segment of my life called "Circus" off my curriculum vitae.

My plan, desperate, idiotic, or otherwise, did work. Two weeks after spotting that alluring white train in the grimy Providence train yard, I arrived in Albuquerque. It wasn't easy dodging my landlord; in fact I spent the final two nights before departure sleeping at the airport. I landed in Albuquerque with $7—and here is where luck kicked in; here is where a truly romantic notion surfaced, a notion that there is a benevolent God somewhere watching over idiots, drunks, children, innocents of all types. Certainly I fit the category. If the circus people had turned me away in Albuquerque that day, I don't know what I would have done with $7 and no return ticket. As it was, I had been worried about where the circus building was located and how I would get there, and lo and behold, divine intervention, the old Albuquerque civic auditorium, long since torn down, was within sight of the airport. The circus was in full view when I stepped off the plane into the dry New Mexico heat.

You are thinking here, *This is where it turns romantic, right? Now we get the story as seen on TV:* My Season Under the Big Top. But no. I did get a job that day. I found Bobby Johnson. He seemed only mildly surprised to see me, and he turned me over to a Mexican who handed me a heavy red board with twenty-five puffy beehives of cotton candy stuck to it. "Fifty cents," he said. "Come back when they're gone."

"Come back?" He pointed to blue doors leading into the arena. I heard the music blasting, the ringmaster's garbled exclamations, the applause and exhortations of the crowd. I headed out, *in* actually, to the beginning of my circus career. I stayed ten years. That first day I earned about $2, and it was harder than brick washing. My last day, just shy of my twenty-eighth birthday, I declined a contract guaranteeing me six figures over ten months where I would work a total of sixteen minutes a day. By then I had had about every circus job available except animal training. I was on concessions, wardrobe, ring curb, transportation, rigging. Finally, high-wire walking was as high as I cared to go. I could have gone for a management position, show director, or a job at the main office in Washington, D.C.; I could have made a life of it. Ringling is a solid organization, the core of Feld Entertainment, the largest producer of live family entertainment in the world. They own all the ice shows you have ever heard of, as well as Disney on Parade, plus permanent shows in Vegas and Atlantic City and two traveling units overseas. Working for them is not much different from working at AT&T or Walmart. They have benefits and retirement plans, a credit union, organizations to protect retired animals and performers, and lobbyists to check the PETA people. But I had had enough of it. In ten years on the show, I had saved enough money to pay for a college education, and that was what I wanted. So I ran off to join a school. It has worked out. I am still here. After fifteen years, I am no longer a first-of-May teacher: I have tenure, people call me "Professor," and I no longer succumb to the allure of white trains.

It is not that romantic notions didn't crop up along the way, especially with the wire walking; it was just that when they did, I found them hard to relate to, absurd even. Once, being interviewed by a young blond newspaper reporter, I let it slip that my wire-walking days were nearing an end. The poor girl, wide-eyed, wouldn't accept it. "No," she said. "It's your life!" Well, okay, if that was what she wanted to believe. When seeking to charm young blond newspaper reporters, any romantic notion will do. But it wasn't my life. It was something I learned by steadfast practice, worked at for seven years, got paid well for, and quit.

About romance there are a lot of misconceptions.

Back in the eighties, I knew a hairdresser in New York, a young man with his own shop on the Upper East Side, a great business, appointments a month in advance, no new clients—this guy was talented and booked solid, $85 haircuts. One day, while cutting my hair, he told me he was closing the business, moving to Orlando, Florida. I naturally figured he was going to a more lucrative market. "That's sad news for me," I said, "but great for you, cutting the hair of Disney stars at two hundred bucks a pop."

"Oh, no," he said. "I'm done with hair."

"What! You're a genius stylist. You've got people begging you to cut their hair. How can you give up something you're born to do?"

He flabbergasted me by stating that he had enrolled in lion-training school. Citing my circus background, I expressed doubt about the existence of such a thing. "It exists," he told me. "Magicians and wild cats, like Siegfried and Roy, making tigers disappear and whatnot."

Realizing he was serious, I suggested that such an outlandish, long-shot, unstable vocation was a major departure from the dependable occupation he enjoyed as a topnotch New York hairdresser. "Hairdresser," he said. "Big deal."

"Think of your future, man!"

"That's what I'm thinking about," he said. "I'm married. I'm going to have a kid." He stopped cutting and pointed his scissors at me. "And no kid wants a dad who is a hairdresser." He paused, stared up at the ceiling, as if at any moment the spotlight might find him. "A lion tamer," he said. "That's something a kid can state with pride. 'My dad is a lion tamer!'"

It was hard to argue.

That was the end of a great hairdresser. I don't know if he ever made it in the land of Siegfried and Roy. Even Siegfried and Roy didn't make it in the land of Siegfried and Roy, whose show, by the way, was owned by Feld Entertainment. The problem with romantic notions is the notions part. Notions are fleeting; they go away. One minute you are making a tiger vanish; the next moment he is having you for dinner. Being eaten by tigers is not romantic.

I knew another guy, a fifth-generation circus performer in Italy, who dreamed about running away to join a town, an American town, specifically, Reno, Nevada. He wanted to dress up like an Old West gambler with a black vest and bolero tie and deal cards in a casino. That was his dream. All day, when he wasn't working in his family's show, he practiced card tricks, card shuffling, card manipulations. He was good at it. But he couldn't leave his family, because for two hundred years they had run this tent show all over Europe. The family needed him to work. It wasn't in his blood, his parents told him, to emigrate to America and become a cardsharp. He was a circus person, of an old and respected family; it was inconceivable that he slip fate and fly to Reno. There was a loyalty issue; he felt guilty for abandoning his family even in spirit. The circus bored him to death, literally; he became depressed, and after many years committed suicide. His way of running away, I guess. Suicide is not romantic.

Some people, usually young males, think it is romantic to go to war, to be honorable and brave with your buddies in glorious battle. But when your balls are blown off, it is not romantic. What will Dad say to the guys at the VFW? My son got his nuts shot off? Even if Dad's own balls are sufficient to say that, it won't be glorious. He will cry in his beer. His buddies will think, *Poor bastard,* and pat his back. That is not romantic. That is pitiful. How will Junior get a girlfriend now? How will Dad be a grandpappy? How will progeny be maintained? What will Mom say to the neighbors? There are many questions when romantic notions are dashed.

Maybe romantic is going out to Wyoming and roping a wild bronco. But after you get out of the hospital, you have to feed the son of a bitch. He bites and kicks and doesn't take kindly to the saddle, and after you get out of the hospital again, you neglect and abandon him, and the PETA people haul your ass into court —there is no romance in court, ever.

Maybe all this romantic crap is Hollywood's fault, our need to escape by sitting before a television. In real life, romantic heroes are unclean. Cowboys, pirates, explorers, soldiers—those guys never bathe. Audie Murphy was famous for playing himself in movies. Who knows Robert L. Howard or Joe Hooper? Both are soldiers more decorated than Murphy. Sports heroes are sweaty and full of chemicals. Astronauts in tight capsules do not have Jacuzzis. In real life, heroes stink. But we have Hollywood to keep them fresh and wholesome. John Wayne was a bigot, but not on the big screen. His white hat didn't even pick up dust when he rode across the desert; he didn't bleed or sweat. Ted Williams was too cheap to eat at restaurants; he gave Boston baseball fans the finger. Joe DiMaggio was moody and mean-spirited. He was mentally cruel to poor Marilyn, one of our most fragile and enduring romantic legends.

When I questioned my poet friend carefully, it turned out that his grandfather, age eighteen, hadn't actually *run off* at all. His mother knew exactly where he was all the time. In fact, he saved his dirty laundry in a duffel bag until the circus came within hoofing distance of his home, and then he would meet Mom and exchange his dirty clothes for clean and folded. Mom probably had an apple pie and a couple sandwiches in her cache as well. "Why did you say 'run off'?" I asked the poet. He suggested the circus, like gypsy life, is simply associated with footloose freedom by those of us earning a living in cubicles and classrooms. "Metaphorical freedom," he said. "We're susceptible to it." Thomas Moore, author of *Care of the Soul,* seems to agree. "Circuses attract that element in the psyche that craves symbolic and dreamlike experiences. When work, facts, and literal issues are our main focus, we have a desperate need for liberation."

My esteemed colleague admitted the cliché of it all, the romantic nonsense of the possibility of escaping who we are. He told me about walking his dog outside on a very clear winter night. He lives out in the country, and he was dazzled—actually, literally starstuck—by the vivid constellations. He said words were not failing him; he kept thinking *dazzling, alluring, glittering, transcending.* He thought, *Andromeda. Cepheus. Ursa Major, Canis Minor.* And then he thought, *What the hell am I thinking? I can't write a poem about the stars! That's the ultimate cliché, the most romantic nonsense going. I'm turning into one of my students. What's next? Hallmark cards?* He chuckled and called his dog. "Where are you, hound major?" He walked home, watching his snowy boots.

As a writer, I spent years hiding and denying my connection to the circus because I had the romantic notion that fiction writers simply made things up out of thin air or their intrinsic, God-given genius. An idea, I see now, about as crazy as running away to join the circus.

VANESSA VESELKA

Highway of Lost Girls

FROM *GQ*

IN THE SUMMER OF 1985, somewhere near Martinsburg, Pennsylvania, the body of a young woman was pulled from a truck-stop dumpster. I had just hitched a ride and was sitting in a nearby truck waiting for the driver to pay for gas so we could leave. When they found her, there was shouting. A man from the restaurant ran out and started yelling for everyone to stay away as a small crowd gathered around the dumpster in the rain. Word filtered back that the dead girl was a teenage hitchhiker. I remember thinking it could be me, since I was also a teenage hitchhiker. Watching the driver of my truck walk back across the wet asphalt, a second thought arose: It could be him. He could be the killer. The driver reached the cab, swung up behind the wheel, and said we should get going. He said he didn't want to get caught up in anything time-consuming. Stowing his paperwork, he released the brake. Neither of us said anything about the dead girl. As we pulled away, I looked once more in the side mirror. They were stringing crime tape around the dumpster just as another state trooper rolled into the lot.

That ride turned out to be fine. We drove up to Ohio drinking Diet Coke and listening to Bruce Springsteen. The trucker bought me lunch and didn't even try to have sex with me, which made him a prince in my world. Several days later, though, heading south on I-95 through the Carolinas, I got picked up by another trucker, who was not fine. I don't remember much about him except that he was taller and leaner than most truckers and didn't wear jeans or T-shirts. He wore a cotton button-down with the sleeves rolled neatly up over his biceps and had the cleanest cab I ever saw. He must have seemed okay or I wouldn't have gotten in the truck with him. Once out on the road, though, he changed. He stopped responding to my questions. His bearing shifted. He grew taller in his seat, and his face muscles relaxed into something both arrogant and blank. Then he started talking about the dead girl in the dumpster and asked me if I'd ever heard of the Laughing Death Society. "We laugh at death," he told me.

A few minutes later he pulled the truck onto the shoulder of the road by some woods, took out a hunting knife, and told me to get into the back of the cab. I began talking, saying the same things over and over. I said I knew he didn't want to do it. I said it was his choice. I said he could do it in a few minutes. I said it was his choice. I said I wouldn't go to the cops if nothing happened to me, but it was his choice—until he looked at me and I went still. There was going to be no more talking. I knew in my body that it was over. Then he said one word: *Run.* Without looking back, I ran into the woods and hid. I stayed there until I saw the truck pull onto the interstate. It was getting dark. I was still in shock, so I walked back out to the same road and started hitching south. I never went to the police and didn't tell anyone for years.

This spring a friend sent a news-story link about a serial killer with the subject line "Is this your guy?" The serial killer's name was Robert Ben Rhoades. Rhoades was a long-haul trucker, in jail since 1990, who had recently been convicted of a couple of new "cold cases." I didn't recognize him from the initial photos, but as I found pictures of him as a younger man, his face came to seem more familiar. The glasses were the same, the curve of the cheekbone, and something about the expression, particularly the set of the mouth. It had the same neutral arrogance. Rhoades looked like the guy who picked me up. But then, Rhoades looks like a lot of guys. He would have been only thirty-nine at the time, and I remember the trucker as an older man with light brown or graying hair. To a teenager, though, someone pushing forty is pretty old, and hair often looks darker in photos. The light in my memory is strange too. It was a cloudy day just before a summer storm, and everything in the truck is cast in gray.

After receiving my friend's e-mail, I left messages with the FBI but was relieved when they were not returned. The memory was twenty-seven years old, and nothing in it was actionable. The photos stayed in my head, though, and with them came questions: What if the man who pulled the knife on me really did murder the hitchhiker? Why did he let me go? Who *was* the girl in the dumpster? Why didn't I go to anyone? I needed to understand what my responsibility was and to find my own answers, if nobody else's, so I began to look.

I have no fascination with serial killers, so I didn't realize that Rhoades was famous. There are articles, TV episodes, and books on him—*Driven to Kill, Roadside Prey, Killer on the Road*—and from these sources I learned that every grim and secret fear I have about the human race is manifest in Robert Ben Rhoades. Rhoades was a sexual sadist. He kidnapped women, tortured and raped them for weeks before killing them. What is known about him in the 1980s is murky. He was involved in the BDSM and swinger scene in his hometown of Houston. He was married. When he was caught, he said that he had been "doing this" for fifteen years, which would put the onset of his murders back into the 1970s. His trucking logs place him in the area of fifty unsolved murders in the three years prior to his arrest alone. While not all fifty cases have been tied to Rhoades yet and Rhoades himself has admitted to only three murders, the FBI has strong reason to believe that at his peak he was killing one to three women a month.

Rhoades was first arrested when an Arizona state trooper found a screaming woman named Lisa Pennal* chained in the back of his cab. He was charged with kidnapping and assault. What put him away for life, though, was the rape and murder of Regina Walters, a fourteen-year-old girl from Pasadena, Texas. Rhoades picked her up along with her boyfriend, Ricky Jones, in February of 1990. Jones was promptly killed, and his remains were discovered later in Mississippi. Rhoades kept Regina for at least two weeks. He shaved her head and pubic hair, pierced her with fishing hooks, dressed her up in a black dress and heels, and photographed her in moments of terror, then killed her with a garrote made of baling wire, leaving her one-hundred-pound body to decompose in a barn in Illinois off Interstate 70.

Behind the tragic elements of Regina's story, like some kind of pentimento, I saw my own. Like me, she left home with her older boyfriend. Also like me, Regina became dependent upon the grace of truck drivers. In her weeks with Rhoades, many driv-

---

* Some of the victims' names have been changed.

ers saw her, but somehow no alarm was raised. She passed through that world as if she were invisible.

In 1985 my biggest problem was sleep. There was no safe way for me to get it. I left home in early January, hitchhiking south from New York City with my twenty-one-year-old boyfriend. We had $60 and a Smith & Wesson five-shot with one bullet in it, which we accidentally fired off in a field in Maryland during a discussion about whether the safety was on. I had a guitar and a knapsack full of souvenirs of my girlhood: notes from friends, earrings, and song lyrics. I was fifteen.

People don't leave home because things are going well; they leave because they feel they have to, and right or wrong, that's how I felt. I lived with my mom in New York, and the fights between us were growing in intensity and emotional violence. I don't think either of us knew what to do about it. There was talk of me going to live with my dad in Virginia, where I had traditionally spent my summers. By then, though, I had been kicked out of two schools for absences and was cutting myself regularly. My emotions were a planet around which I spun like a moon. As I saw it, it didn't matter if I left, because in so many ways I was already gone. On my way out, I destroyed every single picture of me over the age of twelve so that there would be nothing to give to the police.

That first night my boyfriend and I stayed in an abandoned barn in Maryland. It was off the side of the freeway and probably very much like the one Regina Walters was found in. The barn had a loft with wind coming through broken slats and was surrounded by the same kind of brown grassy field and frozen mud. Like Regina, I also had a little journal and probably wrote something in it that night, because it was far too cold to sleep. We were back on the road before dawn, walking down a highway covered in black ice, shivering in our hoodies. A trucker picked us up at daybreak, and I rode in a semi for the first time.

Being up high, warm, and looking out over the traffic was a great improvement. The trucker bought us chicken-fried steak, chatted amiably, and let us nap in the cab while he drove. While we were asleep, he pulled into a small truck stop, and I woke to his hand down my shirt. I kept my eyes closed, stayed still, then rolled away from him, pretending I was still asleep. A few minutes later, I got up like nothing had happened. The trucker went to pay for

gas, and my boyfriend and I went to use the bathroom. When we
came back, the truck was gone and every reminder of home with it
—my guitar, my knapsack, everything except the Smith & Wesson,
which we sold later in New Orleans.

That first ride was a preview of how it would often go for me
with truckers—dodging sex and getting stranded—but I had
learned one crucial lesson: when a truck slows down, you get up.
Getting sleep was pretty easy with a boyfriend, because one of us
could always stay awake. Six weeks later, though, we parted ways.
Somewhere in Arizona we had a fight in a gas station off I-10,
and we each climbed into separate trucks, and that was it. I was
on my own. Without fake ID, I couldn't stay in a shelter. Sleeping
by myself on the street made me a target, and having sex with
some creepy old guy for a spot on a mattress also held little appeal. So I went back to hitchhiking in circles and discovered a state
of half-consciousness wherein I could be asleep and not asleep at
the same time. I could rest but not dream. I could tell you the last
three songs played on the radio if you asked, but only if you asked.
If you didn't, I had no memory of them at all.

I stuck to trucks because they were safer than cars. When you
get in a truck at a truck stop, everyone notices. They chatter about
it on the CB, and you are driving off in what amounts to a huge
billboard advertising the name of the company. I needed visibility
to stay alive. But it was also a dangerous form of brinksmanship,
because if a trucker was going to cross the line, the higher stakes
meant he was going to do it for real. There was a gap before that
line, and most truckers wouldn't take it that far. I lived in that gap.

Truck stops in the 1980s were closed worlds where what went
on passed unnoticed on the outside. The stores were dimly lit
and filled with smoke, radically different from the family travel
plazas of today. Magazine porn often dominated the aisles—gloss-
ies like *Hustler* and *Barely Legal* but also newsprint rags with cheap
color covers. Bottles of isobutyl nitrite and rotgut aphrodisiacs like
Locker Room and Spanish Fly crowded the counters by the register, along with the iconic bumper sticker ASS, GAS, OR GRASS
—NO ONE RIDES FOR FREE.

Back then, though, my thoughts weren't on misogyny; they
were on logistics. I needed to find rides and usually couldn't get
into the restaurant. The general rule was that you were a prostitute until proven otherwise. And then you were still a prostitute.

Waitresses were the first to kick you out. That forced me into asking for rides in the hallway by the showers. Over time I learned safer ways of getting rides by having truckers navigate the CB radio for me. Women couldn't really get on the "zoo channel," as they called it then, because the sound of their voice would trigger twenty minutes of crass chatter. There was only one word for *woman* on the CB, and that was *beaver*. Even the guys who were trying to help had used it. They had to make up stories for me: "I got a beaver needs a ride to Flagstaff for her grandma's funeral don't want no trouble, c'mon back." There was always a sick mom or dead grandparent involved, and I was almost always abandoned by my jerk of a boyfriend, who'd made off with all my money and my car.

Through these stories, I jumped from truck to truck. Like a lemur in a canopy of trees, I barely saw the ground. Even so, it still wasn't safe to sleep. Adhering to my rule (that the only safe truck was a moving truck) meant I woke when a truck took an exit. I woke when it slowed for traffic. When it turned, when it downshifted, when it drifted toward the shoulder—I woke. Wearing down from lack of sleep and trying to get a handle on my risk level, I began to work off a 1-to-5 scale of sexually aggressive behavior:

1. You (the driver) kept your urges to yourself.
2. You asked me to have sex and offered to pay.
3. You told me I owed you sex for the ride and chicken-fried steak and threatened to drop me off some where dangerous.
4. You dropped me off somewhere dangerous.
5. I had to jump when you slowed down because you were going to rape me.

Most truckers occupied the middle of the scale, but the trucker who resembled Rhoades didn't have a place on it. Anybody who pulls a knife on you in an enclosed space like a truck is terrifying. But beyond that, it was the man's demeanor that was so chilling. He wasn't nervous, angry, or excited. He was grave and methodical, as if preparing to dress a deer.

From reading about Rhoades, I knew that he preferred hitchhikers to prostitutes and specifically targeted runaways. I also knew the first thing he did was to get them into the back of his sleeper cab, which had anchor points for shackles. But I hadn't seen any

shackles. I only saw the man with the knife. "It has to be him," a
friend said. "How many of those guys could there be?"

According to the FBI, quite a few. In 2009 the feds went public with a program called the Highway Serial Killings Initiative in
response to a rising number of dead bodies found along the in-
terstates. Some of these were women left in dumpsters. Narrowing
the field to those last seen around truck stops and rest areas, the
bureau counted over five hundred bodies, almost all women. Of
the two hundred people on a suspect list, almost all of them were
long-haul truckers.

But nobody had to tell me that people like Rhoades killed people like me and got away with it. Going through the truck stops,
I'd heard about women getting their throats slit or strangled. I'd
heard of at least one who got hung up on a meat hook in the back
of a refrigerated trailer because a trucker thought she'd given
him VD. At night I listened to the voices of prostitutes on the CB,
barely intelligible between streams of name-calling: "Hello, honey.
It's me, Sugar Bear, in party row. Anyone want to party?"

"Lot lizards" is what truckers call prostitutes who work truck stops,
and since many drivers don't distinguish between hitchhikers and
prostitutes, I was a lot lizard too. If we went missing, months could
pass before a report was filed, and by then there was little to connect
the missing person in one state with the decomposed remains in
another. When the Illinois state trooper who was trying to identify
the body of Regina Walters, the girl Rhoades left in that barn, put
her forensic description out on the national teletype, he was totally
unprepared for the response. He requested information on missing
Caucasian females thirteen to fifteen years old who had disappeared
six to nine months earlier. He got over nine hundred matches.

If there was any way to connect my story to Rhoades, it would be
through the body of the girl in the dumpster. Records on her
would provide a date and a place that could then be checked
against Rhoades's trucking logs. To at least one of my questions—
was Rhoades my guy?—I'd have a clear answer, a simple yes or no.

I began by Googling things like "dead girl truck stop Martinsburg." Nothing came up, but that wasn't too surprising. Her murder happened twenty-seven years ago and was essentially pre-In-
ternet. I pulled up a map of Martinsburg, Pennsylvania, and that's
where things started to get hazy. Martinsburg was nothing but a

pinprick, just a dot on a minor route feeding into a midsize highway on the outskirts of Altoona, Pennsylvania, not the sort of place
you'd expect to find a busy truck stop. Had I confused the state?
I did a search on towns named Martinsburg. There were seven
within range—Indiana, Iowa, Ohio, Pennsylvania, Missouri, West
Virginia, and New York—all less than a day's drive apart.

A week before the girl was found in the dumpster, though, I'd
gone to see my dad in Virginia. At the time he was struggling himself, living with several other guys in a house where you flushed
the toilet with a bucket of water and working what little construction there was in the county. I quickly realized I would have been
nothing but a burden. The morning I left, I asked him to take me
to the closest truck stop so I could get a ride going toward California. It was a made-up destination, a *Grapes of Wrath* narrative of
brighter futures. I was sure he would remember where he took me
back then, so last spring I called him. I didn't tell him about my
recent inquiries at first; I just asked where he'd dropped me off.
Without any hesitation he said Martinsburg, West Virginia.

"Were there any murders that summer?" I asked him.

"There was that hitchhiker. You called and left a message a day
or so after I dropped you off, saying I was going to read about a
dead seventeen-year-old hitchhiker they found in a truck stop and
that it wasn't you."

My whole body relaxed. My memory may have been bent by sleep
deprivation, but I was not crazy. There was a Martinsburg truck stop
somewhere in my story, and there was a dead seventeen-year-old
hitchhiker. She had existed enough for me to call my dad all those
years ago and warn him about what he would read. And if it happened, she could be found. It was just a matter of looking harder.

The original Rhoades investigation had woven a complex web, en-
tangling local and federal agencies in five different states. Eventually the locus shifted to the Houston FBI, because at some point
every thread ran through Texas. Rhoades was from Texas. His wife,
Debra Davis, was from Texas. Regina Walters and Ricky Jones were
from Texas. He picked up two of his other victims in Texas.

I flew to Austin to meet with two retired FBI men, special agents
Mark Young and Robert F. Lee, who'd both worked on the case.
Young was a profiler for the Bureau as well as a field agent. Over
lunch at a local sushi place, he taught me the difference between

a mode of operation and a signature. Modes of operation change. They are more like habits, he said, and can adapt to circumstances or mood. Rhoades, for instance, used guns and ligature strangulation and probably knives too. A signature, however, does not change. Sexual sadists in particular work off erotic maps established early on. They get more nuanced and elaborate, but the basic topography remains the same. One of Rhoades's signatures was shaving the head and pubic hair of his female victims. Piercings around the breasts, bruising, and other signs of torture were also frequently found.

Young, a six-foot-four Texan and third-generation lawman, opened his laptop and pulled up a picture of a woman named Shana Holts. Only days before Regina Walters was taken, Rhoades had been detained by the police in Houston for the possible sexual assault and kidnapping of Holts. She'd been picked up in a truck stop, shackled into the back of the cab, tortured and raped for weeks. She'd escaped when Rhoades pulled into a Houston brewery. I'd always read that she got away because Rhoades forgot to chain her in, but I found out from Young that she'd not been shackled when she escaped. Rhoades had told her to "sit there and be a good girl." But Holts, eighteen years old, had been on the street since she was twelve. By her own account, she had been raped at least twenty times and had already had a baby. She knew how to survive. Whatever the man thought he had broken in her had already been broken and healed back stronger. She didn't do what he expected. She ran. She brought the police right back to Rhoades's truck but then balked at pressing charges, so they had to let him go. The story was that she was too scared, but I wondered if there was more.

I looked at the picture on Young's computer. Shana was a pretty girl with freckles and blank blue eyes. Her thick red-blond hair had been cropped close to her head with a knife or scissors and was now growing back. With all her freckles, she looked very Irish. Around her neck was a dog chain with a padlock attached to the ring that had been used to restrain her neck. But in the picture, with her inch-long hair and dog collar, she looked like a gutter punk, like any girl you might see in any university district.

Young then showed me some photos of Rhoades in the 1980s that had come from his wife. In one he relaxed on the grass in a park. The natural light brought his hair closer to the color I remembered, and again, the side view heightened the key similarities, his cheekbone shape, glasses, the expression; but as I had learned from the echo chamber of Martinsburgs, memory is strange territory. By now papers and photographs were spread out all over the table, and Young was waiting for me to tell my story. Although I'd told it more in the preceding week than in the past two decades, I still wasn't used to doing it, and the nausea still came.

"One thing I always did," I told Young, "was rifle through a trucker's cassette case as soon as we were out on the highway." This gave me a screen behind which to observe drivers when they thought I was distracted. It allowed me to pretend not to hear scary red-flag comments so I could act dumb and get away later, and this is what I was doing that day, going through a tape case, chatting like an idiot and watching the driver—which is why I saw him change. I told Young about the Laughing Death Society. He'd never heard the phrase. I asked about the knife. Every trucker I ever met had a gun, so the knife seemed significant. He said a gun was about control but a knife is personal. I'd seen the page from Regina's little notebook on which Rhoades had drawn a picture of a gun and a huge dagger dripping blood next to the words RICKY IS A DEAD MAN.

"So was the trucker I met a true psychopath?" I asked.

"What I find interesting is that he told you about the body of the girl and talked about the Laughing Death Society while he was still driving. You were not under his control. This tells me that he liked manipulating through terror. That it turned him on, just like Rhoades."

"But a real serial killer wouldn't have let me go, right?" I asked.

"Maybe he didn't think you'd run."

Even at the time I'd wondered if my running was part of the game. Rhoades was a great lover of games. His favorite book was *Games People Play*, wherein each social encounter is treated as a transaction or "game." One game in the book is called "Courtroom." Another is called "Beat Me Daddy," another "Frigid Woman." In that one, driven by penis envy, a woman's inner child taunts a man into seducing her so that she can be freed from guilt for her own "sadistic fantasies." *Games People Play* was a bible for Rhoades. He talked about it frequently and applied its ideas. In a letter to his wife on the subject of psychological games, he wrote:

"I always told you there were three things you could do: *play, pass,* or *run.*" The phrase *play, pass, run* is used twice in the letter. Reading it, I found it hard not to hear the man telling me to *run.*

On the table in front of Young was a snapshot of Regina Walters that I hadn't seen, taken not very long before she was abducted. In it she's sitting in the back seat of a car. The sun is coming down on her long hair, and she's laughing. She looks like any other skinny kid just out of middle school. She looks happy. The picture was given to Young by Regina's mom. Initially agents had disagreed over whether the young girl on Rhoades's film was Regina. It was Agent Young who recognized the small gap in Regina's teeth and noticed that a few freckles were in the same place.

Young pulled out one last picture and slid it across to me. The photo was of a beautiful young girl, possibly Native American. "She was on the end of the roll with Regina," he said. She's shown sitting in Rhoades's truck wearing a gray hoodie. Her eyes are partly closed, as if she's stoned or sleepy. Rhoades must have just picked her up, because he hasn't cut her hair yet. It is glossy black and long.

No one knows who she is.

On the phone, agent Robert F. Lee was civil and to the point but not overtly warm. I arrived at his door melting in the hundred-degree heat. He welcomed me into his spacious living room. Tall and square-jawed, Lee looked like he could probably still tackle a bank robber. Behind him was a shoulder-high pink plastic castle.

"Granddaughter," he said.

On the couch beside me was a large pillow with the FBI seal.

"That's from my old SWAT jacket." He grinned. "They don't use that emblem now. Looks too much like a target."

The question of what you do with your old SWAT jacket when you retire had never entered my mind. Clearly the answer is, make a throw pillow.

I got the sense Lee appreciated brevity, so I dispensed with small talk and went straight to my questions, but he stopped me.

"I just want you to know," he said, looking me squarely in the eye, "that what Rhoades did to women, he did to women. You didn't do it."

Everything I expected from Bob Lee changed in that moment. I had not told him or anyone else how I felt about failing to go to the cops. These were my private feelings. The idea that I might have been responsible for what happened to girls like Regina was devastating, and Lee's directness startled me. It was a raw moment. So I told him the truth, which I had not told others—that I didn't say anything because I didn't think anyone would believe me.

"Well," said Lee, sitting back after I finished, "you're probably right. Look at Lisa Pennal."

Pennal was the woman chained into Rhoades's truck when they arrested him in Arizona. When rescued, she was wearing fuzzy lion slippers, talking secret prisons and being on a mission to see the president—just the kind of testimony that makes most detectives stop taking notes, since they're looking at someone who can't stand trial. Her statement was videotaped the night she was freed from Rhoades's truck. Lee still uses the tape when he trains police detectives in interrogation. He shows it and asks what they think is going on. Most say she's a prostitute and that it's a "transaction gone bad." Between Pennal and Rhoades, it's Rhoades they believe. "Of course," Lee says, "Lisa was talking all sorts of crazy stuff. Microchips in her brain. Holes in the ozone layer. She was wearing those slippers—but she was telling the truth."

I had a vision of Lisa Pennal as a truck-stop Kali roaming the back lots in her denim skirt and fuzzy slippers with an ozone hole for a halo. She would be easy to dismiss. Rhoades intentionally chose women who lacked credibility. Sometimes, as with Shana Holts, the girl who had escaped in the brewery, the sense of not being credible was internalized. Lee told me that the final lines of Holts's police statement read, "I don't see any good in filing charges. It's just going to be my word against his. If there was any evidence, I would file. I would file charges and sue him."

It took me a second to understand those last sentences. What evidence was she lacking? She was found running naked, screaming down a street in Houston with DNA all over her body, her head and pubic hair shaved, still with his chain around her neck. How could she lack evidence? But I thought about what she'd said—"It would just be my word against his," which was clearly followed by the unvoiced thought, *And who is going to believe* me? I could easily imagine my own teenage voice whispering those same words.

The more I learned about Rhoades, the more I saw parallels between us. It wasn't lost on me that while I was hitchhiking and he was driving, we would both have struggled with some of the same challenges—sleep deprivation and the hypnotic dullness of going through identical locations over and over, a world constructed of boredom and violence. And while I was getting more adept at survival, he was very likely getting more adept at killing. We both had our own systems, our own rituals, and our own beliefs about what people were really like and how they acted under pressure.

I'd put off writing to Rhoades, mostly because I didn't want him to write me back. The time had come to do it anyway. Mark Young said Rhoades likes to feel like an expert and that I should ask him to "educate" me, so while writing my letter I used permissive language, saying I wanted him "to teach me what I did right and what I did wrong" when I was traveling. Knowing the capacity of his sadism made this unbearable. Rhoades didn't live a double life as much as a shadowed one. There's a picture of him in leather and chains that floats around the Internet. It's actually from a Halloween party in Houston where he went as a "slave," led on a chain by his wife, who was dressed as a dominatrix.

Debra Davis and Rhoades met in the early '80s at a Houston bar called Chipkikkers. Rhoades was dressed that night as an airline pilot, and it was months before Davis found out he wasn't one. The remarkable thing is that when she did, she didn't dump him. But Rhoades was cunning and highly charismatic. When the FBI extradited him to Illinois, he was able to get a phone number off a waitress while shackled hand and foot and wearing an orange prison suit. This obviously doesn't recommend the waitress's judgment, but at least some of the credit has to go to Rhoades.

I finally got to Davis through Agent Young. He sent me a text just as I was leaving Texas saying that "Debbie" was ready to talk. I called as soon as I landed. Today Davis lives in College Station, Texas, and her kids, the product of a previous marriage, are grown. She occasionally speaks on domestic violence at conferences and in classrooms at A&M. She's tried to put the years with Rhoades behind her but still gets letters from him sporadically. Sometimes they're threatening, sometimes cajoling, but always manipulative.

According to her, in the summer of 1985 Rhoades was driving for a trucking company based in Georgia that had an office right on I-95. I ran my story past her. When I got to the part about the sudden switch in his behavior, she got excited. "That's him! That's exactly like him!" she said. She also said Rhoades often left his

gun at home in the beginning and could have used a knife. There
were other points where she saw similarities and would say, "That
sounds like Bob," but these were less emphatic, and it was hard to
tell what she really thought. Like Young and Lee, she had never
heard of the Laughing Death Society, and since it had featured so
strongly in my experience, I thought it salient.

"Don't you think that fact starts to rule him out?"

"Oh no, not at all!" she said. "Bob was fascinated by secret soci-
eties."

Davis mentioned the case of Colleen Stan, a twenty-year-old
hitchhiker who had been kidnapped in 1977 by a couple who tortured her and kept her as a sex slave for seven years while she slept
in a box under their bed. Eventually she was left unbound. They
kept her from running away by convincing her that a secret society
called the Company would find her and bring her back. "Bob was
obsessed with how they used an imaginary secret society to keep
her from running away," Davis said.

It made sense. As a true sexual sadist, Rhoades would have been
interested in a level of submission requiring no chains. He'd told
Shana Holts to "sit there and be a good girl." Regina Walters had
been seen in Chicago standing freely outside his truck in a public
place.

"Do you remember what he was wearing?" Davis asked quietly.

She was the only person who asked me this, and of course I did.
Or rather, I remember what he was not wearing. He was not wearing
jeans. He was not wearing a T-shirt. He was not wearing flannel. His
clothes were gray or blue, but that may have been the light. Debra
told me that "Bob" always wore matching Dickies, usually dark blue.
"He liked people to think he was in uniform," she said.

The airline pilot's outfit came to mind.

"Do you remember what his cab looked like?"

"Meticulously clean."

"That sure sounds like Bob. When I first saw his apartment, I
thought I'd walked into the showroom of a furniture store. Even
in jail, his shirt and pants were always ironed and pressed."

In Martinsburg, West Virginia, where the truck stop should be is
a massive Walmart stretching flat and endless along a parking lot
the size of a lake. Five years ago the truck stop was demolished,

along with its restaurant. The only thing they neglected to take down is a website with the words *Martinsburg TravelCenter of America*™ flashing like a beacon online.

The whole thing seemed so uncanny. Everywhere I looked, evidence of these girls was disappearing. I hadn't been able to get a copy of Shana Holts's police report because I was told there was no official suspect. Lisa Pennal's full statement, it turned out, had been destroyed for file space. Now the whole Martinsburg truck stop had been swallowed by a Walmart Supercenter.

I knew from talking to the Martinsburg police that the truck stop had been under the jurisdiction of the Berkeley County sheriff. I called the office. A chipper recorded voice told me to press 1 for taxes, press 2 for guns—"all other callers stay on the line!" I finally spoke to a woman and asked if they had a homicide record for a girl who may have been found in the Martinsburg truck stop during the summer of 1985.

"We don't have any records," she told me.

I thought she meant digitized.

"I can come down," I said.

"We don't have any records."

In the 1990s the Berkeley County sheriff's department's computer crashed and burned. The paper records had been destroyed for file space, and so nothing from the 1980s remained. I asked to speak to any senior officer who might have been there at the time. She told me there was only one and he had gone fishing.

I spent a week on the road in Appalachia, visiting truck stops, interviewing the older truckers and waitresses. At first I would ask about the girl in the dumpster, but no one had heard of her, so I asked if there had ever been any women found in truck stops. Wherever I went, I was told nothing "like that" ever happened, which was remarkable given the numbers of bodies the FBI had tracked over the past thirty years. The newspapers were equally silent. It seems our profound fascination with serial killers is matched by an equally profound lack of interest in their victims. One library archivist explained that I was looking for the kind of news nobody wanted to read. The girl, he said, "wasn't one of our own. She was a drifter." I'd never heard the word *drifter* used in earnest. It touched a nerve I didn't know I had. I had been a drifter. If what he said was true, the trail I was on had disappeared into a field.

Out of desperation I made one last attempt and swung by a

smaller truck stop in Hancock, Maryland. I spoke to a woman who had worked there a long time and told her about the dead hitchhiker while she fingered the gold cross on her neck and listened. Had she ever heard about it? I asked. She shook her head; then her eyes clouded some. "Wait a minute. There was that one girl. She was a prostitute. They found her near a dumpster behind the restaurant at the Gateway Travel Plaza in Breezewood. She had a stocking down her throat, I think. That was way back in the early seventies, though."

It wasn't the early '70s, it was 1987, and the woman killed was nineteen-year-old Lamonica Cole. I found her in the *Pittsburgh Post-Gazette* later that night. She had been strangled at Breezewood. Another prostitute had been grabbed there as well, in 2006, but was found farther down the road with her throat slit. Neither of these women were the one I was looking for, but a sentence in the article caught my attention. It said there had been a string of prostitute murders in truck stops in the area beginning in June of 1985, which was right on the edge of my time frame.

The next morning I drove to the Gateway Travel Plaza in Breezewood, Pennsylvania. I thought that maybe in a truck stop where known murders had occurred, people would be more forthcoming. Maybe they would remember something the others hadn't. I parked in front of the family travel plaza, then walked back past a sign that read TRUCKS ONLY. The store for professional drivers was clean and quiet. I asked around until I found someone who had been there in 1985. It was a woman, probably in her mid-fifties. She came over and gave me an open smile. I asked her the same question I was asking everybody: *Did you ever hear about a hitchhiker in a dumpster?*

"No," she said.

"Did you ever hear of anything like that at all, in other times, any other bodies of women found along this stretch of I-70?"

I was in the one place where I knew for certain women had been found, one less than a hundred yards away from where she was standing. "No," she said, "I never heard of anything like that anywhere."

Listening to her, it occurred to me that this investigation of mine wasn't a detective novel. It was a ghost story. The prisms of Regina Walters, Shana Holts, and Lisa Pennal refracted into a set of icons—one in the back seat of a car laughing as she leans on the headrest, one with the shorn red-gold hair and an expression

of resilience, one slightly crazy and ready to fight—each casting
her own light, each a hologram of girlhood.

Recently the New Jersey State Supreme Court handed down a
statement on memory, describing it as complex and often unreli-
able. The ruling went on to question the admissibility of eyewit-
ness testimony. "Human memory is not like a video recording,"
they said. And they're right. It's more like a set of still photos. I
remember coming down through the Blue Ridge Mountains in
a truck with its brakes on fire and dropping over Chester Gap
in the middle of the night when it was still hot and the air was
loud with the chirping of bugs. I remember sitting in the drizzle
in a truck while the crime-scene tape was strung around a dumpster. I remember driving around Ohio howling along with Bruce
Springsteen and buzzed out of my brain on Diet Cokes and being sad that the ride ended because it was a safe one and I had
almost been able to be myself for a second, but that second had
passed. I remember a fuel island in the blue morning light and
a driver with a white shirt that stood out like a flag, and later,
in another ride, taking the turn back east, then south, and a
gray day just before a storm so pressurized my ears hurt. And I
remember being in the woods off I-95. I only ran about a hundred yards before I turned and hid, because I didn't know if I
was being chased and needed to see. I crouched on netted twigs
and breathed into my shirt to muffle the sound. The woods were
blue in the gray light, which was either dusk or a coming storm.
At the center of everything was my own breath. The birds went
silent, and I didn't know what it meant. I watched the truck idle
on the side of the road until it finally pulled off.

One snowy night several months later, I was hitchhiking through
Amherst, Massachusetts, and a carful of students from Hampshire
College picked me up and let me stay with them. In the morning
they talked me into applying to the college. I was accepted, and
that provided a thin strip of pride on which to stand while I made
contact with my family. My mother was happy to pay for school.
Being sixteen and in college is an easier thing to talk about. It was
a solution that worked for both of us and looked like redemption
but didn't last. The dissonance between my emotional world and
the one around me was still too great, and soon I left again, but
in a more sanctioned way. I hitchhiked in Europe and settled in

Vienna for a few years. I lived among artists in the Lower East Side squats. These are narratives we know. Unlike those of other young women on the road, my story was now recognizable.

When I got home from West Virginia, a letter from Rhoades was waiting. It said he would see me if I promised never to say that I had seen him or what had passed between us. It was just the kind of promise a sexual predator or child molester would try to extract. He also wanted $500. I wrote him back and told him that journalistic standards wouldn't allow me to pay for interviews. I expected that to be the end of it, but I got another letter. Young was right. Rhoades liked to think of himself as an "expert," and now Rhoades suggested he be paid as one. But an expert in what, I thought—killing? At the bottom of the yellow legal paper, scrawled in all caps, he wrote, "IT WASN'T ME!!!" I looked at the letter. He may be right, but certainly not because he's innocent. I imagined for a moment flying to Illinois. I go through the paperwork, get fingerprinted and led through a channel of air-locked doors into a room with him. He's there with his neatly pressed shirt and colossal arrogance. We do the interview, but I don't take notes. It doesn't matter what he says. After all, it's just going to be his word against mine. And who's going to believe him? That's where my fantasy ends, in a game of "Who Is Credible Now?"

The same week that I got the letter from Rhoades, the senior officer from the Berkeley County sheriff's department who had been fishing returned. He said that no girls had ever been found in a dumpster at the Martinsburg, West Virginia, truck stop, and I had no reason not to believe him.

One story Debra Davis told still haunts me. She was on a trip with her husband, Bob, the last she ever took in his truck. They were heading west on I-10 and stopped somewhere in Arizona at a busy truck stop. By the restaurant door was a young woman with a baby, trying to get a ride. Debra said she looked about eighteen or nineteen and desperate. Debra wanted to give her money or do something. Her own sister had been on the street, and she was overwhelmed by the woman at the door and didn't want to just walk away. Rhoades saw what Debra was looking at. He came around behind her and grabbed her shoulders. He turned her slowly toward the girl and pointed. "You see that, Debbie," he whispered in her ear. "She's one of the invisible people."

MATTHEW VOLLMER

Keeper of the Flame

FROM *New England Review*

ON THANKSGIVING MY FATHER asked me if I wanted to visit
the Nazi. That's what my father—a dentist to whom the Nazi had
entrusted the care of his teeth—called him, what he'd always
called him: "The Nazi." As in: "Did I tell you who came into the
office this week? The Nazi." And: "Did I tell you that I talked to the
Nazi?" And: "You'll never guess what the Nazi told me." And so on.

The Nazi to whom my father referred was not a real Nazi—
and, as far as I knew, my father didn't call him "the Nazi" to his
face. Neither had this so-called Nazi served under Hitler in World
War II. Back then, the Nazi my father knew had yet to be born.
And though my father had a pretty good idea of where this Nazi's sympathies might lie, all my father said about him was that
he had money, that he'd written a book about the Wewelsburg
castle in southern Germany (the one that Heinrich Himmler had
attempted to restore); that he'd built a castle of his own in a remote location in the mountains of southwestern North Carolina;
that he, like my father, had an affinity for snakes, had fed white
mice to copperheads he'd kept in terrariums; that he'd taken to
leashing one of these serpents and walking it as one would a dog;
and, finally, that his curatorial impulses and an affection for artifacts once belonging to members of the Third Reich had led him
to build a private underground museum in the belly of the afore-
mentioned fortress—a vault of ominous artifacts that my father
convinced me I needed to see.

*

I'd spent a good part of my childhood visiting my father's dental patients, many of whom lived deep in the mountains, in houses that might or might not have electricity or phones. During one visit I'd watched a man yank intestines from a slaughtered hog. I'd been towed, with my sister, down a gravel road on a wooden sled roped to an ox. I'd gathered eggs in shit-strewn barns, run cobs of corn through grinders that worked by cranking a handle and spinning a wheel so that the kernels poured out of one rusted chute and naked cobs out of another. I'd been bucked from the back of a horse; I'd been charged—no kidding—by a yak. I'd sat on a quilted bed in the front room of a house owned by a man who, at sixty-some years of age, had not only installed his first phone but had also been receiving, as a result, vulgar calls from a woman who lived down the road, words so filthy he claimed he wouldn't repeat them.

But I had never before visited the Nazi.

After my father and I had driven out of town, on a narrow two-lane road winding past ramshackle houses and trailers using sheets for window curtains, over narrow bridges spanning rushing streams and onto a gravel road where we passed multiple signs announcing that we were now on private property and that potential trespassers would be shot; after we'd reached the heavy-duty chain-link fence running the length of this property; after my father had dialed the Nazi's number on his cell phone; and after the front gate glided backward on lubed wheels—we drove inside and the house came into view. The Nazi's house did, in fact, resemble a castle. It wasn't exactly Neuschwanstein, but it had rock walls and turrets and wooden doors with wrought iron hinges and arched windows. It had a fountain and an impressive series of stairs leading to the front door. The whole thing looked like something a government —though certainly not our own—had erected centuries before.

We left the truck. I had the feeling we were being watched, that our movements were being recorded—that somewhere inside the castle, a bank of TVs flickered, monitoring different zones of the Nazi's estate.

My father grabbed me by the arm. "See that house over there?" he said. He pointed to the mountain opposite the one where we were standing. Glass glinted through the trees. I could make out a roof.

"Yeah," I said.

"He bought that."

"Who bought it?"

My father said the Nazi's name.

"Why?" I asked.

"Privacy," he said.

"Privacy?" I repeated. "What does that mean?"

My father shrugged. "I guess he doesn't want anyone seeing what he does over here."

I frowned. "What does he do?" I said.

My father made a face and shrugged.

I could not think about the Nazi, could not reflect upon him and his ilk, without also thinking about other people with similar ideas who had retreated to secret places in our mountains. While these mountains—which belong, in name, to the Blue Ridge—might have lacked the remote and indifferent grandeur of, say, the Rockies, they had other notable qualities, and precisely because they exist in a temperate region and are well watered by frequent rains, they have produced a semi-penetrable jungle of trees and shrubs —more varieties of plants, in fact, than anywhere else on the continent, home to all manner of wild creatures, from bear and deer and grouse to ticks, serpents, wasps, and skinks. So dense are these forests during the warmer months, so thick and verdant, that in many wild places a human who wishes to pass through them must do so either by crawling on his or her belly or by peeling back layers of briars and limbs and leaves.

It makes sense that these mountains have been—for centuries —a place for people who want to hide from the rest of the world, people who believe in boundaries and in drawing imaginary lines along a piece of earth and not only calling it theirs but believing firmly in the right to defend that piece of earth, and convinced that anyone who crossed that boundary had committed a crime that justified the firing of bullets or buckshot in someone's general direction. This is not to say that all or even most people in the mountains will shoot trespassers, or that mountain people are not, on the whole, friendly or kind or generous or selfless, but it is to say that there are many people who seek out remote coves and hollows and other secret places with the explicit intent to do things that are not done within the sightlines of others, and that these mountains have had a reputation for attracting people with strange ideas. Take Nord Davis, for instance—the leader of a Christian militia who not only believed that the Holocaust was a fabrication devised in part to create sympathy for the Jews but who also believed, thanks to a rather acrobatic interpretation of the book of Genesis, that Adam and Eve were white-skinned and blond-haired, that dark-skinned people were animals without souls, and that Jews were the literal spawn of Satan, who had possessed one of these dark-skinned people and beguiled (or, in Davis's interpretation, *impregnated*) Eve. Mr. Davis, who is now dead, also apparently took credit for ending the Vietnam War and ran a 130-acre military training facility not far—as the crow flies, anyway—from where the Nazi's castle now stands.

The Nazi's garage door—like the front gate—opened automatically, by some unseen force, and after it slowly retracted itself, my father and I entered. Seconds later another door opened, and the man himself—the Nazi—appeared. I'd been nursing the image of a slight man with pale skin: a malnourished weakling with a head of dark and greasy hair. But this guy was not small. He was tall and hearty, with a head of dirty blond locks cut in a quasi bowl cut, with long bangs that flapped around when he moved. In a lineup of possible Nazis I would not have chosen this man—a fact that probably reveals my own naive, preconceived notions about Nazis and their possible permutations. His wife, on the other hand, looked like she might've been created in a laboratory funded by the Third Reich: her hair—so blond it was nearly white—fell in a luminous sheet down her back. She was tall and wide-eyed, her lips crimson. She introduced and immediately excused herself, and our tour began.

The interior of the Nazi's home could not have been described as regal, but it was without a doubt immaculate. Not only had it recently—if not immediately prior to our entering—been cleaned, but it was also completely clutter-free. There were no stacks of bills or mail on the counter, no dish of change, no stray pens, no stacks of coasters, no knickknacks on the windowsills, no stained-glass butterflies affixed to the windowpane above the kitchen sink. No family photographs—no photographs of any kind—hung from the walls. Papers and pictures and notes and calendars had not been affixed via magnets to the fridge, whose door remained utterly blank. Empty tabletops—devoid even of napkin holders or salt and pepper shakers—gleamed. The place felt sanitized, sterile. Here, at the home of the Nazi, a person seemed unlikely to catch any sort of disease. Rooms had been reduced to the bare minimum. Stuff—if stuff existed here—lived behind closed doors.

I'd expected the Nazi to be effusive, perhaps even charismatic. I'd been told on several occasions that the Nazi had enjoyed seeing photographs my father displayed in his dental office of my towheaded, fair-skinned son, and that he, the Nazi, had jokingly and not-so-jokingly congratulated my father for laying claim to a grandchild with such striking Aryan features. Today, though, the Nazi didn't mention my son, made no inquiries concerning my family or me. The Nazi was not, it appeared, interested in small talk. He knew why we'd come, understood the nature of our visit, which had less to do with the sharing of personal information and more to do with viewing "the collection." And so, immediately after exchanging lukewarm pleasantries, the Nazi led us out of the kitchen.

In the living room, as we stood upon plush white carpet, the Nazi cleared his throat and began pointing to various objects as he spoke—an oil painting of a Prussian king, an innocent-looking set of china that, upon closer inspection, revealed swastikas orbiting the rims, and a mantel into which some apparently profound sentence—in German—had been engraved. Meanwhile, the Nazi was giving a history lesson, explaining how the founders of the Third Reich had taken it upon themselves to do away with the Catholic Church and ignite a renaissance, to pay homage to their true heritage, which was pagan.

I tried to listen, to take it all in, so I could remember it later—I had a movie camera in my pocket, a digital HD recorder the size of a cell phone, but I was too timid to ask if I could take pictures and too chicken to attempt to capture footage surreptitiously. I kept zoning out, trying to figure out how I could ask my most burning question, which was, basically, "So, like, are you *really* a Nazi?" Only I couldn't think of a polite way to word it. Also, I knew that the artifacts in the living room were just the tip of the iceberg, and I wanted him to hurry up and get to the good stuff, which, as my father had told me before we arrived, was downstairs.

In order to go down, we had to go up. That is, we had to climb to the second floor, to a balcony overlooking the living room. Up there, the Nazi opened an impressive wooden door—all the doors in the house were arched and hinged with wrought iron—to reveal yet another door, this one constructed from what appeared to be bomb-shelter-grade metal, and upon whose surface the words *Danger: High Voltage* had been emblazoned. The Nazi unlocked and then swung open this hatchlike door, and we descended a steep spiral staircase, passing near the top a recessed statue: a sculpted head of a soldier wearing an SS helmet. Down, down, down we went, around and around we wound, so far in fact I could feel a significant change in temperature. Once we'd reached the bottom, the Nazi unlocked an iron gate and swung it open.

Until I'd entered the Nazi's house, the only genuine Third Reich artifact I'd seen had been the one I owned, the one my grandfather, who'd served as a major during World War II, had given to me. I could no longer remember the occasion—my grandfather was long dead and now buried in the family plot in the woods behind my parents' house—but somehow and under some circumstance—perhaps he was cleaning out a drawer in my presence—he had given me a button, upon which the Totenkopf, or death's-head skull, had been engraved, and which, as the story went, my grandfather had plucked from the field jacket of a dead Nazi. Now the button lived, as it had for the past couple of decades, in a black plastic box with crimson felt lining, a box that once housed a Remington Micro-Screen Rechargeable Electric Razor. Now the box held a bunch of coins that my missionary relatives had brought back from foreign countries, a smooth stone that I'd picked up from the Mauthausen concentration camp, which I'd visited with my family as a teenager, on a trip through Europe, and the Totenkopf button. Over the years I had opened the box and I had held the button in my hand, and I had imagined my grandfather yanking it off the coat in which the dead body lay, and I had thought to myself, *This came from a real Nazi.* It wasn't just a button. It was a relic from an evil empire—the guys who, in *Raiders of the Lost Ark,* had gotten their faces melted off because they wanted to see something they shouldn't have. They had—in Hollywood and real life—gone too far, wanted far too much.

The Nazi flipped a switch. The resultant *clack* reverberated. Light flooded the room, revealing a cathedral-like space with thirty-foot-high ceilings and a marble floor bearing the image of a sun wheel, which, if you aren't familiar with sun wheels, resembles a swastika whose ends appear to have been lovingly bashed in to give the thing, overall, a more rounded shape.

At one end of the room hung a massive tapestry bearing the image of the Tree of Life, which had, the Nazi claimed, as a pre-Christian pagan symbol been important to the founding members of the Third Reich. Beneath this, a pulpitlike table displayed two wooden boxes, each bearing lightning-shaped *S*'s. These boxes, the Nazi had explained, had been made especially to hold copies of *Mein Kampf* and served as gifts for SS officers on their wedding days: a token of the Führer's appreciation.

Elsewhere: glass shelves of Hitler Youth daggers, polished and dangerously sharp; an SS officer's ring, into which had been carved a grinning Totenkopf; ceramic platters embossed with Runic symbols; a hand-carved wooden plate depicting the Wewelsburg Castle, where Himmler hoped to reconvene the Arthurian Knights of the Round Table; a chair from the same castle's great hall, leather bolted to its back and seat; a set of silver, whose handles had been engraved with Sig runes, and which had purportedly come from the Eagle's Nest—the alpine chalet presented to Hitler on the occasion of his fiftieth birthday.

My father glanced over his shoulder at me and emitted a wheeze-burst of laughter—an exhalation intended to express disbelief. He had led me to an underground vault containing the artifacts of the last century's most brutal regime, and he now seemed downright giddy. I, on the other hand, didn't know what to think or what to say. I found it difficult to process what any of this meant. That is, I didn't know why it was here, how it had gotten from where it had been made to where it was now. Were we in the presence of some kind of monster? Or had he created this space for stuff he deemed historically significant, buried it in a moisture-controlled vault because he fancied himself one of history's unbiased curators? Was this the product of an obsessive and sympathetic mind, one which interpreted the mainstream records of history as having been unduly cruel to the Third Reich, which had been a movement, in his eyes, about nationalism, about ancestors, about revering and honoring the past? I didn't know. And, honestly, I was afraid to ask.

The Nazi handed me a black German helmet and explained why it was rare: all helmets of this particular kind, once the war started,

had been recalled and painted in field colors. To find one that
remained unaltered was exceedingly uncommon. And *exceedingly
uncommon* translated into *quite valuable*. The helmet, if the Nazi
saw fit to sell it, might fetch upwards of $30,000.

Normally, my father explained, as if to help me better appreciate the objects before me, collectors of Third Reich militaria collected one—or mostly one—kind of artifact, attempting to amass
an assortment of one specific relic. The Nazi nodded. Some collected knives, some helmets, some field jackets, some medals. The
difference in this collection was that it wasn't a collection of only
one thing. It was a collection of many things. The scope of this
collection was greater. And therefore it was more singular.

For example, there were the mannequins.

There were four mannequins, actually, each dressed in a different uniform. The uniforms included field jackets, pants, medals,
shoes, knives, and belts. Apparently, the Nazi had purchased these
mannequins from various department stores and carted them back
to his castle, where he sawed off the heads. He then fashioned new
heads—the Nazi, in another life, had worked in advertising and
was something of an artist—and then, as if they were his own personal life-sized dolls, he'd dressed them in SS uniforms.

But the thing about the mannequins was that each represented,
as far as was possible, a painstaking reconstruction of a particular
soldier. That is, the Nazi had found a uniform and tracked down
as many records of the actual soldier to whom it'd belonged as he
could find. He'd identified and tracked down other possessions
that belonged to the solider. He knew the soldier's rank, his shoe
size, his hair and eye color, knew exactly how many medals that
particular soldier had received as well as the occasions upon which
they had been awarded. The Nazi could tell you what this soldier's
favorite food had been, whether he'd been sick or injured or
killed, and whether he'd suffered disciplinary action.

I would like to say that I was disgusted, that the sight of the Nazi
clothing and gear stirred some powerful revulsion, but down there,
underground, I felt the seductive pull of visual design. The clarity
and symmetry, the contrast of the red and white and black, the crisp
lines and borders, the mysterious symbols, the glossy belts, the gleam
of polished buckles—these uniforms, tools, weapons, helmets, and
flags had been put together by intelligent artists from the finest and
heartiest earthly materials. I hated to admit that these things were

beautiful, but I had no other choice. *Not* to say they were beautiful would be to diminish the sense of their power. And their power—however awful—demanded to be recognized.

"This," my father said, "is history."

That is, he might've said, "This is history." I don't know. My memory can't be trusted. I know I was there at the Nazi's house; I know I went up and then went down; I know that I wandered in a cathedral-like space and looked dead mannequins in the eye and feared that they would, if I continued to stare, awaken. But I can't remember everything—or, honestly, much of anything—that was said. What struck me more was the mood. The mood of my father: gleeful, reverent, inquisitive. The mood of the Nazi: not cheerless and not cheerful but rather, despite being intently focused, coolly detached. I do know that my father had said, as the Nazi retrieved for us some glittering knife or piece of china, that "it always makes me nervous" when he, the Nazi, reaches in and takes something out of the case—meaning that he worried that one of these artifacts might be harmed. But the Nazi did not approach these objects with reverence. He didn't need to. The space in which they existed had already assured their status as objects to be revered.

Before we left the Nazi's sanctuary slash museum slash dungeon and ascended to the kitchen, where the Nazi's wife poured us coffee and offered us a platter of cookies; before the Nazi took a cookie, saying they never kept this kind of stuff—meaning sweets—in the house; before the Nazi's wife reminded us that there had also been concentration camps in America, that it had been a time of war, that of course the camps had been such terribly awful places, but awful things had gone on in so many places the world over; before any of that happened—the Nazi wanted to show us one last thing. This last thing was kept inside a glass case with a glass lid, which the Nazi opened. He secured the lid so that it wouldn't fall, then opened an old leather-bound book and began flipping through its yellow pages. It was a ledger of sorts, and inside it were the names of hundreds of SS officers. Finally he pointed to a column of names. The surname was the same as the one that belonged to my father and me. The Nazi didn't say, "Looks like your Uncle Walt was an SS man." He didn't say, "See, you do have Nazis in your family." He just tapped the name with his finger. It was as if he wanted this—the fact that people with the same surname as ours had served under Hitler—to sink in on its own. To show us that whatever we might think about the Nazis, we were in fact connected, by the very name that I'd thought, as a child, separated our family from everybody else's.

The sun had fallen below the ridgelines by the time we left the Nazi's castle. My father drove us home. He wondered aloud what would happen to the Nazi's stuff when the man met his demise, wondered if the Nazi had insured all those relics, and where his last will and testament—supposing he'd drawn one up—stipulated they would go. My father seemed concerned about the Nazi and his legacy, partly because he admired the lengths that the Nazi had gone to in order to amass such a collection, and partly because he seemed to think of the man as a friend. "A friend?" I said. I was incredulous. I said no way could he be friends with a man he merely humored, that true friends weren't afraid to say what they thought, which was that the Nazi was (at best) misguided and (at worst) a lunatic; that he had constructed, unbeknown to all the people living in trailers and cabins along this road, a private shrine to the Third Reich; that he apparently thought Heinrich Himmler was a character worthy of admiration; that he obviously thought the Holocaust hadn't existed —at least not in the way most understood it; and that unless my father had come out and said what he truly believed, he was silently endorsing the Nazi's viewpoints. I can't remember how or even if my father defended himself against these accusations, but I know he didn't say what I'm thinking now—that I was in no position to talk. I'd said very little—if anything—during our visit. Though my mind had been lurching most of the time, seeking any sort of anti-Nazi argument, I'd feared that nothing I could drum up would be able to contend with the Nazi's own encyclopedic knowledge. I'd even begun to wonder how I'd come to know what I thought I knew, and how it was that I could prove beyond a shadow of a doubt that the Nazis were guilty of the crimes of which they'd been accused. In short, I had done nothing and said nothing to give the Nazi one single reason to think I wasn't on his side. For all he knew, I might've been a man on a pilgrimage, coming to pay homage to the ephemera of a lost and once glorious empire. After all, he had pointed to my name in a directory listing the names of former Nazis—and I hadn't protested. I had thought, *Wow, that's messed up;* but I had said not a word.

WILLIAM MELVIN KELLEY

Breeds of America

ONE DAY DEEP IN SUMMER in a time when automobiles went away and stayed all day my friends and I sat on the curb and compared skin color. Jackie, a rare kid of German ancestry on the block, had turned red. Guys whose parents came from the boot of Italy had turned tan. But Salvatore, a son of Sicilians, who grew up to become one of New York's Bravest, had turned, as Jackie put it, brown, like Billy. I still remember Sal's embarrassment. Under his brown skin, he blushed. This troubled me. Why should the comparison of his brown skin to my brown skin make him blush?

So did I first meet the concept of race. Before that day, I can't remember anything about it, though my eyes told me that people came in different shades.

I have had to rethink race since the arrival of my grandson, a half Albanian. According to the one-drop rule, his three-sixteenths African blood makes him 100 percent Negro; in today's parlance, a light-skinned black, an obvious absurdity.

So how should we list him in the census? Who divided humanity this way? Nobody comes into the world knowing anything about race. We all have to learn about it. So I've begun to remember how I started becoming Negro.

Contrary to conventional misunderstanding, in my time growing up in New York, Negroes did not talk much about race. Striving Negroes wanted to transcend it. We did not tell our children they would not succeed because of their skin color. We waited until race clobbered hopes, then we'd try to explain the situation: Most Euros did not like us, so we had to overcome by working harder. We had to work twice as hard to get half as far. Accept that fact and don't complain. No one ever explained the economic system of slavery, though we knew about our slave ancestors.

Of course, we also had alternative views. In the 1910s and '20s Marcus Garvey had enlightened us to our position as oppressed people under a worldwide tyranny, and in the 1930s and '40s Elijah Muhammad had begun to see the world through militant Islamic eyes. These views skirted the subversive. My father kept his Garvey and J. A. Rogers high up in his bookcase with his Frank Harris, *My Life and Loves*. He made Dunbar, Hughes, McKay, and Cullen more accessible, on lower shelves.

I grew up in the Northeast Bronx with the children of Italian immigrants, who mostly embraced me. Several things aided me in my acceptance. My Roman Catholic Creole grandmother and mother attended the same churches as my neighbors, St. Mary's and Our Lady of Grace. Besides, I knew and could sing all of Frank Sinatra's songs in a clear boy-soprano voice. Summer evenings I held small groups of boys spellbound. *Put your dreams away for another day and I will take their place in your heart.*

My Italo friends much preferred me to most Irish kids. (At that time not everybody considered Italians to be whites.) One day one of a group of Irish kids passing through our block called me a nigger. My Creole mother had armed me against this, without going into it very deeply: anybody who called me a nigger had simultaneously demonstrated his ignorance and his inferiority. I should dismiss the comment as I would dismiss the utterance of a parrot.

So when the Irish kid called me a nigger, I assumed an attitude of superiority and condescension. This did not satisfy my Italo friends. The Irish kid, whom they'd caught while his companions ran away, had insulted me, and they would back me up while I gave the offender a beating. But I demurred, had already lost interest. Why strangle a parrot? But Bobby, Jimmy, Sal, Jerome, and Joey would not have it. They gave the kid a beating and ran him from the block.

I had encountered the word *nigger* before this incident, but coming out of the mouths of Africamericans (united, not hyphenated). One of my father's poker comrades, Mr. Timothy, used it all the time—this nigger this and that nigger that—and my mother and grandmother considered him coarse and rude. My father wanted to leave niggerdom behind in segregated Tennessee, and my gentle mother, who read *Vogue* and the *Ladies' Home Journal,* considered it a curse word. Nobody with any class or breeding would ever use it.

In 1944 I started attending Fieldston, a Euro and predominately Jewish progressive private school. Having repeated first grade, I was older and bigger than my twenty Euro classmates, and my boy-soprano voice made me a star. Over the next twelve years I went wherever my class went, to the Met and MoMA, to Carnegie Hall, to see Scribner make pulp paper for special editions, to the bar mitzvah of a classmate at Temple Emanu-El. I went through the front entrance when I went to visit my friends on Fifth or Park Avenue. Their parents had warned the Irish doormen not to turn me away.

At Fieldston Lower, much of the kitchen staff had brown skin. Lila and Bessie, both cooks, treated me especially well. We youngsters had to help with the serving, taking turns going into the kitchen to get a dish of peas or mashed potatoes for the table, where the teacher would spoon it out. Whenever my turn came, Bessie and Lila made a fuss over me. "Here's our Billy." They gave me extra cake and cookies. Gently and joyfully they let me know that my attending Fieldston made them proud. I represented them.

My mother and my grandmother told me our family history from the unorthodox point of view of Creoles of color. *Creole* comes from the Spanish *criollo,* meaning a native of a country, and denoted persons born in the Americas as distinct from their ancestors in Africa or Europe, but later came also to mean persons of mixed blood, often those who were not visibly so. The African might lurk three or four generations back, forgettable behind Berlioz and good brandy.

According to my mother, Narcissa Agatha Garcia Kelley, and my grandmother Jessie Marin Garcia, before 1900 America acknowledged not three but four races. The word *race* comes to English from medieval Italian *razzo,* meaning any given breed of horse. Dogs, cattle, and horses had different breeds, the first Portuguese slavers must have mused in 1444, so why should not humans too have a *raça?* One breed originated in Europe; another came from Africa; a third, the Indians, inhabited America; and the fourth breed, also from America, developed as a mixture of the first three.

In 1613 the Dutch left ashore on the island of Mannahatta a free man of color named Jan Rodrigues, who established trade with the Indians. A man alone, he pretty quickly got himself an Indian wife. Many others must have followed, because in 1638 the Dutch government outlawed sex with Indians.

A four-breed America made sense to my young eyes. (On the radio, the Lone Ranger would put on the berry stain to pass as a half-breed.) Still, I could already discern differences between the swarthy Sicilian Sal and the sunburned German Jackie. Within my own family, though we all answered to the designation Negro (except when we didn't), we came in different shades, ranging from Nana Jessie's white-chocolate color to milk-chocolate-colored me. And my father's friend, the foulmouthed Mr. Timothy, had that disease that made him look like a calico cat.

Yet the world outside our house, excluding American Indians and Asians (another breed), had clearly divided itself into colored and noncolored, to borrow from J. O. Killens. (We had not become black people yet, though some already liked Afro-American.) Any challenge to the two-breed equation met with incomprehension and disbelief. For instance, when Nana Jessie and I went out, people would sometimes come up to her and ask her in Italian or Spanish perché porque she had a piccolo pequeño nero negro ragazzo niño with her. Nana Jessie would answer that she spoke only English, though her dead husband had come from Ponce, Puerto Rico, and she would claim me as her grandson. The Puerto Rican kind of explained my brownness, and the interrogator would drift away.

Neither did my Italo friends accept that Nana Jessie's grandfather Colonel F. S. Bartow of Savannah, Georgia, had fought and died for the Confederacy in the Civil War.

"Was he a Negro?"

"No, he was white."

"If he was white," they'd ask, "how could he be related to you?"

"He was white. And very brave. General Beauregard described him as gallant and impetuous."

Bartow died in July 1861 rallying his troops at Manassas, waving a banner, shot through the heart. The Confederates won the battle. So he became a martyr and a hero. Georgia named a county after him. Nana Jessie's mother, Josephine (age thirteen), had heard him, her father, make a speech before going off to war, promising to il-lust-rate Georgia and keep the niggers down.

Such revelations usually had a chilling effect on pink folks, Italo or otherwise. It slowly dawned on me that people did not want to confront that all this sex, much of it forced, some of it not, had taken place. No wonder my father kept his J. A. Rogers—whose research had unearthed several American presidents with either African or Native blood, and lots of evidence showing how freely the breeds had mixed in America—up on the top shelf with Marcus Garvey and Frank Harris.

Or take Sally Hemings and the confused hypocrite Thomas Jefferson. Everybody makes a big deal out of her breed (Creole in the contemporary context) and her youth (about fourteen when they got started in Paris), but they ignore that mistress Sally and Jefferson's wife had the same father. Jefferson hooked up with his dead wife's half sister.

In sixth grade, in 1950, I started to feel special affection for a girl in my class I'll call Dolly-Jan Issanoff. She had a sweet personality and a shapely blossoming body. We would walk through the halls of school holding hands, until the principal issued an edict forbidding public displays of affection. At the time I did not take this edict personally, but in retrospect I see it as the first in a series of messages designed to enforce an important lesson of Negrohood: don't mess with Miss Cholly.

Later that year I found myself uninvited from our grade's first couples party, an obvious snub. Everybody knew that Dolly-Jan and I were together. Once again came the lesson: don't mess with Miss Cholly.

Through newspapers and dinner conversation I learned about segregation, that if you wore a brown skin you couldn't get served at certain places in New York. Josephine Baker was snubbed at the Stork Club. I wondered whether they had real storks there. And my parents couldn't tell me about Josephine Baker without telling me about her naughty naked banana dance.

Early on, blessed with an ear for the variations of spoken English, I realized that I lived in four linguistic worlds. In my house we spoke standard, grammatically correct American English, all our *be*'s and *have*'s in the right place. Outside my house on Carpenter Avenue in the Northeast Bronx, where I spent my time when I returned from Fieldston in the West Bronx, the guys spoke working-class New York English tinged with many Italianisms. Like they would say "close delight." At school we spoke standard American English with an emphasis on long French-rooted words and slight Yiddish intonations. On weekends when my father took me to Harlem I found a broad spectrum of speech generally tied to skin color, though dark-skinned men like Paul Robeson and Roland Hayes might speak in an international English, British consonants and American vowels. Ethel Waters rolled her *r*'s. My dentist, Dr. Bessie Delany, spoke standard with a southern accent. Sometimes poorly educated light-skinned folks would speak Africamerican vernacular (Ebonics) as well as did dark brown people. I couldn't speak it then, but I loved listening to it and recognized its expressiveness.

The Negroes who spoke this Africamerican Creole seemed to catch hell. Nobody in my immediate family spoke it, so we didn't catch hell, we just had no money. Only my aunt Iris, a native of British Guiana, didn't sound American. Nana Jessie and her sister, my great-aunt Charlotte (who passed for Euro in her business life and some of her private life), both sounded like the elderly Savannah society women I heard one time on TV. My father had worked hard to eradicate all vestiges of Negroness from his voice. He sounded like a radio announcer, and sometimes his brown skin would surprise people who had first encountered him on the phone.

In 1947 they let Jackie Robinson play in the major leagues. I had never seen my father more excited about anything. That summer my father took me to Ebbets Field to see Robinson. Along with the many brown-skinned people in the stands, we cheered his every move. Just about every Negro in America became a Dodger fan. Still, having been raised in the Bronx, I remained a Yankee fan even when they met Brooklyn in the World Series.

Since I couldn't mess with Miss Cholly, I realized that if I wanted to date, I would have to find some brown-skinned girls. My integration into the broader Africamerican society had begun.

Southeast of where I lived in the Bronx with my Italo friends, a Negro neighborhood had developed. As a baby I had actually lived in this new 'hood before the end of the Depression drove my father, my mother, and me to Carpenter Avenue, where widowed Nana Jesse lived with her brother Joe, who would sneak off to New Jersey to spend time with his dead wife's Irish relatives.

Though my mother had baptized me Catholic, I decided to attend the Sunday school at St. Luke's Episcopal Church—for the girls. So for the first time in my life, except for trips to Harlem, I found myself surrounded by Negroes.

I did not assimilate into Negro society immediately, and in some ways, though I have lived exclusively with brown-skinned people since November 1968, I have never completely assimilated. The standard American speech coming out of my brown face made my Africamerican contemporaries uneasy, though their parents liked the way I spoke. After a while I met other private-school Negritos who spoke standard like me. Not quite the same: their accents sounded more middle-class and southern than my own, which had a working-class Italo tinge, kind of like Frank Sinatra, whose singing and manner I continued to revere.

Further, I had never learned how to dance properly. At Fieldston I always danced better than my Euro classmates. In any group of Negroes, I danced like an animated man of tin, or like the esteemed President Obama. I confounded the one-drop rule. If one drop made me 100 percent Negro, then why hadn't my seven-sixteenths African blood taught me to dance? (Years later I learned that slave owners had used the one-drop rule to preclude their enslaved sons and daughters from claiming inheritance of property or land. Mr. Cholly gave us race to talk about so we wouldn't talk about the money.)

And another thing: I didn't know the music. I hadn't heard "Earth Angel," "One Mint Julep," or "In the Still of the Night." I knew Sinatra, Vic Damone, Frankie Laine, and Bing Crosby. I did know the Ink Spots and a little Armstrong (only as a singer) and some Nat King Cole (as singer and pianist), but no rhythm and blues, and no blues at all. The first time I heard Muddy Waters, his ferocity frightened me. Creoles traditionally did not relate to the blues.

Also, I didn't know the food. Fried chicken, collard greens, black-eyed peas, candied yams with marshmallows, and mulatto rice all seemed exotic to me. Nana Jessie had never learned to cook that well. She usually scorched the rice. Her mother had trained her as a seamstress. After her husband, Narciso Garcia, died, she worked in sweatshops and in freelance as the breadwinner and left the cooking to her mother, Josephine Bartow Marin, who had come north to help her. My mother had learned to cook at Evander Childs High School in a home economics class, standard American stuff. My father cooked well, but only breakfast food and roasting. As a teenager he had worked on the railroad and greatly admired the Pullman cooks and porters for their cuisine and exquisite manners. He always made perfect pancakes, never scorched, one side just as golden as the other.

In the summer of 1952 my father took me to Tennessee to visit his birthplace and where he had grown up. He never said as much, but I think he wanted me to see the segregated South. However, in planning the trip he used a very informative guidebook produced by the National Urban League that told the brown-skinned traveler exactly where to stop and to stay and so avoid rejection and embarrassment. Thus I saw only the Africamerican South—sandwich shops and motels, colleges and universities, and the spacious houses of my uncles. I loved the South I saw. The brown-skinned girls had fabulous legs because they walked a lot. Their twangy voices made me swoon.

When I encountered my first COLORED water fountain, on Lookout Mountain, in Georgia, to my private-school mind it seemed absurd, two fountains to dispense the same water. What did Euros want to demonstrate? Did they fear they would contract Negroness? Yet, though nobody watched us, we did not drink from the WHITES ONLY fountain.

Only in southern Illinois did we meet segregation face to face, in the year Adlai Stevenson, governor of Illinois, ran for president. A woman barred us entry to a coffee shop. "I'm sorry, but we don't serve coloreds here." My father sputtered, angry but mostly bewildered. I wondered why she said "I'm sorry." Land of Lincoln.

Then in summer 1955 came the murder of Emmett Till. Damn.

His courageous mother made us look at his battered, bloated face. *See what you've done to my boy.* I saw myself in Emmett Till, an outgoing and adventurous fourteen-year-old from Chicago who considered racism and segregation a crazy joke, who was accustomed to talking boldly to anybody, even to some policemen, not realizing the COLORED and WHITE signs really meant something, complimenting a pretty girl I did not know, like in Chicago and New York. *Hey baby,* Emmett Till said to Miss Carolyn. *Hey baby.*

The murder of light-skinned Emmett Till made me feel like a real Negro. Your skin shade, your manners, your voice didn't matter. Say the wrong thing to the wrong Euro and you'd end up brutalized, beaten, hanged, shot, drowned, killed, dead. Underneath it all, Euros hated us and thought nothing of killing us. I became aware of other indignities—somebody giving Dr. Ralph Bunche some grief, Miles Davis getting beat up by police for standing in front of his workplace, Birdland.

After Emmett Till, living the life of a Negro became a serious business. For the first time I began to feel an emotion that had probably dogged my father and his father, born in bondage in 1858, the son of his owner, nineteen years old when the federal government betrayed the freedmen and we lost our American Dream of forty acres and a mule and a chance at true economic equality. Dread. Dread came into my life, and futility. *Don't matter what you do and don't matter what you say, / If Mr. Cholly feel he want it, he can take all your shit away.*

Dread and the unpredictability of violence. Euros could turn on you in an instant, even after years of kindness and affection. If your friends' parents didn't alert the doorman to your arrival, you would have to go around to the service entrance. When it came time to dis-integrate you from the party, you didn't get an invitation and nobody objected. They all went. You stood outside looking in. When some Euro wanted to beat you or even kill you, nobody did anything to stop him. They might arrest somebody for it, but he would get off.

Euros lived in a democracy; Africamericans lived in a police state. But most Euros didn't see the contradiction. By then we had finally studied the Constitution, and nobody seemed bothered by the way its high moral rhetoric contrasted with the loopholes some Founding Fathers had created to keep Africans in chains. Euros had accepted and justified slavery among the Greeks and Romans —something about the price of a Great Civilization. Suitably Jeffersonian.

In September 1956 I went away to Harvard, hoping that in the rarefied intellectual atmosphere of Cambridge, Massachusetts, race and racism would evaporate. For the first few months it seemed it had, though a teacher in whose class I did poorly seemed to resent me personally for squandering the great opportunity that the college had bestowed on me.

When it came time for the Harvard-Yale game, I got into the spirit of the great event and invited my brown-skinned girlfriend up from New York. Sometime in October I phoned the big hotel up near Radcliffe and made her a reservation for the weekend. The man who took the reservation assured me that I had done all I needed to do to secure it; I didn't have to put down a deposit or anything. "Just show up on Friday night, sir, and you'll find the young lady's room ready for her."

My girlfriend came up on the train and I went to Back Bay Station to meet her. We stopped in Harvard Yard, where all freshmen lived, and had a drink with my roommates. Around eight o'clock we walked up Mass Ave to the big hotel, finding the lobby jammed with arriving young ladies and their dates. We struggled through the crowd and reached the front desk, told the avuncular desk clerk that we had a reservation under the name of William Kelley for Avis Brown. He went away for a minute, then returned and, in the politest way, apologized and told us that the hotel had misplaced our reservation and by now all the rooms were gone. Disappointed but accepting the clerk at his word, we left the big hotel. We returned to my room in Holworthy Hall and made phone calls and found my girlfriend a place to stay in a Boston suburb. Of course this disrupted our other plans—it took so long to get to Cambridge and back that we never got to see the game.

I forgot the incident and for decades never questioned that a mix-up had occurred. Some twenty years later, after I'd made a daring escape to the island nation of Jamaica and lived for several years in a mostly brown-skinned country, I found myself sitting on our small verandah watching my two golden-brown daughters playing with nannybugs in the dirt. My thoughts drifted back to November 1956. The Harvard-Yale game that I never got to see. Fog dissolving from my memory, I realized, and exclaimed aloud, "Holy spaghetti! On the phone they thought I was Frank Sinatra!"

MAKO YOSHIKAWA

My Father's Women

FROM *The Missouri Review*

WHEN I DROVE my sisters back to town from the lawyer's three days after our father's death, it took a while for us to arrive at the subject of his women. The lawyer had given us a rundown on the will—no surprises, 20 percent to each of us, a little more to his final companion and a little less to his two stepdaughters from his second marriage. We knew that his estate, which included a parking lot in a commercial district in Tokyo as well as a summer house near Mount Fuji, was considerable. Yet none of us had any idea where the right documents were, and for some time our conversation shuttled from where to look for them to what kind of service to hold to how to clear the house of its clutter to when to see the body and how best to lay it to rest.

At last we grew quiet. We were tired, still jolted from the call that had yanked us from our lives.

My older sister broke the silence. "Out of all those girlfriends and wives," she said, "out of all the women he had, who did he love the most?"

I glanced at her. Overcome by the shock, she had cried at the lawyer's, but she looked composed enough now.

My younger sister said Ellie, hands down. His second wife, the love of his middle age, his partner in bowling and church dinners. She reminded us of the episode he'd had after her death and the long hospitalization that had followed. "That was a bad one, even for him."

I shook my head. "That was just because her death was so unexpected. Don't you remember how they used to fight about God?"

Rousing herself, my older sister nodded. "He'd point out all the places the Bible contradicted itself."

"And all the ways God was a logical impossibility."

"She'd get so mad she couldn't speak."

"Besides," I said, "since when did any of his episodes occur for a reason?" It was obvious: he was happiest with Toshiko-san, his last companion. So what if she hadn't gone to college? Our father, Shoichi Yoshikawa, had been a Princeton University physicist and a world leader in fusion energy research. None of his women —a category that included us, Ivy League graduates all—had understood physics on his level; very few did. Toshiko-san had made him laugh, no mean feat, and they had had Japan, not to mention Japanese food and the Japanese language, in common.

"But if he loved her so much," my younger sister shot back, "why didn't he marry her?"

To which I had no answer.

It was November 2010. We were in our late thirties and forties, and although we had taken our time about it, we were all finally settled or married, one sister with a nine-year-old, the other pregnant. We had grown up in Princeton and had left it as soon as we could, the two of them hightailing it to California. I had stayed in the Northeast, but in the last two decades I had seen our father almost as seldom as they, my neglect rendered more glaring by my proximity and the fact that I, a childless novelist and professor, had more time to spare.

Systematically we went down the list of the women who'd passed through Shoichi's life: girlfriends whose names we could barely recall, drinking partners, one or two con women who were after his bank account or citizenship papers or simply the cash in his wallet. But we dismissed those as infatuations. Of course none of us suggested his first wife, our mother.

My older sister had fallen silent, her eyes fastened on the landscape, at once familiar and strange, whipping by outside the window.

I pulled to a stop at a traffic light. "You okay?"

Her head still averted, she said, "Do you ever wonder—"

Her voice was husky. Our father had been seventy-six. He had a heart condition, but when he last saw us—we had all seen him, though at different times, in the spring—he'd assured us it was under control.

She cleared her throat. "Do you think it's possible that he never loved any of them?"

Behind us my younger sister released a breath. I gazed ahead. The sky was overcast, but the trees along the road were rinsed with fall color.

Then the light changed to green and I pressed on the accelerator, and my older sister turned from the window and asked where we should stop for lunch.

He was born in Tokyo, the scion of a wealthy family descended from samurai. The only son, he was cheeky, cheerful, and unusually smart, and his parents, sister, nursemaids, and tutors doted on him. On his fifth birthday his mother died of pneumonia; two years later World War II began. His father, who was well educated but impractical, did not know how to supplement their rations, and during the war years Shoichi suffered, his stomach swelling with malnutrition.

With the end of the war his life resumed its rightful course. He acquired a stepmother, a Juilliard-trained pianist who cherished him, and later two half siblings who looked up to him. He became interested in stamps, and at the age of eleven began traveling across Japan on his own to find and collect them.

He was a handsome boy, tall and skinny with an oversized head topped by a thick brush of hair. He had large, dark eyes and a searching, restless gaze; his grin was bright and sudden and took up his whole face. He received the highest marks in the country on the national exam to enter Tokyo University; while there he won awards, acclaim, and finally a fellowship to MIT. When he decided to take it, articles, one or two in Japan's biggest newspapers, deplored the "brain drain" that was taking a mind such as his to America. He completed his doctorate in three years and in 1961, at the age of twenty-seven, began working at Princeton University's Plasma Physics Laboratory.

At PPL, a hive of physicists, engineers, and technicians worked to create an energy source that was clean, limitless, and safe. Their plan was to use nuclear fusion: they would merge the nuclei of two hydrogen atoms into a single nucleus, as the sun does, and the stars. The new nucleus would be smaller than the original two, and the difference in the mass would convert into energy. Shoichi accepted their offer and stayed at the lab for forty years.

My sisters and I held his memorial service in a small room at the local Hyatt. We had looked into using the university chapel, with its stained-glass windows and soaring ceilings, and had been secretly relieved to find that it was booked for holiday festivities through December. The chapel, which seats two thousand, would have echoed even more than usual with only a handful of mourners in attendance.

In the end more than fifty people came, so many that we almost didn't have enough chairs. Most of them were world-class scientists, three Nobel Prize winners in their midst. My mother's old gang was there, as well as Ellie's family, some former neighbors, and a few friends Shoichi had acquired since retirement—quiet men, shy and perhaps lonely, whom he had met through MIT's alumni association. It was the turnout from the lab, which numbered more than two dozen, that had thrown off our count.

At the service, one of the last speakers said that Shoichi used to ask his women to make dishes for their church dinners. "Because," she added, drawling, "of course he always had a woman."

I winced. The audience laughed, but the remark seemed in poor taste, given that Toshiko-san was in the room—in the back row, where she had insisted on placing herself.

The service had been stocked with surprises, one or two even more startling than the fact that my father had continued the practice, initiated by Ellie, of attending church dinners. There was the letter, translated and read out loud by my older sister, from an old high school friend in Tokyo. Some of what the letter said I knew —tales of Shoichi's effortless brilliance, for instance. But much of it was new. I hadn't known that in high school he was popular with boys and girls alike, and friendly and generous to those less favored than himself. For as long as I could remember, he had been a poor conversationalist, an aggressive and mean-spirited debater, and a teller of boastful, embarrassing stories, the kind of person people avoided at parties and dreaded bumping into in the street. I hadn't known that he always came in last in the 100-meter dash, and that his genial indifference to his lack of athleticism somehow added to his popularity and his aura of cool. I hadn't even known that he still kept in touch with anyone from high school—sixty years ago!—let alone a man who would weep at his passing, write such a letter, and then round up every single graduate of their high school he could find so they could hold a memorial service of their own in Tokyo.

Another surprise was the picture that emerged of Shoichi as a young man. One after the next, his colleagues and former students told the same story: in the '60s and '70s, the lab was the premier center for fusion research in the world, overflowing with hope, idealism, and bright young men fired by the conviction that the discovery of a clean energy source lay within their grasp. And in that august company, Shoichi stood out. His brilliance—"that's a word," the first speaker from the lab said, "that I'm betting you'll hear more than once today"—was legendary. If he was a little arrogant, prone to making mincemeat out of those with less ability—well, another speaker said with a shrug, with a mind like that, who could blame him?

They spoke of traveling across the country to study with him, quaking when they had to answer his questions, and angling for invitations to dinner at his house. They told of trusting that his genius would win the day for them, the lab, and mankind.

Shoichi had shared in their idealism. In the early '60s, one speaker said, he had turned down a career in the barely nascent field of computers, even though he was certain that was the wave of the future. He'd been equally certain he could create a clean energy source and had deemed that the more critical step for humanity.

My father had been nine when atomic bombs decimated Hiroshima and Nagasaki; it made sense that he would grow up dreaming of harnessing nuclear power for peaceful and productive ends. But I hadn't realized people once thought the lab might change the world. In the late '80s, which is when I remember it best, it seemed quiet and a little sleepy, a place where smart men toiled dutifully over equations and tinkered with equipment. The optimism had leached out of them by then; they knew that if the lab did achieve its goal, it would not be in their lifetime. The problem was not that they had been wrong. They could, and did, create energy from fusion. But it took immense pressure and heat for the process to work, and the energy required to produce those conditions was always more than they could create. Theoretically they were on target, but for all practical intents and purposes they had failed.

Nor had I known that adoring students and colleagues once surrounded my father. The image clashed so violently with what I remembered that had my mother not said later that her memories of those times matched the speakers' exactly, I would have assumed they'd made it all up. Shoichi lived just a few miles from the lab, but most of his colleagues hadn't seen him for years. With each breakdown and hospitalization, their friendship with him had cooled, and when he retired, in 2000, it must have seemed easier to forget him. I can't blame them. By then illness, medication, and electroshock treatments had done their damage. His mind was diminished and his body bloated. His hands shook, and his gaze was restless but no longer searching.

I wondered at first if the speakers were waxing nostalgic about Shoichi to compensate for their long neglect. But then I realized that they too had been disappointed by their careers. They weren't famous; none of them had won the Nobel Prize. Their nostalgia was not for Shoichi so much as for those heady days at the lab when their ambition and their idealism had run side by side and success had seemed around the corner. Or if the nostalgia was for him, it was for the man he had been as well as for their own younger selves.

The fact that my father had "always had a woman" was not a surprise. He had liked the company of women, the more the merrier. Toshiko-san knew it, and probably many in the room did as well. He was boastful enough that it was difficult not to know this about him.

"Toshiko-san is the primary mourner here," my older sister said in her opening remarks, "no question." More than once I turned around to search for her, a trim, plainly dressed woman with an open face, fighting tears by herself in the back. But the room was too packed; I could not see past the fourth row.

Despite my sister's words, at the reception afterward it was to us, the daughters, that the guests came to pay their respects, never mind that we hadn't been involved in our father's life in any serious way for years. Indeed, Toshiko-san probably received fewer expressions of sympathy than my mother, who had flown in from England to attend the service.

When they met, my father and Toshiko-san were both widowed and in their sixties. She had grown up dyeing kimonos with her family in Kyoto, hard work a fact of her childhood. During the Occupation she met an American soldier—an African American from Alabama and, as it later turned out, an alcoholic with a temper—who took her home with him. Together they had six children, one of whom she lost to pancreatic cancer. Not an easy life, yet somehow Toshiko-san emerged with her good humor intact.

She had moved in with Shoichi early on, but without ever giving up her own apartment, and for reasons that were never clear—his breakdowns, his moods, his untidiness, or his roving eye?—moved back into her own place after about a decade. He took her on trips to Japan, Europe, and Canada and cruises to beaches in sunnier climes; they ended their relationship more than once but always found their way back to each other. When I came to visit, they would take me to their favorite Japanese restaurant, where we'd share large boats of sushi. She would have too many beers and clamber to the front of the room to sing karaoke, mostly sappy songs, Christopher Cross and the like, her voice wavering in and out of tune, as my father watched and smiled, nodding his head ever so slightly to the beat.

She never called him by name. Instead she used the term *sensei*, an honorific title meaning "professor"—a sign of respect, maybe, or a joke, a way to gently mock him and bring him down to earth. I was grateful for it, since it made him laugh.

In the last two years of his life, he and Toshiko-san saw each other only once a week. They met every Friday for about an hour at a mall on Route 1 that stood almost exactly between their homes. Yet even if they saw little of each other, they talked. Toshiko-san told us after his death that he would call her twice a day, at nine in the morning and nine at night. She didn't have to explain the reason for this ritual. The archetypal absent-minded scientist, Shoichi was indifferent to the progress of the clock. If he insisted on such precise times, it was because he was worried about his body lying there, undiscovered, for hours or even days.

As it was, the funeral home director said that based on the decomposition of his body, a full day must have passed before he was discovered. Shoichi had not phoned at night, but since that had happened before, Toshiko-san decided to wait for the morning call. When that didn't come, she had flown into a panic and sped the eight miles to his house.

She banged on the door and then ran around tapping on all the windows. She had the key but was too frightened to use it. She went to the neighbors, a nuclear physicist and his wife. They had lived next door since I was a baby and were used to helping out; the last time my father was found raving in the backyard, clad in nothing but boxer shorts on a brisk February day, it was they who called me.

With them, Toshiko-san went into the house to find Shoichi dead on his bed, the television blasting.

Five days later, my sisters and I assembled with Toshiko-san at the funeral home for a viewing of the body. Shoichi had requested a cremation; the viewing was just for the four of us.

He was dressed in a gray suit. His face looked sunken. The room was cold and dimly lit.

It was a while before I realized that Toshiko-san was talking. "Look like he's sleeping, *neh*." She was rocking back and forth, her eyes streaming. "Wake up, *sensei*. Wake up. *Itsumo nebo*. Look at him, so handsome in his suit." She turned to us, and we—huddled silently together in a corner, my younger sister red-eyed—gaped back. "You see how handsome he is?" she said. Then she turned back to the body. "What'll I do without you, *neh*, *sensei*? Who's gonna take me on nice cruises?" Reaching into the coffin, she gave him a push on the shoulder, hard enough to leave an indentation. "Wake up, *wake up*."

When she and Shoichi met at the mall on Route 1, they would stroll, look into store windows, and chat. Sometimes they would have lunch or a snack, but this was never the primary purpose of the visit. She would reminisce about events from her past as well as theirs, catch him up on her children, grandchildren, and great-grandchildren, and scold him for scrounging at flea markets and accumulating yet more clutter. He would ask a question or toss in a remark here or there; at times he threw his head back and laughed, something he did rarely in the last few years of his life, and then only with her. He'd have little news to impart of his only grandchild, whom he had met just two or three times; in his last decade he and my older sister were seldom in touch. But I like to think that at least once during those weekly walks he broke his customary silence to speculate about his granddaughter and that Toshiko-san wondered with him. Did she still play with stuffed animals? Had she mastered fractions yet? How tall had she grown?

An Asian man and an Asian woman, stooped and gray-haired, their conversation slipping from Japanese to English and then back again: anyone seeing them would have taken them for a long-married couple, out shopping for a toy for a great-grandson.

*

Toshiko-san had loved my father. But my younger sister was right—his feelings for her were open to question. He had been resolute in his refusal to marry her. Whenever I'd ask him about it, he reminded me that she was seven years older than he was. He didn't want to bury another wife. Ellie's death, from complications resulting from diabetes, had been too hard. He couldn't go through that again.

I'd point out that Toshiko-san was in great health and that women usually outlived men. And besides, isn't it better to live for the moment? Was there something else he wasn't telling me?

It made no difference what I said. He wouldn't change his mind, nor would he explain further.

So perhaps he hadn't loved her. Was it possible, though, that he hadn't loved any of his women?

At the end of the memorial service one of his MIT friends had come up to me. He said that in the weeks leading up to his death, Shoichi had remarked that manic depression had ruined his life. I hadn't been able to collect myself enough to respond, and the man ran off before I could find out his name, so I couldn't call him later to ask what aspects of his life my father had meant. I assumed at the time that he had been referring to his career. Only later, and only because of the train of thought that the talk with my sisters had started, did I wonder if he could have been talking about his personal life too.

That my father had not fulfilled the academic promise of his early years—that he, unlike the nuclear physicist next door, had not been summoned to Sweden to dance with the queen and receive the Nobel Prize—was old news. I had made my peace with that disappointment long ago, even if he never could. But the idea that love had also eluded him was new, and harder for me to accept.

He had sacrificed his homeland, his health, and his family for his career. If it had gone as well as he'd hoped, I wouldn't mind as much that his love life had not. Then too, I knew from my own experience what balm relationships could provide. Struggling with my third novel, I had taken refuge in the company of my husband as well as my mother, sisters, and friends. Had my father not had recourse to this solace?

If only I could believe that his failure to love, like his inability to work with consistency, get out of bed every morning, and keep his temper in check, was a matter of faulty brain chemistry. But

I couldn't. Over the years I'd grilled my father's psychiatrists, internists, and nurses and read clinical texts, scientific papers, and memoirs about manic depression. I knew about the controversies surrounding its diagnosis. I knew the difficulty of understanding how exactly it affects the brain, and the many problems associated with lithium, the most reliable medication currently available. I knew that alcoholism is a symptom, that travel can trigger a manic episode, that studies link the illness with creativity, and that it runs in families. I knew that it could make people say and do things they didn't mean and hurt themselves as well as anyone else in the vicinity. I knew how Van Gogh walked into one of the wheat fields he had been painting and shot himself in the chest; how Woolf weighted her pockets with stones and waded into the Ouse; how Hemingway pushed the barrel of his favorite shotgun into his mouth and blew out his brains; how Plath stuffed wet towels into the cracks of the doors in her kitchen and her children's bedroom before turning on the oven and sticking her head into it; how both Rothko and Diane Arbus took barbiturates and sliced their veins with razors; how Anne Sexton put on her mother's old fur coat, closed the garage door, and started her car; how Kurt Cobain fled rehab, hid out in Seattle for days, and then went to his garage to shoot himself in the chin; how Spalding Gray jumped off the Staten Island Ferry into the East River; how David Foster Wallace hanged himself on his patio, and how the designer Alexander McQueen, taking no chances, overdosed on cocaine and tranquilizers, slashed his wrists, and then hanged himself in his wardrobe with his favorite brown belt.

But nowhere had I heard that manic-depressives can't love. On the contrary, Andrew Solomon writes that even though deep depression might temporarily impair one's capacity to give and receive love, "in good spirits, some love themselves and some love others and some love work and some love God."

If my father had not loved any of his wives or girlfriends, it was a decision he had made. He had opted for isolation. Unexpectedly, when I considered this possibility, what I felt was not grief or even pity but fear.

So I wrote to Ellie's younger daughter. We had gone to high school together, and though I hadn't seen her for years, we had reconnected at the memorial service. I asked if she thought that my father had loved her mother. I begged her not to sugarcoat. What I wanted, I told her, was the truth.

Yes, she wrote back, *I think he did love her. With men, it's sometimes hard to separate love from pride, and I think he was very proud to have her as a wife.* They had fought a lot, especially over money, but they had enjoyed their church community and loved their trips to Japan. *He was not a simple man and, consequently, a simple happiness was not in his nature,* she concluded, *but I did know him to have moments of simple pleasure and obvious joy.*

She was trying to reassure me, that was clear. But there was truth in what she said. Shoichi had been proud of Ellie. He had always admired large, fleshy women—a hangover, I'd always thought, from the near starvation he had suffered as a boy in wartime Japan—and Ellie had been huge, her flesh straining against seams and spilling out of shirt openings. I'd forgotten that they had argued about money as well as God, but perhaps the good times had outweighed the bad; perhaps pride did equal love.

Yet I didn't believe it.

I called my younger sister in San Jose. Five years younger than I am, she was just nine when our parents separated—too young, she says, to remember much about our father's whiskey-fueled rages. They hadn't been close, but her relationship with him had been less complicated than mine was, and as a teenager she had spent a lot of time with him and Ellie.

"You said you thought he loved Ellie more than anyone else," I said. "Why?"

For a moment she was quiet. Then she laughed. "Process of elimination." She was seven months pregnant, glowing and huge, and her laugh sounded happy. She does not look much like our father—none of us do—but she has his grin, sudden and bright. "Think about it. Who else is there?"

"Oh," I said. "Oh. I thought that maybe you knew something about them. Maybe from when you went on vacation with them, at the beach."

"I remember—" She stopped.

I pictured her eyes growing distant, as they do when she wants to guard her thoughts.

It took some prodding, but eventually she told me about a fight she'd overheard them having, just a few months after their wedding. From what she could gather, Ellie had been trying to get him to pay a credit-card bill. He had told her that since she, as his wife, was now on his health plan, all of her diabetes-related expenses covered, she had no right to expect anything more. "It went on," my sister said, "but that was the gist of it. So I'd say that the marriage probably sucked—though maybe less than his other relationships."

"Maybe things changed," I said, knowing even as I spoke that they hadn't. "They had ten more years together after that. That's a lot of time."

"Maybe. But it was a bad fight." She paused. "Listening to it, I thought about what you'd told me about the fights he and Mom used to have, and I was glad I didn't remember much about them."

It was with scant hope that I turned to the only candidate left. My mother is an artist and writer, hard at work now on her eighth book, an account based on interviews she has conducted with Japanese veterans of World War II. In this and everything else she has the unflagging support of my stepfather, a smart, well-read business executive whom she has been married to for over twenty years. In England for New Year's, I went to see her in her study. I told her I wanted to hear about her relationship with Shoichi, and she nodded as if she had been expecting the question. The story unfurled slowly.

"I could see he was special," she said, "the day he showed up on our doorstep." He had come to call on her parents at their summer home near the mountains of Karuizawa. He was seventeen, she a year younger. He was stamp-collecting in the area, and since his mother was a distant relative of her father's, he had decided on impulse to pay them a visit—so what if they had no idea who he was? He had shaggy hair, a balloon of a head, and the easy sophistication of a Tokyo boy. He had been confident, personable, outgoing—"Yes, that really was your father back then," my mother said, nodding, though I had not stirred—and her parents were much taken with him. He spoke only with them, as if he were an adult, but she eavesdropped on their conversation and heard enough to be impressed.

In the fall he traveled from Tokyo to Nagoya to have dinner at their home. By winter he was a regular guest. My mother, already in love, sought out his company whenever she could. They struck up a correspondence, their relationship progressed, and she thought their future together was assured.

But he held back. Maybe, my mother said, because of a girl he still liked from high school. Then one day he wrote to say he would marry her only if she promised always to obey him. Unnerved, she stopped writing for a while, but he continued to send letters, one containing a proposal without qualifiers. She began writing again, although she held off on a response, and she was there at the airport when he left for Boston in 1958. Another year would pass before she finally said yes.

"So I boarded a plane from Tokyo to Boston," she said, "a daikon stashed in my purse."

I nodded. The story of how she had flown halfway around the world carrying almost nothing but the daikon, the white Japanese radish my father had been longing for, was lore in our family, the sweetness of her gesture unsullied and perhaps even heightened by the years of acrimony, abuse, and infidelity that followed.

"We had a few good years in Cambridge and when we first moved to Princeton," she said. "It was when we lived in Japan for those two years that he began to lose his mind." She said that Shoichi woke her up one night and told her to alert the authorities. He needed five hundred soldiers to come and surround the house: the enemy was coming and they were prepared for attack. He was an alien, a prince who had fled from another world in a small computer. But the alien enemy had found him at last, and hiding was no longer an option.

Shoichi became angry when she refused to call the police. All night he kept talking about the enemy; every time my mother fell asleep he would jerk her awake. He stayed at home in this state for three days, until finally she had to call the authorities.

This was in the early '70s; I was seven. I didn't think I remembered any of it when my mother first began speaking, but as she continued there was a flicker, a memory of my father standing on a table, backlit by the Tokyo sunset, and yelling as my sisters and I scurried around on the ground and cried.

When she went to visit him in the hospital after he was committed, he greeted her with a look of polite confusion. Then his face cleared. "Oh, I know you," he said. "You have three daughters, don't you."

To reassure herself more than him, she reached out to touch his hands. They were so cold that for a moment she wondered if he was in fact an alien.

They would stay together for seven more years. He would take to wandering outside the Imperial Palace in Tokyo, saying that he had important secrets to impart to the emperor. She would fly out to Italy to rescue him when, instead of delivering a paper on the levitated superconductor multipole experiment, he ranted to hundreds of stunned physicists from all over the world that he needed to see the pope because he was Christ reborn. He would end up in the hospital again and again, and at his family's insistence my mother would explain to colleagues and friends that he was there for a heart condition, a lie that would become the truth more than three decades later. We would return to Princeton because she, missing America, put her foot down, something my father never forgave her for, and they would fight and have affairs. At PPL colleagues and former students would shun him and dismiss his ideas, citing his megalomania and illness, and he would drink too much, grow increasingly violent, and become a regular at the local mental institution, and one rainy day in April, when he was away on one of his long trips to Japan, we would pack up and move away, leaving just a note behind.

But it was when he failed to recognize her for the first time that my mother realized that in order to survive, she would have to pull away from him.

"It was hard at first, and then—" Her voice, when she continued, was low. "Then it wasn't."

I knew she had been struggling since the memorial service, wondering whether she should have stayed, and if she could have saved him.

"You were right to pull away," I said. "If you hadn't left him, you wouldn't be around now, and who knows where we'd be. You know that, don't you?"

She brushed aside a phantom wisp of hair and looked down at her hands. In her mid-seventies she is still beautiful, the delicacy of her features undiminished by age. "I know."

I took a deep breath. "Just one last question," I said. "Do you think—" Somewhere along the way my eyes had filled. I slashed at them with an arm. "Did he ever love you?"

She glanced at me before looking away again. Then she said the phrase that I thought of as the refrain of my childhood. "He was really sick."

I nodded. "But that didn't mean he couldn't—"

"And he loved physics so much," she said. "There wasn't a lot of space left after that." Her eyes met mine. "So no. No, I don't think he ever did."

She spoke without bitterness. It was a long time ago, and she knew as well as I did that if my father had not loved her back, it was his tragedy rather than hers.

I was lugging my suitcase down the stairs on the last day of my visit when my mother called to me from the second floor. I looked up. Her face was flushed, and she was waving a small black book. Back in Princeton, she said, Toshiko-san had given her Shoichi's address book so she could call family members who needed to be informed of his death. She'd been going through it and had just discovered a current address for Masako-san, the girl he'd liked in high school. "You know, the one that made him reluctant to marry me."

She had seen her once, she said, at the airport on the day Shoichi departed for Boston. A host of his friends had gathered to see him off. Masako-san had been the only other girl in the crowd, and my mother had known at once who she was.

She was small, smaller even than herself, my mother said, and lovely and poised. She had a Mona Lisa smile, and she had smiled a lot at my father that day, though she had cried too.

She had lupus. Shoichi's parents had forbidden him to marry her because they feared that his children would inherit the condition. Other Japanese parents would have felt the same, which was why my mother knew that Masako-san could never have married.

She waved the address book again. "Don't you see, he kept in touch with her," she said. "He never forgot her."

I was still, imagining my father bent over a girl even smaller than my mother, a crowd of his friends pressing in on him as the time for his departure drew near. I thought of him writing to her, going to see her when he was in Tokyo, and missing her when he was away.

"Maybe he loved her all his life," my mother said.

She looked hopeful, even though what she was saying was that the relationship that had consumed twenty-four years of her life had been a sham from the start, and I knew that somehow she had sensed what was behind all my questions.

"Maybe he always missed her," she said. "Maybe all the other women in his life somehow fell short."

I smiled. For a moment I'd been swept up by the story. But a high school crush that had lasted all his life—it was the stuff of movies. What she'd handed me was a Rosebud moment, and I was too earthbound to believe that my father could be explained by it. "I don't know about that," I said.

"You sure?" she asked, but the hopeful look was already fading. "Well, maybe you're right. It's hard to know anything about anyone, isn't it?"

"Especially him," I said.

She laughed. "That's true."

Looking up at her, I had a sudden urge to tell her everything. That I was guilt-stricken about never having returned my father's last phone call to me, three weeks before his death. How shocked I'd felt when my father's MIT friend said that Shoichi had believed manic depression ruined his life: perhaps I was naive or optimistic or in denial, but I hadn't realized that he considered—that he knew—his life had been ruined. I wanted to confess to her how small I'd felt at the funeral home, when my own grief had proved a pale, flimsy thing next to Toshiko-san's, and what I had just understood, that behind my research into my father's relationships lay my own guilt and fear. Because if my father had never loved the wives and girlfriends who had loved him and nursed him and stayed by his side, what hope was there for me, the daughter who had fled his home and returned as seldom as she could? If I relayed these thoughts to my mother, perhaps she could untangle them and smooth them back into something less terrible.

Yet nothing she could say would explain my father. Whether because of his devotion to physics, his illness, or a deficiency deep inside him, he had never loved any of us, at least not in any way that mattered. Besides, she had suffered enough because of him; there was no reason to add to the guilt she felt for all the ways his life shadowed my sisters' and mine. Far better to tell her the one definite conclusion I had reached after my two-month inquiry into my father's life and loves: that he linked me to her, and for that I would always be grateful.

But the airport taxi was crunching gravel outside; with a sigh she was beginning to make her way down the stairs toward me. For now we were out of time.

So I squinted up at her instead. "Masako-san, huh?"

She shrugged. "It's nice to think so, isn't it?"

And I told her that it was, and I wished with all my heart that I could.

WALTER KIRN

Confessions of an Ex-Mormon

FROM *The New Republic*

I DON'T REMEMBER the missionaries' names, only that one was blond and one was dark, one was from Oregon and one was from Utah. They arrived at our house on secondhand bicycles, carrying bundles of inspirational literature. They smelled, I remember, of witch hazel and toothpaste. The blond one, whose hair had a complicated wave in it and whose body was shaped like a hay bale, broad and square, wiped his feet with vigor on our doormat and complimented my mother on our house, a one-story, ranch-style affair in central Phoenix that never fully cooled off during the night and had scorpions and black widow spiders in the walls. The boys—because that's how they looked to me that evening, when I was thirteen and my brother was eleven and my parents were in their mid-thirties—shook hands with us and sat down in the living room, where my mother had set out lemonade and cookies and my father had turned off the television so we could talk. They smiled at us. They smiled with their whole faces. Then they asked, softly, politely, if we could pray.

It was 1976, the Bicentennial, and not a good time for my family. We were sinking, mired in gloom, isolation, and uncertainty. We'd moved to Phoenix a few months earlier, driving a U-Haul truck from Minnesota that wouldn't go faster than 50 miles per hour and didn't have room for all of our furniture. We'd left the small river town where I'd grown up because my father, a corporate patent lawyer who loved to hunt and fish in his spare time, had soured on the Midwest. He felt bored there, constrained by dull conformity; a vision of fierce desert freedom had come over him. In Arizona, a land of opportunity, booming and unfenced, he planned to enter private practice and spend his weekends outdoors under the sky. He'd fly-fish in the mountains, he'd shoot quail, he'd buy a Chevy Blazer with four-wheel drive, and he'd take us deep into the red-rock canyons to hike and camp and hunt for rocks and fossils. We'd love it, he told us. Our fresh American start.

But it didn't turn out like that. My father cracked. Too much longing and space, too little guidance.

It began when his own father died of lung cancer after a horrifying, swift decline. When my father returned from the funeral in Ohio, his legal practice was failing for lack of clients. Some mornings he didn't bother to go to work, just sat on the bench at his bus stop and browsed the paper, waving on the bus drivers when they pulled over. He started talking to himself in public, while eating in restaurants or buying shotgun shells. The tone of his ramblings was punitive, exasperated, like that of an angry coach. Addressing himself as Walt, in the third person, he charged himself with foolishness and weakness. "Walt, you pathetic idiot," he'd say. "Walt, you ridiculous stupid little ass." Sometimes strangers heard him and turned to stare.

The story of how the Mormons came was this: Headed home from a job-hunting trip to Blackfoot, Idaho, while changing planes in Salt Lake City, my father suffered a breakdown in the terminal. His haunted mind attacked itself, nearly paralyzing him at the gate. He pulled himself together and boarded his flight, where he found himself seated beside a handsome young couple who radiated serenity and calm. They sensed his despair and started talking to him about their church, the center of their lives, and about their belief that the family is eternal, a permanently bonded sacred unit. (One reason he listened to them, he later told me, is that there had just been a terrible flood in Idaho—the deadly Teton Dam disaster—and he'd heard stories of how thousands of Mormons had immediately dropped what they were doing and convoyed in from states across the West to perform acts of cleanup and reclamation.) The next morning, in his bed at home, he woke up thrashing from a nightmare. My mother threatened to leave him; she'd had enough. Flashing back to the couple on the plane, he opened the phone book, found a number, dialed it, and said he needed help. This minute. Now.

The Church of Jesus Christ of Latter-Day Saints must have been used to fielding such distress calls. They dispatched a rescue party instantly: another couple, retired, in their seventies. Within an hour they were at my father's side. They talked to him all morning behind closed doors and convinced him to go to church with them that Sunday. The service soothed him, lightening his mood. My mother saw this, grew hopeful, and didn't leave him. The bicycle-riding missionaries showed up a few nights later.

"Dear Heavenly Father," their prayers began. They sat hip to hip on our sagging old blue sofa, and milky beads of talcum-powder sweat ran down their temples and their cheeks. They blessed our family, our home. They blessed the lemonade. They asked that we hear their message with open minds. On the first night, they showed us a movie about a boy, Joseph Smith, who, one day in 1820, prayed in the woods behind his parents' farm and found himself face to face with God and Jesus. The lessons that followed described what happened next, from Smith's translation of a golden scripture that he found buried in a hillside to the trials of his early disciples. Seeking peace to practice their new faith, they traveled west from settlement to settlement, harassed by mobs of brutal vigilantes, who finally murdered Smith in Illinois. His people stayed strong, though. Under a brave new leader, Brigham Young, they undertook a 1,000-mile trek that brought them to Utah, their Zion in the wilderness.

The missionaries kept coming for six weeks, always at night, always hungry for our cookies. On Sundays they sat next to us at services, one on each side of us, like gateposts. And then it was time; they told us we were ready. Standing in a pool of waist-deep water, dressed in white robes, we held our hands together as if to pray, let the missionaries clasp our wrists, leaned back, leaned back farther, and joined the Mormon Church.

Last winter I sat drinking coffee in my living room, watching Mitt Romney speak on television after narrowly winning the Michigan primary. The speech was standard Republican stuff, all about shrinking the federal government and restoring American greatness, but I wasn't concentrating on Romney's rhetoric. I was examining his face, his manner, and trying—if such a thing is possible —to peer into his soul. I was trying to see the Mormon in him.

My motives were personal, not political. I'd never been a good Mormon, as you'll soon learn (indeed, I'm not a Mormon at all these days), but the talk of religion spurred by Romney's run had aroused in me feelings of surprising intensity. Attacks on Mormonism by liberal wits and their unlikely partners in ridicule, conservative evangelical Christians, instantly filled me with resentment, particularly when they made mention of "magic underwear" and other supposedly spooky, cultish aspects of Mormon doctrine and theology. On the other hand, legitimate reminders of the church hierarchy's decisive support for Proposition 8, the California gay marriage ban, disgusted me. Deeper, trickier emotions surfaced whenever I came across the media's favorite visual emblem of the faith: a young male missionary in a shirt and tie with a black plastic name badge pinned to his vest pocket. The image suggested that Mormons were squares and robots, a naive, brainwashed army of the out-of-touch. That hurt a bit. It also tugged me back to a sad, frightened moment in my youth when these figures of fun were all my family had.

As for Romney himself, the man, the person, I empathized with him and his predicament. He no more stood for Mormonism than I did, but he was often presumed to stand for it by journalists who knew little about his faith, let alone the culture surrounding it, other than that some Americans distrusted it and certain others despised it outright. When a writer for the *New York Times,* Charles Blow, urged Romney to "stick that in your magic underwear!" I half hoped that Romney would lose his banker's cool and tell the bigoted anti-Mormon twits to stick something else somewhere else, until it hurt. I further hoped he'd sit his critics down and thoughtfully explain that Mormonism is more than a ceremonial endeavor; it constitutes our country's longest experiment with communitarian idealism, promoting an ethic of frontier-era burden-sharing that has been lost in contemporary America, with increasingly dire social consequences. Instead, Romney showed restraint, which disappointed me. I no longer practiced Mormonism, true, but it was still a part of me, apparently, and a bigger part than I'd appreciated.

Sometimes a person doesn't know what he's made of until strangers try to tear it down.

A few months after our baptism in Phoenix, having recovered the basic power to function, my family moved back to rural Minnesota, to a town about 40 miles from St. Paul where Mormons were few, and we promptly began to lapse. My little brother got all caught up in sports, my father resumed drinking wine and beer with meals, and my mother immersed herself in a new job as a nurse at a famous addiction clinic devoted to the gospel of the twelve steps. I remained faithful, however. I hung on. To abandon my family's deliverers so quickly seemed risky to me, not to mention impolite. What's more, I'd become a believer.

The teaching dearest to my young heart related to the transit of the soul through time and space and beyond them. The version of heaven familiar from my childhood, instilled in me by occasional attendance at a Lutheran Sunday school, had always struck me as sterile and impersonal—a cavernous amphitheater of clouds where rank upon rank of stranger-angels sang the praises of a seated wizard—but the Mormon afterlife seemed homier, a sort of family reunion among the stars. Like Dorothy waking from her dream of Oz, I would find myself resurrected with my close relatives, all of us smiling and at the peak of health.

One evening at church, a participatory play was staged to help us envision this reassuring place. Following a simulated plane crash that involved cutting the lights throughout the building and broadcasting sounds of chaos on the PA system, the congregation was ushered down a dark hallway into a room where the bishop and his wife stood dressed in white garments, illuminated by spotlights. Their arms were extended in welcome. Soft music played. Behind them were posters of galaxies and planets and a banner that read, THE CELESTIAL KINGDOM.

Another source of uplift was my new status as a deacon of the Aaronic Priesthood, a junior spiritual order open to all faithful adolescent males. Chief among my duties as a deacon was the ritual shredding of loaves of Wonder Bread into little sacramental chunks. Every Sunday my teenage pals and I would file down the aisles of our modest chapel distributing this holy meal, which also included paper cups of water filled from a tap concealed behind the pulpit. In my powder-blue suit and shiny brown clip-on tie, I felt handsome, useful, and respected. I also felt included, a new sensation for a kid worn-out from changing schools. As I moved through the congregation with my tray, the grateful faces in the pews, male and female, young and old, dissolved my chronic feeling of separation and convinced me I'd found my place.

The strongest force binding me to the church, however, wasn't religious but hormonal. I found the girls of my ward more attrac-

tive than the girls at school. Perhaps because Mormon custom en-
courages young folks to marry permanently and early, often when
they're barely out of their teens, the girls were precociously skilled
at self-enhancement, favoring leg-slimming, grown-up-looking
shoes and eye-catching, curling-iron-assisted hairstyles. They also
permitted discreet erotic contact that stopped just short of actual
intercourse. The girl I liked best of all was Carla H., a hell-rais-
ing cheerleader two years my senior. Carla had sinful menthol-
cigarette breath and a scandalous reputation. A couple of months
before I fell for her at one of the ward's monthly Saturday night
dances, she'd run away from home, the story went, and shacked
up with the married manager of the franchise restaurant where
she worked. The better-brought-up boys avoided her because of
this, but I, a new convert, was undeterred.

Carla's family, whom I'll call the Harmons, was Mormon royalty.
It traced its ancestry to pioneers whom Brigham Young had dispatched to southern Idaho to irrigate the desert and start farms.
The pious stoicism of these tough people was still discernible in
Mr. Harmon, a midlevel corporate accountant with a lean gray
face and hollow eyes who rarely spoke directly to his children, just
mentioned them in mealtime prayers. Above the desk in his orderly home office hung a rack of rifles and shotguns, and after
dinner he'd pull a chair up under them and organize the ward's
books for hours on end while Carla and I watched television in
the next room and Ken, her nineteen-year-old brother, smoked
marijuana and tinkered with his Camaro in the garage. I felt bad
for the man. He seemed defeated. One evening he emerged early
from his office and caught me and Carla with our shirts half off,
but instead of saying anything, he walked silently past us into the
kitchen, where I heard him turn the faucet on and splash water on
his face. A few moments later he went by again, still ignoring us,
holding a glass of milk.

My problem was that Carla wasn't loyal. I was her Mormon boyfriend, not her main one. Her main one was older than me and
twice as tall. I glimpsed him once, at the counter in her restaurant, dressed in a letter jacket covered in pins. I knew from his
posture somehow that he and she had gone places I hadn't. My
consolation was knowing that in theory, she and I had a serious
future together. In only three years I'd serve my mission, sent by
the church to wherever they'd choose to send me—England, I

hoped, because I was bad at languages but pined for foreign lands —and when I got home, I'd be urged to take a wife. It might be her. She'd hinted as much one night. "I'm getting this out of my system," she confided while we lounged in her brother's Camaro smoking dope. "Don't think this is permanent. I love the church. I just can't give all of me right now."

I too had begun having trouble giving all of me. To my parents, the backsliders who no longer knew me, I was a scripture-reading wonder boy whom the elders sometimes invited to speak at services on topics such as "Teamwork" and "Moral Purity," but I knew better. I'd turned into a sneak. At my most recent bishop's interview—a ritual grilling required of every Mormon above a certain age—I'd been asked a series of questions that opened, absurdly it seemed to me, with this one: "Have you committed murder?" No, of course not. "Theft?" No again, though it depended. "Have you masturbated?" I started lying then. I lied right on down the remainder of the list. What's more, I was pretty certain that we all did. So why put us through the whole confusing ordeal? To be asked if you lied and be forced to lie again was annoying and dispiriting. It prevented you from pretending you were good, which is sometimes, with kids, what helps you to be good.

The summer I turned sixteen, I joined my youth group for a ward-sponsored bus tour of the midwestern Mormon holy sites. The site I most looked forward to visiting was the spot in Independence, Missouri, where I was told that God would establish his everlasting kingdom around the time of the Second Coming. The way I'd heard it from a clued-in buddy who'd grown up in the faith, we would be called, via skywriting or trumpet blast, to gather at this consecrated place and erect a temple with our bare hands. We would go there on foot, the way the early saints had crossed the plains to settle Salt Lake City. It sounded like fun to me, and my buddy said it would occur within our lifetimes, after a period of shattering destruction. We didn't need to fear this havoc, he said, because of the stores of food and other supplies that the church encouraged us to stockpile. I didn't let on that my family hadn't done this.

We left St. Paul and followed the Mississippi down along the continent's great valley of primitive fertility and mystery. In the buses, especially as evening fell, a cloistered sense of boy-girl possibility caused sweaty hands to wander in the rear seats, beyond the view of the chaperones up front. In the morning we strolled through Nauvoo, Illinois, the city where Smith and his followers sought refuge after being chased out of Missouri. Our attention was directed to a hill where Smith had begun the construction of a temple, the rites and ordinances of which, my buddy whispered, were based on ceremonies Smith had witnessed in a Masonic lodge that he belonged to. "He stole them?" I asked. "So they say," my buddy said. "They say it was Masons who killed him, for taking their secrets."

Below the hill, on the flats along the river, was a cluster of wooden stores and houses restored by the church as a living history lesson. Standing some distance from Carla to fool the chaperones, I watched with pretended fascination as reenactors dressed in coarse, dull fabrics rendered fat to make soap and spun thread on wooden wheels. The impression I gained was that we—spoiled modern teenagers—were in some manner heirs to these simple, cheerful drudges. When the going got tough after the Day of Judgment, we would shed our luxurious individuality, take up their tools and their rough-hewn way of life, and set out on the overland march to Independence. I could almost imagine this transformation in my case—my parents' house was surrounded by dairy farms, I'd been working at an auto shop that summer—but I doubted that Carla would make the grade.

On down the river we drove, into Missouri. The buses pulled over in a parking lot overlooking a leafy summer cornfield bordered by a tangled hardwood forest. We filed out and were made to stand in silence before what one chaperone, balding, tall, and stern, declared to be Eden, man's childhood home. It was also the spot where Jesus would return to rally the elect, he said. We were shown the broad rock where, according to our guide, the Savior would stand and speak. We were encouraged to stand on it ourselves. The boy who preceded me in line was crying when he stepped down off the stone, one hand pressed on his stomach as though it ached. As Mormons, we'd learned that a burning in our bellies meant we were in the presence of the Spirit, whose job was to confirm for people in doubt the truth of propositions their minds resisted. This was one of those. Eden in a cornfield? It had to be planted in something, I supposed, but then there was the matter of its size. For Adam and Eve it was spacious enough, perhaps, but could it hold all the Mormons who'd be left after the tribulations of the Last Days? Only if they packed in awfully tight.

As Carla and the others watched me, I mounted the rock in my untied tennis shoes and awaited intestinal confirmation of a story I suddenly found preposterous. Other tales from the trip had strained belief, but I'd strained back and managed to accept them. This one was different, though. This one hurt to think about.

What happened next surprised me. As I gazed at the field and struggled to imagine a sea of faithful saints gathered to take instruction from God's son as nuclear mushroom clouds billowed on the horizon and vultures circled above the woods, my stomach cramped. Not a strong cramp, but a cramp. Was this the same as a "burning"? Well, say it was. What prompted it, though? I feared I knew: pure tension. The tension of glancing over at my friends and wondering if I could conceal the look of emptiness that comes from finally losing one's spiritual innocence.

Paranoia overtook me afterward. When I boarded the bus and headed toward the back row where Carla and I had sat on the way down, enmeshed in our comfy, conspiratorial romance, I saw that she wasn't there, that she'd changed seats. She'd plunked herself down across from a male chaperone, in a zone of good conduct where nothing could happen between us. She seemed to avoid my eyes when I approached, then turned around to face my chatty buddy in the seat behind her. I walked on past her and sat by myself with a radio I'd brought. It may have been all in my head, the change in Carla, but the change in me felt real. Later on, when we reached Independence, I played sick and listened to the Bee Gees on the bus while my friends continued with the tour.

Beverly Hills, California, 2008.

I'm forty-six, which is all grown up and then some, and I'm scanning a list of online classifieds for an affordable guesthouse or apartment where I can stay while pursuing a new relationship with a woman I met over the Internet and drove all the way from Montana two weeks earlier to meet for a first date. I have other business in the area—shooting is about to start on a movie of one of my novels, *Up in the Air*, and the director and I have things to talk about—but I can easily finish up tomorrow, at which point I'll face a choice: stay on in my costly, claustrophobic hotel room, secure a monthly rental, or say goodbye to Amanda (for now? for good?) and head back north toward Montana up I-15.

I narrow my list to three places, all guesthouses, and hastily arrange to meet their landlords. My lousy credit scores will be a problem. My life has been spiraling down these past few years. A divorce from the mother of my two kids. Fat medical bills from repeated bouts of kidney stones, which are one of those puzzling ailments you blame yourself for because the doctors can't tell you what else to blame. A dwindling income due to a contraction of both my stamina and the publishing industry. I'm using Ambien to sleep, Ritalin to yank me back awake, and three varieties of narcotic pain pills to keep me from going fetal on the sidewalk when the stones start axing through my ureter. I should talk to my father, who has been where I am now and took extreme measures. But those measures aren't open to me—I closed them off—which may be one reason I'm in this mess.

I never served my Mormon mission. Decision time came when I was seventeen, the year I left Mormonism altogether and began my college education rather than postponing it to proselytize. The disenchantments of the bus tour had savaged my testimony but spared my spirit, allowing me to rebuild my faith around elemental principles of love and forgiveness, charity and sharing. What finally separated me from the church was a loss of nerve, not a crisis of belief. My time in the ward had shown me at close range that God doesn't work in mysterious ways at all, but by enlisting assistants on the ground. I saw sick people healed through the laying on of hands, not suddenly and magically but gradually, from the comfort that comes of feeling the group's concern. I'd heard inspired messages spoken in common English, sometimes from my own excited lips. This proximity to the sacred scared me off. Too much responsibility, it felt like. Too much pressure to side with the miraculous, which places demands on a busy, modern person. You sit down on a plane beside a gloomy lawyer who's cursing himself under his breath, and instead of ignoring him and reading a book, you have to ask his name and offer solace.

My stated excuse for sneaking away from Mormonism was skepticism about its doctrines, but I'd learned that most Mormons don't grasp all the teachings of Joseph Smith—nor do they credit all the ones they do grasp. After the bus trip to Eden, holy Missouri never came up again in conversation. As for the future temple in Independence, I found out that the spot where Smith said it would rise belonged to a Mormon splinter sect with a U.S. membership of about one thousand. The "sacred underwear"? It was underwear. Everyone wears it, so why not make it sacred? Why not make everything sacred? It is, in some ways. And most sacred of all are people, not wondrous stories, whose job is to help people feel their sacredness. Sometimes the stories don't work, or they stop working. Forget about them; find others. Revise. Refocus. A church is the people in it, and their errors. The errors they make while striving to get things right.

But I didn't have the patience, or the humility. I wasn't a son of stubborn pioneers. I was the son of the lawyer on the plane who'd suffered the breakdown I thought I could avoid. I left the church as abruptly as I'd entered it. No formalities, no apologies, no goodbyes.

When I meet with the first two landlords in Beverly Hills, they've already seen my credit files and don't seem to want to know much more about me other than why I'm standing on their property. At my third stop, I speak into an intercom and wait in suspense for an electronic gate either to slide open, meaning yes, or fail to budge, meaning time to hunker down, kick the opiates, and pay my bills.

"Great to meet you, Walt. I'm Bobby Keller. You want a Sprite or something? You look all hot. My sister, Kim, who you talked to on the phone, is at a church thing with our other housemates, but I can show you the place we hope you'll rent."

You can scoff at their oddities, skip out of your mission, run off to college, and wander for thirty years through barrooms and bed-rooms and courtrooms and all-night pharmacies, but they never quite forget you, I learned that day. How had Bobby discovered my secret? My Wikipedia page, written by some stranger. It was loaded with mistakes (it said I was still married, a detail that may have given Bobby pause when Amanda stayed over the next night—not that he said a single word), but the fact that got me a lease without a credit check and rescued my new romance was accurate: my first book, a collection of short stories that opened with a tale of masturbation and ended with one about a drunken missionary, had won a little-known literary prize from a broad-minded Mormon cultural group.

I furnished the guesthouse with chairs and shelves and tables that my new housemates had stored in the garage and not only gave me but helped me clean and move. My latter-day Mormon double life began. Away from the shady, walled-in canyon com-pound that I nicknamed Beverly Zion, I plunged into the arcade of bright temptations that my single and in-their-twenties new friends (Bobby, a personal trainer turned surfing photographer; Kim, a runway model turned mortgage broker; Sophie, a TV talent show contestant; and Lisa, a sales rep for a cosmetics firm—identities that I have tweaked for the sake of privacy) had presumably banded together to resist. I patio-postured at the Chateau Marmont. I Sunset-Stripped until the bands went home. What I didn't do was go back to church. Unnecessary. Mormonism, the religion of second chances, the faith that makes house calls, had come back to me.

In a way I remembered from my teenage years, my housemates did everything in groups, with friends from their Santa Monica "singles ward." They hit the beach for all-night bonfire parties and convoyed off to a giant monthly flea market held at the Rose Bowl in Pasadena. At least once a week they threw a backyard cookout: burgers and chicken, rolls, potato salad, lettuce salad, Jell-O salad, ice cream. When everybody finished eating, we'd gather inside the main house's soaring living room to watch that week's episode of Sophie's talent show or one of the bloody, hard-boiled action movies that Bobby couldn't get enough of. The mood was casual and disheveled, reminding me of a fifth-grade sleepover. I was faintly aware of crushes within the group, of certain young men who had eyes for certain young women, but there was no withdrawing into pairs. Everyone paid attention to everyone else.

I'd forgotten that social life could be so easy. I'd forgotten that things most Americans do alone, ordinary things, like watching television or listening to music or sweeping a floor, could also be done in numbers, pleasantly. One night I sat on the floor next to a kid, muscled and tall, rectangularly handsome, who turned out to be a quarterback for UCLA. I learned this from Kim; he'd never bothered to mention it. Too absorbed in the goofy talent show, too busy barbecuing chicken breasts or squirting Hershey's Syrup on bowls of ice cream, assembly-line style, while someone else stuck spoons in them. At Beverly Zion, that's how it worked: pitch in, help out, cooperate, cooperate. Divide the labor, pool the fruits. This reflexive communalism went way back in Mormonism and underlay a frontier economic system known as "the United Order." It had also inspired the early Mormons' symbol of themselves, the beehive. In Brigham Young's Utah, where speculative self-enrichment was explicitly discouraged (along with the mining and trading of precious metals, which Young decried as a barren, corrupting enterprise), the direction of the pursuit of happiness was toward the advancement of the common good.

It dawned on me that the purpose of Beverly Zion was not to seal out Hollywood at all, but to provide a setting for the enjoyment of a mutualistic way of life familiar from childhood homes and churches. Well, good enough: It kept me fed. It kept me company when I wasn't writing and when Amanda, also a writer, was on assignment. It provided me with a car when mine broke down, with a truck when I bought a used sofa and had to fetch it, with laundry supplies when I ran out of them, and with dog-sitters for Amanda's poodle when we flew to St. Louis to watch the filming of *Up in the Air*. It also provided me, thanks to Bobby's father, a product designer for a Big Three auto company, with an insider's discount on a new car that saved me a sweet four thousand bucks. And in repayment for these kindnesses? Nothing. I asked. Just help finish this Jell-O salad.

"I mean it: Are they for real?" Amanda kept asking me. She'd grown up a Roman Catholic in Chicago and felt guilty about accepting favors that she couldn't instantly return. Beverly Zion soon overwhelmed this attitude.

One ninety-degree afternoon in the backyard, Bobby held a fashion shoot for a publication named *Eliza* run by one of his sister's pretty friends. ("America's leading modest fashion magazine" was how Kim described it to Amanda, meaning no short skirts or low-cut tops.) The theme of the shoot was summer athletic wear, and playing a golfer was a slim Korean girl who looked terrific bending over a putter and aimlessly tossing back her long, thick hair. Three weeks later Bobby informed the house that he and the model, a Mormon, were engaged. Soon afterward, they married.

Amanda and I, who'd already been dating longer than Bobby and his bride had known each other, attended the wedding reception, which was held in the gym of a suburban church and reminded me of my adolescent dances. Abundant pink punch, a blend of juice and soda. Cakes and cookies and yet more cookies. A zany mood of juvenile abandon and a prayer at the end for safe trips home.

Afterward, in the car, on a dark freeway, Amanda said, "I give up. I want to join."

"Don't give up," I said. "We aren't them. We aren't."

"Maybe I'm not. You are, though," she said.

I didn't argue with her. Much as they had in 1976, when the

Kirns lay awake in their broiling house, the Mormons had seen me through an ugly low patch, only this time they'd appeared unbidden. My checks had stopped bouncing. So had my moods. I'd knocked off the Vicodin, flushed away the Ambien, and replaced them with comfort food and group TV nights. I'd met George Clooney but given up trying to be him. When I climbed into bed in the guesthouse after the wedding, I nodded off faster than I had in years, safe behind the walls of Beverly Zion.

Driving home from Los Angeles to Montana recently, I stopped for the night in Salt Lake City with the secret intent of showing Amanda, to whom I'd become engaged a few months earlier, that Utah wasn't the sensory exclusion zone of late-night comedy legend. We turned off the freeway onto a broad street originally laid out by Brigham Young to accommodate passing teams of horses, looked for a restaurant, saw nothing but KFC (past ten o'clock; too late for anything fancier), and pulled up in front of the Monaco Hotel. Having spent the weekend in Las Vegas flinging money at the roulette wheel and attending saucy cabaret shows, we were exhausted, but only she was sleepy. My easily excited ex-Mormon metabolism was still jazzed from the Strip and two truck-stop energy drinks.

At 1 A.M., with no one on the street, I left the hotel and walked up to the temple, a blazingly well lit granite edifice built by stalwart pioneers and completed about 120 years ago, after 40 years of work. I sat on a bench regarding its eastern face and the trumpeting gold angel on its main spire: Moroni, the being who directed Joseph Smith to the spot where the golden Book of Mormon lay buried. I was after something, I realized. A lift, a boost, a spiritual burning in the stomach. I'd never given up chasing that sensation. I tried to force things by praying with closed eyes—or not praying exactly, focusing my willingness. Nothing. The roar of big trucks on I-15, the pounding of my caffeinated pulse. Then I opened my eyes and saw something I'd missed: a simple carved symbol above the temple's entrance that other religions might not have thought to put there. It told a story, it summed it up in stone. My father's story. A lot of mine. And, from what I knew, much of theirs—the Mormons.

Nothing mysterious. Nothing cultish. Just a handshake.

KEVIN SAMPSELL

"I'm Jumping Off the Bridge"

FROM *Salon.com*

PEOPLE USUALLY JUST ask me where the bathroom is or if we are hiring. Sometimes they ask where they can find the latest Dan Brown novel or "that book they just talked about on NPR." On this day in late 2007, however, while I worked at the front info desk at Powell's Books in Portland, Oregon, a frazzled-looking young guy stood silently in front of me.

"Do you need help?" I asked.

He shifted his weight from one leg to the other. "I'm going to go jump off the Burnside Bridge," he said.

Every cell of my body lit up, but something in my head told me to play it calm.

"Why are you going to do that?" I asked. About fifteen feet in front of me, three cashiers worked a small but steady line of happy book buyers. I leaned in a little, trying to create a private space between us. He was wearing a T-shirt and no coat, not enough clothes for the chilly fall day. He smelled toxic. But I could tell he was handsome. I could picture him in a cheap and earnest suit.

"Nobody needs me," he said.

"Who's nobody?" I asked. But then I wondered if that sounded insensitive.

"She won't let me see my daughter," he said.

I noticed a customer coming my way for help. "Hey, what's your name?" I asked him, and he told me it was Chris. "Stay right here, Chris," I said. "I want to talk to you more."

All he had to do was walk out the door, take a quick left, walk ten blocks down Burnside, and find a high place to jump. But he stepped back and waited as I helped one, and then another, customer.

When I had finished, I called him back over to the desk. I called him by his name. He told me his girlfriend didn't want to see him anymore. He told me he'd been up for three straight days, wired on some kind of drug that must have been mixed with something else. He seemed just as surprised about this as I was. "Maybe I should get a book," he said, and for a second I thought everything was going to be okay, but he grew anxious again. "I gotta go somewhere. I have to lie down or something."

He took a few steps toward the door. "Wait, Chris. Hey, hold on," I called out. When he turned toward me, I could see the color drain from his face. He looked like he was already dead, like he had washed up on the banks of the Willamette River with his eyes open and his body bloated. There was something inside him that I couldn't stop. "Let me call someone that can help you out," I said. I was fully aware that I sounded like a character in an afterschool special. I was using·the nonthreatening, sterilized language of the do-gooder. Plus I was saying his name a lot, which I always thought sounded unnatural. ("Hey Chris, can I help you find a book?" "How's your day going, Chris?")

I called one of the managers to the front desk and walked over to Chris, standing between him and the door. "I think you need more time to think," I said. "I'm sure that no one wants you to die."

He took out his wallet, and I thought he was going to give me something. His ID and credit cards, his money and a pile of tattered Post-it notes. But he took out a photo of his daughter and showed it to me. I was glad he didn't hand it to me. It meant he still wanted to hold on to things.

At that moment the manager walked up and gently ushered him into the security office to talk. Thirty minutes later, an ambulance arrived, and Chris was carried out on a folded-up stretcher. He was going to be okay, at least for today.

Afterward, I felt such a strange pride about the whole situation. It was an endorphin rush that shook my voice as I told people about it. "I talked a guy out of killing himself today," I told them. Or, "I saved somebody's life at work."

Maybe I was saying these boastful things because it just feels good to help another human being. Or maybe I was saying them because by then my own life was spinning out of control.

I had been with my girlfriend for about five years, and I felt myself becoming more and more unhappy. It was almost like something had physically happened to me—like I had been in a car accident or suffered a concussion from falling down the stairs—and my chemicals had been jarred somehow. I woke up depressed. One morning, while my girlfriend and I were out eating breakfast, I began crying without knowing why. We paid the bill and sat in my car talking about therapy, about help, about what might be buried inside me.

On the day I convinced Chris not to jump off the bridge, I thought maybe I turned a corner, maybe I could embrace positivity again, maybe I could hear the words I had said to him: "I'm sure that no one wants you to die."

I went to my friend Lynne's house and told her what had happened. She and I had a complicated history. I'd briefly been close to her at nineteen, but we'd lost touch over the next twenty years. She had recently moved to Portland with her husband, and our connection had rekindled. I thought of Lynne often. We exchanged e-mails almost daily. She told me about problems with her husband, and I confided in her about my own problems and the uncertainty in my life.

The more time I spent with her, the more conflicted I became. I felt a sweet glow of nostalgia with her, and we talked about the small town where we both grew up. I sensed a pull toward her, even though I knew she wasn't right for me. Not as right as the girlfriend I already had whom I had built a life with and whom I was more compatible with and more attracted to.

As I was telling Lynne the story in her kitchen while she washed dishes, I broke down and cried. Like that morning in the restaurant with my girlfriend, I wasn't sure why it started. But something broke inside me, and I was gasping for air. I closed my eyes, but tears still poured out. If I shut them tighter, my eyelids would have blown up like water balloons. My whole body shook, and I felt like collapsing.

I felt Lynne's hands on my shoulders. My arms reached out blindly, wanting to pull her to me, wanting to be held. I felt my knees bend, and then reflexively straighten up. I thought of what it would be like to bend my knees on the ledge of a bridge. Would I actually jump, or would I just lean forward and fall? Would the freefall be scary or thrilling? I could imagine my body twisting and somersaulting until it shattered against the water, but I couldn't fathom what would be going through my mind.

"You did a good thing," Lynne said. "You saved a life." She put her sleeve up to my face, softly brushing away my tears. And then her husband walked in the door, home from work.

I wondered if I would see Chris after that. If he would stop in the store and thank me for saving his life. I wasn't sure if I wanted him to. I looked through the newspaper more carefully for the next few days, lingering over the obituaries. I never heard a thing.

I split up with my girlfriend shortly after that. We had gone to see a couples counselor who was far away, in an unfamiliar suburb. I felt uncomfortable and confined during the session. On the drive home, on the freeway, I told my girlfriend I was giving up on the relationship. I drove to Powell's and got out of the car, and she moved to the driver's seat. We were both crying, barely able to talk. I knew I was being an asshole. I was going back to work, like it was a normal day. I did all this on my lunch break.

We would talk about her moving out, how we would separate stuff, and how we would tell my son, later.

My son. I had a son. He was fourteen when this happened. I told myself that he was resilient. I had broken up with his mother when he was about three, and then I married someone else that same year. Five years later my wife asked for a divorce, and he had an ex-stepmom.

He was a good kid, but I worried I was setting a bad example. Telling your kids about another breakup is wrenching work. It's like you're looking at a younger version of yourself and confessing that you are weak at heart, that failure is inevitable, and that sometimes you try so hard and want to seem heroic but you are not. I am weak at heart. I have failed. I am not heroic.

My girlfriend and I told my son, and we could hardly breathe. He sat there with an earnest look of concern. He tried to form a comforting smile on his face. I wasn't sure if the smile was for us or him. That was probably the saddest moment of my life.

The next day at Powell's, I was on autopilot. Completely numb. I was in back where we sort through books. A woman I work with whom I barely know put her hand on my shoulder. I think she could sense something was wrong. She asked if I was okay. I said the words, "Not really." Then I started weeping.

By the time New Year's Eve rolled around, I had decided to

write my will. I wrote it like a letter, like an apology. It almost felt ridiculous to say who got what. I didn't have much to give anyway. Books to that person, CDs to that person, my crappy dishes and old computer. My clothes. Whom would I put in charge of distributing my clothes? Who would want to wear the clothes of a sad, dead man?

The girlfriend I had broken up with had a friend who'd (sort of) committed suicide a few years before we met. He was a policeman, and one night, after an argument, he went to his girlfriend's apartment and waved his gun around, distraught. He turned the gun on himself, and it went off. His girlfriend tried to help him, but it was no use. The girlfriend told her friends afterward that she tried to hold his head together. The girlfriend told people she heard the sound of his blood glugging out. The girlfriend would later tell people that she could no longer listen to the sound of someone pouring wine.

After the funeral, his friends split up his possessions. My girlfriend got a bunch of his CDs. They were mixed into our combined music collection when we lived together. They had his name written on them. She would never sell them. Sometimes we would listen to them with just slightly more reverence than usual.

One of the strange things about this guy's death was that it was on a New Year's Eve, which was the same date I was writing my will on. It's the day when you look back at the year and try to figure out if it was good or not. This was not a particularly good year for me. I mean, part of me realized that I had taken some important steps to learn more about myself, but another part of me knew I was hurting the most important people around me and that I was worn-out. I thought to myself that the bad stuff in my life outweighed the good and that I had turned into a negative force. I thought maybe this was where it should end. I told myself I had done all I could do in my life. I knew how Chris felt now. *Nobody needs me.* I wanted to get it over with.

I didn't know how I would do it, though. I was by myself on New Year's Eve, and it was early evening. I didn't have a gun, and I didn't think I was strong enough to plunge a knife into my gut. I didn't think I could hang myself, because I don't know how to make a noose out of bed sheets. I thought drugs would be nice, but I didn't have enough money to buy sleeping pills. I had imagined, during an earlier depressed period, that running into traffic would work. Maybe I could jump off an overpass into traffic. But what if I didn't time it right, and I bounced off someone's hood and broke my back instead? What if I became paralyzed?

I sat in the dark most of the night wondering what to do. I thought about my parents and what they would say if I died. I was never that close with my parents, so I came to the conclusion that they wouldn't care. I mean, they would care, but it wouldn't shatter them. I thought about my friends and concluded the same thing. I'm not sure why, but I figured they would be sad for a few fleeting moments and then they would move on. These were my pity party thoughts.

My son was a different story. I couldn't pretend this wasn't going to affect him. All I could do was think of my son in the future and imagine what it would be like for him to always tell people that when he was fourteen, his father committed suicide.

Fourteen. An age when every emotion you feel is magnified ten times over and misunderstood a hundred times over. An age that will be frozen in time if anything terrible happens within its sweaty, painful, pubescent months. Those teen years are when the scars happen. The scars you have to tend to the rest of your life, hoping they heal or fade away.

I grabbed a photo album full of school pictures and snapshots of my son. I thought about Chris showing me the photo of his daughter and how he wouldn't let it go.

My son looks like me when I was a kid. You can see it in photos. There were some old photos of me mixed into the album I was looking at, and I held them side by side with photos of my son. We had the same pimples, broad shoulders, and awkward grin. Our clothes were even sort of similar—mine from the 1970s, his from the 2000s. You can even see how we had the same toys: Hot Wheels and Legos.

I showed him *Star Wars* when he was ten, the same age I was when I saw it. I showed him Winnie the Pooh and Little Critter books. I played football with him in the park. I taught him how to hit a baseball. We wrestled in the living room. I took him to Dairy Queen, and sometimes we walked to get doughnuts on Saturday morning. I played board games with him, and even though I don't like board games, I was glad we spent the time together.

I wanted to do more with him. I wanted to teach him how to drive. I wanted to give him money for a date. I wanted to go to his graduations. I wanted to give him advice on something. I wanted to go to a bar with him. I wanted to do something for him that would always be there. I wanted to make him proud of me.

Just after midnight I went to bed. I had decided to tough it out. I decided to live. I sent my son a text message as I listened to people celebrating outside my window. It said: *Happy New Year. Let's make it a good one. I love you.* Less than a minute later, he responded: *Love you too.*

I got in bed and wrapped my blankets around me like I was in a cocoon. I let those words sit in my heart for a long while. I breathed in deep, sucking in gulps of air and crying more. Then I tried to make my mind go blank until the morning. I pretended that everything would be okay when the sun came out.

The next morning I woke up and shaved and took a shower and drank my coffee. I went to work and took my position behind the info desk. The store opened two hours late because it was New Year's Day. Customers came filing in, looking for books, looking for stories. Looking for the bathroom. I sat there, feeling fresh-faced and feeling like a survivor. I was ready to help anyone who needed it.

EILEEN POLLACK

Pigeons

FROM *Prairie Schooner*

NOT LONG AGO I went back to my elementary school, a Gothic
brick-and-mortar fortress whose Escher-like stairs dead-end on
floors that lie halfway between other floors and whose halls branch
off into mysterious tunnels that suddenly disgorge a student into
the cafeteria, or the girls' locker room, or the balcony of benches
overlooking the auditorium that doubles as the gym. Like most
people who hated school, I wasn't surprised to find my younger
self crying at the back of this or that classroom, or staring up at
some adult whose behavior had left me baffled, or wandering the
gloomy stairwells, wondering if I would ever find my way out to a
sunnier, less confusing, less confining life outside.

What startled me was how often I glimpsed the ghosts of classmates whose existence I had forgotten, the ones whose lives, even
then, must have been far more troubled than my own, and who
—even though there were fewer than one hundred students in my
class—disappeared from my consciousness long before the rest of
us had moved on to high school, let alone to college. Seeing those
ghostly classmates, I wanted to bend down and comfort them, as I
had comforted my own younger self. I wanted to assure them that
everything would be all right. But I felt the way a doctor must feel
approaching a patient who is waiting for a pathology report the
doctor knows contains devastating news.

My own malady wasn't fatal, although it felt so at the time. The
symptoms started in third grade, the day a stranger appeared at
our classroom door and summoned me to the hall. My classmates

and I were making cardboard headbands on which to glue the feathers we had won for good behavior. A good Indian was defined by her ability to walk to the bathroom without speaking to her partner or digging a finger in his spine. (That was the year we discovered just how vulnerable the human body is. Twist a thumb between two vertebrae and watch your victim writhe. Place the tip of your shoe at the back of his rigid knee and effect complete collapse.) The edges of my headband kept sticking to my fingers. Not that I had any feathers to paste on the cardboard anyway.

"This is Mr. Spiro, the school psychologist," my teacher said. "He wants to talk to you in his office." Then she went back in and shut the door.

I had been causing a lot of trouble. The year before, my teacher had joked that she was going to bring in her dirty laundry to keep me occupied. In reality, Mrs. Hoos had the sense to let me do whatever I wanted, as long as I didn't disturb my neighbors. At the start of each day, I stowed a dozen books beneath my seat and read them one by one, looking up to see if she was teaching us something new, which she rarely if ever was.

I still love Gertrude Hoos, who was as lumpy and soft as the bag of dirty laundry I gladly would have washed if only she had brought it in. But my third-grade teacher, Mrs. Neff, was made of starchier, sterner stuff. By God, if we were reading aloud, paragraph by painful paragraph, I was going to sit there with my book open to the appropriate page and not read a word ahead. If we were learning to add, I would sit there and learn to add, even if I already had learned that skill at home by keeping score when my grandmother and I played gin.

Mrs. Neff gave me a workbook in which I could teach myself to multiply, but working in that workbook was a privilege and not a right. The more bored I grew, the more I misbehaved, for which I lost the privilege of working in my workbook. Multiplication began to seem like a meal I would never get to eat, because I was too exhausted by my hunger ever to reach the plate. This continued until Mrs. Neff and I each wished the other gone. And since she was the teacher, she had the power to make her wish come true.

Warily, I followed Mr. Spiro to the third floor of our building and then down the main hall, where we entered a narrow door, traversed a short, dark passage, and climbed a few more steps. The room was oddly shaped, with slanted, low ceilings that met at a

peak on top. We were in the belfry! You could see it from the playground, where the older kids frightened us with stories about the
vampires who lived inside. There was an open window along one
wall, but the office was so hot I could barely breathe.

Mr. Spiro settled behind his desk and motioned me to sit beside it. Bushy black curls exploded from his head like the lines a
cartoonist draws to indicate that a character is confused or drunk.
Mr. Spiral, I remember thinking, which is how, four decades later,
I can still recall his name. His heavy black brows, gigantic nose,
and thickly thatched mustache seemed connected to his glasses,
like the disguises you could buy at Woolworth's. His suit was white,
with thin red stripes, like the boxes movie popcorn came in, and
he wore a bright red bow tie. This was 1964. I had never seen a
man in a shirt that wasn't white or a suit that wasn't dark or a tie
that called attention to itself, and I felt the thrill and dread any
child would feel at being selected from the audience by a clown.

He must have sensed that I distrusted him. "Would you like
some Oreos?" Mr. Spiro asked, then slid a packet across the desk.

I can still see those cookies, so chocolaty rich and round, the
red thread around their cellophane cocoon just waiting to be un-
zipped. But a voice in my head warned me to be careful. It was as
if that clown had motioned me to sniff the bright pink carnation
fastened to his lapel.

"How do I know these cookies aren't poisoned?"

Those bushy black brows shot up. "Do you really think I would
poison you?"

"Well," I said, "you're a stranger. How do I know you wouldn't?"

I don't remember what happened next. He probably reassured
me that the Oreos were fit to eat. I don't remember if I ate them.
All I know is that he changed the subject. In a falsely jolly tone, he
said, "So! I hear you want to be an authoress!"

If he had asked if I wanted to be an *author,* I would have told
him yes. But I had never heard that word, *authoress,* and it seemed
dangerous as a snake. *Authoress,* it hissed, like *adulteress,* a word I
had encountered in a novel and didn't quite understand, except
to know I didn't want to be one. "Who told you that?" I demanded.

"Why, your teacher, Mrs. Neff."

"That's because she doesn't like me," I said. "She probably told
you a lot of other lies, but those aren't true either."

He began scribbling on a pad, and even a child of eight knows that anything a school psychologist writes about you on a pad can't be any good. Outside, on the ledge, a pair of plump gray pigeons bobbled back and forth like seedy vaudeville comics (this was the Catskills, after all), pigeon variations of Don Rickles and Buddy Hackett, who sidestepped toward each other, traded a dirty joke, bumped shoulders in raunchy glee, and shuckled back across the stage.

"Well then." He finished writing. "I hear you're a very bright little girl, and I would like you to take some tests that are designed to show if you're smart enough to skip a grade."

Tests? I thought. *What kind of tests? Who had suggested I skip a grade?*

Then it came to me: Mrs. Neff. If she couldn't get rid of me any other way, she would skip me a year ahead. I would miss Harry and Eric, the boys I couldn't resist jabbing in the spine as we walked double file down the hall. But fourth grade had to be less boring than third. *Bring on the tests!* I thought, expecting a mimeographed sheet of addition and subtraction problems or some paragraphs to read aloud.

Mr. Spiro brought out a flipbook. He showed me drawing after drawing, asking me to describe what was missing from each. But how could a person know what was *missing* from a picture if there was nothing to compare it to? Did *every* house have a chimney? Was the daisy *missing* a petal, or had someone merely plucked it?

After we finished with the flipbook, Mr. Spiro brought out a board fitted with colored shapes. He would flash a pattern on a card and ask me to reproduce it. As I recall, he timed me. But as vivid as my memory is for people and events, I have a terrible time remembering patterns and facts. Had the purple triangle been positioned above or below the line? Had the rectangle been blue or green? And who had decreed that playing with colored shapes should determine if a child was ready to skip a grade? It wasn't enough to be smart; you needed to be smart in the ways grownups wanted you to be smart.

Finally Mr. Spiro presented me with a test like the ones I was used to taking. "If you want to buy three pencils," he began, "and one pencil costs four cents, how much would it cost you to buy all three?"

I was about to add three and four when I realized that this prob-lem required a different kind of math. I could have figured out the answer by adding four three times, but something about being so bored that I had misbehaved, which had denied me the chance to work in my workbook, which had denied me the chance to learn to multiply, which seemed to be preventing me from going on to fourth grade, where I might be less bored and less tempted to misbehave, made me cry out, "That isn't fair!"

But when Mr. Spiro asked me *what* wasn't fair, I couldn't put my grievance into words. We sat in silent stalemate until a pigeon flew in the room. It flapped around our heads and beat its wings against the walls. But this struck me as no more strange than anything else that had happened in that room; for all I knew, Mr. Spiro had trained that pigeon to fly in on cue and test some aspect of my psychology I would need to pass fourth grade. The safest response, I decided, was no response at all.

Mr. Spiro, on the other hand, leapt up on his desk and started waving his arms and shouting. Imagine sitting in a chair looking up at a full-grown man in a red-and-white-striped suit who is standing on his desk flailing at a pigeon. I might have understood if he had been flailing at a bee, but what harm could a pigeon do?

At last the pigeon found a crevice at the very top of the belfry and disappeared inside. My final glimpse of its bobbing rear is the image I still see whenever I hear the word *pigeonholed.*

Mr. Spiro smoothed his suit, climbed down from his desk, and asked me why I hadn't been more upset. Hadn't I noticed a pigeon was in the room?

All these years later, I still remember what I said. "Why should I be upset? This isn't my office. I'm not the one who has to clean up after it."

Then I remember nothing more until a disheveled Mr. Spiro led me back to class. Later he told my mother that I wasn't *emotionally ready* to skip a grade. The experience left me more resentful than ever. I misbehaved more and more. The following year, my teacher grew so impatient with my incessant talking that in front of everyone else she said, "Eileen, has anyone ever told you how obnoxious you are?"

Obnoxious, I repeated, delighted and appalled by the toxicity of the word. *Obnoxious,* was I? Fine. I shunned the company of the other girls and hung around with the roughest boys, who were even more obnoxious than I was. I still did well on tests—what was I supposed to do, pretend that I didn't know how to add (or multiply, for that matter)? But I refused to act the part of the well-mannered little lady the grownups wanted me to play.

I looked for Mr. Spiro, but I never saw the man again. I searched in vain for his secret office. From outside, on the playground, I could look up and see the belfry. But the windows were now boarded up, and the pigeons, like me, couldn't find a way to get inside.

That is, until the first day of sixth grade. Climbing to the third floor of our building, I followed the directions I had been given to the dead-end passage to my class, where I saw a small alcove that led to what once must have been Mr. Spiro's office. My teacher that year—let's call him Mr. F—had persuaded the administration to let him board up the windows and use the belfry as a darkroom. Or he hadn't bothered to ask permission and simply had gone ahead and done it.

Mr. F seemed even more bored by school than I was. At least once a day he would put his feet on his desk, tell us how desperate he was to quit his teaching job and work full-time as a photographer, then lovingly describe the Hasselblad camera he was saving up to buy. Unfortunately, my parents and Mr. F's parents were friends. If one of my classmates misbehaved, Mr. F pushed him in the darkroom and we heard terrible bangs and crashes. But nothing I did, no matter how unruly, earned me so much as a timid reprimand. My status as the smartest girl, coupled with my complete disregard for other people's feelings and my lack of social grace, would have made me a pariah anyway. But Mr. F brought that fate upon me even sooner by handing back a test on which I had scored an A, asking me to stand, and demanding of my classmates that they try to be more like me.

Complaining about being praised is like complaining about being pretty. Even then I knew it was better to be me than Pablo Rodriguez, whose parents were migrant farmers and who, in sixth grade, could barely read or write, or the Buck brothers, Phil and Gregory, who seemed to get punished for no other reason than being large and male and black. But if *I* was so unhappy, it defies me to imagine how much angrier and unhappier kids like Pablo or Phil or Gregory must have been.

A few weeks into term, I developed a crush on the boy across the aisle. He was handsome, thin, and lithe, with curly red hair and freckles. His name was Walter Rustic, which is why, whenever I read that ballad about the passionate shepherd wooing his lass ("Come live with me and be my love/And we will all the pleasures prove"), I imagine Walter Rustic saying those lines to me.

All of us were at the stage where we chased each other around the playground and tried to throw each other down in that hysteria-tinged way of not-quite-adolescents who don't know any other means to touch or be touched. I was wearing a brand-new coat, which Walter had grabbed to slow me. As ecstatic as I was that he found me worthy of pursuit, I was upset that he had ripped the lining. My mother was always scolding me for ruining my clothes, and I was sure to get in trouble.

I hate to think that I squealed on Walter. I prefer to believe that Mr. F saw the ripped coat and asked me who had torn it. Either way, I watched in horror as he tugged Walter by the ear into that dreadful belfry—the *darkroom*, I suddenly thought—and we listened to the thwacks and grunts of a grown man throwing a boy half his size against a wall. I covered my ears and wondered what had happened to that pigeon. Had it made a nest inside that wall? What could it find to eat? Perhaps it subsisted on the crumbs of Oreos left by children who had accepted Mr. Spiro's gift.

Then Walter disappeared. Not that day. Or the next. But he didn't graduate from high school with the rest of us. My lack of popularity had reached such spectacular heights by then I couldn't be bothered to consider that anyone else might be miserable for better reasons. But miserable they must have been. Kids killed themselves and killed each other. One of my classmates hiked out into the woods, put his rifle in his mouth, and pulled the trigger. Another set fire to her house with her family asleep inside. A carload of boys died in a drunk-driving accident. But no matter who disappeared or how, no one saw fit to discuss the matter with us. The job of a school psychologist isn't, as people think, to offer counseling for troubled kids; it's to administer IQ tests.

I have no memory of Walter Rustic after we left sixth grade. If I hadn't gone back to my elementary school, I might have lived another forty years without wondering where he had gone. As it is, I called a friend who had been in that sixth-grade class. Walter? she said. Hadn't I heard? He'd had a problem with drugs. Maybe mental illness had been involved. She didn't know all the facts—she had gotten the information secondhand from her brother, who had been friends with Walter's older brother, Frank, before Frank left town for Vegas. But Walter had been living on the streets in Corpus Christi, Texas, and he had fallen asleep in a dumpster. A garbage truck came along and turned the dumpster upside down and Walter's skull got crushed.

Walter? Homeless? Crushed?

I called his brother and left a message, but Frank didn't return my call. I Googled Walter and found a record of his arrest for attempted robbery in Queens, New York, in 1980, when we would have been twenty-four. But that created more mysteries than it solved. The records indicated that Walter had served two years of his sentence before being released "to another agency." Had anyone helped him kick his habit? Treated him for mental illness? How and why had he moved to Texas?

I called the paper in Corpus Christi (I realized as I dialed that the name means *body of Christ*), and the editor sent me Walter's obit. I hoped there would be a photo so I could see what the handsome, redheaded boy on whom I'd had a crush looked like as a man, but the only photo showed a body in a bag being handed down from a trash compactor.

According to the story, on December 22, 1986, Walter had crawled inside that dumpster behind Incarnate Word Junior High, trying to keep warm and sleep. The next morning the sanitation workers hooked the dumpster to their truck and tipped it back. A groundskeeper at Incarnate Word saw a man trying to scramble out of the dumpster and screamed for the workers to stop, but the roar of the engine prevented his warning from being heard. The lid came down on Walter's neck. The fire department needed an hour to remove his body. When they did, they saw that he was barefoot and wearing rags. They were able to figure out who the man was only because he was wearing a hospital ID around his wrist. Apparently Walter had visited the ER the night before to have a swollen ankle x-rayed. There was a bottle of antibiotics in his pocket. He hadn't been in town very long. A few days earlier he had been arrested for refusing to give his name, but he had listed his address as the Search for Truth Mission. Not that anyone there remembered him.

An article published on Christmas Day ("Officials close the book on man's grisly death") added only that Walter Rustic had been a "native of Liberty, N.Y., a town of 4,293 near the Catskill Mountains," and neither his mother nor his brother could be reached for comment. And so, the reporter wrote, "The sad case of the man who died in a dumpster is closed." Except the sad case had a happier coda. In 1988 a shelter for homeless men was opened in Walter's honor not far from where he died. The Rustic House for Men offers a hot meal and a place to sleep for vagrants, although most people probably assume that the name is intended to connote a rural retreat rather than to honor the ragged, barefoot man who died in a dumpster a few blocks away.

I figured I had the facts. But I still seemed to be missing something. I dialed Walter's brother one last time. An elderly woman answered and told me that she was Walter's brother's mother. Which meant she was Walter's mother too.

"You knew Walter in sixth grade?" she said. "He's been in your mind all these years?"

I wanted to lie and say I had been thinking about her son for forty years and was very, very sorry he had been beaten up on my account. Instead, I asked if Walter ever talked about Mr. F. But his mother said Walter never talked about school at all. He made it to junior year before he dropped out. I wanted to ask her why, but it's hard to press a dead friend's mother as to whether he had been mentally ill or addicted to drugs. All she would say was that Walter had loved to travel. He had traveled from state to state to state, calling her now and then to say hello and ask her to send him money so he could get something to eat. His favorite place had been Tupelo, Mississippi, where he visited Elvis Presley's birthplace. Another time he called her on New Year's Eve and told her that he had been picked up as a vagrant, and the police liked him so much they invited him to join their party and share their pizza.

Then, on Christmas Eve 1986, she was sitting in her house in North Carolina—she had moved there a few years earlier—wrapping a present for Walter when she got "the horrible phone call" telling her that he had died. She hadn't even known he was in Texas, but she flew to Corpus Christi and spoke to the sisters at Incarnate Word, who told her that her son had died in the arms of two nuns, and she got some comfort in hearing that, as she still derives comfort from knowing that the Rustic House for Men takes in vagrants like her son "and gives them a hot meal and a warm clean place to sleep and keeps them there a while until they're ready to get a job or go out on the road again."

I have no doubt that Walter would have ended up homeless or dead even if he had been blessed with a more caring sixth-grade teacher. I was only twelve years old. I don't hold myself responsible for the beating that Walter received that day. But being thrown against a wall doesn't do anyone any good. It isn't much fun to occupy any of the circles of hell to which all but the most popular and well-adjusted students find themselves consigned. But schools fail different children in different ways. Kids like Pablo grow up unable to read and write, with no way to earn a living. Kids like Walter Rustic grow up to be dead.

And kids like me? We make it through. We end up who we were meant to be. Sometimes we end up someone better. Despite Mrs. Neff's refusal to allow me to work in my workbook, despite Mr. Spiro's decision that I wasn't ready to skip a grade, despite a similar decision the following year to advance the two smartest boys while leaving me behind because—as the principal claimed—girls don't finish courses in science or math, I studied those courses on my own and got accepted to Yale, where I earned a degree in physics. I was too far behind my classmates, too angry and confused and lacking in confidence to go on to physics grad school. But I'm not sure how much I care. What gadget might I have invented, what small theorem might I have proved, that could have mattered half as much as my being forced to learn compassion? I gave up the chance to spend my life multiplying and dividing so I could become an authoress and tell the stories of all those poor pigeons who didn't make it out of school alive, who survived childhood but not adulthood, who are missing from our community. Although how can we measure what we have lost? To what can we compare their absence?

JON KERSTETTER

Triage

FROM *River Teeth*

OCTOBER 2003, BAGHDAD, IRAQ. Major General Jon Galli-netti, U.S. Marine Corps, chief of staff of CJTF7, the operational command unit of coalition forces in Iraq, accompanied me on late-night clinical rounds in a combat surgical hospital. We visited soldiers who were injured in multiple IED attacks throughout Baghdad just hours earlier. I made this mental note: *Soldier died tonight. IED explosion. Held him. Prayed. Told his commander to stay focused.*

In the hospital, the numbers of wounded that survived the attacks created a backlog of patients who required immediate surgery. Surgeons, nurses, medics, and hospital staff moved from patient to patient at an exhausting pace. When one surgery was finished, another began immediately. Several operating rooms were used simultaneously. Medical techs shuttled post-op patients from surgery to the second-floor ICU, where the numbers of beds quickly became inadequate. Nurses adjusted their care plans to accommodate the rapid influx. A few less critical patient beds lined the halls just outside the ICU.

The general wanted to visit the hospital to encourage the patients and the medical staff. We made a one-mile trip to the hospital compound late at night, unannounced, with none of the fanfare that usually accompanies a visit by a general officer in the military. After visiting the patients in the ICU, we walked down the hallway to the triage room.

One patient occupied the triage room: a young soldier, private first class. He had a ballistic head injury. His elbows flexed tightly in spastic tension, drawing his forearms to his chest; his hands made stonelike fists; his fingers coiled together as if grabbing an imaginary rope attached to his sternum. His breathing was slow and sporadic. He had no oxygen mask. An intravenous line fed a slow drip of saline and painkiller. He was what is known in military medicine as *expectant.*

Some of his fellow soldiers gathered at the foot of his bed. A few of them had been injured in the same attack and had already been treated and bandaged in the emergency room. These fellow soldiers stood watch over the expectant patient. The general and I stood watch over them. One soldier had a white fractal of body salt edging the collar of his uniform. One wept. One prayed. Another quietly said "Jesus" over and over and kept shaking his head from side to side. And another had no expression at all: he simply stared a blank stare into the empty space above the expectant patient's head. A young sergeant, hands shaking, stammered as he tried to explain what had happened. The captain in charge of the expectant soldier's unit told the general and me that this was their first soldier to be killed—then he corrected himself and said this was the first soldier in their unit to be assigned to triage. He told us that the soldier was a good soldier. The general nodded in agreement and the room was suddenly quiet.

The general laid his hand on the expectant soldier's leg—the leg whose strength I imagined was drifting like a shape-shifting cloud moving against a dark umber sky—strength retreating into a time before it carried a soldier. And I watched the drifting of a man back into the womb of his mother, toward a time when a leg was not a leg, a body not a body, toward a time when a soldier was only the laughing between two young lovers—a man and a woman who could never imagine that a leg-body-man-soldier would one day lie expectant and that that soldier would be their son.

As I watched the soldiers at the foot of the bed, I noted their sanded faces, their trembling mouths, their hollow-stare eyes. I watched them watch the shallow breathing and the intermittent spasm of seizured limbs and the pale gray color of expectant skin. I took clinical notes in my mind. I noted the soldiers—noted the patient. I noted all the things that needed to be noted: the size of the triage room, the frame of the bed, the tiles of the ceiling, and the dullness of the overhead light. I noted the taut draw of the white linen sheets and the shiny polished metal of the hospital fixtures. A single ceiling fan rotated slowly. The walls were off-white.

There were no windows. The floor was spotless, the smell antiseptic. A drab-green wool army blanket covered each bed. Three beds lay empty. I noted the absence of noise and chaos, the absence of nurses rushing to prepare surgical instruments, and the absence of teams of doctors urgently exploring wounds and calling out orders. There was an absence of the hurried sounds and the hustle of soldiers in the combat emergency room one floor down. Nobody yelled "medic" or "doc." Nobody called for the chaplain. Medics did not cut off clothing or gather dressings. Ambulances and medevac helicopters did not arrive with bleeding soldiers.

The *American Heritage Dictionary* defines *triage* as "a process for sorting injured people into groups based on their need for or likely benefit from immediate medical treatment. Triage is used in hospital emergency rooms, on battlefields, and at disaster sites when limited medical resources must be allocated." All dictionary definitions refer to the origin of the word *triage* as deriving from the French verb *trier,* to sort. The essence of the meaning is in the sorting. In the context of battle, a soldier placed in a triage room as *expectant* has been literally sorted from a group of other injured soldiers whose probability of survival was deduced by a sort of battlefield calculus implemented by a medical officer or a triage officer. The sorting occurs rather quickly—usually with minimal, if any, deliberation.

A military physician trains for triage situations. I trained to make combat medical decisions based on the developing battlefield situation and limited medical resources. I read about triage. I role-played it in combat exercises. When I first learned about the role of triage in combat, I reasoned, *Of course, triage is necessary. It's part of war. You do it as part of the job of a medical officer.*

More than twenty years ago, when I was a newly minted captain, I attended the two-week Combat Casualty Care Course at Camp Bullis, Texas. The course was designed to teach medical officers combat trauma care and field triage techniques. The capstone exercise included a half-day mass casualty scenario complete with percussion grenades, smoke bombs, and simulated enemy forces closing on the casualty collection point. The objective was to give medical officers a realistic setting in which to perform triage decisions and to initiate medevac protocols according to standard operating procedures. About twenty moulaged patients mimicked battlefield casualties ranging from the minimally injured to those requiring immediate surgery. Each medical officer in training was given five minutes to perform the triage exercise and to prepare an appropriate mede- vac request. Providing treatment was not an option: the exercise focused exclusively on making triage decisions.

All the participants could have easily completed the role-play within the time limit. Nothing, of course, is that straightforward in army training. There is always some built-in element of surprise to test how well trainees cope with chaos. In this case, the ele- ment of the "unexpected" was a simulated psychiatric patient who was brandishing an M16 rifle and holding a medic hostage while threatening to commit suicide. In order to maintain the element of surprise, the doctors who had finished their turn were whisked out the back of the triage tent, not to be seen again until the after- action review some hours later.

My turn. I entered the tent at the shove of my evaluator. The mock psych patient was screaming and threatening to kill a nearby medic. Other medics were pleading with the disturbed patient to lay his weapon down and let the wounded get on a helicop- ter. I was to take charge and get control. I did. I approached the screaming patient with quick, confident steps. I got about halfway through the triage tent when he pointed his rifle directly at his hostage medic and yelled, "One more step and the medic is dead." I backed off slowly, turned sideways, and quietly pulled my pistol. In an abrupt and instantaneous movement, I reeled around and shot the psych patient with my blank ammunition. "Bang—you're dead!" I yelled. A nearby evaluator took his weapon and made him play dead. One out-of-control psycho eliminated. I finished the triage exercise within the five-minute time limit. My evaluator laughed. "Damn," he said.

I felt great. I had control.

In the after-action review, I was asked about my decision to shoot. "Time," I answered. "I only had five minutes, so I maxi- mized my effectiveness by eliminating a threat. It's combat," I ar- gued.

One fellow doc asked if I would really shoot a patient in com- bat. A debate ensued as to the ethics of my decision. Nobody else had shot the psych case. Nobody else finished the exercise in the allotted time. Some trainees had considered shooting the crazed soldier but had failed to act. Some managed to talk the psych pa- tient into giving up his weapon. Those physicians had taken nearly fifteen minutes to complete the exercise—minutes in which some of the simulated patients died a simulated death. In the end, it was decided that my decision to shoot, while potentially serving a greater need, may have been a bit aggressive, but that it was in fact *my* decision, and my decision met the needs of the mission. All ethical considerations aside, I felt that I understood the necessity and the theory of triage. I understood it as part of my job.

Military triage classifications are based on NATO guidelines and are published in numerous websites and Department of Defense publications. The triage categories in the third edition of *Emergency War Surgery*, the Department of Defense bible of military medicine, are listed below:

Immediate: This group includes those soldiers requiring lifesaving surgery. The surgical procedures in this category should not be time consuming and should concern only those patients with high chances of survival.

Delayed: This group includes those wounded who are badly in need of time-consuming surgery but whose general condition permits delay in surgical treatment without unduly endangering life. Sustaining treatment will be required.

Minimal: These casualties have relatively minor injuries . . . and can effectively care for themselves or can be helped by nonmedical personnel.

Expectant: Casualties in this category have wounds that are so extensive that even if they were the sole casualty and had the benefit of optimal medical resource application, their survival would be unlikely. The expectant casualty should not be abandoned, but should be separated from the view of other casualties . . . Using a minimal but competent staff, provide comfort measures for these casualties.

The text of *Emergency War Surgery* further notes, "The decision to withhold care from a wounded soldier, who in another less overwhelming situation might be salvaged, is difficult for any surgeon or medic. Decisions of this nature are infrequent, even in mass casualty situations. Nonetheless, this is the essence of military triage." Triage requires assigning patients to those various categories based upon a rather quick and semi-objective assessment of a patient's injuries. If the triage officer calculates that a patient falls into the *expectant* category, treatment is withheld in order to allow medical teams to concentrate more efficiently on those soldiers with potentially survivable injuries. Preserving the fighting force is the central tenet of the process.

I have read and reread the official triage definition. I suppose I might have used it in a classroom of medics that I instructed. I am intimately familiar with the words that describe each category and with the professional commentary about the mechanics and ethics of sorting injured patients, yet I repeatedly come back to those words that try to clarify exactly what might be involved in the process of triage. I find the words weak and innocuous. They undercut the gravity and scope of a real-time triage experience. Here's the rub: the official commentary about the decision process focuses on the essence of triage as being the *difficulty* of making that decision. The difficulty is a given, but I think there is more. I think the essence of military triage is the *necessity* of making the decision when the combat situation demands it. It is the necessity of triage that requires medical staff to assign expectant soldiers to their death in order to provide an accommodation to a calculated greater good—a cause measured by the number of combat survivors. It is an accommodation that has not changed since the trench warfare of World War I.

Modern military medicine provides battlefield casualties with more sophisticated treatment and much faster aeromedical evacuation than in prior wars, but the process of triage remains essentially raw and unrefined as a standard combat operating procedure. Combat physicians encounter an overwhelming number or complexity of casualties. They make a rapid medical assessment, render a decision based on incomplete information, assign a triage category, and move to the next patient. Done. If they are particularly adept, they can triage several critical patients simultaneously.

Saving lives is the endpoint of all triage. Let one life go, save three others, or five, or maybe ten. The ratios don't matter, the benefits do. And a benefit in war always comes at a cost. On the surface, of course, the ultimate cost of a triage decision is a soldier's life. One decision, one life; perhaps one decision, several lives. But there are other costs not so easily calculated, like the emotional cost to survivors or the psychological cost to soldiers who make triage decisions. Textbook definitions are silent on how military physicians prepare for, or react to, the demands of making a triage decision. No chapter in a military textbook instructs combat physicians in the multidimensional complexity of decision making that serves to deny lifesaving interventions for soldiers. There are chapters on why triage decisions must be made and chapters on how to apply established medical criteria in making those decisions. But what to do next, after the triage decision has been made—not covered. And that vacuum of knowledge leads to a feeling of exposure and vulnerability, both of which cannot be tolerated in war.

The act of triage is subsumed under the assigned duties of medics and physicians. I am not suggesting that the process fall to someone else or that the criteria used to make triage decisions should be discarded for a different process. I know of no other way of quickly sorting and categorizing patients when the critical nature of combat demands that it be done. I am, however, declaring that the practice of triage obligates doctors and medics, whose principal duty is the saving of lives, to perform tasks which share in the brutality and the ugliness of war—tasks that are tantamount to pulling a trigger on fellow soldiers.

In the final analysis, the decision to withhold medical care is not a decision that can be practiced, and rehearsed, and fully prepared for, outside of the realm of combat. How could that ever be accomplished with any modicum of reality? Could a medical officer simply say, as I did in training, "Bang, you're dead" or "Put the black tag on this one," and with that feel the same gut-ripping tension that combat evokes? No, the reality of triage tends to hit more like the force of a bomb blast. In an instant, fragments of stone and metal explode through the air with such velocity that when they hit a human target, even if the target is not killed, it is stunned and bleeding and breathless. It is that environment in which a military doctor or medic makes a live-fire triage decision and then must stand against the ballistic force of its consequences.

Somewhere in the process of making notes about the expectant patient, I paused and moved toward the middle of the bed. I put my hand on the patient's leg, just as the general had done. I laid it there, let it linger. From where I stood, I stared directly into the expectant soldier's face. I watched his agonal breathing, a long sighed breath followed by an absence of movement, and that followed by three to four shallow breaths. I matched his breathing with my own breathing. I timed the slowing pattern with my watch. I made some mental calculations, then looked away. Once again I noted the quiet of the room and the whiteness of the walls. I noted the empty beds, and the ceiling, and the antiseptic smell. Again I watched the expectant soldier, who was oblivious to all of my watching.

I stood at the triage bedside thinking if this were my son, I would want soldiers to gather in his room—listen to his breathing. I would want them to break stride from their war routines, perhaps to weep, perhaps to pray. And if he called out for his dad, I would want them to become a father to a son. Simply that: nothing more, nothing less—procedures not in Department of Defense manuals or war theory classes or triage exercises.

I moved to the head of the bed, placed my right hand on the chest of the patient. And my hand rested there with barely any movement. I turned to the other soldiers, gave them an acknowledgment with a slight upturned purse of my lips, then looked away. I lifted my hand to the patient's right shoulder and let my weight shift as if trying to gently hold him in place. I half kneeled, half bent—closed the distance between our bodies. I noted the weave of the fabric in his skullcap dressing and the faint show of blood that tainted its white cotton edges. I lingered. I prayed for God to take him in that very instant. I whispered, so only he could hear, "You're a good soldier. You're finished here. It's okay to go home now." I waited. I watched. I saw the faces of my own sons in his: was glad they were not soldiers.

I finished, stood up, and walked to the foot of the bed. One of the soldiers asked me if there wasn't something I could do. I said no. I meant no. I wanted my answer to be yes. I faced the captain and put my hand on his shoulder, told him that we were finished, that his soldier did not feel pain, that he would be gone soon, and that everybody had done everything they could. The tone of my voice was neither comforting nor encouraging, neither sorrowful nor hopeful. It was, as I remember, military and professional.

I think about that expectant soldier so often. I know I would have seen his name in his hospital chart or been told his name by his commander. I did not take the time to write it down anywhere, and that bothers me. It bothers me because years later he remains nameless—just like so many other soldier-patients I encountered —and I think I equate that namelessness with a form of abandonment for which I feel personally responsible. I do understand, in a professional sense, that the patient was not abandoned, that his triage was purposeful, and that it allowed an ascent to medical efficiency which, in the end, saved other soldiers' lives. But I also understand that the theoretical basis of triage quickly erodes when confronted with the raw, emotional, human act of sorting through wounded patients and assigning triage categories. In my mind, the theoretical and the practical wage a constant battle, so that whenever I participate in a triage decision, part of me says *yes,* and part of me says *no.*

I sometimes find myself wanting to speak with the expectant soldier's mother and father. I want to tell them that their son did not die alone in a triage bed—that he was not simply abandoned or left as hopeless in a secluded corner room of a distant combat hospital. I want to assure them that he died in the company of men who stood watch over him as if guarding an entire battalion and that we tried to give everything we could give—that we tried to be more than soldiers or generals or doctors.

When I tell the story of this particular soldier to my medical colleagues, I always mention that triage is a necessary part of war. I tell them it's a matter of compassionate medical necessity and the entrenched reality of combat—that it's the exercise of a soldier's final duty.

Occasionally, though, I think about telling them how I wished I could have done something, anything. But then I realize I cannot tell them that, because in fact I did do something, and I am left with the nameless face of an expectant soldier and countless sheets of history filled with decisions made by doctors at war. I am left with my own understanding that we who are soldiers are all triaged.

I want to remember the expectant soldier as a person with a name, but I have come to accept that I cannot. I remember instead the triage room. I recall the general who placed his hand on a young man. And I see the drifting once again—the fading of a soldier back into the womb from which he was born into life. I see him loved. He is a soldier. Wounded. Triaged. Expectant.

MARCIA ALDRICH

The Art of Being Born

FROM *Hotel Amerika*

IN WHAT I HOPED would be our final appointment with the midwife, she guessed you weigh eight pounds and four ounces and that you will come soon.

I woke up late, having spent the night beached on the couch in the living room, memorizing the distinguishing signs of every rash chronicled in Dr. Spock's baby book, until nodding off around six. The book lay open to cradle cap, flaking patches of skin on the tops of newborn heads, which might be "cracked, greasy, or even weeping."

I'm ten days past the date you are supposed to arrive and too uncomfortable, too wrung out with anxiety to sleep. In the last weeks, after an hour or so of tossing in bed each night, I've been shuffling to the couch so that your father might sleep undisturbed. In the mornings I lumber into the shower, stand under the spray, and cry. I brace my arms against the shower walls and let the water rain down my face and stream over my breasts and enormous stomach.

This morning I waddled to the bedroom and sagged in the doorway. Your father took one look at my forlorn figure and said, "Come on, let's get out of here."

We wound our way slowly down Twenty-second Street to the entrance of Ravenna Park, and inside the park to the old-growth ravine with freshwater springs welling from the tall walls and flowing into Ravenna Creek.

As we entered the muddy trail down to the creek, Richard took my hand in his to brace me for our descent. We walked at a glacial pace, mimicking the first untroubled humans, on the path that looped through the waterlogged ravine, Richard consciously slowing his pace, me trying to move myself forward. At the end of the mile loop, we huffed up from the ravine and emerged by the tennis courts, where we rested a bit, sitting on a bench beneath a bracelet of blooming cherry trees, the branches dipping down around us. Though it was only noon, I lay on my side on the bench and put my head in Richard's lap. Sitting on the bench, we spoke of our anticipation, and wondered how much longer we had to wait until you, our first child, would be born. At that moment we weren't anxious. How could we be anxious, sitting on the warm bench, the world alive and green, and the branches of the cherry framing our hopes?

I'm telling you this because few events are more momentous than birth. Every child wants to know about her birth and asks, *Where did I come from?* Many are answered with a birth story that speaks to the child of who she is and will be and that sets her life in motion in a particular way. Mothers know the story and tell it like a favorite fairy tale to the child, who rests her head on her pillow, on her way to sleep.

But sometimes the stories of origin are troubled, riven with complexity and unanswered questions, and bespeak a cloudy future.

My parents never spoke of the circumstances surrounding my birth, and I am in possession of only a few meager facts.

I was born on February 26 in the dead of winter.
No baby pictures were taken.
No baby book, where the important milestones are recorded, exists.
I was installed in a wood-paneled room down a long corridor at the back of the house.

The absence of any information made me puzzled about my place in the family. When visiting friends, I couldn't help notice the gallery of framed photos chronicling their life from birth and wonder what it meant that there was no documentation of my life displayed in my house. Luckily I wasn't asked to produce an autobiography or photo collage at school, and so the lack of material didn't become a public issue, only a private worry. I was the only child of my mother's second marriage. As a young woman she had married and given birth to two daughters in quick succession, and then her husband died unexpectedly. My sisters were separated by less than two years and formed a strong unity around my mother, as was only natural given the circumstances. Their births were well documented, and two ornately framed photos, one of each of them, sat on my mother's dresser, directly across from her bed. After struggling for years on her own, my mother married my father, and four years later I was born. Ten and twelve years separated my sisters from me, a gap that could not be bridged. Though we lived under one roof, it was as if we had been born into two different families. The first family was short-lived but cast a long shadow.

One winter evening after dinner while we were washing up the dishes, I asked my mother what she remembered about my birth. She was taken aback by the question and responded as if she were the subject of a police interrogation. "You were a small baby, only five pounds, and had to stay in the hospital several weeks before you could come home."

"What was wrong with me?"

"Nothing lasting," she said as she wiped the counter for the second time. I couldn't understand why she didn't want to share the details of my birth, why she seemed to be keeping something from me. "Your birth weight was a little low," she reluctantly continued, "and doctors were more cautious then than they are now. Mothers routinely spent two weeks flat on their backs after giving birth." She finished in a matter-of-fact tone. It didn't occur to me then to ask why I was so little or to question her about her pregnancy and prenatal care. It wasn't until I became pregnant myself with you that I began to wonder about such details. But that night in the kitchen I could only think to ask, "Do you remember anything else?"

She said, "You weren't born as planned," and she looked at me hard, as if an old anger had been stirred out of the corner. "You were two weeks past your due date and in the middle of the night my water broke."

I didn't have the foggiest idea what she meant by waters breaking. She seemed angry, angry at me. The words *water breaking* were part of a puzzle called my birth I had to assemble.

"Anything else?" I pestered. I wanted to know what happened after the waters broke.

That was it. She was done telling me the story of my birth. She hung her apron on the handle of the oven door and joined my father in the den to watch the nightly news.

My mother's defensiveness on the subject of my birth led me to believe that the day, the event, my first entrance onto the stage and into my mother's life, was complicated by emotions I didn't understand and would never understand. I came to think, perhaps irrationally, that from my mother's point of view my birth was a mistake, and that was why all the memorializing forms were blank. Instead of caressing the event in memory, she entered a state of amnesia from which she never awoke. That winter evening after dinner was the only time in my childhood that I pried even the slightest sliver of information from the wound.

In high school, on the bus ride, while some of my girlfriends were making up the names for their future children, I'd make up stories of my birth, as if I were a character in search of a play. The births I imagined all took place out of doors, as if I were a wild animal—

> *In fields*
> *In meadows*
> *In mountains*
> *In a valley*
> *In the woods*
> *In a ravine*
> *By a stream*

And my mother and I were always alone, mother and daughter, the essential couple.

Here is one story I made up:

On a Sunday morning in September, my mother drove out of town, by herself, deep into the country of farms and pastures and ponds, until she reached an orchard. The orchard was on a rough incline, under an open sky. She was in the midst of pulling apples down from the branches and putting them in her bag when she sank down among the dropped apples and I was born.

This story is preposterous on many levels. I wasn't born in September. I never knew my mother to pick any fruit by hand, and certainly the apples we ate were all store-bought. You can tell I didn't know the first thing about birthing. Imagining my mother making a bed below the boughs and giving birth to me as if she were a doe and I her fawn is a fairy tale. I don't ever remember my mother lying in the grass or on the ground of any sort. We never even had a picnic at a table. Yet despite its utter lack of veracity, this was one of my birth stories.

After my mother's death, my father discovered a cache of photographs she had stashed away. All the photos were a revelation; just their existence required me to rethink my portrait of my mother. But one photo stood out: it was a baby picture of me. No one is holding me, neither my mother nor my father. I'm lying awake on my mother's bed, the one place where I most longed to be as a child. In this photograph I seem to be looking up at the person taking the photo. It must have been my mother's shadow pointing the camera. The bedspread is white and the blankets I'm swaddled in are white. I look small and dwarfed among the snowy folds. I'm holding my hands up in a defensive position, and even then my hands were clenched. I can hardly say what I felt looking at this picture after having spent the bulk of my life believing no pictures of me as a baby existed. And here I am, at long last, on my mother's bed. It's just a little square photo, so small it could easily have disappeared and never been recovered. But it has; it is a fact, and like other facts, it complicates everything.

I thought I was the wounded party. It never occurred to me that perhaps I wasn't the only one who had been deprived of a birth story, or a story one would want to share. It never occurred to me that there were no baby pictures because my mother was denied access to me in the first weeks. In my mother's proper middle-class circle, birth wasn't talked about. Women didn't share the gritty details of birth, the bloody show. A doctor and medical staff kept women medicated and deadened to the actuality of birth. Perhaps my mother never spoke of my birth because she didn't know the details. In some ways she wasn't present for my birth—she was the vessel that carried me. She was knocked out, there's no other way of putting it. She only saw me through the nursery window, too heavily sedated to hold me. My mother went home without me. In the case of my birth, my mother had little say in her experience and little to say about her experience. And she never talked about what had been denied her.

*

After our afternoon appointment with Patricia, our midwife, in which she announced your weight, we returned home, ate dinner, and watched the Sonics playoff game on our tiny black-and-white TV, which Richard set up on a bench in front of the couch. Around halftime I started having contractions. Just in case this was the real thing, I packed my bag, a blue suede overnight bag, and put it by the door. In the bag was my hospital reading, Nietzsche and Schopenhauer, which I needed to get a grasp on for my upcoming comprehensive exams. I can imagine you shaking your head and laughing—I obviously knew nothing about labor or hospital stays.

Unlike my mother, who took no class and had no birth partner, we had prepared for your birth by taking a class offered through the midwife's clinic that included drafting a birth plan. Yes, we had a plan. We paid scant attention to the physical exercises but spent an inordinate amount of time figuring out what music we wanted to hear during labor, as if it were a dance party requiring a playlist. The birth plan called for a teddy bear as a focal point for me to concentrate on, a tape player and tapes, a mat to lie on, and a baby bag full of clothes and blankets for you. When it started looking bad for the Sonics, Richard hauled all the birthing assemblage to our car, filled with boxes of books we had neglected to clear out.

The time between contractions was shortening and they were intensifying, rapidly and uncomfortably so. It seemed like real labor, what we had been waiting for, not a false alarm, not the practice Braxton-Hicks contractions. We called Patricia and were told to come on in. Back into our little Civic we went, packed now as if we were heading on safari.

The ride, our second in not many hours, was excruciating. The rhythmic bounce of the car as it passed over each seam of the bridge shot pains through my body. Richard tried to listen to the basketball game through my groans. Back to the parking lot that five hours ago seemed like heaven, only now I could barely lift myself out of the car or walk across the lot. If I didn't move, the contractions might not be so bad or might not come at all.

When Patricia measured my cervix, it was as it had been at my office visit earlier in the day. She wasn't certain I was in real labor. Without declaring labor, I couldn't be admitted to the hospital, couldn't be assigned my own room. I was instructed to walk up and down the back stairwells to stimulate labor. The optimism of the morning and afternoon had vanished.

At eleven o'clock I was measured once again. Slight progress, but not enough to declare active labor. Patricia sent us off wandering once again. Midnight came, and still I hadn't been formally admitted. We climbed a few stairs, only to have me fall against the cement wall and slump to the steps when a contraction seized me.

You should know that contractions operate in stages like a thunderstorm. You feel them rumbling toward you from far off, tremors building incrementally until they arrive dead center.

At full strength, you feel as if every inch of your brainbodysoul has been taken captive by the seizure and there's nothing you can do but give in to its superior power.

And then, when you feel you have been wrung out, it lets you go and rumbles off until the next tremor begins.

When this contraction lifted, Richard hauled me to my feet and we once again climbed the stairs. Up and down we went, stopping and starting until we exited the stairwell and staggered by the nurse's station like beggars searching for a handout.

"Couldn't someone do something? Give me something to move the labor along or ease the pain?"

"No," replied the nurse manning the station, referring me brusquely to my birth plan, which was pinned on her clipboard. The plan firmly stated my opposition to drugs. I had wanted a natural birth, to be awake and alert, to feel everything. "What you are going through is perfectly normal," the nurse said. "Not an emergency."

I screamed—I'm sure I screamed—"But I didn't know what labor was when I wrote the plan. Give me something, *please*." She offered me ice chips. Richard rubbed my back. I cried.

I thought I was going to die and that you would never live through this. How could something so painful result in you? How could babies survive the turmoil of birth, the violence of it? Because make no mistake, labor is violent: it squeezes the air out of you. In the moments between contractions, when pain waited in the wings, I thought about women who had given birth before me, women who were at this very instant giving birth alongside me, in fields, in hospitals, in apartments, in elevators and makeshift infirmaries, women of all colors, sizes, shapes, who spoke languages

I couldn't understand and ate food I had never tasted. We were united by this scorching labor.

At 12:30 Patricia rechecked me. I had progressed and was officially declared in labor and admitted to the hospital. I was going to have you after all. Finally we moved to the birthing room we had toured nearly nine months ago, decorated like a bedroom at home, with pictures on the walls, rocking chairs, and a flower-patterned quilt. The walls were mauve with a burgundy border —rich and warm.

Unfortunately, by this time labor was so advanced that I was barely conscious of the decor that had been so important to me in the planning stages. I lay down in the quilt-covered bed but had even more difficulty getting through the pain. I tensed up, gripped Richard. I forgot about the quick shallow puffs of breath I had practiced in birthing class. I cried and looked to Richard, who was the only person in the room. I refused to let him go, even to bring our birthing accoutrements in from the car. I was long past teddy-bear focal points or playlists. I looked into his face during the contractions as he dutifully chanted, "Breathe, breathe, breathe." When the contraction was over, I drifted out of consciousness. Far away.

Spent, and traveling out of the body, I returned to the apple trees of my earlier birth fantasy. This time the trees were in blossom, in sunlight, under a pale blue sky, and my friend Elizabeth, who had her daughter Emma a year before, stood beneath them. In between contractions I went to this place with Elizabeth and Emma. They seemed to be welcoming me. Emma was perched at her mother's waist, stiff legs supported by Elizabeth's cradled arm, while the apple tree's canopy of branches crowned Emma's head. Elizabeth grasped a branch, pulling it down as Emma pushed on her stomach to reach the blossoms waiting above them both. Early in pregnancy women can forget they are pregnant for an hour or two, a day perhaps. They can walk the fields at their usual pace, bend down and lift laundry baskets easily. They can hop, skip, jump, and run after a bus pulling away from the curb. In the last trimester every second is colored with the knowledge that you have something living inside you and it's growing—it's pushing against your being. When you turn on your side, you are turning for two. Nothing about me remained as it was.

Our midwife suddenly noticed Richard—how shaken and pale he was. He looked like he was going to faint. He alone had been my companion in labor; it was his face I looked at when trying to focus through the contractions, his hands I gripped, his voice trying to talk me through the pain, and it was his frame upon which I collapsed. There was no one else in the hours between arrival and admittance.

"Go down to the cafeteria," Patricia said. "Get some coffee, something to eat. It's going to be some hours before the next stage." I let go of his hands that I had been holding on to like a life raft in a storm.

When Richard came back I was in transition, that period between the first stage of labor and the last, when you push the baby out. I had been drifting in and out of consciousness, when suddenly I got up, went to the bathroom, and threw up. Then the mucus plug that blocks the opening of the cervix was expelled and my water broke. It was as if a small balloon had burst and out came the water in one big gush. And then I had to push. There was no stopping, no slowing the need to push, a push that originated somewhere else, far behind me, a great epic push and I was the instrument of it.

I had been steadfastly uninterested in having children. Nothing moved me from my refusal, not holding a newborn in my arms or the transformative tales of motherhood. I was too wrapped up in the trouble of being a daughter forever waiting for her mother's love that would never come. I was surprised when I was seized by a great longing for a child.

Husband, midwife, and nurse huddled about the fetal monitor in the birthing room, because it had started to register distress. Something was wrong—I could hear it in their voices, in the low tones, though I couldn't hear what they said. I was concentrating on pushing. I had to get out of my bed and lie on a gurney being rolled in. Then away I went, wheeling toward an operating room. Patricia was trying to slow down my pushing—there was talk of a C-section, getting you out quickly, calling a surgeon. But I couldn't stop pushing, and you crowned. Richard said he could see your head. I had never heard such excitement in his voice. Out you rushed, with your umbilical cord lassoed around your neck. That's what was causing the distress. Each time I pushed, the cord tightened around your neck, cutting off oxygen and blood. Later

I wondered if this was the origin of the term *mother knot*. But what could have been dire was not. As you crowned, Patricia was able to unloop the cord from around your neck, and all was well. It was 4:19 A.M. on April 18 and you weighed eight pounds, four ounces.

Richard wiped you off, wrapped you in a blanket, and put you in my arms. And a new story was born, a story I am passing on to you. And while I hope you live in the here and now, in a present so full that you have no reason to look back in puzzlement about how you came into the world, remember I know the story of your birth by heart.

CHARLES BAXTER

What Happens in Hell

FROM *Ploughshares*

"SIR, I AM WONDERING —have you considered lately what happens in Hell?"

No, I hadn't, but I liked that *lately*. We were on our way from
the San Francisco Airport to Palo Alto, and the driver for Bay Area
Limo, a Pakistani American whose name was Niazi, was glancing
repeatedly in the rearview mirror to check me out. After all, there
I was, a privileged person—a hegemon of some sort—in the back
seat of the Lincoln Town Car, cushioned by the camel-colored
leather as I swigged my bottled water. Like other Americans of my
class and station, I know the importance of staying hydrated. And
there *he* was, up front, behind the wheel on a late sunny Saturday
afternoon, speeding down California State Highway 101, missing
(he had informed me almost as soon as I got into the car) the
prayer service and sermon at his Bay Area mosque. The subject of
the sermon would be Islamic inheritance laws—a subject that had
led quite naturally to the subject of death and the afterlife.

I don't really enjoy sitting in the back seat of Lincoln Town
Cars. I don't like being treated as some sort of important person-
age. I'm a midwesterner by location and temperament and don't
even cotton to being called "sir." So I try to be polite ("Just call
me Charlie") and take my shoes off, so to speak, in deference to
foreign customs, as Mrs. Moore does in *A Passage to India*.

"No," I said, "I haven't. What happens in Hell?" I asked.

"Well," Niazi said, warming up and stroking his beard, "there is
no forgiveness over there. There is forgiveness here but not there.
The God does not listen to you on the other side."

"He doesn't?"

"No. The God does not care what you say, and he does not forgive you once you are on that side after you die. By then it is over."

"Interesting," I said, nondirectively.

"It is all in the Holy Book," Niazi went on. "And your skin, sir. Do you know what the God does with your skin?"

"No, I don't," I said. "Tell me." Actually I was most interested in the definite article. Why was the deity referred to as *the* God? Are there still other, lesser gods, minor subsidiary deities, set aside somewhere, who must be differentiated from the major god? I drank some more water as I considered this problem.

"It is very interesting, what happens with the skin," Niazi said as we pulled off the Bayshore Freeway onto University Avenue. "Every day the skin is burned off."

"Yes?"

"Yes. This is known. And then, each day, the God gives you new skin. This new skin is like a sheath."

"Ah." I noticed the repeated use of the word *you*.

"And every day the *new* skin is burned off." He said this sentence with a certain degree of excitement. "It is very painful, as you can imagine. And the pain is always *fresh* pain."

Meanwhile we were proceeding through downtown Palo Alto. On the outskirts of town I had noticed the absence of pickup trucks and rusting American cars; everywhere I looked, I saw Priuses and Saabs and Lexuses and BMWs and Volvos and Mercedes-Benzes and a few Teslas here and there. The mix didn't include convertible Bentleys or Maybachs, the brand names that flash past you on Ocean Boulevard in Santa Monica. Here, ostentation was out; professional-managerial modesty was in. Here the drivers were engaged in Right Thinking and were uncommonly courteous: complete stops at stop signs were the norm, and ditto at the mere sight of a pedestrian at a crosswalk. No one seemed to be in a hurry. There was plenty of time for everything, as if Siddhartha himself were directing traffic.

And the pedestrians! Fit, smiling, upright, well-tended, with not a morbidly obese fellow citizen in sight, the evening crowd on University Avenue appeared to be living in an earlier American era, one lacking desperation, hysteria, and Fox News. Somehow Palo Alto had remained immune to what one of my students has referred to as "the Great Decline." In this city, the businesses were thriving under blue skies and polished sunshine. I couldn't spot a single boarded-up front window. Although I saw plenty of panhandlers, no one looked shabby and lower-middle-class. I noted, as an outsider would, the lines outside the luxe restaurants—Bella Luna, Lavanda, and the others—everyone laughing and smiling. The happiness struck me as stagy. What phonies these people were! Having come from Minneapolis, where we have boarded-up businesses in bulk, I felt like—what is the expression?—an ape hanging on to the fence of Heaven, watching the gods play.

And it occurred to me at that moment that Niazi felt that way too, apelike, except that I was one of those damn gods, which explained why he had to inform me about Hell.

"You burn forever," Niazi said, drawing me out of my reverie. "And, yes, here we are at your hotel."

Sir and *Hell:* the two words belong together. After arguing with the hotel desk clerk, who claimed (until I showed him my confirmation number) that I didn't have a reservation and therefore didn't belong there, I went up to my room past a gaggle of beautiful leggy young men and women, track stars, in town for a meet at Stanford University, where I'd been hired to teach as a visiting writer. They were flirting with each other and tenderly comparing relay batons. Off in the bar on the other side of the lobby, drugstore cowboys were whooping it up, throwing back draft beers while the voice of Faith Hill warbled on the jukebox. Nothing is so dispiriting as the sight of strangers getting boisterously happy. It makes you feel like a stepchild, a poor relation. Having checked in, I went upstairs and sat in my room immobilized, unable for a moment even to open my suitcase, puzzled by the persistence of Hell and why I had just been forced to endure a lecture about it.

Rattled, I stared out the window. A soft Bay Area rain was falling, little dribs and drabs dropping harmlessly, impressionistically, out of the sky—Monet rain. A downmarket version of an Audubon bird—how I hate those Audubon birds—was trapped and framed in a picture above the TV.

I am usually an outsider everywhere. I don't mind being one —you're a writer, you choose a certain fate—but the condition is harder to bear in a self-confident city where everyone is playing a role successfully and no one is glancing furtively for the EXIT signs.

In his writings and his clinical practice, the French psychoanalyst Jacques Lacan liked to ask why any particular person would *want* to believe any given set of ideas. He initially asked the question of behavioral psychologists with their dopey experiments with mice and pigeons, but, inspired by Lacan, you can ask it of anyone. Why do you *desire* to believe the ideas that you hold dear, the cornerstones of your faith? Why do you clutch tightly to the ideas that appear to be particularly repellant and cruel? Why would anyone *want* to suppose that an untold multitude of human souls burn in extreme agony for eternity? Having left a marriage and now living and working alone, I found myself in that hotel room experiencing the peculiar vacuum of self that arises when you go on working without a clear belief in what (or whom) you're working *for* and are also being exposed randomly to the world's cruelties.

The idea of Hell has a transcendently stupefying ugliness akin to that of torture chambers. This particular ugliness is fueled by the rage and sadism of the believer who enjoys imagining his enemies writhing perpetually down there in the colorful fiery pit. How many of us relish the fairy tale of endless suffering! Nietzsche claimed that all such relishers are in the grip of *ressentiment,* whereby frustration against the rulers and anger at oneself are transformed into a morality. Ressentiment is what happens to resentment once it goes Continental and becomes a metaphysical category. After Marx, injustice no longer seemed part of a natural order. And if injustice *isn't* part of a natural order, then ressentiment will naturally arise, the rage of the have-nots against the haves, the losers against the winners. Sometimes the rage is constructive, sometimes not. For Nietzsche, in *On the Genealogy of Morals,* the unequal distribution of power is simply a condition of things-as-they-are:

> It is not surprising that the lambs should bear a grudge against the great birds of prey, but that is no reason for blaming the great birds of prey for taking the little lambs. And when the lambs say among themselves, "These birds of prey are evil, and he who least resembles a bird of prey, who is rather its opposite, a lamb,—should he not be good?"

If you're a loser, you might as well get used to your loserdom and sanctify it. Thus Nietzsche. The eagles will come down sooner or later and grab you and eat you. It's how nature works.

But if you, the lamb, claim a superior virtue to the eagle, and you band together with other lambs and consign the eagles to a sadistically picturesque Hell, you will, in another life, find yourself behind the wheel, working for Bay Area Limo, instructing the hapless pale-skinned passenger from Minnesota about the manner in which some will find themselves scorched forever on the other side, forever and forever, oh, and by the way, here we are at your hotel.

In one of Alice Munro's stories, a character observes that the Irish treat all authority with abject servility followed by savage, sneering mockery. Ressentiment has its comic side, after all.

After washing up, I came back downstairs through the lobby—more beautiful track stars, more flirting, and a little microportion of ressentiment on my part against their beauty and youth and sexiness—and ambled to the Poolside Grille, where I ordered the *specialité de la maison*, blackened red snapper (California cuisine: black beans, jasmine rice, salsa fresca, lime sour cream), the snapper itself an endangered species. I hastily gulped down my chardonnay and, like a starving peasant, devoured the fish without tasting it. Gulping and chewing and swallowing, I watched the athletes in their skimpy garb promenading around the hotel, as graceful as swans. Ned Rorem on youth: "We admire them for their beauty, and they want us to admire them for their minds, the little shits." All the while Niazi's voice was in my head: "Every day the God gives you a new skin so that he can burn it away." I paid the bill and returned to my room. Fresh pain! What a phrase. I couldn't read, so I watched TV: *CSI: Crime Scene Investigation*, Captain Jim Brass confessing to human failings, played very well by Paul Guilfoyle. Or did I watch another show, some prepackaged drama interchangeable with that one? I can't remember. I do remember that I drifted off to sleep in my street clothes. There was no one around to tell me not to.

I didn't see Niazi again for another four weeks. On a Wednesday morning in April, he was to meet me in front of my Stanford apartment at 9:30 to take me to the San Francisco Airport so that I could fly back to Minneapolis. I had been commuting almost every week. At 9:25 I stood out in front with my suitcase beside me, waiting for him. I saw his black Lincoln Town Car in the visitors' parking lot. He honked, pulled up, and rushed out to put my suitcase in the trunk.

"Good morning, sir," he said. "How are you?" His eyes, I noticed, were heavy-lidded and puffy. He looked like a box turtle.

"Fine," I said, settling into the back seat and snapping on the lap-and-shoulder belt. "How about you?" I looked around for a bottle of water. There were two little ones.

"Very tired," he said, checking his watch before flopping in behind the wheel. "I could not sleep last night. I have been in this parking lot since eight-thirty."

"You should have called me," I said. "We could've left early."

"No no no," Niazi corrected me. "I have been trying to take the nap."

"Are you still drowsy?" I asked, noting again his nonstandard use of definite articles.

"A little, somewhat," he told me. "But when I am that way, I think of the Holy Book."

"Ah."

He drove us up to Interstate 280, back in the hills, an alternative route to the airport. Here the rain was falling harder, and I noticed that Niazi didn't bother to turn on the car's windshield wipers. The rain spattered violently against the glass in an almost midwestern manner. I felt right at home. Stroking his beard, Niazi gazed out at the highway, and after about ten minutes I saw that, with his eyes half closed, he was moving his head back and forth, shaking it slowly, as if . . . *Was this possible? Was I actually seeing what I was seeing?* He was driving the limo, with me in it, while sleeping.

My brother Tom used to get drowsy behind the wheel and, one winter night in 1961, almost killed himself outside Delano, Minnesota, when he dozed off. Another irony: Delano's major business in those days was the engraving of cemetery monuments, and the town's motto was "Drive carefully. We can wait." Unable to walk away from his accident, his car in the ditch, my brother had to drag himself on all fours out of the wreck across a snowy field to a farmhouse. As a boy, I was quite accustomed to my brother's sleepiness behind the wheel and would keep him entertained and awake with bright patter, for which I have a gift. So: "Niazi!" I said. "Do you have many jobs today? I'll bet you do!"

"Oh, yes, sir," he said dispiritedly. "Many. Two this afternoon." Maybe he wasn't asleep after all.

The rain fell harder, unusually hard for northern California. I looked around at the interior of the Lincoln Town Car, thinking, *We're going to crash. But at least this limo is a very solid car.* With the irony of which life is so fond, I thought of two lines of a creepy song I had heard a few months before, by the group Concrete Blonde. The song was "Tomorrow, Wendy," and two lines serve as the song's refrain:

> Hey, hey, goodbye
> Tomorrow Wendy's going to die.

And just about then the car began to fishtail. When a car fishtails, you take your foot off the accelerator and tap the brake pedal. Fishtailing occurs often in icy conditions (think: Minnesota winter), less often in rain. But California drivers aren't used to precipitation, so when the car began to lose control, Niazi woke up and slammed on the brakes, throwing the Lincoln into a sideways skid, and when the rear-wheel-drive tires acquired traction again, they pushed us off the freeway, onto the shoulder, and then, very rapidly, down a hill, where the car flipped over sideways and began to roll, turning over and over and over, until it reached the bottom of the hill, right side up. From the moment the car began to lose control until it came to rest, Niazi was screaming. All during the time we turned over down that hill, he continued to scream.

Reader, this essay is about that scream. Please do your best to imagine it.

Men don't scream, as a rule; they bellow or roar with fright or anger, but male screaming is an exceptionally rare phenomenon, and the sound makes your flesh crawl. A woman's scream calls you to protective action. A man's scream provokes horror.

Inside that car, I was holding on to the door's hand rest, clutching it, and I was as quiet as the tomb. I wasn't particularly scared, although things were flying around the car—my cell phone had escaped from my coat pocket and was airborne in front of me, as were various other items from the car, including those free little bottles of water and a clipboard from the front seat—and I heard the sound of crunching or of some huge animal chewing up the car. I thought, *Let this be over soon.* And then it was. They say everything slows down during an accident, but no, not always, and this accident didn't slow down my sense of time until we were at rest and I heard Niazi moaning, and more than anything else I wanted to get out of that car before the gas tank exploded, but my door wouldn't open—the right rear door—but the left rear door did, after I pushed my shoulder against it.

Around and inside the car was a terrible smell of wreckage, oil and burned rubber, and another smell, which I am tempted to describe as sulfurous.

"Niazi," I said, "are you okay?"

"Oh oh oh oh," he said, "yes, I am okay"—he clearly wasn't—"and you, Mr. Baxter, sir, are you okay?"

"Yes." Where was I? Without a transition, I seemed to be standing in the rain outside the car, and Niazi, making the sounds that precede speech in human history, was trying to get himself off the ground, blood streaming down his face; and his shoes, I noticed, were off, which (I had once heard) is one of the signs of a high-velocity accident. Amid the wreckage, he was barefoot, and blood was dripping onto his feet. I reached out for him.

Suddenly witnesses surrounded us. "You turned over four times!" an Asian American man said, clutching my arm. His face was transfixed by shock. "I saw it. I was behind you. Are you all right? How could you possibly be all right? Surely you are not all right?" He opened his umbrella and lifted it over my head, a perfect gesture of kindness.

"I don't know," I said. I looked down at my Levi's. The belt loops had snapped off. How was that possible? I stared in wonderment at the broken belt loops. I looked at the man. "Am I all right?"

He simply stared at me as if I had been resurrected.

The usual confusion followed: EMT guys, California Highway Patrol guys, witness reports. An off-duty cop from San Marino, another witness to the accident, said he couldn't believe I was standing up. He touched my arm with a tender gesture as if I might break. Someone asked me to sign a document, and I did, my hand shaking so violently that my signature looked like that of a third grader. And what was I worried about? My *laptop*. Had it been damaged? Furthermore, I thought, *I'm going to be late for my airplane flight!* In shock, we lose all sense of proportion. My signature on another official document looked like someone else's, not mine. And now Niazi was standing up, still bloodily barefoot, talking. He appeared to be in stable condition, though they were putting a head brace on him and then lowering him onto a wooden stretcher, as if he had been smashed up. The Asian American witness who saw our car turn over four times asked me where I was going, and I said, "To the airport."

"I will take you," he said. "Just put your suitcase in the back seat. We will have to drop off my father-in-law in Millbrae. Do you mind?"

"No," I said. "Thank you."

The driver and his father-in-law spoke Mandarin all the way to Millbrae, the driver politely interpreting for me so that I wouldn't be left out of the conversation. "My father-in-law thinks you must be badly injured," the driver said. "I told him that you said you were fine." Thanks to this gentleman, I arrived at the San Francisco Airport in time for my flight. My ribs hurt, and my back hurt, and I gave off an odd panic-stricken body odor, but all I wanted to do was to get home. At the same time, I was still disoriented. Near the entrance to Terminal One, I noticed, was a sign with a name on it: NOSMO KING. It appeared to me as graffiti on behalf of a deposed potentate. Who was this oddly named Nosmo King? King of what? We were in northern California! No kings here! Not until I was seated on the airplane did I calm down and realize that I had misread the sign and that, like other public places, the San Francisco Airport did not tolerate lighting up or puffing on cigarettes.

My back still hurts sometimes, especially on long flights. Niazi called me at home a few days later and left a message on my answering machine. His voice was expressive of deep despair combined with physical pain. "Mr. Baxter, sir, I am worried about you. I am . . . I am not all right, but I am lying down, recovering. Would you please call me?"

No. I would not call him, and I did not. I still haven't. I heard from someone else that he had broken his back. Guiltily, shamefully, I left him uncalled, and my inability to dial his number and to ask him how he was recovering surely serves as a sign of a human failing, a personalized grudge that will not be appeased. But all I could think of then and now was, *That expert on Hell almost got me killed.*

The insurance company has promised to send me $500 to compensate me for my pain and suffering.

*

In another version of the accident, the one I sometimes told my-self compulsively, I sit silently while Niazi screams and the car rolls over down the hill. But I didn't just tell myself this story; I told everybody. The accident turned me into a tiresome raconteur. A repetition compulsion had me in its tight narrative grip. I had be-come like a character in one of my own stories, the sort of madcap who buttonholes an innocent bystander to relieve himself of an obsession. Some stories present themselves as a gift, to be handed on to others as a second gift. But some more dire stories have a certain difficult-to-define taint. They give off an odd smell. They have infected the person who possesses them, and that person peevishly passes on the infection to others. In the story in which I am the victim, I am not an artist, but a garrulous ancient mari-ner who has come ashore long after his boat has been set adrift and long after his rescue, which does not feel like a rescue but an abandonment.

From the airport I called my wife, from whom I was—and re-main—separated, to give her the news. She met me at the airport, and we hugged each other for the first time in months. Near-death trumps marital discord but does not heal it. Then she took me back to my apartment, where she dropped me off.

I sat alone in the apartment for a few days, trying to read, but mostly writing e-mails. At night I would fall asleep to the remem-bered sound of Niazi's screams. I announced my accident on Facebook, curious whether any of my FB friends would press the "like" button. A few did. I picked up the phone and started calling people. "Let me tell you what happened to me," I would say. I had become strangely interesting to myself. One friend has called my compulsion to talk about the accident a form of "vocational impe-rialism," though I think he means *avocational* imperialism. After all, I am a mere tourist in the landscape of Islam. As an unsteady humanist, I don't believe in much, and the virtues that I do believe in—goodness, charity, bravery—abandoned me in the moments after that accident.

All I thought as we tumbled down that hill, as I have said, was the hope that this awfulness would be over soon. We die alone, even if someone else is dying beside us. And—this was my fleet-ing wish in the back seat of that violently rotating Lincoln Town Car, in the wondrously dark clarity of thought produced by the

unexpected, as the plastic bottles of water were flying around
my head and my cell phone twirled in the air in front of me—I
prayed that the car would land right side up or, if this was to be
the moment of my death, by fire as the gas tank exploded, that
it be quick.

ANDER MONSON

The Exhibit Will Be So Marked

FROM *The Normal School*

A COUPLE OF YEARS AGO, I asked friends and family to make me a mix CD for my birthday, hoping to get thirty-three mix CDs, one per year I'd lived. I got fifty-nine, including some, pleasingly, from strangers. Somewhat predictably, though not unpleasantly, there were a number of Jesus-Year-themed mixes, though fewer Jesus-themed songs. I also put out the call to friends to pass it to anyone they thought might be interested in sending a mix CD. I made it a project to listen actively to each of these mix CDs and to respond by annotating, riffing on, and responding to the selections, and sending a note with my response to the mix-maker, or I suppose we should call her an arranger, since therein is the art of the mix.

The idea I had about this was that the collective mix CDs would somehow represent the network of friends and family I was in close contact with—or close enough. I thought I'd be able to divine something about myself from how others viewed me, what they thought the best approach was to making the mix, whether they used the mix as an opportunity to impress, to educate, to colonize, to woo, to irritate, to posture, to stake out some emotional territory between us. I'd done all these things in the past, usually with an emphasis on woo. I'd made hundreds, I'd guess, maybe a thousand, though I'm not obsessive enough to have kept track of all of them—their recipients, the occasion for the mix, the strategies I employed, if any, and the track lists over the years. Whether an individual mix meant anything was hard to say, but it would be tough to avoid making some conclusions about the first third (I hope) of my life from the aggregate information contained on these compact discs.

One disc arrived cracked, so only the first few tracks were playable. Another mix, this one pie-themed, arrived so broken that only the track list was readable. Another was virtual, a ghost mix, a list of the worst thirty-three songs in her iTunes library without any actual music to inflict said songs on me. One was all songs written and recorded when the artist in question was thirty-three. One, also impressively, was only songs released in 1933. The length of one disc added up to exactly thirty-three minutes and thirty-three seconds. My brother sent me, in lieu of a mix, a box set of Americana from Rhino, which says quite a bit about our relationship. Another mix consisted of songs that I had never heard before. One, maybe the most meaningful in the way mixes can be, collected songs by bands that the mixer and I had seen in concert together. Perhaps in a bid to piss me off, several featured "Sweet Home Alabama." More than one included a Bon Jovi song. I am not sure why.

Then one mix CD was not a CD at all. It arrived in a regular business-sized envelope. It was a microcassette without a case. Sent in an unpadded envelope, it too arrived broken. I filed it on my shelf with the others. It did not fit in the box with the others because the box was designed for CDs. The envelope it arrived in was a plain business envelope, you know the sort, designed for holding a letter-sized sheet of paper folded in three parts. It had no return address. Addressed to me with a barely readable postmark from Nebraska City, Nebraska, the tape was an enigma. Did it have anything to do with the mix CD project? I did not know. It was broken and unplayable. As I listened to the other mix CDs and wrote about them, or in response to them, I thought more about what might be on the broken tape. I filled the room with thought. I paid attention to the songs on the listenable discs and tried to correlate them with my relationship with the person who made the mix. My head was elsewhere as I contemplated the moonlit limbs of the sumacs visible from my office window, the invisible network of roots converging at the base of the trees, and waited for snow to come.

Nebraska City, Nebraska, is the official home of Arbor Day, the last Friday in April (in most states—sometimes differing climates lead to different dates), a "day to celebrate trees," according to the Arbor Day Foundation website. You've heard of it. Maybe you've celebrated it. I'd guess that only a few of us, though, have revered it. Founded in 1872 by Julius Sterling Morton, a journalist and politician originally from Michigan, Arbor Day is surely the least sexy national holiday. (It is a postal holiday, but only in Nebraska.) While it's odd to think about the burned, windswept prairie of Nebraska as the birth of the day of tree celebration, Nebraska Citians are pretty serious about Arbor Day.

From what I can see of it (which, thanks to the Internet and Google Earth, is extensive in a way that would not have been possible even a decade ago), Nebraska City, Nebraska, appears undistinguished. Just south of I-29's intersection with I-80, it has the usual stuff of American towns: golf courses, churches, monuments, Super 8 motels, a hospital, townhomes, Buick LeSabres, football, insurance agents, a sewing store, a mostly abandoned downtown, quilts, sadness, pretty girls, fields and fields, a factory outlet store, one or two Chinese restaurants, a Mexican restaurant with wack burritos, the smell of farms, a Friends of Faith Thrift Shop, scattered signs of both doom and joy. When you start to look at what distinguishes cities from each other, particularly in the American Midwest, it's pretty easy to despair of our culture for its portability, its replicability, its easy genericism.

Nebraska City, Nebraska, is one of those State Name City cities that feel peculiarly American and complicate schoolchildren's memorization of the states and their capitals: Oklahoma City, Oklahoma, may be the capital city of Oklahoma, but Iowa City is no longer the capital city of Iowa (as of 1857). You've probably never even heard of Ohio City, Ohio, or Minnesota City, Minnesota, for good reason. I'd reckon about half the states have a State Name City, and a few have cities named after other states, often straddling state lines. As such, Nebraska City, Nebraska, could be —though it is not, except maybe in a few lonely dreams—the center of the center of the country.

The Midwest is an odd place when you look at it closely enough, though it gets caricatured as Norman Rockwellville, a place of the safe and boring, hard work, religion, football, "family values"— whatever they are. My experience with the Midwest belies these broad brushstrokes: most of the Midwest is much stranger, darker, more hollow, anger- and treasure-filled. You find serious evidence of weirdness in the abandoned factory steam towers and knock-off Dairy Queen—called Kastle Kreme—in Galesburg, Illinois (they'll make a blizzard out of anything you bring in, including salted pork), or the closed Blue Bird School Bus assembly plant in Mount Pleasant, Iowa. Zeeland, Michigan, has the highest incest rate in the state. You find the World's Biggest Ball of Twine in a small town: Darwin, Minnesota. Another contender for the crown is in Cawker City, Kansas, with at least one more in Wisconsin and inevitably one in the weirdest town in the greater Midwest: Branson, Missouri. Looking closer at Nebraska City, you learn that it is the oldest incorporated city in Nebraska and has the only Underground Railroad site in the state. Then there's the legacy of Morton's Arbor Day—thousands of trees lining the streets of Nebraska City, thousands of saplings in kids' hands about to be planted; or maybe those are metaphors: the hands, the kids, the trees, Nebraska City.

Strange enough on the ground, then, but from the air it must seem like the least identifiable city in one of the least identifiable states, identifiable only in its display of absence, the sort of place where someone mysterious might hide and send out strange microcassettes or bombs.

Every move across the country, and every visit, if it's a good one, if you pay attention: these force you to recalibrate your sense of place and what you thought the place might be or mean. When I moved to Tucson, Arizona, a couple years later, I was surprised by just how green it was, belying the broad brushstrokes that "Tucson, Arizona," brings to mind. My vision/version of the place was of the flat, swaled infinity that you might see in Riyadh, Saudi Arabia, where I lived briefly as a teenager, or in the Sahara, where much of my consciousness of what *desert* means was born. Not much grew in the desert around Riyadh. But the part of the Sonoran Desert surrounding Tucson (a valley city, surrounded by mountain ranges) is comparatively speaking a celebration of the tree, particularly the Martian green–skinned palo verde, Arizona's unreal and prickly state tree. And Tucson isn't technically in a desert at all: the area gets enough rain (twelve inches a year most years, though a little less in the last decade's ongoing drought) to be considered only semiarid. Landscapes are filled with the famous saguaro cacti that only grow in the Sonora, the green spray of blooming ocotillos, a song is important to southerners, particularly Alabamans, partly for its famous fuck-off to the Canadian Neil Young, "Southern man don't need him around."

By the time I heard it covered in Atlanta, the song had lost whatever meaning it might have once had for me as a result of sheer oversaturation. But I listened hard to all the mix CDs. Doing so, I found that I don't really *listen* very often to songs anymore. Perhaps it's a product of the MP3 age, in which we trade off fidelity for convenience, the immersive and social experience of the album for the portability, downloadability, and immediacy of the digital single, but whether we love songs, hate songs, or disregard them, more typically when we press Play, we press Play on our memory of the song or what it represents, how it makes us feel, who we were when we first heard it or made it part of our lives. We don't listen to the song *itself*. (Well, we're never listening to anything itself, without consideration of context, genre, history, personal experience, and so on, but that road leads to a neurotic infinity.) Instead, I found that when I actually listened to it, "Sweet Home Alabama" is actually a pretty catchy song. This raises uncomfortable questions about what my taste in music actually means, but I can't think about that too hard, too often, if I want to maintain any sense of what self means.

This last year tornadoes destroyed much of Tuscaloosa, including both of the places I lived in when I was in grad school there: an apartment complex named, in an attempt to ape the patrician South, Charleston Square, and a house situated about five miles distant on a street called Cedar Crest, though there were no cedars anywhere in sight. I remember seeing the damage on television, trying to reconcile the images in the media with my memory of the place. *What corner is that?* I asked myself—only to realize, holy shit, that was the street on which I lived: and it was entirely wiped out in a mile-wide stripe, just erased, like magnetic tape. You could tell it was Cedar Crest by the railroad tracks, the decimated Krispy Kreme, and the few remaining individual trees, which are numerous and often very old.

Tuscaloosa has long been called the "Druid City," for the preponderance of water oaks lining its many leafy streets, and my memory of entering the South for the first time was largely one of being engulfed in trees, in near-total forestation, surprisingly

dozen different palms, yuccas, mesquites, and thousands of
trees bushing out of backyards throughout the city, to say not
of the other hundred succulents and varieties of cacti, though
many of Tucson's denizens, both flora and fauna, many are ha
native to the region.

I found the fruit trees particularly fascinating, since the ora
trees spectacularly line the Third Street Bike Path that dead-e
into the campus of the university where I teach. Being from Mic
gan, and spending much of my life in the cold realms, I fetishiz
fruit trees, fetishized cacti, images from vacation postcards, te
vision, and deep winter dreams. Fruit trees especially were ti
directly into the myths of California and Florida, Disneyland ai
Disney World, twin visions of escape from the endless snowbou
heart of Upper Michigan.

Like many orange trees planted on public property, the Thir
Street trees produce oranges that are incredibly bitter. They offe
only visual sustenance—glossy nests of leaves cradle orange orb
When they fruit, they become more of a nuisance than anything
else, dropping inedible oranges that rot in the street and taun
hungry students and passersby who fetishize fruit globes.

I have a problem with inedible things—particularly soaps and
bath products, though the sour oranges qualify—that smell or
look like something edible. If sufficiently hungry, I will disregard
sense and eat them, or try to, and spit out a mouthful of soapy
chemical mess or too-sour fruit. I am no smarter with age. Biking
down that street, I've been tempted. Too often, desire is a more
powerful force than restraint.

At the request of a pair of conventionally rather attractive Alabama
sorority girls, the Scottish indie rock band Belle and Sebastian
once covered "Sweet Home Alabama" at a concert I attended in
Atlanta. It was a glorious, if ill-fated, collision, the sort you look for
in a cover situation. After all, Belle and Sebastian was a famously
shy and media-elusive band in its youth, so the prospect of them
inviting requests for covers was a funny surprise. I was shocked
that the guitarist knew the riff at all, though the band didn't know
all the lyrics. Said sorority girls were pulled up onstage to sing.

University of Alabama alums know that the proper way to sing
the song is with a "Roll, Tide, Roll" inserted like a virus in the chorus. As a northerner in the South, you understand quickly that this

similar to my home in Michigan, with echoes of *Deliverance* and red dirt everywhere.

A couple months before the tornado, an Alabama football fan was arrested for poisoning a stand of 130-year-old oak trees 160 miles away in Auburn, Alabama, commonly called Toomer's Corner. These oaks are among the oldest of Auburn's trees. There are 8,236 on the campus. According to tradition, fans would festoon the oaks with toilet paper after important football victories.

Alabama and Auburn have a longstanding and especially bitter rivalry, but the poisoning of the trees by sixty-two-year-old former state trooper Harvey A. Updyke Jr. is certainly a new low. Evidently he had problems with mental illness, though you could argue that the degree of obsession that hardcore Alabama fans often exhibit borders on crazy. Rarely do you get a sense of restraint overriding desire when it comes to Alabama football.

Updyke used a powerful herbicide called Spike 80DF—"80 percent tebuthiuron (the active ingredient) and 20 percent inert ingredients," according to a *Huffington Post* news article on the subject, farmed certainly from some other website in the way of modern aggregated media. The same article suggests the herbicide "kills from the roots up." As a result, it might take years for the stand of oaks to die as they shed, regrow, and reshed their leaves like past lives, past iterations of selves suggested by mix-tape track lists and embarrassing letters written to girls we yearned for. It's not yet fully certain whether they will live or die, but the prognosis for the trees is not good.

The prognosis for my old neighborhood is worse: it's since been bulldozed, the rubble and uprooted parts of trees removed, along with the few remaining halves of houses and the graves of the many stray cats my wife and I fed and tried to save. You can only do so much. The roots of my memories there are now erased entirely, along with the house next door to ours that (we were informed by an obsessive football fan who came to our house to take photographs) once housed football star Joe Namath.

According to the July 7, 1936, issue of the *Toledo News*, comedian Hugh Herbert was the first inventor of a particular mix tape of a tree, the "fruit-salad tree": "[He] is developing a horticultural marvel to be known as a fruit-salad tree, or Herbert's Folly. On a grapefruit tree his [*sic*] has grafted oranges, avocados, peaches, apples, plums, and walnuts." Two months later, the *Christian Science Monitor* ran an article about McKee Jungle Gardens, almost two hours southeast of Orlando, in Vero Beach, Florida (now McKee Botanical Garden), which had a fruit-salad tree of its own ("the Mexican salad fruit tree . . . pineapple, strawberries, and bananas combined").

These Frankentrees are made by grafting parts of different trees onto one trunk in order to maximize the variety of fruit grown on the one tree, and also for novelty or entertainment. Contrary to the *Toledo News,* these fruit-salad trees, also called fruit-cocktail trees, probably predate 1936, since the technique of grafting branches tree on tree has been around since antiquity, and someone surely had the idea before 1936. Circa 300 BCE, for instance, amateur botanist Theophrastus writes, in *De Causis Plantarum,* that "it is also reasonable that trees so grafted should bear finer fruit." He goes on to explain the technique of grafting in detail. Much of his discourse in "Propagation in Another Tree: Grafting" could more or less be copied-and-pasted directly into any contemporary manual on the subject, since the techniques have not changed much. It's hard to believe that as an experimental botanist, he or his contemporaries wouldn't have mixed multiple fruits on one tree.

By this time pretty much all of our domesticated trees, particularly citrus, are hybrids, only reliably reproducible via grafting. All fruit trees are Frankentrees. So it shouldn't be surprising that the fruit-salad tree would later be developed by the University of California at Riverside, and more recently commercially popularized by the Fruit Salad Tree Company out of Emmasville, Australia, which distributes four fruit-salad tree varieties (Stone Fruit, Citrus Fruit, Multi-Apples, and Multi-Nashis—Japanese pears) that are ready to plant, tend, and fruit.

A mysterious and unmarked tape arrives . . . straight out of a noir novel.

Was it a message? Was it from a stalker? A crazy Alabama football fan? A former lover? A family member?

I asked the most likely suspects. Then I asked everyone I knew. No one claimed responsibility.

The actual magnetic tape was not broken, though its casing was.

I headed to Radio Shack to procure some new microcassettes in hopes of nerdily dismantling the broken casing and rethreading the old tape through an unbroken case. None of them turned out to be openable without some mystic wizard moves.

A couple months went by. I thought about other things, worked on other things, as I do. Watched the trees out my window lose their leaves and wind down, spectral, for winter. I thought more about it. The hacker in me said I had to fix the tape myself. The reasonable person just said, *Eh, forget it.* But I couldn't just forget it. Eventually I sent it out to a specialty audio restoration company that fixed the tape, burned it to a CD, and mailed it back.

It sat in its package on my desk. *Should I listen to it?* I wondered. What if the mystery disappointed me, and it was just some heavy breathing? (Actually I'd take heavy breathing. It could connote anything.)

When I think of mystery, I think of the Paulding Light, the most famous unexplained phenomenon of Michigan's Upper Peninsula. At one point, *Ripley's Believe It or Not!* offered a $100,000 reward for anyone who could definitively explain the light. It was even featured on an episode of Robert Stack's redundantly named television show *Unsolved Mysteries* and a more recent Syfy network show.

The Paulding Light is in the Ottawa National Forest, south of Bruce Crossing, about an hour and a half from the town where I grew up and in which my parents live. Driving south, it's off an old mining road on the right of U.S. 45, a couple miles before you get to Watersmeet. You drive in at night and park where the other cars are, among millions of towering pines. Most nights there will be a dozen or more people sitting on the hoods of their cars, often with binoculars or telescopes, looking north at a series of lights that emerge, slowly move down a hill, and disappear. The locals have stories of these balls of light getting within a hundred feet of the viewers, floating, moving, changing colors, spinning, and splitting up. The official U.S. Forest Service sign (adorned helpfully, surely unofficially, with an illustration of Casper the Friendly Ghost) reads as follows:

> This is the location from which the famous Paulding Light can be observed. Legend explains its presence as a railroad brakeman's ghost, destined to remain forever at the sight [*sic*] of his untimely

death. He continually waves his signal lantern as a warning to all
who come to visit. To observe the phenomenon, park along this forest road facing North. The light will appear each evening in the
distance along the power line right-of-way. Remember, other people
will be visiting this location. Please do not litter.

In a place adorned with a long history of suffering (the miners, mostly, and the families of miners, many of whom died in the
mines or in related accidents, or in the Italian Mining Hall disaster
of 1909, and the Ojibwa before them, who suffered in ways all too
familiar to students of American history), the Paulding Light is a
cryptic and appealing experience with a speculative and storied
past. Though there have been several scientific explanations offered for the light, including some sort of power phenomenon
involving the electrical lines, swamp gas, headlights on a highway,
and so on. Though several other television shows and paranormal
investigators and experts have been deployed to investigate the
light, most have concluded that the phenomenon remains unexplained. In 2010 a group of Michigan Tech University optics students claimed (with a good claim to fact) that they had proved
that the light was a result of headlights in the distance. I have my
doubts. It's not just that I love the mystery of it, but that after having experienced the light myself on several occasions, the optics
explanation doesn't fully track. Or perhaps I just resist its attempt
at closure. The roots of a mystery like this run deep.

Was it worth $40 to get the broken microcassette fixed? It turns
out the answer is yes, if only to know. It is always worth $40 to
know. That's what makes me a crap poker player. I want to see
everyone's cards, to see the flop, the turn, the river, to see how it
turns out. And in poker you have to pay to find out. And I almost
always pay to find out. Now you know.

So. I popped it in and gave it a listen. It appeared to be a recording from the judge's microphone in a murder trial set in Upper Michigan. There is no real identifying information beyond the
names of the attorneys (Mr. Biegler and Mr. Dancer; there is also
apparently a Mr. McCarthy who is mentioned) and the fact that
the original judge on the case, a Judge Maitland, was taken ill, and
the new judge was from Lower Michigan. There are references

to this being a sensational trial. Here is an excerpt from my transcription:

> I come here on assignment from Lower Michigan to sit in place of your own Judge Maitland, who is recovering from illness. Now I have no desire to upset the folkways or traditions of this community during murder trials or whatever they may be. I had not realized that there were so many among you who were such zealous students of homicide. In any case I must remind you that this is a court of law and not a football game or a prize fight.

Beyond this there are the judge's exhortations to the attorneys and the gallery to quiet down, to act more civilly; a couple rulings on objections and witness testimony; and a congratulations to the prosecutor on a particularly spectacular prosecution: "This is the first time in my legal career that I have seen a dead man successfully prosecuted for rape." The actual prosecution, the actual witness testimony, the actual objections—in short, any voice aside from the judge's—is not in evidence. There are only short silences during the spaces where other people apparently responded, indicating that this is an edited version with the long silences and other voices removed. I didn't know what to make of it. It felt like there was a decent chance that this was a recording from the courtroom of the murder trial on which I based some of my first book. Strange. *Maybe I'm reading too much into it,* I thought, *making everything about myself.*

A damaged tape. An audio recording of a section of an Upper Michigan murder trial. The trial, the trail—they both appear to end here.

Then there is more: "I suggest that both of you gentlemen invoke a little silence and let the witness answer. In fact I order you to."

"I'm going to take the answer."

"Take the answer."

"Gentlemen, gentlemen. There has been a question and an objection. And I must make a ruling, which I cannot do if you keep up this unholy wrangling. We are skating on thin ice, I realize. But in all conscience, I cannot rule if the question is objectionable. Counsel is not asking for the results of any polygraph test, but the opinion of the witness based upon certain knowledge possessed by him. Take the answer."

You want to give it a listen? The MP3 is on my website at other electricities.com/vp/mix.html.

It's pretty freaky, actually, when you just listen to it, not knowing what it is. Turn the lights out. Look out the window at the canopy of whatever deciduous tree you see and the moon rising spookily through its bare wintry branches. Make sure no one is paying attention to you.

I listened to it over and over, filling the silent hisses with speculation.

So I spent a couple hours trying to look up information on the murder trial of the man who killed my high school acquaintance, just to see if this was it. I found very little. Having taken place before the explosion of the web, there's almost nothing online about it. I wonder whether the trial transcripts are public record, whether they're available for researchers. The court transcriptionist surely did her (I've never seen a male transcriptionist, but they must exist) job for a reason. Surely these transcripts are open at least to lawyers who might want to prepare an appeal or something. I resolved to find out more about this, then promptly forgot about my resolution.

The roots of the tree that should, in nature, grow the sweet oranges that most of us enjoy eating or juicing are susceptible to a bark-destroying virus. The roots of the sour orange tree, however, resist the virus. So in Texas or Florida, for instance, growers graft sweet orange branches—scions—onto the trunks/roots —understock—of sour orange trees for protection. Farther north, orange scions are usually grafted onto rough lemon understock for a similar result. Oranges are now so hybridized that the seeds of a given orange will usually not grow the same kind of orange tree if planted.

For those of us who fetishize the tree as the epitome of *natural*, understanding that the modern citrus is essentially a remix, a cut-and-paste job, comes as a bit of a surprise. There's not a whole lot natural about domesticated anything anymore, which is one reason why "natural" on food packaging doesn't usually denote very much. (Neither the USDA nor the FDA has rules for what "natural" may or may not refer to.) Like most of us who eat, I don't spend much time close up with my food, and certainly not fruit trees, and haven't bothered to investigate the joints where the understock meets the scion.

It is not particularly difficult to make your own fruit-salad tree if you're adept at grafting. Though it does take a lot of care and careful pruning, since fruits mature and fruit at different rates and times, and you risk having one fruit take over your tree or become too heavy, unbalancing your tree and bringing it down.

The term for grafting scions on the understock of a different tree is *topworking*.

Maybe six hours later, after feeling entirely engaged in the mystery, I figured out what might already be obvious to you, what would be obvious to denizens of Upper Michigan (or aficionados of film or murder mysteries) of a certain age—that the microcassette recording is in fact a greatly condensed and edited version of the audio from the 1959 film *Anatomy of a Murder*.

It took me a while to get there. My wife suggested that there's no way anyone was recording the trial from the inside. True, I thought. It's suspiciously articulate, and I didn't hear the accents and Canadianisms, the *ya*s, the trills of *eh*s and dropped prepositions that usually signify the Upper Michigander, or as we call ourselves, the Yooper. And the more I thought of some of the lines, the more they sounded like written dialogue. At that point I had not yet seen the film, though the book on which it is based is set in Upper Michigan and is probably the most famous rendering of my peninsula, if you don't count the crappy Ben Affleck heist movie *Reindeer Games*.

And with that revelation, the door slammed closed, one part of the mystery solved. But then: Why only selections from the replacement judge character's comments?

And why unmarked? Why a microcassette? Why from Nebraska City, Nebraska?

And who sent it?

Where I am from there are a lot of unexplained things: that Paulding Light, the Mining Hall disaster, the strange phenomenon of paradoxical undressing, crimes unsolved, disappearing girls, unresolved deaths. In a relatively remote place like my part of Michigan you learn to live with the fact that not everything is understandable. That's part of the irreducible mystery of the state, itself obscured much of the year by weather of one sort or another.

Much is obscured by trees and snow on trees, falling to cover over our tracks as we set out for a winter ramble among the fallen trees, the rabbit tracks on snow, the marks that suggest the occasional wolf or moose had come through here just before or after us. Some of it is clouded by history or the passing of time; some is erased by willful obfuscation. The speculation we engage in to get at the roots of those stories and selves now lost to history is memory topworking.

My favorite mix tape I ever found, which I no longer own, sadly, because it was lost in a move, was a mix tape created by a guy I don't know for a girl I don't know. It was staged as a radio show, with commercials and bits and jingles that the guy improvised himself, using different voices, between the songs. It was an impressive gesture, clearly scripted and rehearsed, technically very sophisticated. Since I found it at the decrepit St. Vincent de Paul Thrift Store in Grand Rapids, Michigan, it must not have been sufficiently beloved by the recipient. Or possibly the recipient died. Or was killed. Or maybe it was never sent—the gesture discarded in a moment of hesitation and second-guessing, a sweet, powerful regret that most of us know all too well. Or perhaps it was well loved at the time and was only later discarded as she forgot about the he, or didn't care, or maybe got rid of her tape player and either committed it to digital format, or more likely didn't—that's the feeling I got, perhaps because the mix tape seemed a little excessive, by which I mean obsessive, which is the way that all mix tapes are if you're serious about making them. As a social ritual it's still a lovely but strange one, and it's not always welcome, as you find out if you've made enough mix tapes, or if you've misread the social cues preceding the presentation of the mix tape, which you might have done because you were concentrating so hard on the mix tape you were making.

Though I use the terms *mix tape* and *mix CD* interchangeably, I probably shouldn't, since the technologies are so different. The track-by-track skippability that the CD brought us, along with its futuristic laser shimmer and Sharpied CD title, differentiates it from the mix tape, which required much more work to produce: you had to do it manually, cuing and taping each song from the other source, being careful about song times, splicing here and there, adjusting intros and gaps, taping over things so that occasionally you got a little history of your magnetic tape poking through the hiss that signified silence.

Erasing an analog object like a mix tape is never a full erasure.

With the CD, an actual silence—a digital zero—can be achieved. We give up the two-sidedness of the mix tape; we give up the physical act of having to flip the tape and press Play. We give up occasionally having to wind or rewind the tape manually when the tape gets messed up. We forget these things in our desire for the convenient format of the CD, which is, of course, on the wane now too, in favor of the (frankly superior, let's be honest) format of the MP3, where the music has little to any physical presence at all. It's not a shock to see the CD discarded. I've thrown away so many burns I've made because they don't last either, not more than a few years, often even when they've not been scratched up or used accidentally as coasters. Finding someone else's mix CD in the thrift store or on the street, or even receiving one, still gives me a thrill, but it's not quite the same as the weird analog and homemade intimacy of the mix tape with the handwritten track list.

Thus the mix tape is a particular devotion offered not just to the recipient of the mix tape but also to the technology itself, an offering from and to the double tape deck itself, and to posterity. I often made copies of the mix tapes I made for friends because I liked them so much. They're abandoned now, rashly, probably, after I decided that my CDs were the future, which have now been replaced by my return to vinyl and the ethereal format of the MP3. I think of those tapes sometimes, given to the trash for future dumpster divers or anthropologists to sort through. They've been donated too to Salvation Armies, Goodwills, Alabama Thrift Stores, St. Vincent de Pauls, the White Elephant in Green Valley, AZ, Lutheran Thrift, Deseret Industries Thrift, Humane Society Thrift, 22nd Street Thrift Store, Casa de los Niños, Miracle Center Thrift, flea markets, and installed in various libraries around the country. Perhaps one ended up in the Nebraska City, Nebraska, Friends of Faith Thrift Store, on Central Avenue, just across the street from the Otoe County Courthouse, between L. Brown Cabinetry and an Allstate insurance office, where my tape might be speaking to someone else this very moment, perhaps even you, reader.

Making mix CDs, then, is thus a kind of long play for the future, but also a convenient fudge, a topworking of one technology on top of the techniques implied in and learned by dabbling with the other.

One of the reasons I love shopping in thrift stores is the history, the happenstance of it. Many things at thrift stores are messages placed in bottles for whomever to find, whether or not the giver or recipient knows it. Maybe you can call it providence. There are plenty of ecological and economic reasons to shop secondhand also, but I'm in it for the surprise.

What do we leave the world? What marks do we leave in snow among the trees? What magnetic trace do we erase or tape over? Which tapes are spared the magnet or the scissors or the heel of the boot? What books have we written? What websites have we created? Will anyone read the crappy poems we posted on rec .arts.poetry in the early days of the Internet, or will they persist as ghosts, the not-checked-out-for-decades copies of obsolete research on metallurgy I page through in the university engineering library before they're on their way to storage and probable discard or pulp? What music offerings have we left, hopefully, our faces lit with hope, with expectation, for potential lovers or friends, or in some cases perfect strangers? What have we grafted onto what rootstock; what have we planted for some future resident of this space to enjoy? What have we plastered up in the walls of our old houses that we remodeled? What scrawls in wet concrete sidewalks of our old neighborhood? What initials have we paired our own with, cut in hearts on bark of the biggest trees out back of the school? Does our thinking of the future imply that we believe in a future after the world has heated, combusted, blown up, forced our civilization off it? Have we left answers, or will we leave questions?

Coda: Three years later I figure out the second big question, who you are, mix-tape sender, mysterious stranger, crypto–Upper Peninsulan, old friend. Chatting, our housesitter mentions that she was at a writing residency last year in Nebraska City, Nebraska. A small door opens in my brain.

I inquire. It turns out there's an artist/writer residency there, the Kimmel Harding Residency. A residency? In Nebraska City, Nebraska, home of Arbor Day? Yes, a residency. They have a list online of their previous residents along with their dates of residency. I scan the names. It has to be someone there on a residency. That makes so much sense. You do strange things on residencies. Hide things in public spaces. Conduct interventionist art. Post random projects to friends anonymously. When you limit your inputs like you often do at a residency, you start to generate more unusual outputs. *See also* Oulipo. (*See also* the essay "Space" on my website, otherelectricities.com, under *Vanishing Point.*) You want to have a personal conversation with others who have shared the space, or who will occupy the space after you.

I know a lot of the names. I don't know what that says about me. But one in particular catches my eye, and the dates line up, and that last big question of the mystery is solved (a few of the smaller ones continue on, like a grace-note ghost). Of course my friend from Alabama, Alicia, is the culprit. Well played, Alicia.

I'm in Tucson when I figure it out at last, contemplating the sound of wind through the windmill palms that tower with the ocotillo in my front yard. It's a lovely sound, one that you just don't get in the north. I love the sound of wind through pines too, or the rustling of the maples, oaks, and poplars in the fall as they go brilliant and lose their leaves, suggesting the approach of winter. But the palms have a peculiar beauty. They don't need much. You don't want to water your palms, since the roots will rot. They're designed to catch and hold their water in the crown of sharp leaves, where the heart of palm resides, rising with each year's new growth. Trying to transplant a small palm from my backyard to my plant-obsessed friend Jon's makeshift Japanese garden, we had to cut its root ball away from its wide network of roots. In this part of the Sonoran Desert, plants' roots spread wide, not deep, because of the caliche, a superhardened clay that's everywhere a foot or two beneath the surface—so transplanting saguaro cacti, for instance, is nigh impossible.

Pulling it out, we drew blood too, since everything in the desert is sharp, thorned, serrated, spined, resistant to meddling. We left a little of our analog selves in the space left after we got it out. After a year, the palm died in his yard. We're still not sure why. He will presumably pull it up and replace it with something native and gorgeous and complicated, since that's his wont. The memory of those new roots, those old roots, will be gradually erased.

It's bittersweet, I suppose, to close this open door of mystery, but more sweet than sour, as I am the agent of the solution, lucky in my stumble. The world offers so few of these rewards for our attention that we best take them when they're offered, before they disappear back into the trash, the sidewalks filled with other rotting oranges, the thrift store, the lumber pile that might get pulped to paper in Wisconsin, on which we might write or rewrite history, the whiteness of blizzard or memory. I'm going to take the answer.

ANGELA MORALES

The Girls in My Town

FROM *Southwest Review*

1.

Here in the middle of California—in this sun-bleached, hardtack landscape—we have no choice but to search for beauty. The soil, dun-colored and rock-hard, erodes into a soft layer of silt that covers the town every time the wind blows. All across California's farm belt—this land between the Sierras and the Pacific—rows and rows of cotton bolls, apricot and walnut trees, grapevines and tomato plants, roll out for hundreds of miles. But then the rain ceases. Two years pass. Three years. Early morning dew brings the smell of manure that lingers in our neighborhoods, a smell that grows stronger with every passing month. Winter brings no rain but only a thick layer of tule fog that traps us further in a damp white haze. Bitter particles of pesticides hang in the air. We drive on Highway 99 in search of something to look at and find FOR LEASE signs, abandoned western-themed restaurants, and peeling billboards advertising brand-new housing developments that never panned out—a picture of a two-story tract home adorned with a Spanish tile fountain, a father holding a plump toddler, a chemical-green lawn, a happy yellow dog. Between aqueducts and waterways, mazes of irrigation canals and ditches, we try to improve our minds. We enroll in classes at the community college and vow, once and for all, to see it through.

But our library—a big, sad building—houses old, second-rate books, and the librarians seem tired as they thumb through ladies' magazines and gaze wearily over the tops of their reading glasses. This library, unlike some libraries with summer reading programs and cheery children's wings containing beanbags and puzzles, is not a happy place. Here the hours are limited. Erratic. Now think of the brutally hot sun. You worry about dogs not having any shade. That dog chained to some little leafless tree in the back of somebody's junkyard. That dog whose water bowl is covered in green slime and sits about six inches from the end of his leash. You worry about dogs and children. (Cats can generally take care of themselves.)

2.

Francisco, a beautiful boy, sits at the front of the classroom—center stage. When the girls arrive, they circle around him and slip into desks nearest to him, glancing his way and trying not to giggle every time he makes a comment. He leans forward with folded hands, his feet planted solidly on the floor like some goody-goody schoolboy. When he asks a question—usually something ridiculous—the girls turn completely around in their seats to stare at him. I say, "The midterm exam will be next Tuesday at ten—don't be late!" And he raises his hand and asks stupidly, "Uh . . . Miss? Is there a midterm for this class?" Then one of the serious, not-so-beautiful boys murmurs, "*Pendejo!* Open up your ears," and beautiful Francisco will wink at me and yawn. His eyes, translucent and emerald green, make me uneasy. He resembles Johnny Depp but speaks with a slow rising cadence that reminds me of my grandfather—my grandfather who ended up with seven kids and a gambling habit. Francisco tries to flirt with me by calling me *profesora* in that lazy melodic lilt, though around here—at age thirty-two—I am old enough to be his mother. I wonder which girl will get to him first and then whether he'll pay child support or if he'll want to get married *ever,* being so beautiful and all.

3.

Our neighbors across the street whom we call the "Meth Joads" remind us of Steinbeck's Joads because they drive around in a patched-together pickup truck that teeters under the weight of a perpetual mass of junk: wooden pallets, broken bicycles, miscellaneous car parts. Unlike Steinbeck's Joads, however, they are most definitely meth addicts, with the telltale tense jaw, the broken shorn-down teeth, the deep bronchial laugh that inevitably turns into a coughing fit. The Meth Joads have a teenage daughter who sits on the front porch and talks on the cordless phone. One day she's out there talking and I notice that Misty Joad's belly has grown big as a watermelon and is now straining against the seams of her tank top. A few days later, Mr. Meth Joad hauls in a yard-sale crib from his pickup truck. *It's all good,* he says, straining under the weight of the crib, a cigarette between his teeth. The girl, Misty Joad—no more than sixteen and heavily pregnant—paces the sidewalk and talks languidly on that phone like she's waiting for somebody to pick her up and take her somewhere. Every few days a red-faced teenage boy shows up and the two of them drive away in his Mustang. Then the boy stops coming. Eventually Misty Joad walks the sidewalk with her newborn baby. But imagine her power. Even with dirty bare feet and no plans, her body has declared a coup: *If you won't love me, here's a person who will.*

4.

We live down the street from the continuation high school. When we first moved to the neighborhood, Patrick and I referred to it as the "bad-boy school" because that is what my grandpa used to call the school on his street in Boyle Heights. At that bad-boy school in Boyle Heights, enormous pigs lived belly-deep in black muck —muck that emitted an odor so foul that we tied bandannas over our noses and gagged anyway as we rode our bikes past the pigs' enclosures. I'd spy on those bad boys in their rubber boots as they shoveled muck and slops, and I was glad that, being a girl, I would never have to shovel shit or get my ass bit the way that rogue hog had once bitten Grandma's ass (after it had chased her around the neighborhood for a good forty-five minutes). That pig had gone *hog wild.*

The bad-boy school in this town, though, turns out to be a bad-*girl* school, with a special program for pregnant teens. Sometimes

I see those girls exercising on the track—twenty or thirty of them —a whole herd of teenage girls walking around in circles, hands supporting their lower backs, bellies sticking out a mile. Merced gets hotter than hell, so usually the girls pant dramatically and fan themselves, periodically squinting and shielding their eyes from the merciless sky. After their babies are born, most of these girls will come back to school for a few months, and then the majority of them will drop out of school altogether.

I push my own baby in her stroller and observe the girls through the chain-link fence as they complete their one-mile forced march. One starts brushing her hair. The teacher cajoles her and momentarily she quickens her pace, but as soon as the teacher turns around, she slows down again. Looking at them, I try to imagine the moment of love or rage or revenge that brought them here. Most of their babies' fathers will not marry them. Most will continue living in poverty as single mothers. The majority of their children will have learning and behavioral problems. Some of those babies will end up right here back on this very same track.

In the Teen Parent Program, girls are taught life skills, like how to eat healthy foods such as carrot sticks and cottage cheese rather than a *machaca* burrito (two out of three girls are Latinas) and the three-pack of Hostess Ho-Hos. (And who knew that a bacon guacamole Whopper had 1,020 milligrams of sodium and 43 grams of fat?) They watch filmstrips in which fetuses unfurl their tiny limbs; black guppy eyes grow human eyelids; a prehistoric fin separates into ten toes. Later the girls learn about scary conditions like pre-eclampsia and gestational diabetes and suddenly they understand why so-and-so's cousin gave birth to that extraordinary thirteen-pound infant, the one with doughy, waterlogged skin and a protruding tongue.

They learn how to change a diaper and how to hold a baby's head so it won't bob off to one side. They learn about the soft, downy triangle called the fontanel and how their babies' brains, soft as cream cheese, can be felt by gently placing a finger on that eerie soft spot. They learn about shaken baby syndrome and sudden infant death syndrome and then they are given stickers with emergency contact numbers—school counselors, social workers, paramedics. They are told that they will not be alone and that caring for a child requires both strength and humility. *We are your support system,* the girls are told. *We are here for you.*

Across the street from the bad girls' school on the corner of 20th and G Streets, Rollins' Donuts emits the thick, cloying scent of golden doughnuts as they bob around in the fryer. After school the girls disregard what they've learned in health class and line up out the door, shifting their pregnant selves from foot to foot while absent-mindedly massaging the undersides of their bellies, bellies now covered by maternity jeans with spandex tummy panels. Some girls, the rebels, forgo the secondhand maternity clothes altogether (too *old-ladyish!*) and let their bellies hang over the elastic bands of their sweatpants.

Just downwind from Rollins, at the government-approved WIC grocery stores, girls can cash their WIC vouchers for Similac, double-wide boxes of Cheerios, and big hunks of cheese.

In the hospital after my daughter was born, the nurse had brought me yet another stack of forms to fill out. "Here," she'd said, handing me a pen. "You'll definitely want to fill these out." I hoisted the baby onto one shoulder, and just as I had begun to write my name in the first box, I saw that I was about to fill out a Women, Infants, and Children Assistance application.

"Oh, I don't need this," I said. I tried to give back the pen, but she wouldn't take it. "Oh, but you *have* to," she said. "You get free food like bread and milk and formula. Formula's expensive! You'll see! You can get WIC vouchers until the baby is five years old! Imagine five whole years of free food!"

"No, that's okay, really . . ." I said again. She pressed on.

"Why the heck *not?*" she said, leaning close, giving me a conspiratorial look. "Almost everyone gets approved. Well, just think about it."

After she left, I crumpled the forms and shoved them into the trash can. Certainly, I thought, WIC is for *very* poor women — single mothers, teenagers, and migrant farm workers. Being of sound mind and body (or so I tell myself) and having a job, I knew I would not need such assistance, and now I admit to being slightly offended that the nurse had automatically assumed that I needed WIC at all. Based on what? Based on my dark hair and my last name? But in her defense, the odds that a Latina with a newborn baby would need government assistance are, in this town, indeed, very high. Here, population 60,000, one in four women and children is enrolled in WIC. That's a lot of formula. A lot of cheese.

Every day on my street little girls push strollers with real babies in them. The girls walk with their friends—other young girls with *their* babies—sometimes three or four of them at a time. They walk shoulder to shoulder in the middle of the street like they belong to a fertility parade. Sometimes we have to drive around them, swerving gently to the opposite side of the road. "Careful," I'll tell Patrick as he turns the corner. "It's a stroller brigade." It's an evangelist's nightmare (or would that be a dream come true?).

Times have changed since my grandmother and great-grandmother (with sixteen children between them) dodged the shame of being dark and young and pregnant. Without reliable birth control, access to good schools (only the inferior "Indian schools"), and decent jobs with decent wages, what choices did my grandmothers have? Even if girls did not have babies of their own, they often became mothers by default—by tending to younger siblings, nieces, and nephews. Babies were a fact of life. The wealthy had nannies and nursemaids at their disposal. My grandmothers *were* these nannies.

Fast-forward a hundred years and observe the very same girls —now unfettered by husbands and tradition—now walking side by side in the middle of the street, chattering away as they adjust their babies' juice bottles, talk on their cell phones, and halfheartedly dangle little rattles above the strollers. Unlike my grandmothers, the girls in this town have access to birth control pills, integrated schools with specialized programs, and guidance counselors who are supposed to tout the merits of college—even to the brown and black kids. The girls in my town have more choices, though some people might argue that when you're young and poor and your own mother lives on welfare, those choices are hard to find. Love, on the other hand, is easier to find. Love (or the promise of it) is free. Love makes you feel good, especially if you've never had a father, even if only for a few minutes. Love is beautiful: think of walking hand in hand with the green-eyed Francisco at sunset along some fictional beach. And if you end up getting pregnant, *we are here to support you.* And here's a fact about babies: babies now come with many cute accessories—headband bows for little bald heads; Lilliputian T-shirts imprinted with hip slogans like *Ladies' Man* or *Change My Diaper, Biaatch!;* knit caps with built-in Mohawks and bunny ears; pacifiers with vampire fangs painted onto the mouthpiece.

5.

The obstetrics nurse at Mercy Hospital dims the lights and draws the threadbare curtain across the center of the room, a flimsy illusion of privacy between me and my fourteen-year-old roommate. Both our babies had been born around midnight, and now, with babies swaddled and sleeping inside plastic, wheeled bassinets, sleep seems like a superb idea.

Everyone has gone home, and I'm alone for the first time with my newborn daughter. I can't stop staring at her. She'd been the loudest, angriest baby in the nursery, apparently furious at having been exiled from the womb. With our bodies now separate entities, the world, to me, seems upside-down. Sharp-edged. Somewhere a car smashes into a tree. Airborne bacteria and spiky pollens float past. And who is this little human, anyway? What about her life comes predestined? I try to see the tiny, scrolled-up map inside her skull—the grid within her brain, the catalogue of her choices and, ultimately, her destiny and desires: an aversion to crowds, a deep compassion for animals, a love of money, a penchant for mathematics, a blind left eye.

Meanwhile, my roommate and her boyfriend are lying side by side in bed and watching back-to-back episodes of *Cops*. Crack addicts make excuses, a homeless woman sobs over a lost dog, a teenage girl's baby-daddy just put a steak knife to her throat. My roommate's baby-daddy adds his own running commentary: *Damn*, look at that dude! He's so fucked-up. *Hey! Remember when the cops beat the shit out of my uncle?* My roommate murmurs something in reply. And what's going through her head? I try to remember being fourteen. I try to imagine being a mother at age fourteen.

Then my roommate's baby starts crying. The crying gets louder. Pretty soon the baby wails like a peacock. Ay-*ya!* Ay-*ya!* Suddenly the sound of a crying baby makes me feel crazed, like an animal with its paw caught in a trap about to gnaw off its own foot. My head throbs. My spine aches. I wonder if these fourteen-year-old children know what do with an infant. Do *I* know what to do with an infant? How will we keep these babies alive? How will these

children survive the years ahead? *Jesus, where the hell are the nurses?*
I think. I consider saying something, but I'm too exhausted. I've
got seventeen years on her, and compared to her, I'm already an
old lady.

6.

The Lamaze teacher said, "Visualize that your uterus is a beautiful spring bud, slowly unfurling its leaves, blossoming right before
your eyes." This teacher talked so gently about the body and the
birth process—how childbirth happens every single day—how
women's bodies are designed for birth. Her voice, like a drug, hyp-
notized me as I sat cross-legged with the other pregnant women—
some with husbands, some with boyfriends, some with their moms.
We breathed deeply and traced slow circles across our bellies—a
technique that supposedly calms the body, calms the mind.

At the onset of my labor, then, I successfully envisioned a
Georgia O'Keeffe orchid, a soft swirl of violet petals and leaves.
As labor progressed and the pain intensified—surprise, surprise
—my orchid melted away and in its place appeared an engulfing
blackness. Eventually, as the pain intensified into lightning bolts,
a creature took shape—half man, half goat, with horns, red eyes,
and lobster claws, the whole bit; he could have leapt right out of
a Francisco de Goya painting. By the eighth hour, the beast had
burst right through the floor and had me around the waist and
was trying to pull me into the hole that had opened up in the
middle of the floor.

Lying in my hospital bed in the small-town Catholic hospital, I
decided to surrender myself to the image; in other words, I would
not swim against the current and try to turn the demon back into
an orchid. Instead, I would face my nightmare head-on: I would
grab that son of a bitch by the horns and peer directly into his
flaming eyes. *Ha! Two can play at this game,* I thought. Here's what
the Lamaze teachers don't tell you about childbirth—particularly
childbirth without drugs: the goal is not really to stay calm and
focused; the goal is to stay *alive!* Once, when I was eighteen, a
fortuneteller peered at my palm and said, "Mmm . . . lucky you
live in *these* times. One hundred years ago you would have died giv-

ing birth." In this small-town hospital, though, one hundred years does not seem like that long ago.

So with the fortuneteller's words echoing in my head, I told myself to fight like a warrior. Screaming felt good. I screamed until my throat became sandpaper. Suddenly a nurse grabbed me by the wrist and said sternly, "Dear. You are wasting an awful lot of energy on all that screaming. Why don't you get a hold of yourself? Just *calm* down." I jerked my arm away and glared at her. How dare she tell me how to have a baby? How dare she intrude into my hallucination? Anyway, I thought, she had no idea what she was talking about—all those Lamaze lies, all that childbirth propaganda designed to shut us up—to keep the masses *sedated* so that nurses and doctors don't get headaches.

So I decided that with each contraction I would scream every bad word I knew. *Bitch, motherfucker!* I didn't care what anyone said, not Patrick, not my mother, not even the nuns. It felt good to fight, then, to unleash my rebellious tongue.

Later I wondered about my fourteen-year-old roommate, who had been giving birth at the same time. Why had I not heard her voice? Did she not feel such intense pain? Had she been given an epidural? Was *I* too melodramatic—me with my death-defying warrior fantasy? Now I wish I'd talked to her during those two days that we shared a room. We talked a little bit, but she averted her eyes. Painfully shy. Not much of a talker. I wish I'd asked her how she got through it and whether she dreamed up some flower or some other beautiful thing. What thoughts and images travel through the mind of a fourteen-year-old girl as she becomes a mother?

7.

Carl Jung believed that his schizophrenic patients' hallucinations should be treated with the same respect that one might treat any "real" scenario that one can see with one's own eyes. Jung believed that if a person truly believes that he is being chased by wild tigers in a jungle, you should not remind him that he is actually sitting in a comfortable velour armchair and not running for his life through a jungle. Nor should you tell him that the tigers are simply phantoms or figments of his imagination. Instead, you should help him *to survive*. Instead, ask him, "Have you a spear? Have you a rifle?" Urge him to jump into the river or to grab a big stick. In acknowledging the phantom tigers, Jung believed that he could reaffirm and validate the contents of a mind, those contents being significant in their symbolism and necessary to the survival of their host.

8.

Here is a true story that has become part of our local mythology:

Late one night, fifteen-year-old Benita Ramos pounds on the door of a random house. Crying and begging for help, she says that a man has just kidnapped her son—snatched the stroller right out of her hands. When police arrive, Benita explains that she was visiting the baby's father (age seventeen) at his parents' house, and as she was walking home and pushing the baby's stroller down the dark path, a tall, skinny white guy tackled her from behind and then ran off with the stroller, her baby boy still strapped inside.

That night Benita appears on the eleven o'clock news, slurring her words and begging for the safe return of her baby. Her family—aunts, uncles, parents—all stand behind her with grim expressions on their faces. The girl's story sounds plausible because terrible things happen to children in our town. Imagine a place of planetary misalignment, a celestial crisscross of weird energy. Imagine the Bermuda Triangle on dry land. Our town, home to the Pitchfork Killer and the Yosemite Killer, makes us believe that anything is possible.

Later that night, though, police find the empty, overturned stroller on the muddy embankment of the creek. In the flashlight's white beam, they spot what looks like the baby's body floating face-down in the black, stagnant water. (Bear Creek, a tributary of the Merced River, begins high in Yosemite backcountry; up there, it's gorgeous and rugged and the water rushes across car-sized boulders, all framed by Douglas firs, sugar pines, and sequoias. Look up and see an impossibly blue sky with fast-moving wisps of vaporous clouds.) But here, far away from the creek's source, the baby's hooded sweatshirt is caught on some protruding branches next to an overturned shopping cart. (God only knows what else is down there.)

Eventually Benita confesses, though detectives observe that she is not very articulate; moreover, they say, she acts much younger than a girl of fifteen. Later, by piecing together her confession and forensic evidence, they'll determine that Benita tried to drown the baby in the water fountain at Applegate Park. They'll say that she then threw her baby into the creek and faked the kidnapping.

After this happened, we will always think of Benita's dead baby when we go to Applegate Park, which functions as our town center; we go there most Sundays. Fragrant orange and pink rosebushes surround that fountain, and nearby children can visit a half-blind donkey at the petting zoo or an old bear that paces his enclosure for eighteen hours a day. If Benita's baby boy had lived, surely she would have brought him to ride the miniature train that circles the perimeter of the same park in which she killed him.

But Benita won't say more. She appears to be a broken girl. Detectives claim that because she appears to be mentally disturbed and because she functions below the level of an average fifteen-year-old, they might never get inside her head. What's there to say when you have a baby at age fourteen and your seventeen-year-old boyfriend starts dating some other girl, some little slut from another high school, and now your whole life consists of Pampers and plastic baby bottles, milk-encrusted rubber nipples, and maybe once in a while your life gets supplemented by a Jerry Springer episode and an orange Popsicle?

I just went sort of crazy, she might have said. And, *Having a baby is like really, really hard. Nobody understands.* And if you can love babies when there's nobody else to love, sometimes you hurt babies when there's nobody else to hurt. You don't mean to, exactly—you just can't control it. Maybe it's payback for all that's ever been done to you.

9.

Our mothers tell us the story of La Llorona, which means the Wailing Woman. In the story, La Llorona's husband leaves her for another woman. After being rejected and abandoned, La Llorona plots her revenge.

La Llorona decides to take her children on a picnic next to the river. She brings a quilt and a basket filled with strawberries, hard-boiled eggs, heart-shaped cakes, and honey water (because she really loves them). Imagine a spring day resplendent in all ways: the children play in the tall grass, they laugh, they tumble around.

But oh, what bad luck to have been born a child of La Llorona! (How many times, for how many hundreds of years, have these children had to endure the same fate with variations in details?) Soon she lures the children, one by one, through a low tunnel of shrubs to the river—probably across a raccoon or deer trail. The tunnel, enshrouded by eight-foot-tall reeds, leads to a waterside thicket; here frogs lounge on lily pads and dragonflies dive-bomb the water's surface.

Then she drowns her children, one by one, and afterward she arranges their bodies side by side across the family quilt and kisses each of them in the middle of their cold foreheads. Later, when La Llorona's husband finds the children, his screams can be heard for miles. She's dragged away in chains and put into a dungeon, where she wakes up in shock and realizes what she's done.

For all eternity she will cry out for her dead children. After she dies, her ghost will wander the riverbanks in search of new souls. Our mothers tell us that if we look carefully, we can see La Llorona crouching next to the water, furiously rubbing her hands with sand and gravel. They say that if we listen at night, we can hear moaning and rattling chains. If we're not careful, they say, she might mistake us for her dead children.

Our mothers never talk about any moral of the story. They tell it because it's a good story and they can alter the details as they please. But children are presented with the idea of mothers gone crazy, of mothers who use their children for revenge. Many children have nightmares about La Llorona, because all of our basic fears can be traced to our mothers, whether we realize it or not. During the day she combs our hair and kisses us. At night she's the madwoman in the attic. It's this duplicity that scares the hell out of us. All mothers have dual natures, and La Llorona's pale face and leaf-strewn hair reminds us of this. So we dream about children floating beneath gentle currents, their faces obscured by the water, their small, icy hands floating to the surface. The simple lesson: Stay away from water! Don't go out after dark! Be quiet and go to sleep! The deeper message: Do *our* mothers want to kill *us*? Is it not a question of *if*, but a question of *when*? And most importantly: If our fathers abandon our mothers for the "other woman," should we opt out of the picnic next to the river? (We get these thoughts especially when walking next to creeks or canals or irrigation ditches.)

10.

Once a girl brought her infant to the final exam. She arrived late, all sweaty and exasperated, and I don't remember exactly *why* she brought the baby—probably that her mother couldn't babysit, so I said, *Fine, fine, sit down, take the exam, don't want you to fail on account of that,* knowing these girls have enough problems as it is. So I offered to hold the baby throughout the exam; I jostled it about as I walked up and down the aisles patrolling for cheaters. It was weird, because suddenly I became a mother, teacher, grandmother all at once. I lost a little bit of my authority. I became a relative. A regular person.

Midway through the exam, when the baby started to fuss, I poked the baby's mother on the arm and whispered, *Do you have a bottle?* She dug around in her backpack and (thank goodness) found one. I gave the bottle to the baby while students were bent over their exams. The baby sucked down its formula, making that gulping sound that babies make. They study you, their fat little fingers fondling the edges of the bottle, fondling your fingers, reaching for your nose, their bare toes. This one never took his eyes off me. Once he snapped the rubber nipple with his four teeth and then laughed loudly. The class heard this and then laughed too. The baby wanted us to love him, maybe to improve his chances of survival.

How quickly the border between classroom and home, personal and professional can dissolve! But it felt good to hold a baby in a classroom. I could breathe for a minute. A baby provides comic relief. A baby is funny and random and unscripted. But I could not fully enjoy the moment, because the whole time I was wrestling with ideas like *Is this really a good message to be sending to students? Shouldn't I send her away, saying "No children allowed," because those are the rules? Will this baby distract the other students?* How much do you bend the rules for these girls with their babies, these girls with the odds stacked so high against them?

11.

My teenage students have babies right in the middle of a semester. The San Joaquin Valley has the highest teen pregnancy rate of any region in the United States. My students call me up and say, "Miss, I just wanted to remind you that my baby is due in a couple days . . . so if you don't see me in class . . . that's why." They disappear for a couple days and then reappear, their eyes slightly glazed. *Back already?* I say, because after my baby was born, I'd staggered around for two weeks feeling like I'd just completed the Bataan Death March. But for most teenagers, the body heals itself and springs back into shape almost immediately; life goes on. Evolutionarily speaking, a quick recovery makes sense. Biologically, humans can give birth at a relatively young age; consider that, on average, girls begin to menstruate at age twelve—sometimes as young as age eight. But to what advantage? Do species evolve to produce as many offspring as possible, even at the risk of mothers being socially and mentally immature? Is it better to throw our DNA into the mix as often as possible to improve the odds that at least some of our genetic material will survive? Consider, though, life within a tribe—all those hands, the elders to keep watch, to give advice, to admonish. Perhaps for some humans, the young-mother model works just fine. But without the tribe, without rules, who will watch over the girls in my town—these girls who often need mothering themselves—these girls with their babies in their low-rent apartments with boyfriends who sometimes marry them, most often do not?

After class one girl says proudly, "Look, Miss. I can already button my old jeans!" She holds up her blouse to reveal her small, swollen belly. Any evidence of her pregnancy has all but disappeared. Who would know that an eight-pound baby had recently been expelled from that same body?

At times I'm baffled by the lack of impact motherhood seems to have upon many of my students. Many girls don't appear to be visibly moved by the event of childbirth. Or at least they don't know how to express their feelings about it. Afterward they return to class; I search, but cannot discern any real change in their eyes. *So? Well?* I say. *How did it go?* The girls often shrug. "He weighed nine pounds," they might say, or, "He's already sleeping through the night, Miss." They'll tell me details that they've heard other mothers say, common quips that you hear on TV or in doctors' waiting rooms—bland, unrevealing details that seem scripted. Many of these same girls want to write essays about the births of their babies, but they almost always lack the language to express anything more than a basic plot outline. Example:

> My water bag broke right in the middle of the grocery store. It felt so weird. My mom drove me to the hospital. They put me in bed and got me all hooked up to the machines and then the pain got really bad. It went on for hours. They ended up doing a C-section, thank god. The labor lasted over twenty hours but then the baby was born healthy and now I am so happy. I love my baby so much!

In the margins of their papers, I'll press for specific details and analysis: *Describe the pain! Describe the baby! Do you feel any different? What obstacles do you face now?*

12.

My cousin X. and I practically grew up together. Sometimes she'd stay at our house for seven, eight, nine days, and then I'd stop talking to her. I'd give her the cold shoulder. I just wouldn't talk anymore. She'd say, "Are you mad at me?" I'd shrug. "Are you sick of me?" she'd say. "A little," I'd say. I didn't know how to articulate that I needed my bedroom back. I needed to close the door and read and think. I was that kind of kid. I needed solitude to feel normal. Sometimes I would just lock my door and stay in there the whole day. I'd stare at the ceiling. I remember saying, "I just need to think," not really knowing what I needed to think about. Then she'd say, "Okay, I'd better go home then. I guess I'll call my mom." I loved X. the way only cousins can love other cousins, kids who are thrown together in this world by way of shared mothers, mothers who sometimes turn parenting into an informal commune, the philosophy being *You take them today, I'll take them tomorrow,* the mission statement being *Together we will keep these children alive.* X.'s mother had gotten pregnant when she was eighteen. The guy ended up marrying her and then a couple years later he dumped two-year-old X. and my aunt onto Grandma's front lawn. He tossed their clothes out of the car and all over the grass. Then he drove away. End of story.

So we understood why X. got pregnant at age eighteen. She

started looking for love in all the wrong places—love with surfer guys with names like Travis and Dave. One day she got herself knocked up and her stepfather kicked her out of the house and she moved in with us. "I just can't have an abortion again," she told me. "I won't do it." The born-again Christians had gotten ahold of her, pressing antiabortion pamphlets into her hands, pamphlets that contained gruesome pictures of dead fetuses, their tiny hands awash in fresh blood. She'd convinced herself that her dead baby was waiting for her in heaven and for the time being the baby was being cared for by angels, who had it gently by the hand, and that one day it would be reunited with its mommy-on-earth, but only if mommy-on-earth was willing to call herself a sinner and change her wanton ways. "I'm having this baby," she said defiantly. It was a common trope back then.

But babies get annoying real fast. They get bigger and then they squirm away from you and then they call you names like *butthead* and they take off their shoes and hurl them at you and as soon as you get the shoes laced up again, they pry them off and toss them behind the dresser, and inevitably you lose that shoe and now you've got four mismatched shoes without mates. Toddlers can be hard to take, especially when they start saying NO all the time and that's the only word they know. They poke you in the eyes when you're sleeping and you're dead tired and they always have runny noses and the snot runs into their mouths and they lick at it with the edges of their tongues or smear it onto damp encrusted sleeves. They jump on you when you don't expect it, knees and elbows jamming into your ribs, into your chest, into your cheek-bones, and the more you try to wrench them off, the more they want to jump on you again; sometimes you want to shove them off and maybe pinch their little arms or yank a clump of hair or leave them in the crib even if they're crying and calling you so piti-fully, and you know this borders on child abuse, but it's really hard when there's no father and you are *it*—the kid's sun and moon.

13.

My daughter and my fourteen-year-old roommate's daughter—born on the same night, the same hour—are now thirteen years old. When I look at my own daughter I cannot believe that a girl of roughly her age and temperament could be a mother. She slams doors. She stomps around. She throws up her hands and says, "Are you *kidding* me?" She sketches pictures of horses and then crumples them up. She announces, "I'll take animals over people *any* day" (and she means it). And although her fingers are now longer than mine—her hands more graceful—I cannot, no matter how hard I try, imagine those hands changing a diaper.

Would our daughters have anything in common? My roommate's daughter, according to county statistics (based on her mother's age and ethnicity), will very likely have a baby before she turns eighteen. Then the girl will most likely drop out of school and struggle to care for her child in this place of leached soil turned to clay. My roommate's daughter may never know about the migratory waterfowl such as Canadian geese and whistling swans that once stopped off in our valley marshlands—most of which have been drained to rechannel water for irrigation. And maybe the babies, in some weird way, reflect our need to find beauty once again in this landscape. In any case, I suspect our connection to the land runs deeper than we know.

As for our daughters, the fortuneteller might peer into her crystal ball or examine our girls' palms and see a whole web of alternate realities. *Anything can happen,* she might say. For all of us, the road is wide open.

ZADIE SMITH

Some Notes on Attunement

FROM *The New Yorker*

THE FIRST TIME I heard her I didn't hear her at all. My parents did not prepare me. (The natural thing in these situations is to blame the parents.) She was nowhere to be found on their four-foot-tall wood-veneer hi-fi. Given the variety of voices you got to hear on that contraption, her absence was a little strange. Burning Spear and the Beatles; Marley, naturally, and Chaka Khan; Bix Beiderbecke, Louis Armstrong, Duke Ellington, and James Taylor; Luther Vandross, Anita Baker, Alexander O'Neal. And Dylan, always Dylan. Yet nothing of the Canadian with the open-tuned guitar. I don't see how she could have been unknown to them—it was her peculiar curse to never really be unknown. Though maybe they had heard her and simply misunderstood.

My parents loved music, as I love music, but you couldn't call any of us whatever the plural of *muso* is. The Smiths owned no rare tracks, no fascinating B-sides (and no records by the Smiths). We wanted songs that made us dance, laugh, or cry. The only thing that was in any way unusual about the collection was the manner in which it combined, in one crate, the taste of a young black woman and an old white man. It had at least that much eclecticism to it. However, we did not tend to listen to white women singing very often. Those particular voices were surplus to requirements, somehow, having no natural demographic within the household. A singer like Elkie Brooks (really Elaine Bookbinder—a Jewish girl, from Salford) was the closest we got, though Elkie had that telltale rasp in her throat, linking her, in the Smith mind, to Tina Turner or Della Reese. We had no Kate Bush records, or even the slightest hint of Stevie Nicks, raspy though she may be. The first time I was aware of Debbie Harry's existence, I was in college. We had Joan Armatrading and Aretha and Billie and Ella. What did we need with white women?

It was the kind of college gathering where I kept sneaking Blackstreet and Aaliyah albums into the CD drawer, and friends kept replacing them with other things. And then there she was, suddenly: a piercing sound, a sort of wailing—a white woman, wailing, picking out notes in a nonsequence. Out of tune—or out of anything I understood at the time as *tune*. I picked up the CD cover and frowned at it: a skinny blonde with heavy bangs, covered in blue. My good friend Tamara—a real singer, serious about music —looked over at me, confused. *You don't like Joni?* I turned the CD over disdainfully, squinted at the track list. *Oh, was that Joni?* And very likely went on to say something facetious about white-girl music, the kind of comment I had heard, inverted, when I found myself called upon to defend black men swearing into a microphone. Another friend, Jessica, pressed me again: *You don't like Joni?* She closed her eyes and sang a few lines of what I now know to be "California." That is, she sang pleasing, not uninteresting words, but in a strange, strangulated falsetto—a kind of Kafkaesque "piping"—which I considered odd, coming out of Jess, whom I knew to have, ordinarily, a beautiful, black voice. A soul voice. You don't like Joni?

Perhaps this is only a story about philistinism. A quality always easier to note in other people than to detect in yourself. Aged twenty, I listened to Joni Mitchell—a singer whom millions enjoy, who does not, after all, make an especially unusual or esoteric sound—and found her incomprehensible. Could not even really recognize her piping as "singing." It was just noise. And, without troubling over it much, I placed her piping alongside all the interesting noises we hear in the world but choose, through habit or policy, to separate from music. What can you call that but philistinism? *You don't like Joni?* My friends had pity in their eyes. The same look the faithful tend to give you as you hand them back their "literature" and close the door in their faces.

In the passenger seat of a car, on the way to a wedding. I no longer had the excuse of youth: I was now the same age as Christ when

he died. I was being driven west, toward Wales. Passing through
woods and copses, a wild green landscape, heading for the steep
and lofty cliffs . . . It is a very long drive to Wales. The driver, being
a poet, planned a pit stop at Tintern Abbey. His passenger, more
interested in finding a motorway service station, spoke frequently
of her desire for a sausage roll. The mood in the car was not the
brightest. And something else had been bothering me for several
miles without my being quite conscious of its source, some persis-
tent noise . . . But now I focused in on it and realized it was that
bloody piping again, ranging over octaves, ignoring the natural di-
visions between musical bars, and generally annoying the hell out
of me, like a bee caught in a wing mirror. I made a plea for change
to the driver, who gave me a look related to the one my friends
had given me all those years earlier, though this was a stronger
varietal, the driver and I being bonded to each other for life by
legal contract.

"It's *Joni Mitchell*. What is *wrong* with you? Listen to it—it's beautiful! Can't you hear that?"

I started stabbing at the dashboard, trying to find the button
that makes things stop.

"No, I can't hear it. It's horrible. And that bit's just 'Jingle
Bells.'"

I hadn't expected to get anywhere with this line and was surprised to see my husband smile and pause for a moment to listen
intently: "Actually, that bit *is* 'Jingle Bells'—I never noticed that
before. It's a song about winter . . . makes sense."

"Switch it off—I'm begging you."

"Tintern Abbey, next exit," he said, closed his jaw tightly, and
veered to the left.

We parked; I opened a car door onto the vast silence of a valley. I may not have had ears, but I had eyes. I wandered inside,
which is outside, which is inside. I stood at the east window, feet
on the green grass, eyes to the green hills, not contained by a non-
building that has lost all its carved defenses. Reduced to a Gothic
skeleton, the abbey is penetrated by beauty from above and below,
open to precisely those elements it had once hoped to frame for
pious young men, as an object for their patient contemplation. But
that form of holy concentration has now been gone longer than
it was ever here. It was already an ancient memory two hundred

years ago, when Wordsworth came by. Thistles sprout between the stones. The rain comes in. Roofless, floorless, glassless, "green to the very door"—now Tintern is forced to accept the holiness that is everywhere in everything.

And then what? As I remember it, sun flooded the area; my husband quoted a line from one of the Lucy poems; I began humming a strange piece of music. Something had happened to me. In all the mess of memories we make each day and lose, I knew that this one would not be lost. I had Wordsworth's sensation exactly: "That in this moment there is life and food / For future years." Or thought I had it. Digging up the poem now, I see that I am, in some ways, telling the opposite story. What struck the author of "Lines Written a Few Miles Above Tintern Abbey" (1798) was a memory of ecstasy: "That time is past, / And all its aching joys are now no more, / And all its dizzy raptures." The Wye had made a deep impression on him when he'd visited five years earlier. Returning, he finds that he still loves the area, but the poem attests to his development, for now he loves it with a mellowed maturity. Gone is the wild adoration: "For nature then / (The coarser pleasures of my boyish days, / And their glad animal movements all gone by,) / To me was all in all.—I cannot paint / What then I was." To be back in Wales was to meet an earlier version of himself; he went there to listen to "the language of my former heart." And though it's true that the young man he recalls is in some senses a stranger, the claim that he "cannot paint" him is really a humble brag, because, of course, the poem does exactly that. It's striking to me that this past self should at all times be loved and appreciated by Wordsworth. He understands that the callow youth was the basis of the greater man he would become. A natural progression: between the boy Wordsworth and the man, between then and now. His mind is not so much changed as deepened.

But when I think of that Joni Mitchell–hating pilgrim, standing at the east window, idly wondering whether she could persuade her beloved to stop for some kind of microwaved service-station snack somewhere between here and the church (British weddings being notorious in their late delivery of lunch), I truly cannot understand the language of my former heart. Who *was* that person? Petulant, hardly aware that she was humming Joni, not yet conscious of the transformation she had already undergone. How is it possible to hate something so completely and then suddenly love it so unreasonably? How does such a change occur?

Sidebar: In 1967, another poet, Allen Ginsberg, stopped at Tintern Abbey. He had gone to Wales with his British publisher, Tom Maschler, to stay in Maschler's cottage and take acid in the Black Mountains. Those were the glory days of British publishing. Ginsberg wrote a poem about the trip, "Wales Visitation." The ground he stood on was "brown vagina-moist," and the thistles he saw had a "satanic . . . horned symmetry." In other words, he had a typical Ginsberg epiphany. I like the poem best, though, not when he's describing the things he sees but when he's examining the manner of the seeing; that is, the structural difference between how he normally sees and how he saw that day, attuned, on acid— *What did I notice? Particulars!*

This is the effect that listening to Joni Mitchell has on me these days: uncontrollable tears. An emotional overcoming, disconcertingly distant from happiness, more like joy—if joy is the recognition of an almost intolerable beauty. It's not a very civilized emotion. I can't listen to Joni Mitchell in a room with other people, or on an iPod, walking the streets. Too risky. I can never guarantee that I'm going to be able to get through the song without being made transparent—to anybody and everything, to the whole world. A mortifying sense of porousness. Although it's comforting to learn that the feeling I have listening to these songs is the same feeling the artist had while creating them: "At that period of my life, I had no personal defenses. I felt like a cellophane wrapper on a pack of cigarettes." That's Mitchell, speaking of the fruitful years between Ginsberg at the abbey and 1971, when her classic album *Blue* was released.

I should confess at this point that when I'm thinking of Joni Mitchell, it's *Blue* I'm thinking of, really. I can't even claim to be writing about that superior type of muso epiphany which would at least have the good taste to settle upon one of the "minor" albums that Joni herself seems to prefer: *Hejira* or *The Hissing of Summer Lawns.* No, I'm thinking of the album pretty much every fool owns, no matter how far from music his life has taken him. And it's not even really the content of the music that interests me here. It's the transformation of the listening. I don't want to confuse this phenomenon with a progressive change in taste. The sensation of progressive change is different in kind: it usually follows a conscious act of will. Like most people, I experience these progressive changes fairly regularly. By forcing myself to reread *Crime and Punishment,* for example, I now admire and appreciate Dostoyevsky, a writer whom, well into my late twenties, I was certain I disliked. During an exploratory season of science fiction, I checked Aldous Huxley out of the library, despite his hideous racial theories. And even a writer as alien to my natural sensibility as Anaïs Nin wormed her way into my sympathies last summer, during a concerted effort to read writers who've made sex their primary concern.

I don't think it's a coincidence that most of my progressive changes in taste tend to have occurred in my sole area of expertise: reading novels. In this one, extremely narrow arena I can call myself more or less a "connoisseur." Meaning that I can stoop to consider even the supposed lowliest examples of the form while simultaneously rising to admire the obscure and the esoteric—and all without feeling any great change in myself. Novels are what I know, and the novel door in my personality is always wide open. But I didn't come to love Joni Mitchell by knowing anything more about her, or understanding what an open-tuned guitar is, or even by sitting down and forcing myself to listen and relisten to her songs. I hated Joni Mitchell—and then I loved her. Her voice did nothing for me—until the day it undid me completely. And I wonder whether it is because I am such a perfect fool about music that the paradigm shift in my ability to listen to Joni Mitchell became possible. Maybe a certain kind of ignorance was the condition. Into the pure nothingness of my nonknowledge something sublime (an event?) beyond (beneath?) consciousness was able to occur.

I just called myself a connoisseur of novels, which stretches the definition a little: "An expert judge in matters of taste." I have a deep interest in my two inches of ivory, but it's a rare connoisseur who does not seek to be an expert judge of more than one form. By their good taste are they known, and connoisseurs tend to like a wide area in which to exercise it. I have known many true connoisseurs, with excellent tastes that range across the humanities and the culinary arts—and they never fail to have a fatal effect on my self-esteem. When I find myself sitting at dinner next to someone who knows just as much about novels as I do but has somehow also found the mental space to adore and be knowledgeable about the opera, have strong opinions about the relative rankings of Renaissance painters, an encyclopedic knowledge of the English civil war, of French wines—I feel an anxiety that nudges beyond the envious into the existential. *How did she find the time?*

"On the Shortness of Life," a screed by Seneca, is smart about this tension between taste and time (although Seneca sympathizes with my dinner companion, not with me). The essay takes the form of a letter of advice to his friend Paulinus, who must have made the mistake of complaining, within earshot of Seneca, about the briefness of his days. In this lengthy riposte, the philosopher informs Paulinus that "learning how to live takes a whole life," and the sense most of us have that our lives are cruelly brief is a specious one: "It is not that we have a short time to live, but that we waste a lot of it." Heedless luxury, socializing, worldly advancement, fighting, whoring, drinking, and so on. If you want a life that feels long, he advises, fill it with philosophy. That way, not only do you "keep a good watch" over your own lifetime but you "annex every age" to your own: "By the toil of others we are let into the presence of things which have been brought from darkness into light." So make friends with the "high priests of liberal studies," no matter how distant they are from you. Zeno, Pythagoras, Democritus, Aristotle, Theophrastus: "None of these will be too busy to see you, none of these will not send his visitor away happier and more devoted to himself, none of these will allow anyone to depart empty-handed. They are at home to all mortals by night and by day."

Well, sure—but you have also to be open to them. Because you needn't have had even a whiff of whoring in your life to legitimately find yourself too busy to visit Aristotle. Busy changing diapers. Busy cleaning the sink or going to work. And since, in the contemporary world, we have to place in "liberal studies" not only a handful of canonical philosophers but also two thousand years of culture—plus a bunch of new forms not dreamed of in Seneca's philosophy (Polish cinema, hip-hop, conceptual art)—you can understand why many people feel rather pushed for time. It's tempting to give up on our liberal studies before even making the attempt, the better to continue on our merry way, fighting, drinking, and all the rest. At least then we have the satisfaction of a little short-term pleasure instead of a lifetime of feeling inadequate.

Still, I admire Seneca's idealism, and believe in his central argument, even if I have applied it haphazardly in my own life: "We are in the habit of saying that it was not in our power to choose the parents who were allotted to us, that they were given to us by chance. But we can choose whose children we would like to be." Early on, for better or worse, I chose whose child I wanted to be: the child of the novel. Almost everything else was subjugated to this ruling passion, reading stories. As a consequence, I can barely add a column of double digits, I have not the slightest idea of how a plane flies, I can't draw any better than a five-year-old. One of the motivations for writing novels myself is the small window of opportunity it affords for a bit of extracurricular study. I learned a little about genetics writing my first novel, and went quite far with Rembrandt during my third. But these are only little pockets of knowledge, here and there. I think Seneca is right: life feels longer the more you engage with it. (Look how short life felt to the poet Larkin. Look how little he did with it.) I should be loving sculpture! But I have not gone deeply into sculpture. Instead, having been utterly insensitive to sculpture, I fill the time that might have been usefully devoted to sculpture with things like drinking and staring into space.

Nowhere do I have this sensation of loss as acutely as with music. I had it recently while being guided round an underground record shop, in Vancouver, by a young man from my Canadian publisher who wanted to show me this fine example of the local cultural scene (and also to buy tickets for a heavy-metal concert he planned to attend with his wife). I wandered through that shop, as I always do in record shops, depressed by my ignorance and drawn toward the familiar. After fifteen shiftless minutes, I picked up a hip-hop magazine and considered a Billie Holiday album that could not possibly contain any track I did not already own. I was preparing to leave when I spotted an album with a wonderful title: *More Songs About Buildings and Food.* You will probably already know who it was by—I didn't. Talking Heads. As I stopped to admire it, I was gripped by melancholy, similar perhaps to the feeling a certain kind of man gets while sitting with his wife on a train platform as a beautiful girl—different in all aspects from his wife—walks by. *There goes my other life.* Is it too late to get into Talking Heads? Do

I have the time? What kind of person would I be if I knew this album at all, or well? If I'd been shaped not by Al Green and Stevie Wonder but by David Byrne and Kraftwerk? What if I'd been the type of person who had somehow found the time to love and know everything about Al Green, Stevie Wonder, David Byrne, and Kraftwerk? What a delight it would be to have so many "parents"! How long and fruitful life would seem!

I will admit that in the past, when I have met connoisseurs, I've found it a bit hard to entirely believe in them. Philistinism often comes with a side order of distrust. How can this person possibly love as many things as she appears to love? Sometimes, in a sour spirit, I am tempted to feel that my connoisseur friends have the time for all this liberal study because they have no children. But that is the easy way out. True connoisseurs were like that back when we were all twenty years old; I was always narrower and more resistant. For some people, the door is wide open, and pretty much everything—on the condition that it's *good*—gets a hearing. And I am indebted to my friends of this kind who have, after all, managed to effect some difficult and arduous changes in my taste. I'm grateful for the reeducation, while still fearing that my life will never be long enough to give serious consideration to all the different kinds of wine that can be squeezed out of different kinds of grapes.

With Joni, it was all so easy. In a sense, it took no time. Instantaneous. Involving no progressive change but, instead, a leap of faith. A sudden, unexpected attunement. Or a retuning from nothing, or from a negative, into something soaring and positive and sublime. It will perhaps insult sincerely religious people that I should compare something rare and precious, the "leap of faith," to something as banal as realizing that *Blue*, by Joni Mitchell, is a great album, but to a person like me, who has never known God (who has only read and written a lot of words about other people who have known God), the structure of the sensation, if not the content, seems to be unavoidably related. I am thinking particularly of Kierkegaard's *Fear and Trembling,* and even more particularly of the "Exordium" ("Attunement") that opens that strange book, and which many people (including me) usually skip, in confusion, to get to the meat of the "Problemata." The "Exordium" is like a weird little novel. In it, Kierkegaard summons up a character: a simple, faithful man, "not a thinker . . . not an exegetical scholar," who is obsessed with the biblical tale of Abraham and Isaac but finds that he cannot understand it. So he tells it to himself four times, in different versions, as if it were an oral fairy tale that mutates slightly with each retelling.

The basic details stay the same. (In all versions, the ram, and not Isaac, gets killed.) The variation exists in the reactions of Abraham and Isaac. In the first iteration, Abraham, in order to preserve his son's faith in God, pretends that he, Abraham, hates Isaac and wants him killed. In the second, everything goes according to plan except that Abraham can't forgive or forget what God just asked him to do, and so all joy leaks from his life. In the third, Abraham can't believe how he can possibly be forgiven for something that was so clearly a sin. In the final version, it's Isaac who loses his faith: How could his father have considered the terrible crime, even for a moment? Following each of these retellings, there is a small paragraph of analogy to a quite different situation, that of a mother weaning her child:

> When the child is to be weaned, the mother blackens her breast. It would be hard to have the breast look inviting when the child must not have it. So the child believes that the breast has changed, but the mother—she is still the same, her gaze is tender and loving as ever. How fortunate the one who did not need more terrible means to wean the child!

That's the version following the first story, the one in which Abraham tries to take the rap for the Lord. In these peculiar breast-feeding anecdotes it is not always obvious where the analogy lies. Professional philosophers spend much time arguing over the precise symbolic links. Is God the mother? Is Isaac the baby? Or is Abraham the mother, Isaac the baby, and God the breast? I really haven't the slightest idea. But in each version a form of defense is surely offered, some kind of explanation, a means of comprehending. *It's not that my mother is refusing me milk; it's that I don't want it anymore, because her breast is black. It's not that God is asking something inexplicable; it's that my father wants me dead.* All the versions the simple man tells himself are horrible in some way, but they are at least comprehensible, which is more than you can say for the paradoxical truth: God told me I would be fruitful through my son, and yet God is telling me to kill my son. (Or: my mother loves me and wants to give me milk, yet my mother is refusing to give me milk.) And after rehearsing these various rationalizations the simple man still finds himself confounded by the original biblical story: "He sank down wearily, folded his hands, and said, 'No one was as great as Abraham. Who is able to understand him?'"

When I read the "Exordium," I feel that Kierkegaard is trying to get me into a state of readiness for a consideration of the actual biblical story of Abraham and Isaac, which is essentially inexplicable. The "Exordium" is a rehearsal: it lays out a series of rational explanations the better to demonstrate their poverty as explanations. For nothing can prepare us for Abraham and no one can understand him—at least, not rationally. Faith involves an acceptance of absurdity. To get us to that point, Kierkegaard hopes to "attune" us, systematically discarding all the usual defenses we put up in the face of the absurd.

Of course, loving Joni Mitchell does not require an acceptance of absurdity. I'm speaking of the minor category of the aesthetic, not the monument of the religious. But if you want to effect a breach in that stolid edifice the human personality, I think it helps to cultivate this Kierkegaardian sense of defenselessness. Kierkegaard's simple man makes a simple mistake: he wants to translate the mystery of the biblical story into terms that he can comprehend. His failure has something to teach us. Sometimes it is when we stop trying to understand or interrogate apparently "absurd" phenomena—like the category of the "new" in art—that we become more open to them.

Put simply: you need to lower your defenses. (I don't think it is a coincidence that my Joni epiphany came through the back door, while my critical mind lay undefended, focused on a quite other form of beauty.) Shaped by the songs of my childhood, I find it hard to accept the musical "new," or even the "new-to-me." If the same problem does not arise with literature, that's because I do not try to defend myself against novels. They can be written backward or without any *e* or in one long column of text—novels are always welcome. What created this easy transit in the first place is a mystery; I feel I listened to as many songs in childhood as I read stories, but in music I seem to have formed rigid ideas and created defenses around them, whereas when it came to words I never did. This is probably what is meant by that mysterious word *sensibility,* the existence of which so often feels innate. I feel sure that had I, in 1907, popped in on Joyce in his garret, I would have picked up his notes for *Ulysses* and been excited by what he was cooking up. Yet if, in the same year, I had paid a call on Picasso in his studio, I would have looked at the canvas of *Les Demoiselles d'Avignon* and been nonplussed, maybe even a little scandalized. If, in my real life of 2012, I stand before this painting in the Museum of Modern Art, in New York, it seems obviously beautiful to me. All the difficult work of attunement and acceptance has already been done by others. Smart critics, other painters, appreciative amateurs. They kicked the door open almost a century ago—all I need do is walk through it.

Who could have understood Abraham? He is discontinuous with himself. The girl who hated Joni and the woman who loves her seem to me similarly divorced from each other, two people who happen to have shared the same body. It's the feeling we get sometimes when we find a diary we wrote, as teenagers, or sit at dinner listening to an old friend tell some story about us of which we have no memory. It's an everyday sensation for most of us, yet it proves a tricky sort of problem for those people who hope to make art. For though we know and recognize discontinuity in our own lives, when it comes to art we are deeply committed to the idea of continuity. I find myself to be radically discontinuous with myself —but how does one re-create this principle in fiction? What is a character if not a continuous, consistent personality? If you put Abraham in a novel, a lot of people would throw that novel across the room. What's his motivation? How can he love his son and yet be prepared to kill him? Abraham is offensive to us. It is by reading and watching consistent people on the page, stage, and screen that we are reassured of our own consistency.

This instinct in audiences can sometimes extend to whole artistic careers. I'd like to believe that I wouldn't have been one of those infamous British people who tried to boo Dylan offstage when he went electric, but on the evidence of past form I very much fear I would have. We want our artists to remain as they were when we first loved them. But our artists want to move. Sometimes the battle becomes so violent that a perversion in the artist can occur: these days, Joni Mitchell thinks of herself more as a painter than a singer. She is so allergic to the expectations of her audience that she would rather be a perfectly nice painter than a singer touched by the sublime. That kind of anxiety about audience is often read as contempt, but Mitchell's restlessness is only the natural side effect of her artmaking, as it is with Dylan, as it was with Joyce and Picasso. Joni Mitchell doesn't want to live in my dream, stuck as it is in an eternal 1971 — her life has its own time. There is simply not enough time in her life for her to be the Joni of my memory forever. The worst possible thing for an artist is to exist as a feature of somebody else's epiphany.

Finally, those songs, those exquisite songs! When I listen to them, I know I am in the debt of beauty, and when that happens I feel an obligation to repay that debt. With Joni, an obvious route reveals itself. Turns out that while she has been leading me away from my musical home she has been going on her own journey, deep into the place where I'm from:

> For 25 years, the public voice, in particular the white press, lamented the lack of four-on-the-floor and major/minor harmony as my work got more progressive and absorbed more black culture, which is inevitable because I love black music, Duke Ellington, Miles Davis. Not that I set out to be a jazzer or that I am a jazzer. Most of my friends are in the jazz camp. I know more people in that community, and I know the lyrics to Forties and Fifties standards, whereas I don't really know Sixties and Seventies pop music. So I'm drawing from a resource of American music that's very black-influenced with this little pocket of Irish and English ballads, which I learned as I was learning to play the guitar. Basically, it was like trainer wheels for me, that music. But people want to keep me in my trainer wheels, whereas my passion lies in Duke Ellington, more so than Gershwin, the originators, Charlie Parker. I like Patsy Cline. The originals in every camp were always given a hard time.

I wonder what it will be like to hear the music of my childhood processed through Joni Mitchell's sensibility? I didn't know anything about her "black period" until I started to write this piece and read some of her interviews online, among them a long discussion she had with a Texas DJ in 1998. Now I mean to seek out this later music and spend some time with it. Make the effort. I don't imagine it *will* be such an effort these days, not now that I feel this deep current running between us. I think it must have always been there. All Joni and I needed was a little attunement. Those wandering notes and bar crossings, the key changes that she now finds dull and I still hear as miraculous. Her music, her life, has always been about discontinuity. The inconsistency of identity, of personality. I should have had faith. We were always going to find each other:

> I'm contracted for an autobiography. But you can't get my life to go into one book. So I want to start, actually, kind of in the middle —the Don Juan's Reckless Daughter period, which is a very mystical period of my life and colorful. Not mystical on bended knee. If I was a novelist, I would like that to be my first novel. And it begins with the line "I was the only black man at the party." (Laughs) So I've got my opening line.

BRIAN DOYLE

His Last Game

FROM *Notre Dame Magazine*

WE WERE SUPPOSED to be driving to the pharmacy for his prescriptions, but he said just drive around for a while, my prescriptions aren't going anywhere without me, so we just drove around.
We drove around the edges of the college where he had worked
and we saw a blue heron in a field of stubble, which is not something you see every day, and we stopped for a while to see if the
heron was fishing for mice or snakes, on which we bet a dollar, me
taking mice and him taking snakes, but the heron glared at us and
refused to work under scrutiny, so we drove on.

We drove through the arboretum, checking on the groves of
ash and oak and willow trees, which were still where they were last
time we looked, and then we checked on the wood-duck boxes
in the pond, which still seemed sturdy and did not feature raven-
ous weasels that we noticed, and then we saw a kestrel hanging
in the crisp air like a tiny helicopter, but as soon as we bet mouse
or snake the kestrel vanished, probably for religious reasons, said
my brother, probably a *lot* of kestrels are adamant that gambling
is immoral, but we are just *not* as informed as we should be about
kestrels.

We drove deeper into the city and I asked him why we were
driving this direction, and he said I am looking for something that
when I see it you will know what I am looking for, which made
me grin, because he knew and I knew that I would indeed know,
because we have been brothers for fifty years, and brothers have
many languages, some of which are physical, like broken noses
and fingers and teeth and punching each other when you want to

say I love you but don't know how to say that right, and some of them are laughter, and some of them are roaring and spitting, and some of them are weeping in the bathroom, and some of them we don't have words for yet.

By now it was almost evening, and just as I turned on the car's running lights I saw what it was he was looking for, which was a basketball game in a park. I laughed and he laughed and I parked the car. There were six guys on the court, and to their credit they were playing full court. Five of the guys looked to be in their twenties, and they were fit and muscled, and one of them wore a porkpie hat. The sixth guy was much older, but he was that kind of older ballplayer who is comfortable with his age and he knew where to be and what not to try.

We watched for a while and didn't say anything but both of us noticed that one of the young guys was not as good as he thought he was, and one was better than he knew he was, and one was flashy but essentially useless, and the guy with the porkpie hat was a worker, setting picks, boxing out, whipping outlet passes, banging the boards not only on defense but on offense, which is much harder. The fifth young guy was one of those guys who ran up and down yelling and waving for the ball, which he never got. This guy was supposed to be covering the older guy but he didn't bother, and the older guy gently made him pay for his inattention, scoring occasionally on backdoor cuts and shots from the corners on which he was so alone he could have opened a circus and sold tickets, as my brother said.

The older man grew visibly weary as we watched, and my brother said he's got one last basket in him, and I said I bet a dollar it's a shot from the corner, and my brother said no, he doesn't even have the gas for that, he'll snake the kid somehow, you watch, and just then the older man, who was bent over holding the hems of his shorts like he was exhausted, suddenly cut to the basket, caught a bounce pass, and scored, and the game ended, maybe because the park lights didn't go on even though the streetlights did.

On the way home my brother and I passed the heron in the field of stubble again, and the heron stopped work again and glared at us until we turned the corner.

That is one *withering* glare, said my brother. That's a ballplayer glare if ever I saw one. That's the glare a guy gives another guy when the guy you were supposed to be covering scores on a back-door cut and you thought your guy was ancient and near death but it turns out he snaked you good and you are an idiot. *I* know that glare. You owe me a dollar. We better go get my prescriptions. They are not going to do any good but we better get them anyway so they don't go to waste. One less thing for my family to do afterward. That game was good but the heron was even better. I think the prescriptions are pointless now but we already paid for them so we might as well get them. They'll just get thrown out if we don't pick them up. That was a good last game, though. I'll remember the old guy, sure, but the kid with the hat banging the boards, that was cool. You hardly ever see a guy with a porkpie hat hammering the boards.

There's so much to love, my brother added. All the little things. Remember shooting baskets at night and the only way you could tell if the shot went in was the sound of the net? Remember the time we cut the fingertips off our gloves so we could shoot on icy days and Dad was so angry he lost his voice and he was supposed to give a speech and had to gargle and Mom laughed so hard we thought she was going to pee? Remember that? I remember that. What happens to what I remember? You remember it for me, okay? You remember the way that heron glared at us like he would kick our ass except he was working. And you remember that old man snaking that kid. *Stupid kid,* you could say, but that's the obvious thing. The *beautiful* thing is the little thing that the old guy knew full well he wasn't going to cut around picks and drift out into the corner again, that would burn his last gallon of gas, not to mention he would have to hoist up a shot from way out there, so he snakes the kid beautiful, he knows the kid thinks he's old, and the guy with the hat sees him cut, and gets him the ball on a dime, that's a beautiful thing because it's little, and we saw it and we knew what it meant. You remember that for me. You owe me a dollar.

TOD GOLDBERG

When They Let Them Bleed

FROM *Hobart*

I WAS ELEVEN the first time I saw someone killed. A real someone, that is. Prior to that point, I'm certain I'd seen hundreds,
probably thousands, maybe tens of thousands of fake people die
on television or in the movies and usually in fairly grotesque fashion. This was the autumn of 1982, what I thought of for many
years as the worst time of my life, though later on I'd change that
assessment. What happens is that you stop making absolutes about
such things as the best and worst days, weeks, months, or years
of your life and you're able to view things a bit more dispassion-
ately, once you understand that most things that seem horrible in
the moment can morph into something like experience or blind
chance.

This is particularly true now that I think about how the person
I saw killed wasn't even someone I knew, that I was one of millions
who saw him killed, that what haunts me still about his death is
probably more about my own fears, about how the ultimate good
fortune about that year is that I am still here, still remembering,
still trying to make things right in my mind.

His name was Duk Koo Kim. He was a South Korean boxer,
fighting Ray "Boom Boom" Mancini for the WBA lightweight title
the old-school way: outdoors, under a blistering sun, behind Caesars Palace in Las Vegas. Kim was the most unlikely contender for
the title—no one had really heard of him, but here he was fighting
America's real-life Rocky, an Italian kid from an industrial town,
the son of a failed prizefighter. Two men who found great luck and
that great luck brought them to a roped-off square in the middle

of the desert to fight for a world title. Except, of course, just like all things you realize after a certain age, they weren't really men. They were boys. Ray Mancini was twenty-one. Duk Koo Kim was twenty-three.

This was when boxing was still shown on television for free, back when fights went fifteen rounds, back when boxing was ruled by the likes of Larry Holmes, Sugar Ray Leonard, Marvin Hagler, and Wilfred Benitez, back when even eleven-year-old boys knew who all the contenders were for the major weight classes, back when they still let them bleed.

What I know is true: the heartbreak of one person's bad childhood is not equal to the tragic death of a young man in a boxing ring. The danger of drawing parallels is that some things are always inequalities. And yet I can't think of Duk Koo Kim without thinking about that year, about how I carried a pocketknife with me wherever I went, about how I used to press the point of it into my stomach until a bubble of blood appeared, how I ingested Afrin hourly because I liked the rush it gave me, about how the vision of Duk Koo Kim being carried out of that parking lot behind Caesers Palace on a stretcher, his body limp, stayed with me for years as the face of a real dead person, even when he was only in a coma and wouldn't die for a few days. I can't think of Duk Koo Kim, who weighed 135 pounds and was five foot six and was fighting for the lightweight championship of the world, without thinking about how at the same time I was eleven years old and stood just four foot eight and weighed 135 pounds, about how I would squeeze the layers of fat on my stomach against the frame of my shower and imagine slamming the door hard enough to just cleave the skin off, how it would solve so many problems, how lucky it would be just to melt into the crowd of students at my school, to be an invisible boy.

Duk Koo Kim wasn't famous. He became famous for a few years after he died. Warren Zevon did a song about the fight. Several years later, a song by Sun Kil Moon called "Duk Koo Kim" came out. It was nearly fifteen minutes long. That's approximately five rounds.

Whenever Ray "Boom Boom" Mancini fought after Kim died, someone on the television would say how he wasn't the same fighter since that tragic day, and then they'd talk about Duk Koo Kim's heart or how he'd supposedly left a message scrawled on a lampshade in his Las Vegas hotel room that said "Kill or be Killed" and how prophetic that turned out to be . . . before getting back to the carnage they were there to report on, hoping for an exciting fight, hopefully a ferocious brawl, hopefully a knockout. Because if there was one thing everyone said about Mancini after Duk Koo Kim died, it was that he lacked that killer instinct, that desire to really knock someone out. He was still a very fine boxer, he just didn't have that drive to destroy someone, to put them on their back, to make them lay motionless on the canvas. Maybe, they'd say, this would be the fight where he showed that aggression again. Before the fight with Duk Koo Kim, Mancini was in twenty-five bouts. He went 24–1, with eighteen knockouts or technical knockouts. Afterward he went 4–4 and found himself TKOed twice.

What's a knockout? Technically, it's a stroke. A very small stroke, but a stroke no less. What happens is this: when you get hit with a left or right hook, like the thirty-nine straight punches Ray "Boom Boom" Mancini landed on Duk Koo Kim late in their fight, your head swivels at such a high rate of speed that it actually compresses and constricts your carotid arteries. This is not a good thing if you like having cardiac function or the ability to speak. An uppercut does just about the same thing, though instead of affecting your carotid, the whiplash from the blow compresses the circulation to the back of your brain.

Duk Koo Kim died from a blood clot on the brain caused by a right subdural hematoma. Dr. Lonnie Hammargren, the neurosurgeon who operated on Duk Koo Kim directly after the fight's aftermath, said in the November 22, 1982, issue of *Sports Illustrated* that the trauma was caused by "one punch."

My bedroom back then was covered in pictures from *Sports Illustrated*. I don't remember when I began meticulously removing the covers of the magazines and pinning them to the wall, only that at some point I also began to frame entire issues on my wall, my sense being that one day the magazines would be valuable and that I'd want to keep them in better condition (I can only imagine that this belief stemmed from the start of the baseball card craze that took hold around then, since that's also when I began not to touch my cards anymore, the result being that I have plenty of mint copies of Rusty Kuntz's rookie card).

I received my subscription to *Sports Illustrated* as a gift from my father on my tenth birthday. At that point I hadn't seen him in five years, hadn't even heard from him—via post, phone, or messages sent over the Ouija board, where I sometimes tried to contact him, even though he wasn't dead—in at least three. Yet a month or so after my birthday in January of 1981, my first issue arrived, along with a notice saying it was a gift subscription from my father. At first my mother refused to let me have the magazine, as if somehow the mere fact that my father had paid for it made it part of him. I can still see her, standing in my bedroom, trying to rip the magazine in half. It was the annual "Year in Sports" issue, so it was extra-thick, and thus she only managed to rip through the cover and the first few pages before she became frustrated and opted just to throw it away.

Later that night my sister Karen smuggled it back into my bedroom. "Keep this somewhere Mom won't be able to find it," she said. Karen was seventeen, and her main job then was to serve as a buffer between my sister Linda and me and our mother, who was insane. I don't mean "insane" in a flip way. I mean eventually we'd have her institutionalized against her will. Though that wouldn't happen for another twenty-five years and by that point it was too late.

The magazine was damp and covered with bits of coffee grounds and cigarette ash, but Karen had taped the torn pages for me. I kept it, and for the next few weeks, every single other issue of the magazine that arrived, underneath my bed during the day and only read it at night, after my mother went to sleep. And then one day I came home from soccer practice and all the issues were neatly stacked on top of my bed. My mother never said a word about it, which was unusual, since she tended to have a word about most things.

I can still see the boxing covers in my mind—the ones I remember best are those that prophesied greatness: Thomas Hearns glaring into the middle distance beside a headline that said, BETTER PRAY, SUGAR RAY; Joe Frazier and his son Marvis, years before Marvis would be destroyed by Larry Holmes and Mike Tyson, the words A CHIP OFF THE OLD CHAMP? stretched across their rippled chests; an ebullient Gerry Cooney being carried out of the ring, the banner an understated THE CONTENDER. And then, in August of 1982, there was the cover of Ray Mancini smacking the shit out of Ernesto España beneath a canopy of impossibly blue sky and the words BOOM BOOM BOOMS! Three months later, Mancini would appear on the cover of *Sports Illustrated* for the last time. It's a photo of him smacking the shit out of Duk Koo Kim, a photo eerily similar to the one from August, except this time the headline said TRAGEDY IN THE RING.

I went and looked at the old covers online, to make sure I was remembering them correctly. I was. Five things stood out for me afterward:

1. That there's an exclamation point at the end of BOOM BOOM BOOMS! but not TRAGEDY IN THE RING.

2. In the last decade, there's been exactly one cover of *Sports Illustrated* featuring boxers.

3. Ray "Boom Boom" Mancini had two fights within just three months of each other.

4. After realizing that Mancini fought two huge fights in just three months' time, I went and looked to see when his other fights were in 1982, because I recalled him fighting constantly that year. Between December 26, 1981, and November 13, 1982, the day of the Kim fight, Ray "Boom Boom" Mancini fought five times. Take it back further, and between March 1981 and that day in 1982, he fought a total of ten times.

5. The last active boxer to appear on the cover of *Sports Illustrated*, Floyd Mayweather Jr., has fought ten times since 2005.

Five things I remember about the days before Duk Koo Kim was killed:

1. This was the period of my life when my classmates began calling me by the names of Columbus's ships.

2. A man named Don Olsen moved into our house. My mother met him when she was in the hospital after her hysterectomy and he came to visit the woman my mother was sharing a room with. I don't know the exact algebra that led to this, but at some point during those visits to see his friend, somehow Don Olsen convinced my mother he should rent the room my brother vacated when he went to college. For the first month that Don lived in our house he mostly kept to himself, which

meant he sat in his bedroom smoking cigarettes, eating TV dinners, and drinking beer. It wasn't until the second month that
Don Olsen finally decided I needed a male role model in my
life. He would watch sports with me in the family room—by this
point, he decided that our faux leather recliner was his—and
when we watched boxing, he'd tell me how he learned to fight
when he was in the service and how I could lose some of "that
shit around your belt" if I learned to spar, maybe even kids at
school would think I was less of a "fat pussy."

"You got any man questions, you come ask me," he said.

I told him I didn't have any man questions.

"What about ones about the war? You could ask me about that.
I know you ain't got a father in your life, so fire away."

I thought for a moment and realized I had absolutely no desire
to hear anything Don might have to say about anything. I'd have
been much happier to hear about his experiences getting up off
his ass to change the TV channel, a chore he liked me to do. The
only thing I truthfully ever wondered about Don was what had
occurred to his tongue—a chunk was missing from the tip and
it made his words sounds mushy, but then so did the six-pack of
Milwaukee's Best that he kept in a cooler next to the recliner.

"You know what the best part of war was?" Don volunteered.
"The poontang. I never got more poon than I did in the service.
Get you a nice pair of shoes and a haircut, and whoa, boy, you
could get some poon too. Come here," he said. "I'll show you my
wife." Don reached into his pocket and pulled out a thick wallet
filled with receipts, scraps of paper, a few bucks, and a sleeve filled
with photos. I came and stood beside him and looked down as
he flipped through the pictures. Stuffed between a photo of the
White House and the Golden Gate Bridge was one of an Asian
woman. "That's her. Met her in Taiwan, married her, and then
everything fell to shit and I left her there."

"Oh," I said.

He dug around in his wallet some more and came out with a
condom. "Here," he said. "Take it. Show it off at school and the
other kids will think you're cool. I'm sure they think you're a sissy
right now, right?"

"What happened to your tongue?" I said, because, well, that's
what I said.

"Some poon got drunk and bit it," he said.

"Did it hurt?"

"No more, no less," Don said.

Don stayed with us another three weeks, and each afternoon he tried to engage me in another conversation about sex or about war or about my mother, who, he confided, was a "foxy lady." When he came home drunk one evening and tried to have the same conversation with my mother, his term in our home came to an abrupt end, which was fine by me, since I was due to have my tonsils removed and the only bedroom in the house with a TV hookup was my brother's, which meant I'd get to convalesce in there, eating ice cream and watching TV. Ray "Boom Boom" Mancini was scheduled to fight Duk Koo Kim a few days after the operation. The timing was perfect.

3. I began using the Ouija board by myself. It moved. It answered my questions. It put me in contact with a spirit that said every girl in school had a crush on me. It pointed to "yes" when I asked it if I should keep living. It told me, in painstaking detail, that it was okay if I ate frosting every day. It told me I would one day be president of the United States of America. I swear to God, it moved on its own.

4. At night, after everyone was asleep, I'd microwave pieces of Italian salami and eat them, then lick the grease from the plate.

5. I asked the doctor if anyone had ever died while getting their tonsils removed.

"Of course," he said. "Any time you go under anesthetic, there's a chance you won't come back out."

"What are the odds I'm that person?"

"Not good," he said. He was standing in front of me, listening to me through his stethoscope. He smelled like cigarettes and mint gum. His name is lost to me now, but it was something foreign-sounding and he had a thick accent that was actually rather pleasant. I think he might have been French. "Do you want to talk to me about these marks on your stomach?"

I was seventeen the first time I went to Las Vegas. My mother was there to cover an event—she was a society columnist, so her job was to go to parties for a living—and we stayed at the Sands. This was 1988. I was the only one left at home now, and my mother spent the majority of her time dating guys who owned men's suit stores and who sang or played piano in Italian restaurants and who showed up at our house in cars driven by guys with names like Fat Tommy or Billy the Lip. We'd moved from northern California to Palm Springs, which was like moving from Mayberry to Hollywood, except Hollywood in 1958.

We drove by Caesars Palace, and I remember thinking how strange it was that all of these people were streaming in and out of it, none of them disturbed by the fact that Duk Koo Kim had been beaten to death where they were hoping to win their fortunes.

I've visited Las Vegas maybe fifty times in my life, not including the two years I lived there in the late 1990s. I've stepped foot inside Caesars Palace maybe ten or fifteen times. I've never won a single cent there.

I lived through getting my tonsils removed. I was in the hospital for two days, however, because they also removed my adenoids and then I had a reaction to something—I never knew what—that had me vomiting every few hours. I finally got home on Friday night and got to sleep in my brother Lee's old room. Don had moved out a few weeks earlier, but the room still smelled of his cigarette smoke, sweat, and something that at the time I thought smelled like vinegar. Now I think that I don't want to know what the fuck that smell was.

My mother put a bucket next to the bed and told me that if I got sick, well, I should tell Karen, because she needed to get some rest, she had a party to cover on Saturday. If I was in pain, I should wake Karen up and tell her too. If I needed anything, pretty much I was instructed to let Karen know. The problem was that Karen had left for college two months earlier. My sister Linda, who is two years older than me, sat in the room with me for the next several hours and we ate ice cream and read magazines, and then, in the middle of the night, I threw up mint chip ice cream all over the wall.

Duk Koo Kim didn't actually write "Kill or be Killed" on the lampshade in his room. Whatever he wrote was in Korean. Royce Feour, a former writer for the *Las Vegas Review-Journal*, said in an interview in the paper twenty-five years after the fight that the actual translation was roughly "Live or Die." Either way you cut it, it's a strange thing to write on a lampshade.

What I remember about the fight is that it was extraordinarily entertaining. A brawl from the first bell. I sat on the floor of Lee's room, the smell of mint chip ice cream vomit now mixing with the remnants of Don Olsen, and watched the fight. Unlike fights today, this one took place in the afternoon. Can you imagine? Watching a championship fight in the middle of a Saturday afternoon on CBS? Today it would cost you at least $50 for pay-per-view and you'd need to wade through three terrible undercards just to get to the big fight.

But I didn't know any of that yet. The Ouija didn't give me any information regarding how things would change in the boxing world. So I sat there and watched and ate more ice cream. What I recall is that the two fighters never stopped punching each other. Unlike heavyweight fights, for instance, where there's a lot of stalking around the ring and clinching, the lighter weight classes have always been more electrifying affairs, and in this case, with two fighters of about the same size and weight, it was an unceasing barrage of head and body blows. Mancini looked better—he was more muscular and thick, whereas Kim seemed skinny, owing perhaps to his two-inch height advantage—but once you step into the ring, it doesn't really matter how you look.

The prefight buzz was that Kim was going to be seriously overmatched, that his number one ranking was a joke, that he was lucky even to be in the conversation, much less in contention, but the fight proved his ranking was earned. I recall Linda coming in to sit with me and then getting up and leaving because she thought it was disgusting the way these men were trying to kill each other. I tried to explain to her that they really weren't trying to kill each other, that it was a sport of respect, the sweet science —these were the sorts of things I learned reading *Sports Illustrated,* I imagine—and that they'd hug in the end. Linda said it was gross.

Duk Koo Kim's name was not Duk Koo Kim. His real name was Kim Deuk-gu. His real name was also 김득구.

The last three rounds of the fight—the twelfth, thirteenth, and fourteenth—were absolutely vicious. That's what I remember. Had

I ever even seen the fight since that day? I couldn't recall. I must have, right? No, it turns out, I hadn't. Because no clips were released for twenty-five years, until Bob Arum got Mancini's permission and released the film for use in a documentary. I watched them on YouTube the other day. Duk Koo Kim looks horrible in the twelfth, like he can barely stand, his face is swollen, he's staggering around, it looks like just one punch will do him in. At one point he nearly stumbles and falls, it's over, it's over, but no, it just keeps going. Then the thirteenth comes and Mancini hits him thirty-nine straight times. As a kid, I loved this, I'm sure. As an adult, it sickens me. Why didn't they stop the fight? How can you let someone take thirty-nine straight punches? How can someone survive that?

It turns out they can't.

Three people died because of that fight, actually. There was Duk Koo Kim, obviously. And then, three months later, Duk Koo Kim's mother committed suicide. Eight months later, Richard Green, the referee who let the fight go on even after those thirty-nine punches, also committed suicide.

The fourteenth round started with Mancini storming off his stool. He gets to the center of the ring, and seconds later Duk Koo Kim is flat on his back, and then he tries to climb the ropes, stumbles back, and it's over. Mancini is jumping in the air. Kim is pulled into his corner, loses consciousness, and that's it. Except as a kid, I didn't know that. The camera was on Mancini. CBS interviewed him, he talked about what a fierce competitor Kim was, about wanting to fight Aaron Pryor, there was a commercial, and then, when they returned, Duk Koo Kim was being taken out of the arena on a stretcher. The announcer called him "very game." His mouth was open slightly. He was covered in sweat. One arm hung off the side of the stretcher, the other was across his chest. His eyes were closed, his face swollen. He was completely limp.

Jews have closed-casket funerals, so I didn't see an actual dead body again until college, when two of my friends killed themselves and I attended their funerals. Standing over their open caskets, staring at their painted faces, I thought that they didn't look dead at all. They looked like mannequins. There was no part of them that seemed to have ever been alive. They'd both died alone, one by overdosing, the other by shooting himself in the head, so millions of strangers never saw their final living moments. For many years I have wondered why their deaths don't haunt me as much as this stranger's death, this boy who died by the calculated risk of becoming a boxer, and I can only conclude that it's all about distance. I didn't see either of my friends die—though in some respect I should have at least seen the signs, but I was a boy too, and they were boys, and you can't expect boys to see things like pain and depression as clearly as retrospect would like us to believe—I just stood there in the aftermath and wondered why I was thinking of a dead boxer.

I took down all the pictures.

The last time I saw a person die, it was my mother. I felt lucky to be there, even though I'd spent the previous thirty-nine years of my life wishing her gone. She wasn't a good person, I'm not afraid to say anymore. She was at times cruel, malicious, mentally abusive. At other times she was simply mad. And at other times still, she was the darkness that kept me awake at night as an adult, wondering if I was becoming her.

And yet.

My sister Linda called and said that the doctors were only giving our mother four hours to live, that she'd fallen, that if I wanted to see her before she died, I needed to get to the hospital right away. The hospital was four hours away, with no traffic, but we would be leaving our house right in the middle of rush-hour traffic. We would be lucky to make it there in seven hours.

My wife and I made it there in four hours.

My mother, who'd been dying of cancer for a very long time, was in the hospital bed, her eyes barely open, her face was swollen and black-and-blue from her fall, her mouth agape, one arm was slung across her chest, the other was falling to the side of the bed. She was limp and unconscious.

I sat down beside her and told her it was okay to go. And thirty seconds later she was gone.

I stopped hurting myself after Duk Koo Kim died. I don't know why. I still have the pocketknife, however. It's in an old tackle box that's out in my garage. It's strange: I have a tendency to hold on to things that are relics of bad memories, as if by knowing where they are I'll somehow be able to avoid the unlucky occurrence of running into them and being overwhelmed.

The problem is, you can't mitigate chance. That's what makes this life so pitiless, so unnerving. Duk Koo Kim died at twenty-three, killed in a boxing ring, and by chance I sat and watched it happen when I was eleven. Twenty-eight years later, almost to the day, I sat beside my mother as she died and he came back to me, the vision of him on that stretcher, the congruence of their bodies, their faces, and I wonder if now those last moments of hers will finally replace his in my mind and who, eventually, will replace her.

VICKI WEIQI YANG

Field Notes on Hair

FROM *South Loop Review*

And nothing is less worthy of a thinking man than to see death
as a slumber. Why a slumber, if death doesn't resemble sleep?
—Fernando Pessoa, *The Book of Disquiet*

AFTER THE BRAIN THING* the world became divided spatially
and temporally. There were those who knew the truth about my
illness, and those who knew the easy-to-swallow version that I had
personally lubricated for them. And, as much as I tried to prevent
this, there was the cleavage of my life's short timeline into two
separate but unequal segments: before the brain thing, when I
possessed coveted big-name qualities like Radicalism and Bright-
Eyed Naiveté; after the brain thing, when I lost a little bit of those
things, and also, for several months, a lot of hair.

I suppose I should say now that this isn't a sob story. Within
these lines you will find no hysteric account of how the world has
wronged me or marred my idyllic youth. If I think it, I refuse to
verbalize it and I—I don't think it in those terms except at my
lowest of lows. But still, I carry that scar within my head. There
are phantom visions for me, the way other people have to live
with phantom limbs, and I stand, divided in the wake of a Capgras
delusion in which another me had replaced myself without due
warning. And the encounter, spanning the length of a midwestern

---

* Among friends, I almost always refer to it as such. To do otherwise would endow
it with undue weight.

winter, left behind cold streaks of clarity in an otherwise muddled mind.

Hair loss begins and ends on its own terms.

The whole affair began on a winter weekday, the kind of weekday that, because the school term had come to an end and the absence of the usual regimen left blank vast stretches of time, blended seamlessly from Monday to Friday to Monday. At 3 A.M. I said goodbye to Tonya, whom I had been talking to online, and then I had my stroke. For some reason I like the sound of that—*I had my stroke*, as though I am talking about some private but routine gesture: in the afternoon, I had my coffee, and at the stroke of three (as if on cue, by clockwork) I had my stroke. Tonya, a quiet, warm-palmed Mexican Jew with perpetual bedhead, is one of my college friends who got the lubricated version. She likes to dress nicely, in a cardigan and loose button-down, for the girls she could picture as girlfriends. If you had a bad cold, she'd make you chicken noodle soup and feed it to you too. That's the kind of girl Tonya is: A girl who tripped over your softest falls. A girl who I knew would apologize incessantly for things that were nobody's fault. That's why I could never tell her the truth about any of it, you understand—not about the nature of my illness, nor about the fact that she almost became the last person to see me alive.

So I had my stroke (a splitting headache, waves of nausea followed by vomiting, residual pangs that made me knead my temples hard). When it happened, I didn't realize that it was a stroke. Strokes weren't *had* by nineteen-year-olds. I consulted the wisdom of the Internet with search terms like *differences between stroke and migraine* and came to the unhelpful conclusion that the two often shared symptoms. I tried to go to bed and in the morning had an MRI, which revealed whole areas in my circulatory system that were missing capillaries. So it was back to the blinding white of Chicago. No, not really white.

Light slate. I moved into a shared room with a high school girl whose digestive organs were failing by the day. I heard her moaning through the heavy curtain between us, until I was transferred to a private room. Occasionally I would lumber about the halls with my own leash in one hand and the other clutching the train of my dress: a blushing bride in green with IV infusion sets as my bridesmaids. The halls were filled with construction paper posters for the sake of false cheeriness. NEUROSURGERY WARD WINS AWARD FOR BEST CARE, one might proclaim. Tests, some involving blood and others involving spinal fluid but all of them involving needles, became a routine part of my day (today I *had* a CT scan, yesterday I *had* a lumbar puncture). The nurses clapped hands and complimented me for my "skinny" frame (for an absence of flesh folds made finding veins relatively simple; even so, we were running out of them by the second week). I began looking forward to morphine injections, which made the senses melt deliciously like diluted watercolors.

All of this I learned to take in with serene indifference. I cried at first, because none of the doctors could give a definitive answer. And the radiologist (a studious-looking man with kindly but overworked gray strands) kept averting his eyes. Of all the possible long-term side effects, I dreaded this the most: "a decrease in intellect." What kind of woman would I be without my intellect? Not a beautiful one, I knew. At night I tossed and turned as much as I could without disturbing the plastic needle planted in the crook of my arm. My hair pressed against my face and made it greasy. In the daytime I tried to keep my mind occupied by reading about the upbringing of John Stuart Mill. (He was, of course, infinitely more precocious than I was. Things like this used to make me agonize.)

Embolization One. I took uneasy trips into the REM world and brought back souvenirs. I dreamed of a North Korean footrace through mountains and classrooms with shattered windows. People stepped in the beads of glass dotting the linoleum and hardly noticed the red footprints they left behind. There were many casualties. The winner was awarded with a large medal of yellow brass. If you looked closer, it probably came with a raised etching of the Great Leader—I couldn't tell, since one does not zoom in on dreams.

I came in second, or maybe sixth. I remember there was a small lecture to the ten of us forerunners. The speaker was throwing out jagged pieces of Confucian maxims at us, except he attributed them to Kim Il Sung and I'm not sure if he knew the difference. There was a bony lady (the nurses would have no trouble finding her veins) who had an especially pious countenance, who kept bowing little solemn bows and repeating, "That's very wise, Professor. Ah, yes. That's very wise, Professor."

In the waking world a mere block away, my friends were celebrating the cancellation of classes for the second day in a row. This was a rare event that had not occurred at the university since 1999. A blizzard, so I heard, which had washed over the slate and made the city a true white.

Embolization Two, "stereotactic radiosurgery." It was after that that the hair started falling away in droves. Months later, back in the dorm room that I share with Eliza, I started making a list with everything I knew about hair.

> You cannot tear out hair except from the roots.
> You can cut hair, but you cannot hurt it.

And:

> Mine is black.

Mine is black, but not everyone has black hair. Some have brown, dirty blond, platinum blond, salt-and-pepper. This I learned in Miss Morris's classroom at the age of seven when I moved from Shanghai (where, at the cusp of the twenty-first century, almost everyone's hair was black) to Dallas. When I was younger I used to wonder whether people's pubic hair always matched the color on their heads, so I compared notes with my ginger friend Bryce. I learned a new term that I still find kind of funny: *firecrotch*. At the hospital I met a young man with black hair like mine, except his was wavy and he had dark skin. Like the other resident physicians, he was startlingly handsome. All of the residents at the Medical Center, if they weren't already going to be all sorts of -ologists, could have been models. I fantasize about eating in the hospital cafeteria—when I am better and in something other than pastel-colored hospital gowns—and trying to catch the eye of the curly-haired, dark-skinned ER doctor. When I go back to school, I don't go back to the hospital cafeteria. Not because he's seen me use a bedpan. Not because he's already seen my breasts through the size XXL gown (so that I had one less feminine wile at my disposal), the neck hole of which could fit around my waist.

At my parents' house in Texas, the hair loss came to me like an afterthought several days after the radiation. Nothing happened on the first and second days. I washed my hair vigorously.

2-in-1 Shampoo & Conditioner ≠ shampoo + conditioner

Do you know what they do to you when they come at you with numb, technical-sounding words like *stereotactic radiosurgery*? To be sure, it's not serious the way chemo is, so forgive me for adopting a nihilistic attitude. First they have to affix a crown to your head. They do this by drilling four evenly spaced screws into your head, and they stop when you can hear the screw crunching against the cranium, turning bone into fine powder like pestle on mortar. Then they bring in physicists to crunch out the numbers: at what angle to aim the laser, how wide the blast radius should be, how long the exposure.

"This is not the elegant part of the procedure," the resident doctor, who was preparing my head for the placement of the crown, admitted.

I remember saying to her (a nervous young woman with light brown skin, whose dark frames and tightly scrunchied hair kept her from metamorphosing into the heartbreaker that she might have been), to keep the situation light, "Oh, I am so *screwed!*" She laughed but hastily stopped herself.

Post-radiation hair is thinner, fluffier, and paler than pre-radiation hair.

You become deathly afraid that strangers have x-ray vision. And then you'll grow defiant ("Who gives a shit if everyone can see my bald patch," you'll reason, and then meaningfully leave that knit cap on the bedpost), for there is no room for your dignity to flower into anything except bleary-eyed defiance.

I don't buy a wig. Most of the time a wig serves the purpose of making sure that other people feel comfortable; in my defiance I believed they had no right to that comfort.

Wigmakers are not only selling beauty, but also dignity. But that dignity is fragile.

Later, when the hair has returned, strangers will meet your eyes for the first time. They will say, "Oh, I recognize you." "I've seen you around," they'll say, neglecting to mention that they sat a few rows behind you in Intro to East Asia: Korea and every Monday–Wednesday stared at the back of your yin-yang head.*

Hair is best as a binary. You want hair, true, or you want hair, the absence of. Anything in between looks ridiculous, and the comb-over is not a valid option for girls barely out of their teens.

Good friends joke about bad hair days. Acquaintances ask What Happened To questions. Other people look everywhere but at your head.

There is no inherent shame in this, but it is a curious spatial phenomenon. A sociology professor who had nothing to do with me prior to the brain thing approached me one afternoon and said, *It is different for people like you and me, who have seen the other side.*
"Even the Chicago sky doesn't look so gray."

Baldness, at least the involuntary kind, is not "shiny." You get the shininess from repeatedly wearing down your scalp with blades, as though polishing the edge of a kitchen knife, and from moisturizers. Instead, the baldness of radiation is soft and pink—thoroughly unnerving to the touch like eggshells soaked in warm vinegar. What was once alive now pulsates with vengeance at the living.

The truth about the brain thing is that it will always follow me. I don't mean in an abstract way. I mean that every year I cast a die to determine whether I will have another stroke, and there is nothing I can do about it.

Should I write a will? I suppose it would be heartbreaking if it were ever found—heartbreakingly idiotic (like a child's crayon drawing of her nuclear family, the feet sprawled at impossible angles and the hands like flattened cakes of Play-Doh, created with the intent of saving a doomed marriage) if someone found it while I was alive, but plain heartbreaking if someone found it after my

* Radiation's baldness is true baldness, since hair falls out at the roots. No sign of its former inhabitant.

death. And anyway I have nothing of value to give anyone except my books—the last vestiges of a brain-rose prematurely pruned.

Another time in the hospital, I had a terrifying nightmare. Half of the world had suffered through a gigantic natural catastrophe of some sort and had to relocate. My family was doing the same; everybody's front lawns were littered with possessions, waiting for their turn to be carried into their new homes. All of my books— compacted into four neat bookshelves—sat there unguarded, tantalizing. And amid the chaos of movers and children and carpenters, some clever soul decided to masquerade as the owner of the books and conduct an impromptu yard sale. In vain I screamed *THOSE ARE NOT YOUR BOOKS TO SELL*, running from bookshelf to bookshelf, but I succeeded only in garnering jeers. I grew so flustered that my desperation devolved into violence, and I began hitting book buyers left and right. Most of my blows were harmless, but then I distinctly remember picking up *The Great Latke-Hamantash Debate* and jamming the corner into somebody's eye.

This nightmare bothered me for two reasons:

1) Why did the physical manifestation of knowledge matter so much to me? I was not generous with this knowledge, as I should have been—rather, I hoarded earthly paper and ink as though they meant something on their own.

2) Why did I retaliate violently against innocent people, and was my reaction representative of a ruthless survival instinct in waking life? If so, then that makes me morally decrepit. Or at least inauthentic. It must not be a coincidence, then, that the lesion in my brain is next to the pineal gland. Descartes, although he was mistaken about its location, believed it to be the seat of the soul.

In the mornings, clear packing tape clears hairy pillows. The same goes for hairy consciences.

My neurosurgeon is saying things like *You should be able to lead a relatively normal life aside from your unfortunate propensity,* and then he drops the *but.* But the *but* turns out to be surprisingly tame. "But," he says with a winning smile, "stay away from heavy lifting, scuba diving, maybe things that make your blood pump a little too roughly."

I think of asking about orgasms.

I don't.

On another trip to the dream world, I saw my mother. My mother is an illogical woman, as all mothers are prone to be, because her diet consists of far too much true crime. She's forever drawing lines of causation between what I do and what grisly things happen to young girls like myself on a daily basis. In my dream she is clutching fistfuls of her own hair. She is clutching fistfuls of the doctor's hair. The thick strands turn into snakes when they fall to the floor, until the entire office is a writhing, rippling web—the capillaries that I am missing. I can't stand snakes, so I scream and scream.

I remember to call my mother when I wake up. I tell her, *I should be able to lead a relatively normal life, but I should stay away from heavy lifting and scuba diving.* She hears, *I should stay away from anything that makes me too happy or sad or mad.* She also tries to convince me to take the rest of the school year off, a suggestion that I reject.

> Your mother cares a lot about your hair, and she will cry over its involuntary separation. That's because she sees the passage of time in the blackness of your hair, and every clump in the trashcan is another reminder that her baby is dying.

"But Mom," you say, "hair is inorganic. It can't *actually* die." Wrong. Hair is organic, because it is made from the protein keratin. You would know that if you studied chemistry like Eliza. Eliza is my roommate, and she is a scientist and a positivist—a bright-eyed, golden-headed student with profound faith in things like reason and logic and the triumph of the superior argument. But neither of us are very good mathematicians, and neither of us believe in predestination. I tell her the truth about the brain thing, my brain thing, and we struggle to calculate the likelihood that I'll survive into my sixties without another stroke. She reacts the same way as I did, her eyes fogging up for a moment but then returning to their original clarity: "I think it's a permutation?"

"Wait a second, I think I have to use integration. We just learned this."

And: "If I do figure out the answer, do you want me to tell you?" *Sure,* I say.

Even though half of it is thinner and fluffier than I remember, I have all of my hair now. A bit of it is turning white: a quirk inherited from my father, who started dyeing his head in his late thirties because at that age it already resembled snow and slate.

But I won't dye. A strand here, a strand there. Like so many reminders to live with authenticity.

J. D. DANIELS

Letter from Majorca

FROM *The Paris Review*

LET'S SUPPOSE YOU are a serious person, or you transmit to yourself certain conventional signals of a sort of seriousness: you reread Tacitus, you attempt to reread Proust but it can't be done, you listen to Bartók and to Archie Shepp.

Also: You can't stop moving your bowels, or your body can't. You have a body, you are a body. You don't know what's safe to eat these days, or when. You're so sick that you take off your clothes when you use the bathroom, for safety's sake. That was a hard lesson to learn. Let's stop saying *you*.

I had a body. It was a problem. It hurt most of the time. I dreamed of one world and woke into another. I woke in pain from bad dreams of my divorce, again, and listened to Wayne Shorter's *The All Seeing Eye.* It would see a lot of things, that eye. Think of all it might come to know and desire to forget.

My throat hurt, my stomach hurt, I coughed, I lay in bed and stared at the ceiling and thought about death: I heard its soft footfalls approaching. I had some blood tests, I took some medicine. I spent a lot of time in bed.

At the time I'm telling you about, I was earning some money, not much, as a freelance journalist and a teacher in a university, writing about education, about gun control, about fashion or music, reviewing new novels through a haze of rage and envy, telling myself that *whatever it takes* means *whatever it takes,* doing whatever I had to do to convince myself that I was not a number two schmuck.

The wife tells her husband, *You must be the number two schmuck in the whole world.*

Why can't I be the number one schmuck? he says.

But how could you be number one? she says. *You're such a schmuck.*

There was nothing the matter with me that was not also the matter with everyone else. I was not as interesting as I thought I was. My major problem, inadequate or inappropriate love from my parents, was as common as dirt. And one rainy day, all the boring poignancy of these realizations detonated in me like an atom bomb, burning the dead shadow of each former torment or preoccupation onto solid rock. Those silhouettes, that record would remain: the museum where I used to be.

All right, I thought, *I've had enough. Some other way from now on, but not like that, not anymore.*

And so I quit my university job after shouting at a student until she began to cry. "You're crying?" I said. "Why are you crying?" She ran away.

I had done this to innumerable boys over the years and had considered it good for them, but a girl's tears shocked me and made me see myself as I was: cruel, power-mad, an abuser of children, because in our time twenty-year-olds remain children, and they themselves are not entirely to blame. We have failed them. Let's stop saying *we.*

I shouted at a pretty girl with long black hair. She often stayed after class to discuss her favorite books with me, sitting next to me on my desk, playing with the strap of her shirt and smiling in a way that becomes familiar to every teacher, flattering and dangerous, and when she ran away crying I saw that I had scolded her in order to prevent myself from going to bed with her.

And later, when I realized that her name, she had a man's first name, was also the name of a friend with whom I was angry because I had praised my analyst in his presence and he had applied and been taken on as an analysand, when I realized that by driving my student away I was also murdering her name-twin, my rival sibling, I thought, *These kids deserve better instruction than I am currently capable of providing.*

Once I admitted how much I wanted to kill and eat the children who had been entrusted to my care, I tried to forgive myself for any harm I might have done them over the years, for all the crackling bolts I had hurled from my cloud of self-serving ignorance, and I left that institution of learning to resume my position of nothingness in a world where I had no power to abuse my sub-ordinates because I had no subordinates, where I had no author-ity save whatever I might seize by force or by cunning—where, as each day proves afresh, people will walk smiling through pud-dles of your blood, smiling and talking on their cellular phones. They're going to the movies.

People at parties in Cambridge asked me *What do you do?* with alarming regularity. I had spent the previous thirty years in Ken-tucky, never once having been asked what I did, because what would be the point? I do some task I don't care about in order to be able to afford to stay alive, the same as you do, and then I clock in at my real job holding down a stool at the Back Door or Check's Café or Freddie's Bar-Lounge or Jake's Club Reno.

In Cambridge, at parties, I said whatever came first into my mind.

"I manufacture organic catheters."

"I'm a butt scientist."

"I am an AM/FM clock radio."

For a while, when I sensed they might find it contemptible, I had thrown it into people's faces that I worked in a deli. It was true: once, in Cambridge, I had made a sandwich for Arthur M. Schlesinger Jr. "I think that was Arthur Schlesinger," I said, and the next person in line said, "Who's Arthur Schlesinger?"

And once I made a Reuben for a Weimaraner. Probably I made a lot of sandwiches for dogs without knowing it, but the lady I am thinking of made it clear to me that I was to be careful with her dog's sandwich, take it easy on the Russian dressing.

I was proud of myself on the day I quit my university teaching job. I remembered when I was still a little boy and my father came home from work, too tired and sore to bend over and take his own boots off, and I was so pleased to take his boots off for him, the brown and white laces and the brads and the dry mud flaking onto the floor; and my mother said, "How was work today?" and my father said, "I quit."

We sat down to dinner and we did not speak. Soon the phone rang, and my father smiled. On the phone was someone who had heard about how my father had told the foreman off, good, he deserved it and only you had the guts to give it to him, we always have a job for a man like you, can you start tomorrow. He could.

Now that it was settled, we finished eating our dinner, meatloaf and mashed potatoes maybe, or hamburgers and thick-cut, deep-fried potatoes, my father's favorite. And that night my mother sobbed until she vomited. This happened many times when I was a boy.

I told my girlfriend I had quit my teaching job. "That was dumb," she said.

It was at this time that the captain called me long-distance from Tunisia and said, "I need a man. Get over here."

"I'm sick," I said. "I don't know how much help I can be to you."

"All I need is arms and legs," he said. "Do you still have arms and legs? Then buy a ticket for Cagliari and meet us in Carloforte."

The captain was a gray giant out of Tel Aviv. One holiday I had seen him surrounded by his daughters, by his sons-in-law, his grandchildren, his pretty young girlfriend, and I thought, *This man has something to teach you about what a certain kind of happiness is in life, so learn it, you dummy.*

I already felt *at sea,* as they say, *lost in familiar places* is another thing they say. I decided to spend some time at sea, where my bewilderment might make more sense, because disorientation and chaos would actually be happening.

Why do people feel things and go places, tell me if you know.

That was how my odyssey began. I flew to Heathrow Terminal 4, where a man in one of the many airport bars drank a bottle of Worcestershire sauce, put the empty in his briefcase, and chased it with a pint of ale. A morose Russian paced near Aeroflot. I flew on to Sardinia and hired a car, and soon I was alone, under the moon, without the luggage Alitalia had lost, on the last ferry to the island called San Pietro.

The boat was forty-three feet long and there were five of us, myself and four Israelis, on it for five weeks. I had never been sailing for more than two hours at a time, in Boston Harbor. I didn't understand the captain when he told me to take the French seasickness pill.

There was work to be done, and so after three acid-yellow heavings-up they left me to my fate, sprawled on my back with a bucket nearby. Shattered by nausea and fear, I sweated through my shirt and took it off and wrung it out and wiped myself with it. I was sick all day and night as we crossed from Sardinia to Minorca. I hadn't had a drink in eight years, but hello, vomiting, it is always nice to see you again.

When the captain saw that I could sit up and drink water, he said, "You're a sailor now," and he sent me fore. It wasn't true that I was a sailor, but it was true that a task helped me to focus on something other than my constant boring suffering, something to do with the jib roller, it's all a blur.

I wasn't going to be sick again for more than a month, but there was no way I could know that. As we hobbyhorsed up and down, pitching hard over the waves, I saw first the sea and then the sky, black sea, night sky, burning moon, a foretaste of death.

Both Odysseus and Captain Ahab are heroes of departure and return, for Ahab too returns: to his death-home, in the whale.

Shlomo's English was good. He told me about the Dead Sea Scrolls. He told me about Brazilian agronomy. He told me about Joseph Stiglitz.

Shlomo said, "I ask myself, who are the wisest people in the world? The answer is, the Jews. This is well known.

"And who are the wisest Jews? A moment's reflection reveals that Russian Jews are the wisest.

"Next we must discover who are the wisest of these Russian Jews. And the answer comes back, clearly the people of Odessa.

"So who are the wisest Jews in Odessa? The members of the old synagogue.

"It's plain to see, then, that the wisest man in the world must be Rabbi Loew, chief rabbi of the old synagogue of Odessa. But he's such an idiot."

And Amatsia said, "My brain is fucking." He meant his memory was going bad. Asked for an example, he explained that in the army he had once carried a dead man on his back for two days and now he couldn't remember the man's name. He shook his head. "Fucking," he said.

Amatsia didn't talk much. He smoked. Every now and then he picked up the binoculars and looked at the colors of the flags of other ships and said, "Fucking Germans."

One night, docked, we met a German couple in a Spanish restaurant. "You talk about Jerusalem, I think," the man said, "in your beautiful language. It is so interesting. I too have been to *Yerusha-layim,* so interesting. Yes, and to Haifa also. A beautiful city."

The captain said, "Do you know what we say about the beautiful Haifa?"

"What is that?"

"The most beautiful thing in Haifa is the road to Tel Aviv."

All the Israelis, a little drunk, laughed.

"Yes," the German said, "this is a kind of humor, I think."

Amatsia had sailed across the Atlantic Ocean with the captain ten years earlier. He smoked, and I smoked too, pretending to be him, because I wanted to fit in and because he seemed to be an admirable man, quiet and hardworking, and from time to time the captain snarled at us in Hebrew.

"He says smoking is stupid," Amatsia said.

I smoked a cigar on a bench along the dock and saw a waterfront bum coming from a hundred yards away. He was burned brown and wrinkled by the sun. He looked like a wallet someone had been sitting on for forty years.

"Have you got another *puro?*" he said. "You speak English? You understand me? Don't worry about Spanish. English is the best. A very good language. With English, you go anywhere in the world. All places. If you know Spanish, what does that get you? Tell me, where can you go?" He made a face as he gestured around himself, disgusted by the beauty of his native Spain.

It had been a long time since Señorita Geile had taught me Spanish with her hand puppet named Teodoro, a little bear. I had written the Pledge of Allegiance, *juro fidelidad a la bandera de los Estados Unidos de América,* as a punishment when I was bad, which had been often, and I had memorized *poesía,* but now I couldn't remember one word of it, which is not what *memorize* means. I memorized the Pledge of Allegiance, and I memorized this fact: I am bad.

A cabdriver said to me, "How many languages do you speak? Your Spanish is very bad, we're not going to count that one." He adjusted his eyeglasses and said, "The real money in this cab-driving business is the night shift, the *putas.* Tell me something. How do you say *fucky-fucky* in English?"

I floated in a sea of Hebrew, or in an estuary of Spanish and Hebrew. I made up ways to spell what I thought I was hearing. It's astonishing what you won't need to know in this life. I got by for weeks with nothing but *ani rotse le'echol mashehu bevakasha,* which means, I think, *I want something to eat, please.* I thought about language—speaking in tongues, rebuking the Devil—and I thought about twins: about my new sibling, the fellow analysand I loved and had shared my precious analyst with and now wanted to kill. I would kill him and eat him. Maybe I would eat him first.

There were twins at my high school, nice shy Vietnamese boys. They were king-hell math achievers, but they hardly spoke a lick of English. At first I figured they spoke French at home, or Vietnamese, but I came to understand that they didn't speak those languages either. They'd had one another since birth, before language, and they had never seen the need to learn to speak anything.

The Israelis were competitive in all things, and they soon set out to establish who was the greatest shipboard cook. The contest lasted for weeks and was delicious, but I was often unwell, and there was the small problem of the head onboard. I made it filthy, sometimes twice, because I was unwell, and then I made it clean again, not without some effort. I have cleaned a lot of toilets, I worked as a janitor at one time, and I can tell you land-based toilets are preferable, they do not move.

Shlomo wouldn't take his turn cleaning the head. "It stinks," he said.

"The head smells fine," said the captain. "What stinks is human shit."

We could urinate over the side if the sea wasn't too rough. "One hand for you, one hand on the ship," the captain said, "and no matter what lies she may have told you, boys, one hand for yourself is plenty. Most of the dead men in the sea have their flies open."

On the boat, we did laundry like this. You wore your underwear until you felt you were no longer a member of the human race. Then you turned it inside out and wore it some more.

I found myself thinking about my father, about a time we had gone to a baseball game together. We were in the parking lot. "When are you moving north?" he said. "The forty-third of Delfember," I said, and he laughed, and then he said, "Help me," and I turned around and my father had shit in his britches.

He'd been out the night before with his best friend, Jeff, a bartender who was blind in one eye and drunk in the other and tended to wear a black T-shirt that said *Vietnam Veteran,* in case any onlookers happened to wonder if Jeff might be a veteran and if so, of what conflict.

And when I say *tended* I mean he wore that shirt to funerals, a T-shirt at a funeral, that was Jeff all the way. When his own brother, when Jeff's brother, Sarge, had died, my father had lent him my mother's car and Jeff, already crocked at ten in the morning, had almost run it off the road on his way to the service, scraping it along the guardrail and snapping off its side mirror. My mother said nothing, which was not her habit.

My father too was a Vietnam veteran. So were a lot of men in my family. One of them was my uncle, who died of Agent Orange–related complications. "Let that be a lesson to you," my father said. "Don't join the service, and don't let your friends join the service. Because they tell you what to do. They tell you where to go, they tell you what to eat. They tell you when to die. And then you're dead."

In that parking lot, my father was right to trust in my expertise. I was well acquainted with the problem at hand. I was a promising young drunk, bad with women and an easy vomiter, and occasionally I had to shit as well. I had shit the bed once and kept sleeping and got up in the morning, going happily about my day off, and had not noticed until my then-wife came home from her job and asked me what it might be in our bedroom that smelled so much like shit. And, of course, it was shit that smelled that way. That was the answer.

And so I was prepared to aid my father. As in so many endeavors, the first step is to lie: I said everything was going to be just fine. I told him he had to be brave for a few minutes, could he do that, could he walk, if not we could find some other way but that would be the simplest, and he said he thought he could.

We walked past the parked cars and trucks and the yellow paint on the asphalt toward the gray concrete of the arena and its public restroom. I got my father into a stall and stood outside and told him to take his shoes and socks and jeans and underwear off. My father hated public restrooms. Once, when I was a little boy, I had noticed he did not wash his hands after urinating and asked him about that habit and he had given his explanation, saying, "I'm confident that my penis is the cleanest thing in this environment."

His drawers were not so bad after all, but I threw them in the garbage just to seem like I was doing something to help. I passed him handfuls of paper towels. "Check your legs down to your ankles and feet," I said. "Check your socks. How are your pants? We want to keep them."

"What if we can't?"

"Then you wear my shirt around your waist like a kilt until we get back to the truck," I said. But he washed and dried himself and put his pants and socks and shoes back on. And that was that. It was nothing he could not have done on his own if he had given it a moment's thought, instead of willing himself to helplessness, to asking for help. *Orders make you stupid,* the captain told me, *figure it out for yourself.*

What do you know, I'm finally shitting my father. God knows I ate enough of him. I am thirty-seven years old, five feet, ten inches tall, 180 pounds, a hairy man like Esau with an increasing amount of gray in my chest, a miniature facsimile of my father is half extruded from my rectum, otherwise I am in good health.

The past is behind me, burning, like a hemorrhoid. My parents will not die if I wish them dead. They will die because life is finite.

When I was in college, one of my teachers said, "What's the matter with you? Are you waiting for your parents to die before you write something honest?" and I said, "That is the dumbest question I have ever heard."

My mother calls collect from Hell. She rides her bike and goes swimming. There are a lot of ibises in Hell. She sends me a picture. It's pretty. I'm shouting into the telephone, I'm trying to shout but it's hard to make a noise, my jaw won't work, my teeth are long and getting longer, they break against each other, everywhere I turn I'm biting something. I bite the telephone, biting.

My parents are not dead. I mean hell on earth, plain old regular real hell. You know that hell? That's the one I'm talking about. And even when they are dead they will live on in me, burning in my hell-head, it's so crowded in here, still yammering about what I ought to do: *Now I see how it is, you drop a coat hanger on the floor and if no one is watching you don't pick it up, that's the kind of man you've become.* My dead father in particular is very interested in the proper configuration of everyday household items like coat hangers.

Ibiza was on fire as we approached by night from the sea. A third of the island was burning. We anchored and watched airplanes swoop to fill their tanks with seawater. They flew high over the mountains and dropped water on the burning trees again and again. It was the biggest wildfire on the island in all of recorded history. It was still burning the next day when we left.

Shlomo, swimming just before we pulled up anchor, was stung by a jellyfish. "Do you want me to pee on it?" I said.

"No, I want you to shit on it," he said. "Americans!" he said.

On that boat, surrounded by blank water and blank Hebrew, with a somewhat less blank Spanish awaiting me on shore, I was free from the obligation to apprehend and interpret. If I don't understand what you want from me, I don't have to try to do it, I can't. The sea is incomprehensible and uncomprehending, the sea doesn't care, which is terrific, depending on what kind of *care* you are accustomed to receiving. The sea is wet.

As a teenager I was once waved through a roadblock by a police officer who then pulled me over and ticketed me for running the roadblock. "I don't understand what you want from me," I said, something I had already, at that early age, said many times to many different people.

"What's the matter with you?" the officer snarled, something many different people have said to me, and when my father and I went to court we found I had been charged with attempting to elude a police officer and failure to comply. My father knew the judge, or should I say the judge knew my father: she had been his girlfriend in high school. My father and I were wearing the nicest clothes we owned.

"Well, Mr. Prosecutor, what do we have here?" the judge said, smiling.

"The apple doesn't fall far from the tree," said Mr. Prosecutor, and he was also smiling, and they were speaking to and for my father, not to me, although I had been charged with *attempting to elude a police officer,* for Christ's sake, I still don't understand it. I got off with a fine for making an illegal turn. The judge knew my father, everyone knew my father, just as everyone had known my grandfather, and even people who had not been alive at the time knew that all the lights in Hodgenville, Kentucky, had gone out when my grandfather died. I was not a tree, I was an apple, I had not fallen far from those trees, but I had fallen. Somewhere there had been an apple and a fall. This much we knew.

If anyone wanted something from me on that boat, he said my name; if no one said my name, I was not wanted. And *I was not wanted,* I floated for a month in a sea of unmeaning noise, I was free from the horror of being deformed by another person's needs and desires.

I became a twin, a sibling to myself, and I gnawed myself for nourishment in the red cavern of the womb, relaxing into my own death.

I ate myself until there was nothing left but my mouth. Then I ate my own mouth. Then I died.

But no one ever dies. I got off the boat and hailed a cab and took a train to Madrid.

In Madrid I went to the Prado, where I looked at Goya's *Saturno devorando a su hijo*. There he sat, sickened, with his horrid mouthful, and the whites of his eyes were huge.

I had always thought of Saturn as vicious, as power-mad. I had never realized how frightened he was, how compelled to commit and experience horror against his will. I began to cry. I felt sorry for Saturn. He didn't want to eat anyone. His stomach hurt. He wasn't even hungry.

And I flew home. Last night I dreamed the Devil bit my penis off. This morning it was still there, or *here*. Where I am is called *here*.

JOHN JEREMIAH SULLIVAN

Ghost Estates

FROM *The New York Times Magazine*

IRELAND BEGINS FOR ME with the end of "The Dead," which my father read to me from his desk in his basement office in Indiana. I don't remember what age I was—feels like anytime between the sixth and eleventh birthdays—but I picture the scene with a strange and time-slurred clarity of detail. His offices were always in the basement, because that's where he could smoke his endless, extra-long menthols, exhaling nasally over the rust-red mustache. The air in the room would get so thick with smoke that shafts of sunlight beaming in through the high basement windows took on a slab-like solidity of definition, such that you couldn't believe your hand passed through them so easily. I accept that tobacco is evil, in both health and historical terms, but will always love it on some animal level, because the smell of it was so great a part of the physical existence of my father. I smell it in his sweat when he bends down to kiss me, and I smell it in this room. I also note cat urine, because our vicious, lonely old calico likes to relieve herself on the dark green chair in the corner when stressed, and the scent has soaked into the stuffing, and my father won't throw away the chair, because it belonged to his father. The mottled surface of the desk where he writes is a dark green—the green that is almost black—and bright, glowing green are the little letters on the screen of the primitive word processor the newspaper gave him, and forest green is the cover of *The Portable James Joyce*, my mother's Penguin paperback from college. He's holding it close to his face. He was blind in one eye and couldn't see especially well out of the other, wore dark-framed, vaguely government-issue glasses, but they're lowered. He's turning his head and squinting over the top of them. He reads the famous last paragraph, "The time had come for him to set out on his journey westward . . ." Nothing of the specific language remained with me, except, years later, reading the story at school, there was something like déjà vu at the part where Joyce first says the snow was "falling faintly," and then four words later says it was, "faintly falling." The slight over-conspicuousness of that had stuck, as I suppose Joyce intended.

That memory found me last year, as I sat outside a hotel on the Aran Islands, off the west coast of Ireland, talking to the night manager and having the first cigarette I allowed myself in a long time. For once I'd given in not out of anxiety but from sheer ex-cellence of mood. After four days in the country, my jet lag hadn't corrected by as much as an hour, so it was pleasant to find that the manager, Chris, made good company. Not just that, but he had keys to the bar. In fact, he was also a bartender. If any locals wandered in at 3:00 A.M., as happened more or less nightly, Chris would open the bar and serve them. And if they caught him in the middle of a short nap on the sofa in the lobby, they knew to shake him awake. "It's great," he said. "It makes my night go faster."

He was one of the most authentically Irish-seeming guys I'd ever met, apart from the lone fact of his being Ukrainian. His fam-ily left before the Orange Revolution, and now they were scattered all over. A lot of his (very good) English was perfected in Ireland: his Ukrainian accent had an Irish accent. I can't describe it, but it suited him. He seemed to be going through life quietly, good-naturedly laughing at how charming he was. He set up two chairs in front of the hotel, with a view of the harbor and the moon, which was either full or almost full, the moon over the dark jutting silhouette of the Aran Islands, a thing I'd always hoped to see. He told highly convincing wee-hours bar stories that can't be printed but that had a way of involving "beautiful, insane" tourist women who nearly caused him to be late for work.

A couple of older gentlemen showed up at one point, in jackets and caps. We went inside, so he could take care of them. I sat at the other end of the bar and tried to spy on their conversation a bit, but they spoke in low, grumbly tones, and the English in the western part of Ireland can be so heavily inflected with Gaelic rhythms that it's often hard to tell it apart from the Irish language —you see tourists, having passed some natives and overheard a chance remark, turn to each other and whisper, "That's Irish," when what the woman said, if your ear had been given time to adjust, was something like "Don't open the gate yet, idiot!"

Back outside, I asked Chris about the men, who they were. "Well," he said, "they *used* to be fishermen." But the fisheries had been declining for some time, partly due to overfishing, and "when the Tiger came"—by which he meant the Celtic Tiger, the mainly technology-fueled economic boom that began in the mid-1990s and transformed Ireland before the collapse three years ago of a catastrophic housing bubble—"a lot more tourists were coming here. So a lot of the fishermen sold their boats and bought mini-buses." It was the easiest fishing on earth: you just picked them up at the dock. But it didn't come naturally to the men, dealing with outsiders. "These are island people," Chris said. Often they would all but forcibly herd the dazed and newly arrived visitors onto the minibuses, drive them to a few main sites, mumble some unintelligible words, and drop them off again, demanding payment. Folks complained, but the ex-fishermen complained harder, at the bar. Many of them regret giving up their boats, Chris said, especially now that tourism, post-Tiger, has gone back to the old decent-but-sleepy levels.

The day before, on the way from the dock to the hotel, I had passed rows of these minibuses, each with its own bored-looking owner standing by the open driver's-side door, on the way from the dock to the hotel. One man gave me the look, asking if I needed a ride, but when I said, "I'm just going to the hotel," he said, "Aye," and looked relieved, folding his arms back and looking off, even though it turned out that the hotel was farther than a person would want to walk with an awkward, heavy suitcase and he could easily have talked me into it. Something in him hadn't wanted to. That something is part of what draws travelers to the Aran Islands: it takes an independent and even perverse character to live the way they do, on three spits of barren limestone in the North Atlantic, in a place where you couldn't even grow spuds unless you created your own soil-scrum with a kind of layered-kelp composting. If they were to suddenly offer to braid your hair or be smilingly hustling you onto group tours, it would spoil the effect. You go to the Aran Islands expecting to keep a certain distance from the population. You go to observe their indifference.

There was an obvious affection in Chris's voice as he spoke

about the locals. He saw that they could be funny, but he never made fun. He didn't sound like an outsider. "I feel Irish now," he said. More than that, he felt like an Aran man. "Even Galway seems strange to me now when I go to the mainland," he said. Everyone there looked to be in a hurry. "And I don't know," he said, "they're just different."

He wanted a house, was the thing; he was feeling maybe too old for roommates. And it was frustrating, he said, because there were empty houses on the islands, more than ever in fact. During the Tiger years, many people built and acquired second homes here, and since the crash plenty of these places were empty, "just standing there for years," Chris said. He and some of the other "blow-ins" had approached certain owners and asked to be caretakers, to live there purely in exchange for upkeep. "We said, 'We'll sign a paper that says: "I give up all right to the house once you come back. You show up, I'm out." Plus, your property isn't falling apart.'" But most owners weren't interested. They wanted what was theirs and were clinging to it. Chris looked out at the water thoughtfully, but I gathered he wasn't too worried. His patience was right for this place. He would stay until something happened.

"Marry a girl from Galway?" I asked.

"Or not," he said, and twinkled.

I'd landed in Dublin a few days before, not having been in Ireland, other than the airport, since living there as a twenty-year-old restaurant worker, during whatever you call the life phase in which you try to reconnect with your roots—though what ended up happening, as is common in those cases, was I had my whole idea of "roots" and "heritage" and "blood wisdom" and whatnot smacked out of me in a useful way and exposed for self-serving sentimentality. "Jesus, Johnny, you're more Irish than I am," said Liam, the little red-cheeked, red-haired chef for whom I chopped vegetables in a railroad kitchen in Cork, after I'd unspooled for him once more the glory of my Celtic lineage: Sullivan, Mahoney, O'Brien, Cavanaugh, Considine, my Fenian grandfather, my . . . until he began to berate me for having screwed up the tartar-sauce mixture again, for drinking seven "minerals" on the job one hungover day, or for having brazenly lied about knowing even the most basic, life-sustaining things about food preparation when he hired me.

Nobody cared about "Irish American"; nobody wanted to hear

about it. Were you born here? Then you're not Irish. I remember
the first real Irish bar I ever entered, an old man gave me grief
about it. I'd landed in Shannon with my friend and traveling partner Ben. We had big Barney-looking purple backpacks. We started
hiking out of the airport parking lot. Ben's backpack had a small
orange foldable shovel hanging from it, of uncertain purpose.
Our plan was to camp in farmers' fields; we'd read that you could
do this, and probably Ben meant to dig trenches and latrines with
it. Unfortunately it looked sort of murderous—he described it as
a "cacking tool"—and this made us appear, I realize now, rather
unappealing to passing drivers, who might otherwise have happily
picked us up. Finally a young hippie couple did. I don't call them
hippies derisively; they were real old-school flower children; the
woman had beautiful gold-brown hair that should have had twigs
in it. They told us that recently there had been a terrible murder
in the area—a man had killed a priest, and a child? I don't remember the details. Nobody wanted to mess with hitchhikers, much
less with two carrying a poorly concealed little shovel.

Apart from those helpful hippies, hardly anyone stopped for us.
We walked ourselves into blisters and cramps, but through magnificent, shining valleys, vistas of greens upon greens. Our money,
which had come from selling my car, ran out so quickly that it was
as if someone had put a curse on it, maybe the old Kerry woman
back at the airport in New York, an impishly tiny person who told
us how she'd won a great deal of dough off some airline after she
fell asleep in her seat on a flight and her upper torso tilted out
into the aisle and a beverage cart came along and smashed into
her face. Ben and I kept re-doing the math on where the money
had gone but finally just stopped talking about it.

We did go into this pub, near Killarney. Classic place, dusty,
great wan light. A likely old fellow sat there, with a cane beside his
stool. I was ready to get drunk with him and embrace him as my
kinsman. At one point, while the man was pouring our pints, I put
my hands together behind my back and wiggled around a little,
stretching. I was all messed up from walking so much without any
preparation and sleeping in hard places.

"Oh, *foine*," he spat, holding his whiskey before him. "Do your
exercoises."

We told him our names. We were Irish too!

"Sullivan's an English name," he said, looking down. "O'Sullivan—that's an Irish name."

I was stunned. I told him (as was true, as if it mattered) that my great-grandfather Patrick was a stonemason in Bantry, County Cork, like his father and grandfather before him—I'd seen their illiterate *X*s on parish birth certificates—and their names were Sullivan, not O'Sullivan, and if they weren't Irish, I don't know who—

"I don't know about any of that," he said. "But Sullivan is an English name."

We shouldered our purple packs and kept on toward County Cork. Ben had the decency never to speak of the incident.

This more recent trip was different. When I landed, the first thing I did was rent a car, a tiny violet-colored vehicle called a Micra. It was the smallest car I had ever been inside. I admired its austerity-measures economy and the fact that when I got lost, as frequently happened, I could turn it 180 degrees in about a four-foot radius, like turning yourself on a spinny ride at the fair. As I drove, I kept seeing recent-looking houses and subdivisions, many of which had empty parking lots, as in, all empty. The developments were uninhabited, and they seemed to be everywhere. The phenomenon had actually impinged on the countryside, visually. Large swaths of Ireland had turned beige.

These were the outer fringes of the notorious "ghost estates," tens of thousands of structures, half built and abandoned, or finished but never occupied and swiftly falling apart. They had colonized the island in clusters during the Irish housing madness. One finds them especially near the entrances into cities, where they would (the thinking went) be most conspicuous and status-confirming. Or else they appeared out along the edges of smaller roads, where developers had hoped to plant new townlets (many estates were born with their own ghost pubs and ghost post offices).

In the letters sections of the local newspapers, citizens were offering modest proposals for what to do with these structures. Give them free to returning emigrants and bring the exiles home. Give them to the poor. Or else—and probably most practicable—bulldoze them back into green grass, remove them as eyesores and safety hazards.

I pulled off the road at a few points and walked around in the ghost estates. They were melancholy and menacing-feeling places

—the weeds had started advancing, cracks and holes were opening in the pavement. There was a lot of mold, which couldn't help reinforcing the fungal quality of the estates themselves. Boarded-up windows. In a lot of places the authorities were having a hard time keeping people from stealing building materials from the sites. Stealing from whom, after all? Half the developers responsible for these aborted projects had left the country after the crash. You would hear stories (the Irish relish as topics the hubris and comeuppance of their own) about onetime wheeling-dealing rural builders, having lived high on tax trickery and borrowed money, "and now they say he's living in New Zealand, swinging a hammer like he did before they gave him all that cash!" One of the worst had supposedly gone to Jordan. Meanwhile all these estates were left behind. It had been a dream, like something in a Celtic Revival play: faeries built thousands and thousands of houses in the night. In the morning everybody was poor again, and the houses rotted away.

It was hard to see why the government would allow the ruination of so much open land, which after all is one of Ireland's principal commodities, the "unspoiled" landscape. People go to Ireland for all sorts of reasons, but they mainly go there because it's *pretty*, because it's "not all built up."

From the point of view of the rural Irish themselves, though, this can look quite different. One has to remember that the greenness of Ireland is a false greenness. Not that it isn't green—its roadside views can still make you have to pull off and swallow one of your heart pills. It's that the greenness doesn't mean what it seems. It doesn't encode a pastoral past, in other words, much less a timeless vale where wee folk trip the demesne. The countryside is not supposed to look like that, to be that empty. Ireland was at one time one of the most densely populated places in Europe. In the 1830s there were more people living there than today. What you see in the wide-open expanses the island is famous for are hundreds and hundreds of years of Irish dying and fleeing in large numbers. Famines, wars, epidemics, and a wretched postcolonial poverty drove them into the ports by the millions. It's perhaps not strange that such a people, experiencing their first flush of disposable income, would undergo a mania of home building and land development.

*

In the Aran Islands, in different places including on some of the farms overlooking the ocean, there are curious stone huts, invariably described in guidebooks as "beehive-shaped." They are made out of flat rocks piled atop one another and expertly joined (*corbeled* is the term). Anthropologists aren't in complete agreement about what they are—much less have been the generations of pub-stool antiquarians who'll lay a theory on you for free—but many think that early Christian monks built them. What the monks were doing on three barren slabs of limestone in the freezing sea, why they couldn't pray somewhere near Galway, is unclear. The islands seem to have been an ancient pilgrimage site. Perhaps the huts were shelters for pilgrims. Or maybe people just used them for smoking fish. Or are they tombs? They are as mysterious as they are humble.

The playwright and (less-well-remembered) essayist John Millington Synge writes of walking to see these beehive huts (*clochans* in Gaelic) in *The Aran Islands,* his classic account of living here for several months in the 1890s, when he gathered the material for his greatest plays. No writer is more closely associated with this place and its people than Synge, although in many ways he makes an unlikely representative. He was Anglo-Irish, Protestant in his upbringing, fairly well-to-do, scientifically minded—there could have been, at the time, few Irish people possessing less in common with the peasantry he wound up making his subject and taking for his inspiration. Even in his famed descriptions, and despite their vividness, you sense a remoteness. It was the artist in him, the very thing that made him a great writer. He never loved his own people too much, so as to be unable to see what was grotesque and silly and consequently most human in them. On his walk to the beehive huts, he's following an old blind man named Mourteen, a local storyteller who gave him all sorts of material. The man knows the islands so well that Synge cuts his feet trying to keep up, despite the fact that his guide can't see—"so blind that I can gaze at him without discourtesy," is Synge's phrase. The old man at one point indulges "a freak of earthly humour" and starts talking sex, saying what he would do if he could bring a girl into the hut with him. They pass a house where a schoolteacher lives alone. "Ah, master," the old man says, "wouldn't it be fine to be in there and to be kissing her?" It's just the kind of scene that Synge's detractors hated him for. The heroism of his characters tends to arise from a helpless urge to be themselves, against all better judgment.

Poor Synge. He spent half his adult life thinking he had tuber-culosis, then found out he had Hodgkin's disease. He died when he was not even thirty-eight—I was the age at which he died, on this trip, which fact made the weight of his achievement suddenly palpable. He didn't write his first play until he was thirty-two. Before that he wrote mediocre poems and reviews. It was Yeats who told him to go to the Aran Islands, a place whose people gave him his voice. All of those masterpieces— *Riders to the Sea, The Playboy of the Western World, The Well of the Saints, The Aran Islands* itself—all written in the span of only seven or eight years. It must be reck-oned a true out-flashing of genius in the literature of the twentieth century.

The hike to the beehive huts should have been an easy one, but I had contrived to have with me on the island only one almost-new pair of dress-walking shoes, bought at the airport and nowhere near done chafing; also I radically underestimated the distance to the farm where the *clochans* are (it was miles). After an excessive-seeming time spent walking without finding the heritage-board sign I'd been told to watch for, I figured I must have done some-thing wrong and stopped at a house overlooking the ocean. A man and his son were at work repairing a stone wall. The boy was about eighteen. They dropped their tools and walked over and looked at my map with me. "Well, you're a strange sort of tourist," the man said when I laid out my agenda. I wasn't sure what he meant—that not many people wanted to see the beehive huts anymore, or that not many people would be stupid enough to try it on foot in black leather shoes—but he assured me I hadn't gone too far and that, in reality, I hadn't gone nearly far enough.

Back on the road I passed a water well, one of the "sacred wells" that Synge mentions in his account. It was a little pool that lay un-der the shadow of a limestone outcropping. Brilliant white heads of Queen Anne's lace swayed in the sunshine that struck the water, and blue-gray butterflies flitted around. I didn't see the butterflies anywhere else on the island, only at this well.

You were walking along the coast, with the ocean on your right and the central stony ridge of the island running along high on your left. Up there were thatched-roof houses and long stone walls, joined tightly enough to last for hundreds of years but not enough to prevent sunlight from showing through the gaps and chinks. It gave them a curious filigreed appearance, when you saw them standing against the sky.

Eventually I found the farm, and a carbuncular teenage boy who worked there—who was at that moment preparing to bring some cattle in, for the end of the day—showed me which narrow little path to take. You walk down a long sloping plain toward the ocean. A stark place to live, even for early Christian Irish monks.

I found the *clochans* where the kid said they would be. There wasn't much to think about them beyond their existence, beyond the fact that they were still standing in the open like this after weathering countless wild storms. I crawled inside for a second and squatted. Even the floor was bone-dry.

The city of Cork—the urban center, where all the shops and bars and everything are—is actually an island, a river island. The River Lee splits at a certain place, as it flows toward the sea, and "encloseth Corke with his deuided flood," as Spenser says in *The Faerie Queene.* You can't really sense it if you're there—you just keep feeling like you're running into the river too many times, must be confused, too many bridges, or maybe there are two rivers.

Ben and I worked pretty much every night—it was the price we paid for being allowed to have jobs at all on the cheesy, nonenforceable visas we'd bought from a company in the States. After the restaurants closed we would meet up late and walk home together, stopping at pubs along the way, putting a little punctuation mark on the night, before it was time to head into the hills. Cork city is surrounded by them. From up high you can see that it's nestled at the bottom of a green bowl. Our apartment was on one of the highest hills, a mile's walk up a steepening incline. Once home, there came the final climb, up three flights of stairs. Our rooms were on the top floor. It was literally as high as one could get in Cork. There was a big picture window, where we would stand and watch the cargo ships coming up the Lee. The window offered fantastically little resistance to the wind. When the weather turned cold, the flat was like a place where Poe could have lived. In the middle of the night we would sit there in our sleeping bags, tending a coal fire that had almost zero perceptible influence on the temperature of the room. Our money kept running out—after rent and food, we'd be at zero every month, and neither of us had family checks coming. When it got worst, we had a system, undignified but effective: I would stroll at an appointed moment down the alley beneath the window of the kitchen where Ben worked, so he could drop two baked potatoes down to me. One I'd save for him, the other I'd eat on the spot.

I did the first disciplined writing I'd ever done in that apartment—in a little sitting room with a picture of some long-dead pope on the wall, on a plastic typewriter that my father shipped over to me. Everything I wrote was a tremendously bad imitation of James Joyce, but what was different now was when I looked at it, I saw how bad it was and didn't despair but wondered how it might be less bad, and kept going.

My father visited in the fall. It was the first time he'd ever been to the auld sod, and the last time he and I ever went on a trip together or anything like that. His body was already failing. The few little hikes we attempted, he had to keep stopping over and over. But sit in a pub and drink and smoke and talk about books? That was a miniature heaven, and we spent most of our few days there. We drove down to Bantry, the family omphalos—he proudly demonstrating amazing lefty gear-shifting skills—and found some old family graves. At one point, when we had introduced ourselves to a man in a shop—the sign said Michael Sullivan, my father's name—my father remarked to the man that we were "looking for our ancestors." The man thrust out his hand and said, "I'm your ancestors!"

This trip, on my second day back in the city, I walked down to the neighborhood around University College Cork. In a coffee shop on the campus there, I had a long conversation with four young men just finishing their studies. Brian Burke was thin, with a trim red beard and fiercely skeptical eyes. He had just finished a dissertation on "Mechanisms for Fixing Pay and Conditions in Ireland." There was also a trio of dark-headed guys: Colm, Peter, and Cathal. All had known one another, with different degrees of closeness, during their university schooling. Colm was a big, tall man with a shaved head and glasses, who wanted to do something with an international aid agency, an NGO; Peter was a journalist, doing a kind of temporary gig—something between an internship and a job—at a paper in Waterford; and Cathal hoped to go into business. He already had made plans to leave for London. "But his parents don't know yet," Peter said. The implication was that his parents wouldn't be happy about it. The other three were thinking about emigrating too. Not necessarily in the sense of planning to do it, but thinking about it. For an Irish person, the question is always there, the way it is for, say, a Cuban. To be Irish is to make up your mind about whether or not to leave Ireland.

In some respects, it was like sitting anywhere in the world with young people who are just out of college. Their brains are oiled, they know what's wrong with the world and how to fix it. But in this case, their talk had a kind of baffled stoicism to it, because they were part of a generation that had been bred for a new kind of success. A unique generation in Irish history. They grew up hearing "It'll be different for you." And now they were leaving school, and it wasn't different. It was like before. Among their group of friends—equally well educated—it was considered lucky to have jobs at the local customer-service call center. (Ireland is famously good at doing these centers, like India, something I hadn't known, and the lads had received some training there in how to deal with people's anger and outrage when you told them their phone was being cut off or whatever.)

They asked me if I had heard of the Elysian tower, the "ghost tower." I had seen it there in town, without knowing its story or its name. Built since I lived there, it was now the tallest building in Cork—indeed the only tall building in Cork. Luxury apartments. The rumor in town (details of which turned out to be exaggerated, but only slightly) was that only the penthouse had ever been occupied. And it cost the management company so much to maintain services to the old woman who lived up there, they finally had to move her out. They bought her a house. But for a few months she stayed up there, they said, looking out over the city.

Ben's father was very sick while I was in Ireland this recent time. The thought occurred of inscribing to him an old copy of Synge's collected works I'd brought with me and leaving it at the little library on Aran. The librarian wasn't there—she only works certain days of the week—but a very pleasant lady, when I told her what I wanted to do, opened the door for me and loaned me a pen and let me sit there in a sunny corner.

I felt regret at parting with the book, which made it seem right to leave it there. *The Complete Works of John M. Synge,* 1935 Random House edition, the only one-volume edition I've seen that has all of his stuff. It's worth finding, not just for the sake of having all the plays in one place, but because it reveals a lesser-known Synge, Synge the writer of powerful nonfiction pieces, essays like "The Vagrants of Wicklow" and "In the Congested Districts." He wrote some of the best Irish walking journals ever, and that's not a narrow genre; perhaps only Heinrich Böll's are as good. Before handing over the book, I reread a favorite paragraph from *The Aran Islands*, where Synge describes men bringing horses ashore in their small sailing craft: "The storm of Gaelic that rises the moment a horse is shoved from the pier, till it is safely in its place, is indescribable."

The other good thing about a collected Synge is that you can read the rest of his plays, the ones that didn't become as famous but all of which have moments that are on a level with his best writing. The night before, after Chris had excused himself to do some work—it turned out he did have some duties as night manager, it wasn't all sleeping and pint-pulling—I read *The Shadow of the Glen*, the plot of which came from yet another tale Synge heard on the Aran Islands. A husband decides to fake his own death in order to test the loyalty of his wife—he'll spy on her from his slab, see how she behaves with the men who come to pay their respects. A tramp shows up by chance, and the woman takes a liking to him. During a brief, magical, cursed night, she sits talking to her new friend while the falsely dead husband lies there listening (multiple vectors of betrayal converging: take note, budding playwrights). The woman allows herself to dream about the life she'll have with the money her old man has left her in a sock—not a grand life, but less boring and awful than the one she'd been living with him. When at last he sits up, revealing his ghastly trick, she's so horrified that she doesn't know what to do except prepare herself for death. But the tramp won't let her think that way. "You'll not be getting your death with myself, lady of the house," he says,

> and I knowing all the ways a man can put food in his mouth . . .
> We'll be going now, I'm telling you, and the time you'll be feeling
> the cold, and the frost, and the great rain, and the sun again, and
> the south wind blowing in the glens, you'll not be sitting up on a wet
> ditch, the way you're after sitting in the place, making yourself old
> with looking on each day, and it passing you by. You'll be saying one
> time, "It's a grand evening, by the grace of God," and another time,
> "It's a wild night, God help us, but it'll pass surely."

The speech was reminiscent of Christy's equally great one from the ending of *Playboy*, and of countless other passages in Synge. They are versions of the single great discovery he made in his study of the Irish character—the notion of survival as an act of imagination. Against the unacceptability of the void he pits the howl of irrational humor and the keen. He was too dignified to apologize much for his work to hostile critics, but he might have said, in response to the charge that he was aloof from the true rural Irish, that he shared their unforgotten paganism.

People said he made clowns of the peasants—there are still writers who complain that his dialogue wasn't always true to real Irish folk speech, a criticism that manages to be correct while driving past his achievement, which was to go beneath them, into something even older and deeper, the Greeks. Possessing the mercenary instinct of the artist, he sought not to "capture" the Irish language but to mine it for his English sentences. He had in him something of Gabriel, from "The Dead," who when chastised for not wanting to visit the Aran Islands and learn his own native tongue answers sourly, "Irish is not my language." In his room here at the inn, they say, Synge lay on the floor with his ear to the boards, listening to the talk of the people below, making notes. Out of that stuff, the table talk of the islanders, he made plays that caused riots in multiple countries.

Whatever comes next, after the crash and the austerity measures and who-knows-what that follows, Ireland will have to make itself anew. If it's smart, that is—if it doesn't insist, like us, on desperately trying to crawl back to the conditions that made the bubble. Synge's character knew what it meant to wake up hopeless and get back to it, back to the incomprehensible business of being alive, and not listlessly but with defiant panache. A century after his last works were published, he is again the writer Ireland needs.

MEGAN STIELSTRA

Channel B

FROM *The Rumpus*

FOR THE FIRST few months after my son was born, I called him
The Baby, or sometimes just Him with a capital *H,* huge proper
nouns to illustrate how completely he took over my life. Is he eating, not eating? Pooping, not pooping? What color is the poop,
how long ago was the poop, did I mark the poop on the spread-
sheet? I had spreadsheets. I had *stuff*—white noise CDs and magnetic blocks and this super-high-tech video monitor with a remote
wireless screen and night vision, which made The Baby glow electric green in the dark as if he were a CIA target. It was a little
unnerving, actually. It had two frequencies, an A channel and a B
channel, in case you had two kids in separate rooms, and what's interesting about this is that one of my neighbors must have owned
this same monitor, because on channel A I saw my baby, and on
channel B I saw someone else's.

And if I could see someone else's, then someone else could see
mine.

We live in a third-floor walkup in Uptown surrounded by other
third-floor walkups. Jumping onto a neighbor's Wi-Fi signal isn't
much of a stretch, so perhaps the fact that I could toggle between
babies shouldn't have been a surprise. But it was. It was huge. I was
obsessed. On one hand, it was totally creepy—stalking, even—but
on the other? It was sort of magical, like walkie-talkies and CB radios when you're a kid: connecting with someone across the void,
adding your voice to the collective unconscious, feeling less alone
in this crazy world, and who knows who might be listening?

Who knows who's in that Uptown condo on channel B?

A baby, to be sure, but it wasn't the baby I was obsessed with. It was the mother.

My imagination went wild when I thought of the mother. Did she sit there watching my kid in the dark? Did she question his bedtime? Wonder where I got his pajamas? How might she react if I left a sign in his crib that read STOP LOOKING AT MY BABY, YOU DIRTY VOYEUR!

Or this one: YAY NEW FRIENDS! DO YOU WANT TO MEET UP AT THE PARK? Or the truth: I AM TERRIFIED. I AM SO TERRIFIED THAT SOMETIMES I CAN'T EVEN BREATHE.

Any winter in Chicago is a force to be reckoned with, but 2008 was particularly awful. The Baby was born three weeks early, middle of the night, middle of a snowstorm. My poor husband had to dig out our buried car, shovel the alley, and navigate Lakeshore Drive through a whiteout blizzard, and that relentless, pounding snow stayed through January, February, March, and into April. I'd taken those months off from work, and my husband, a web designer, had picked up extra projects to cover the difference, so for the most part, The Baby and I were alone in our tiny Uptown condo, beyond which, in my mind, was the ice planet of Hoth. Remember Planet Hoth? From *The Empire Strikes Back?* Luke almost freezes to death, but Han Solo pushes him inside a dead tauntaun for body warmth? *That* Hoth.

I joke about it now, but here's the truth: I was scared to go outside. The Baby might freeze. I was scared to fall asleep. He might suffocate. I was scared he wasn't eating, wasn't latching, wasn't gaining, wasn't doing what the books had said he would do, and every morning when I looked in the mirror, I wondered who that girl was looking back. We all have things about ourselves that we know to be true, and suddenly I couldn't remember any of them. I was unbrushed, unwashed, wearing the same yoga pants and empire-waist shirt every day. I couldn't write. I couldn't laugh. I couldn't feed my kid. At the time my understanding of postpartum depression was primarily shaped by Brooke Shields's memoir *Down Came the Rain:* crippling depression, suicidal thoughts. But since what I was experiencing seemed heavy but not *that* heavy, dark but not really *that* dark, scary but not, you know, like *that,* it didn't occur to me to ask for help. I mean, I wasn't going to hurt my kid. I wasn't going to hurt myself. Right?

Now, four years later, I know that the symptoms and intensity of PPD are as varied as the flowers in a greenhouse. I wish I'd told someone. I didn't need to feel that alone: just me in the frozen Chicago winter with my tiny, fragile baby. And channel B. Whenever The Baby would fall asleep, I'd stare at his Day-Glo body on the monitor, making sure he wasn't choking—or levitating or exploding or whatever horrible thing I'd imagine—and then, assured of his safety, I'd flip the channel to see how that other mother was doing. I bet *her* kid was eating. I bet *she* changed clothes occasionally. I bet for her snow wasn't a terrifying apocalypse but rather a Hallmark-like sprinkling of picturesque flakes—"Walking in a Winter Wonderland," if you will. And yes, I know, it was completely intrusive and unethical and, above all, *ridiculous*. Why was I comparing myself to this woman? I never even *saw* her! Mostly there was just an empty crib. Sometimes there was a baby, wiggling and doing baby things, but the mother was a total nonentity. Until one night I flipped over to channel B and heard crying. Not from the baby—he was fast asleep, an angel—but somewhere in his room, a woman was sobbing: heavy, gaspy, gulpy sobs.

They went on. They went on and on. I shouldn't have listened. But it was the first time since my son was born that I didn't feel alone.

What finally changed things was this: *spring*. Birds! Green things! Grilling on the porch! Frozen blender drinks! Short skirts! Outdoor seating! SPF! Lemonade! Which you can get any time of year, but it tastes better in the sunshine! Sunshine! My God, how desperately I'd needed it! I'd wager most Chicagoans feel this way in spring, but for me, May 2008 was a godsend, a great, mammoth hand reaching down out of the clouds and pulling me to my feet.

That May, The Baby became Caleb, smiling, laughing, responding, four months old and learning about the world outside my lap. I'd strap him in a backpack and walk through Uptown—Broadway to Argyle, down to the beach and back up Montrose—finding magic in everyday things. Plastic grocery bags? Amazing. Tapping a glass with a spoon? Kick-ass! Water in a dish? Fun for hours! One morning he reached for a yellow street-cleaning sign stapled to a tree, and all at once I saw yellow as if I'd been blind to it for years: *Brake lights! Parking lanes! Flowers in the neighbors' yard! Taxis! More taxis!*

And in that moment we passed a woman with a stroller. She was pretty, early thirties, wearing yoga pants and a yellow empire-waist shirt. She looked nice. And tired. And interesting, like there were all sorts of secret things about her that were set on pause for the time being. She looked like how I saw myself. We nodded at each other in solidarity. This, I had newly discovered, is the way moms do it: acknowledging the fact that even though you don't know each other, you're still a part of this great cosmic team. And then you check out each other's kids. Hers was grabbing his toes in the stroller—so sweet. So adorable. So . . . *familiar,* and not in that All Babies Are Alike sort of way. I looked closer: yes, I knew this kid, and suddenly I saw him not face to face on Lawrence Avenue but electric green on a tiny handheld screen.

I looked back at the mother. "You know—" I started, then stopped, 'cause, really, what would I have said? *Stop looking at my baby? You want to meet up at the park?* How's about the truth: *You helped save me.*

"Your baby is beautiful," she said.

"So's yours," I said.

We stood there.

We stood there long past what is appropriate for strangers. I like to think it's because she was thinking the same thing I was. That maybe she too had flipped channels in the middle of the night, trying to connect with someone across the void or feel less alone in this crazy world. Maybe she'd overheard me crying in Caleb's bedroom, months ago when everything still seemed so cold, so impossible.

"How are you?" I asked her. I wasn't just saying it. I really, really wanted to know.

She smiled. "I'm getting better."

"Me too," I said. "I'm getting better."

It was something about myself that I knew was true.

DAGOBERTO GILB

A Little Bit of Fun Before He Died

FROM ZYZZYVA

ONLY WEEKS BEFORE, I'd been across the street at the University of Texas at El Paso Museum, working a three-story add-on as a carpenter—the second-highest-paid worker on the job site at $5 an hour. It was because I could also tie steel, an ironworker's trade, that I got this big-time wage. No, it was not good money even then, in 1979, except in El Paso. Yes, I was proud of myself to have backdoored my way into an English department teaching job that included a well-air-conditioned, downstairs office. It really belonged to a full-timer who never used it, and because he liked me, he wanted to help a young writer out. A sweaty carpenter banging nails those weeks ago, now I was banging an electric typewriter, finishing my first novel. I would learn that lots of my new colleagues there didn't really like my having an office. I was only a part-timer —a couple of remedial composition classes I had to learn to teach under the false assumption, theirs, that I had a graduate degree in English. But there I was, a luxurious office completely to myself, with a sweet, picturesque view of the very poorest lean-to shacks of Juárez across the border. Typing. I was not unhappy with the change in my personnel status.

Next door was one of the many and mostly shared offices. I did not socialize much with campus people, so initially I was not very responsive when Bill Ripley, half of my next-door neighbor, interrupted the precious artist-at-work concentration I kept on my first opus. He was bigger than those numbers, six-two. His belly was prominent even then, and that's what I and many called him too, Belly Ripley. He showed much personal abuse all over his body already, beginning with the acne scars from his youth. I don't remember what his exact first words to me were, how he charmed me, but I am sure it had to do with his country-boy grin, and I'm sure it had something to do with him suggesting how both of us surely needed an afternoon toddy. I had never heard the word *toddy* before, and so I certainly had never had one. So I stepped out with him, persuaded, sold, actually smiling about cutting my afternoon schedule short.

I think the word *toddy* didn't only make me want to laugh in itself. It was the way Ripley made the word's fussiness sound even funnier, especially as it echoed in an air-conditioned hall at the Texas-Mexico border. It was so, like, Eastern—at once both sophisticated and classy, yet mocking that pretension. Like drinking hot tea in teacups and saucers with those rings in the middle to secure the cup there and teaspoons (as in, spoons for tea) for, I guess, a lump of sugar. Or honey. Or maybe to stir milk? I hadn't been taught any of this in my youth. El Paso was the most East I'd ever lived. Whereas Ripley, with his Texas drawl, he'd gone to Harvard. I knew what Harvard was like; I knew what the White House was. President Kennedy went to Harvard. Ripley was the first person I ever met and talked to—had a toddy with, which he taught me was just a shot of whiskey at a bar—who'd gone to Harvard.

Not only that, Ripley'd published his first short story in the *Harvard Crimson*, the campus paper. Which was all the more impressive to me, as he thereby became the first person I hung out with who'd ever published anything. He'd turned down a scholarship offer, he told me, to play football at Texas. After Harvard, he got into a law school—I think in Colorado—but he hated law school and loved drugs and therefore lasted only a week, give or take. He moved to Austin. He had title, he would say, to some iddy-biddy acres there in Central Texas, which, like anyone else who'd never been east of El Paso, I assumed was lots of dirt, not what I know now to be Dripping Springs, which is twenty miles west of Austin, in what is the idyllic Texas Hill Country. He began to sell marijuana on a larger scale than many, moving it out of West Texas to the north and east. He had three women drivers who, he claimed, listened to him attentively and loved his cocaine. Women, he explained, were the best drivers because the cops never suspected them. When one of them got pulled over with a few hundred pounds of weed, his theory was proven to be mistaken. Except his stepdaddy was a congressman in Colorado, and he knew a lawmaker in El Paso. His conviction was adjudicated into a sentence of him never leaving the city limits of El Paso without permission while enrolling himself in a master's degree program in creative writing at UTEP.

I knew nothing about creative writing. Until that point, despite evidence everywhere that apparently didn't register in my brain, I thought all writers were dead—not their literature, only them—and therefore I had a good shot at some openings. For years I was the only living person I was conscious of who wrote. What I knew of the contemporary writing business came out of a used copy of *Writer's Market*. In El Paso, with my new job, my outlook was transmogrifying. I had even befriended a much-praised, published poet and teacher who introduced me to Gary Snyder when he visited. We had dinner together at a small table! I watched and heard a spectacular Robert Bly reading—way before his men's movement fetish and probably before that drum-beating-in-a-circle thing. And the faculty at UTEP, my "colleagues," included Raymond Carver. Now there was Ripley: my first fiction-writer role model.

I liked knowing men who were older than me, because I liked learning from them, and so I liked Ripley, even when I wasn't always comfortable with him. First of all, despite being a large landowner in Central Texas (he'd sell an acre now and then when he needed cash), he was always broke and mooching. He would often slump his big shoulders and virtually pull out the pockets of his pants right when he got to the cash register with a bottle of whiskey, looking at me like a puppy dog. I didn't really like whiskey, and though I plead guilty to drinking more of it than I ever had in my life, he drank three to my one. I lived in an apartment with only a wife, a double mattress on the floor we shared, a rocking chair, a TV (black-and-white), and a newborn baby who shared the rocking chair with her and the mattress with both of us. This was the entire expanse of our belongings besides clothes and books. I barely made the monthly rent, and that was with construction side jobs I did.

Along with Ripley's busty girlfriend, whom he called Peaches or Cookies or Creamy—I can't remember—we were once asked to leave a late-night Denny's. They'd been eating their food with too much wet, licking spoons and chewing on forks, too drunk and high, and I did laugh too loud myself, too. Though I'd concede that the noise at our table didn't help, in my opinion the heap of staring was out of a visual taboo—his petite girlfriend, who was in her early twenties, looked fifteen and would often be taken for his daughter if left without an introduction, while he, being overindulgent in every category of intake, had more middle-aged bulk, and his other excesses prematurely lined his face into that of a man in his mid-forties. Not that the two of them couldn't in fact offend. Back in his apartment, little Peachie might jump on his stuffed chair, straddle his lap, and pull up her top so that he could nibble and suckle. I had to tell Ripley that, nice as that seemed even from my distance, could he please take me home?

Numbers of events in his El Camino. I had to tell him often to be careful when he spoke about Mexicans. Always uncomfortable with his cracker side, I would steam about his favorite descriptives. When I'd blow, he'd say I was crazy and exaggerating and being overly sensitive. Once he was driving and another car did something he didn't appreciate. Niggers, he yelled, though none were black. I had to tell him: *Let's be clear, Ripley. You ever have a problem with any black dudes because you just said that, I'm telling you now I do not and will not back you up. You are on your own, and I will make it very well known whose side I'm on.* He could only shake his big head and go like it was me making something of nothing, not getting his humor, while I would wonder what I was doing riding with him. I didn't drink whiskey and I didn't like shitkickers. Maybe it'd be considered exciting to be moving at 100 mph, bouncing high off the small rises on Mesa, that big west-side El Paso street, but I was never drunk enough to not think it was way stupid and beg him to stop. Like slowing through red lights and stop signs, driving too fast was his deal. Maybe the draw for me was that Harvard mix in it. He was going maybe forty-five through Kern Place—a desirable, rich, attractive Anglo neighborhood—and ahead not fifty yards, on the left side of the street, a yardman in a straw hat was raking leaves. Without losing any speed, Ripley steered that El Camino and ran it over the curb and onto the middle of the lawn and into a stop exactly beside the man who could not have moved fast enough. He rolled down his window. As stunned as I was as a passenger, the Mexicano clutched the rake. His mouth might not have been open, even if it seems as though it was to my memory. I swear he didn't blink. I too would have thought I had just survived death were I him. And then, as he did, I started listening to Ripley lecturing on the topic of life's sorrows and expectations after retirement from sports. The yardman, who I don't think was following a word of it even if he knew enough English, didn't move, didn't flinch, made no sound whatsoever. It certainly was not as hilarious as it hit me, drunk enough, but I was crying with shameless and shameful laughter.

Laughter. Laughing was how we wrote a poem one afternoon at a relatively new gourmet-style coffee shop on Mesa Street. Ripley was in a graduate class in poetry and had to write a poem. He didn't write poetry, and no, I certainly could not help him—never an attempt at verse ever. "Come on, Dagoberto." There was always something funny, humor-inducing, about Ripley even saying my name. It alone caused me to grin. Maybe how he made each syllable a drawled word of badly accented Spanish . . . He wrote a line. I shook my head. Then we had to talk and figure until we started laughing about what we were trying to do—you know, scamming out a poem for a class to keep his parole grades up—and it got so that what the poem should be about was us doing this. That is, not working, drinking, high, creating poetry, more cheating on "homework" than making art. Which was the art of it! As true poets, he'd pronounced us, we were so often so very busy "researching" for serious art that it was demeaning to have to write obligatory poetry for a class. Therefore, it wasn't fair. He'd write a line about life not being fair. Once a line made us both laugh, it became a keeper, and more lines piled up. It got so that, toward the end, we were laughing way out of control. A funny poem, the fun, much of it off the page, was that we were writing this at all, and editing it through laughing. We were just messed up, until finally he was downing coffee to get sober enough to type it up and submit it to his early-evening seminar.

The poem was about us sitting there in an air-conditioned coffee shop, in the middle of a scorching desert afternoon in El Paso, having nothing but poetry to do, while everybody else out there in the world was responsibly employed. All we wanted to do—all we had to do—was to have a little bit of fun. That was what Ripley always said, like it was his motto or creed. Especially when he was Rippedly, wasted on drugs or liquor, usually both, which was a lot. Funny, Ripley was a sad, self-destructive, self-abusing man. And when he was really too fucked-up, so gone his mass became a limp blob of can-barely-move, he might get his breath too close to my face, and in his most insincere voice say, "Dagoberto, all I want to do is have a little bit of fun before I die. Now is that too much to ask for? Is it?"

By the mid-'80s, I was the father of a second son and I'd joined the union in Los Angeles as a class-A, high-rise journeyman carpenter. Now I wrote short stories. I thought once I'd published a few, agents or publishers would believe in me as a writer and want that novel I'd finished in El Paso, which I didn't realize yet was simply lousy. I mean, they were in love with Raymond Carver, and if they wanted working-class, well, I actually was still working in that working class more years than I wished I had to.

We lived in a duplex near Micheltorena that overlooked Sunset Boulevard. Next to the building was an empty lot that descended from our street curb down to the sidewalk along Sunset. It was ground-covered in ivy. Which is a jungle paradise for rats. During the fall, it rained so much that the rats were running openly all around in front of our narrow street to get out of their flooded nests. It was sick. I went after disgusting rats like a serial killer. I wrote a story called "The Rat" and I sent it to the literary magazine *Quarterly West*. It was Ripley who turned down the story, saying something like it wasn't him but the rest of them who didn't like Mexicans or literary fiction about them. He'd moved on too. After he'd finished a master's degree in creative writing at UTEP, he went for a PhD in creative writing at the University of Utah.

It wasn't too long after that, he was in L.A. doing a tiny drug transaction, which also coincided with him getting an opportunity to visit his buddy James Crumley, who was in Hollywood to write a screenplay of his novel *The Last Good Kiss* for the director Robert Towne. Crumley had briefly become a creative-writing teacher at UTEP right after I left, and as part of their bonding and mentoring, he and Ripley drank, and so on, a lot. No, not only did I not mind him so wasted when I agreed to drive him to visit Crumley that Saturday afternoon, I was outright excited. At its most lucrative, my life consisted mostly of getting to construction sites by six in the morning and putting in ten or more. When would I ever get to see what it looked like to be put up free in a posh hotel as a writer? But try as I might to finally leave once we'd been there long enough, Ripley sipping more and more, Crumley insisted that Ripley could not be left there. I didn't blame Crumley, but I wasn't expecting to have to care for Ripley the rest of the day either. What else could I do but drive him to the last place he'd been?

Some time before, my wife had been telling me that she thought there'd been a rat in her car, which was a fifteen-year-old Chevy Nova. She showed me our baby's car seat as evidence. I saw how some of its upholstery was shredding at a seam, but I thought there was some other explanation and didn't take it seriously. I was driving Ripley in the Chevy because it was the more luxurious of our poor cars. Ripley was aiming for stupor by the time we left Crumley, and I wasn't especially thrilled. I was afraid he'd gotten the address of the next place we were going wrong, and I would be stuck with his bloat for many more hours. I remember making turns assertively, just, you know, because. If I turned left, the Rippedly would bounce against the passenger door. If I went right, he tipped over to hit my shoulder. I was on the Hollywood Freeway, probably sighing because now I didn't even have anyone to talk to—though I was always tired because of construction work—when I felt his fingers scratching my left shoulder. When I turned my head to him to ask what the fuck, he was drooling with his eyes closed, slumped against the passenger door. I turned my head toward the windshield and felt, then saw, the rat quickly clawing down my left arm, which was attached to the steering wheel. My window was up, but the wind wing was open, turned to allow wind in always because a thief had broken it off its upper hinge and it dangled from the bottom. Ripley! I yelled. The rat jumped from my wrist to the top of the driver's side windowsill. *Ripley!* I yelled. He moaned. The rat scooted to the wind-wing opening. *Ripley, look!* He moaned. The rat held itself there for between one and two seconds, pondering, looking left and right, down at the strobe of the white lane stripes, who knew? And it dove onto the Hollywood Freeway. *Ripley, did you see that?!* "What, Dagoberto?" *That rat, the rat that just jumped out!* "Come on, Dagoberto." *I'm telling you!* I yelled. "Dagoberto, you have rat on your brain." Drunk, he did not believe me. Sober, he never did either, as many times as I recounted that amazing, disgusting rat suicide.

*

Tales of Ripley accumulated. One had him in Central Texas driving wild in the country, with open beers and empty cans in his vehicle, and when he pulled over to pee, he was swarmed and arrested by the Secret Service. President George Herbert Walker Bush was quail hunting nearby. Another had him in Utah at a party where it was either Rust Hills, fiction editor of *Esquire,* or some other big-shot editor like that, drunk and cocained, who battled him in a groveling contest. As Ripley explained, it involved the two crawling across the room to see who was more wasted. When he didn't make it there first, Ripley told the editor that the winner of a groveling contest was he who couldn't get there. The biggest news exclaimed that he had been given a book contract by Atlantic Monthly Press. To me, it was his funniest creative-writing achievement ever. Ripley had taken the stories he had written for a master's degree and linked those into a novel, a creative "dissertation," to earn a PhD and what became *Prisoners,* his only book. Yet as the sales of the publication faded quickly, so did Ripley. No more fellatio-obsessed fictions by him, only more sorry tales of him multiplied, and then he was busted traveling from Texas on his way to Colorado, holding, a large quantity, sales, along those lines. He was weeks in a local jail before his family bailed him out.

But what became the oddest Ripley event ever began back while he was in Utah. I don't know if he had published any previous short stories, but one did appear in the first volume of a series titled *The Best of the West.* I hear echoes of our coffee shop laughter in the opening of this mediocre short story (the Dagoberto character became a snake handler, something like that). What I heard was that it was published because his reputation was consuming Utah. Since I was a figure in his lore, therefore I too seemed to have earned some strange cachet. Which was the only explanation I could come up with for why, one day back in El Paso—where I, my sons, and my wife had returned after Los Angeles—I opened an envelope to find a volume of poetry, which I assumed was for review. By that date, the later '80s, I had published lots of short fiction but only a chapbook-size collection of them, the first book from a new small press in El Paso. I'd never been asked to review or blurb anything, and anyone asking had to be suspicious. And this was a poetry collection from an established press. The author, Wyn Cooper, someone I'd never met, was a young poet, a grad of the Utah program, a protégé I assumed, smitten by the romance of Ripley's debauchery. The only poem that stood out to me, "Fun," I remember well, a liveliness and color and style not in the others, was about Ripley. I left the volume near my bookcase.

Years passed. I'd estimate it was near a decade that I didn't have the slightest inclination to speak to or contact Ripley, because I was so pissed off at something he'd done. I'd hear of him once in a while, sightings and tales, but it was when my friend, author of *Afoot in a Field of Men*, Pat Ellis Taylor (who changed her name to Pat Little Dog), a woman's Kerouac, known all over Austin, whose book was published and promoted alongside Ripley's by the same publisher, that I found forgiveness. Pat did many kinds of the lowest-paying jobs to earn a living and write poetry and live in humid apartment complexes. During the Fourth of July period, she'd open up a fireworks stand. She and her partner would clean out abandoned buildings and suites from failed businesses, and they'd sell the used wares along the side of the highway. One of her more steady gigs was the annual gathering of TAAS test readers and graders. The TAAS test system was Texas governor George Bush's emphasis on testing public school students, and it panicked almost everyone whose job it was to teach the young. The Republicans, in particular, believed these tests would make the schools, rich or poor, accountable, and they were particularly proud. What no one talked about were the test graders, those making sure the kids were good boys and girls—an overeducated social caste who were the most habitually underemployed or unemployable, who saw TAAS as major seasonal income, after which they could return to their various drug addictions, alcoholisms, manias, phobias, severe depressions, marijuanísmos, general unsuitablenesses, and plain weirdnesses. And so it was that Pat Little Dog, regular TAAS grader and reader, told me she had actually sat next to and lunched with Bill Ripley during TAAS grading, where they laughed about their literary success. She told me Ripley said to say hi to me. And I once again smiled about that Rippedly. I was over it. I told her to say I said hello back. I told her to give him my phone number.

Not too much later, I found Ripley was living in a moldy dump in a complex in South Austin. His roommate had been recently released from a penal facility. Ripley had become Dr. Ripley, "the Dark Professor," he called himself. He wrote school papers for a business that catered to loser students who would pay well for them. He liked literary topics the best. His specialty was to offer original compositions that could never be resold. He could also write a B-range paper upon request—sometimes, he explained, suspicions could be drawn if suddenly a student got too smart. But, he said, he was a doctor of creative writing, and he could write in any voice, any style that was desired. Lately he'd gotten to sounding a little paranoid. Working for one of the athletic programs at UT Austin, he heard that somebody thought he saw Ripley geezing outside, or in the bathroom, something like that. Ripley was worried because maybe they were a little concerned about what he knew and what he did and what he might say if they let him go, how much worse if they didn't. And so on.

I hadn't visited him in a long time, but I was making a better-than-average wreck of my own life, an okay time for me to share in his latest troubles. It seemed that the singer Sheryl Crow, living in Los Angeles, was struggling with a song, so to help her out, her producer visited a few used bookstores and bought some poetry books. The producer picked out the same book I'd received back when, the one that had the poem "Fun" in it. She recorded "All I Wanna Do." Though she placed the setting off Santa Monica Boulevard, Ripley's name itself remains inside the lyrics with an evaluation of him.

> *"All I want is to have a little fun*
> *Before I die," says the man next to me*
> *Out of nowhere, apropos of nothing. He says*
> *His name's William, but I'm sure he's Bill*
> *Or Billy or Mac or Buddy; he's plain ugly to me,*
> *And I wonder if he's ever had fun in his life.*
>
> *We are drinking beer at noon on Tuesday,*
> *In a bar that faces a giant car wash.*
> *The good people of the world are washing their cars*
> *On their lunch hours, hosing and scrubbing*
> *As best they can in skirts and suits.*

Ripley was sunk deep into a stuffed couch, books and papers puddled all around, and it was almost as if there was a '50s detective light on him. His face was liquid and sticky-looking, the Texas sweat had caked but was still moist, his graying hair more afraid to relax than simply uncombed and messy, the REM-like flutter of his eyes so quick that human ones like mine took their movement as too slow. His voice was calm, each syllable as distinguishable as the one that preceded and the one that would follow. He'd reached a new dimension of wasted.

"All I Wanna Do" was a hit everywhere, even number one in Germany, as Ripley kept pointing out as dramatic proof of something more. When the rights for the poem were first bought, his excited friend Cooper, Ripley wanted me to believe, offered to pay him half. He wanted to, went his claim, because Cooper always said the poem was Ripley's too. And Ripley agreed, but because it was only a couple thousand dollars, he wouldn't take half that. "He was a friend, Dagoberto," and he wouldn't take that little bit from a friend. He was happy for him then. But now? Why wouldn't he give him some now? He didn't even want half anymore. Just a cut. Fifteen percent was a fair amount, he thought. Cooper refused. He would give nothing. Ripley began to read aloud a too-long and boring letter he had written Cooper, explaining friendship, their friendship, their poem, their agreement according to him. It was a painfully bad letter, the worst Ripley creative writing I'd ever heard.

There was a pounding on the door. Bang, bang, bang. A fist mocking Ripley's speech pattern. He got up like a weightlifter straining for the record. The visitor was a shady dude whose eyes darted. Ripley went through another door and came back. He had the prettiest *colitas* of marijuana you'd ever seen, all curled cute inside a clear freezer bag. The dude, who did not seem like someone into weed, smelled it and rubbed it between his fingers, bought it. When he left, Ripley plopped back into the stuffed couch. He asked if I wanted or knew anyone who wanted an ounce or two of crystal meth. He didn't think so, he said, but he had to ask.

We actually heard the song playing on a radio outside an open window. It was impossible not to laugh. He didn't know what he should do. Ripley said he'd gotten his uncle in Corpus Christi to pursue Cooper. Ripley's uncle was an intellectual property rights lawyer. At that time I didn't even know there was such an item, let alone an attorney for it. Then Ripley clutched what I remember—surely wrong—looked to me like a telegram. It was, Ripley told me, from Cooper or his representative, or his uncle, like that, and said that unless he ceased and desisted in his demands, like that, he would be exposed as a drug dealer and heroin addict. Ripley looked at me like I should be as astounded as he was by the charge. "Why would he be this way, Dagoberto? Why would he want to say these things about me?" I shook my head. What could I add but my laughter?

I didn't keep in touch with Ripley. I have no clue how much fun he had left in him before he died, seven years ago, though he did find a woman and they moved to California. Years passed. Ten more? I got one e-mail from him from there and it was all in caps. It wasn't really screaming at me, being loud, but the opposite. He said he was happy.

MICHELLE MIRSKY

Epilogue: Deadkidistan

FROM *McSweeney's*

I AM CONSUMED most moments by a feeling of sham adulthood, of profound adolescence. Always a late bloomer, I'm dubious as to whether this re-teenaged state in which I find myself is a function of grief and renewal or whether I'm just now finding my way for the first time, admitting that I was never really all that grown-up. Of one thing I am certain: I am not the person I was before Lev died. Nor am I the person I was at the end of the first year, the 365 collected days of which I was supported, carried, sometimes to the point of feeling suffocated—childlike. I became very nearly the ward of my wider world and filled with some kind of crazy uncharacteristic peace and faith in the universe, never alone by accident and never alone by choice.

In year two, the world went back about its business. Lev's tiny legend faded. The well-meaning sympathy of acquaintances soured into something like pity. People listened a little less patiently when I talked about sad things; a feeling of otherness crept on me and fogged me all up, shut me down. I stopped talking about Lev so much. I began to make choices when meeting new people, whether to tell them about Lev at all. I need to decide within a few moments of meeting someone if I want to know that person beyond our introduction. And if I do, I must then find the words to explain my loss and how it's going to be okay. They need to know it's going to be okay, so I tell them it will be. I can tell the whole story of Lev's life quickly and without crying, with a smile even. But it doesn't get easier. It never gets any easier. More often, when meeting new people, I tell them I have just one child (a child with an implied unremarkable medical history). They don't need to know all about me. Lev gets redacted in the interest of everyone's comfort.

For five years I've shown up to work every day in a beautiful, world-class children's hospital. I have a unique unicorn of a job advising the hospital on the experience of being a parent of a patient, working with medical professionals at the top of their respective games, people who are the best in their field at healing children. We work together every day to figure out how to build a better mousetrap from the inside out. I work with men and women of all stripes, from housekeepers to hospital executives to doctors and everyone in between. My job was challenging while Lev was living —switching hats between mother and employee, between problem and solution. Talking with the doctors at Lev's bedside about his heart medication and pacemaker settings and cancer treatment and then meeting those same doctors at boardroom tables to talk about construction projects and hospital policy changes. Sleeping in Lev's room at night and tumbling bleary down to my office in the morning to host family coffee hours for parents of patients, to learn their stories, to feed them back to the system. I used to tell pieces of my story to help parents contextualize the experience of having a sick baby. I was just like them. With Lev gone, I'm two years into my role as the worst-case scenario. As the mother of a child who couldn't be saved, I am a constant reminder of what no one likes to remember: you can't win them all. Like one of the former Soviet republics, the ones whose names you never hear, I'm a casualty of the wider war—a shambled diplomat. I am the ambassador of Deadkidistan. I smile and nod and listen and ask questions. I don't tell my story to the parents anymore.

In the first year after Lev died, the ladies who worked the cafeteria checkout line would occasionally catch me off-guard by asking how I was holding up, how my parents were doing, or telling me they missed seeing my sweet boy. Once and again they would tell me their own stories of grief and ask my advice in solidarity. I'd feel bad in these moments that I didn't know all their names. I didn't know anything about them. But they knew me. And they'd known my son. They knew the sad ending to our story: my son died of cancer and heart disease in a room one floor up from where they serve lunch, one floor down from the gift shop. He died just down the hall from the sunny courtyard where he'd met his brother for the first time three years earlier. He died in a bed a short elevator ride from my office, where I'm about to eat a $4 salad for lunch. Thank you. Have a nice day.

One month to the day before Lev died, I was at a friend's baby shower in Los Angeles. The hosts of the shower arranged the services of a tarot card reader for the party. The guests were abuzz. When the ersatz soothsayer arrived, she looked to be in costume. Dressed in striped thigh-highs and a tutu, her hair in pigtails, she approximated a stripper version of a circus sideshow gypsy: clownish without winking, a performer. The filmy veil of artifice, an extension of the one that mostly envelops my beloved L.A., made me tired on top of tired. No need to make a party trick of predicting my future. My path was clear. The day before the shower, Lev's doctors had confirmed a relapse of cancer, and I spent much of that happy day hiding on the sunporch, trying to keep it together, crying dryly on the phone with Lev's dad. I'd been ruminating on a way out of ruminating. I knew our story had an end, but I didn't want to see it quite so clearly. At the alarm of the relapse diagnosis, I woke up to what Lev faced. I hadn't known I was sleeping, but I had been fast asleep, complacent. Facing the universal truth—just because a lot of bad shit happens to a person doesn't stop more bad shit from coming—helped to put everything in line. The dam between the present and the next place had burst. A river of shit was coming for us harder and faster, nowhere to go but under. I demurred on the tarot reading. I flew back to Austin early the next morning to begin the end run.

After Lev died and the rushing stopped, I took comfort in the idea that life without Lev might be something like filling a cargo ship with experiences, like a treasure hunt, sailing the blue-green ocean of all-things-possible. The image became a totem for me: my life as a boat with Lev as its captain. The first year after Lev's death, I bobbed along drowsily in this gently waved and salt-scented dream. I wasn't particularly curious about the future. I was hungry for it, ready for all of it. I took it as it came. I began to write again and I chronicled year one in a bubble of self-reflection and gratitude, reveling in possibility and potential.

The second year was different. Murky. My vessel felt exactly like a spacecraft hurtling though the blackness of infinity, of possibility to the nth degree. Too dark for me to see a way forward, propelled to the next place by physics I didn't understand, I faced the permanence of the loss I'd experienced. The future was a nebula. A vacuum. The void . . . *And I'm floating in a most peculiar way. And the stars look very different today.*

Two full years out from Lev's death, I feel lost. Which is to say, I feel like myself again: armored, dukes up. I'm past the year of firsts—first birthdays and holidays and anniversaries post-Lev are all past. Everything is old or brand-new. Nothing has more meaning than it should. Yet nothing about Lev's absence has lessened for me with the passage of time. I don't know that I expected my grief to grow smaller, but perhaps I hoped it would grow more manageable. More stable. If anything, living with the pain longer has meant more pain, compounded pain. But one becomes accustomed to the feeling of living with ghosts, gets used to being haunted. I dread the day, soon, when Lev will have been dead longer than he was alive, when I will have lived longer with his ghost than I did with my darling boy.

In the second half of my second year without Lev, I met a woman I'd previously known by reputation and admired, a true renaissance woman, a character and an open book. Event staging! Silversmithing! Painting! Artist modeling! Hunting for (and dealing in!) rare antiques! Officiating weddings!—Angeliska is a woman of all these many talents and more. And yet she manages to be the opposite of intimidating, so warm you feel instantly that you've always known her. She and I had met only once in the backyard of a dive bar, and our rambling conversation touched on death and grief and love and grandiosity of all sorts. After we spoke, we corresponded for the better part of a year about various bits and dreams, halfheartedly planning to reconnect, life always intervening. We'd not yet found the time to have coffee or cordials or to gossip over steaks, but we knew we'd meet again. I'd long known that one of her trades was doing tarot card readings in a 1940s Spartanette trailer in the backyard of her rambling house. The inclination to have a reading done for myself had never so much as flickered, until suddenly—with my birthday and Lev's second deathiversary looming—I found myself seeking clarity with some mounting degree of desperation. Feeling humbled and hopelessly stuck, I was aflame with the need to gain some direction. It was time to close the loop. To feel focused on the future again, instead of always feeling the unrelenting suck of the past, I would face my fortune.

When I sat down with this lovely woman on my lunch break from the hospital, on a crisp and windy Friday afternoon, I felt nervous and teary and self-conscious. She poured me a glass of water and took my hands in hers and we began the series of rituals and careful shuffling choices that make up a reading of the tarot. She wore a head wrap and a sweater befitting the weather and giant claret-colored rope braid earrings that brushed her shoulders. She was not in costume. She was herself, a real gypsy witch: one in a million. The reading Angeliska offered was full of parables and pragmatic interpretation, more like therapy than like a visit to a mystical realm. The array staring back at me was indisputably mine. She suggested I take a photo of the cards all laid out and so I did. The grief card, the hermit, the moon. Rulers and gifts. Wands upon wands. Swords upon swords. The practical and the silly and the divine. "Do this thing. Take these steps. The universe has gifts for you. It's all right here . . ." Year three.

I'm terrible at learning from the past. I make the same mistakes over and over. I wish I could take everything that's happened and synthesize it into something great, something sage, some wisdom I can apply to parenting, to living, to love, to writing. I live with all of the decisions that made me, the choices that got me here to this place of alternating needless and needful worry, this place of adolescent rumination, of camping out inside my head doing nothing but damage. Right now it all feels like a scrambled Rubik's cube. I want to twist it into rightness, feel the parts click into place, see the colors line up. See them fall into order because I know how to fix it, not because I made the surface look right by switching the stickers. Believe me, I've tried. I learned a few things, though. I learned that aces are gifts from the universe. I learned it's easier to meditate with two swords than to hold three in your heart. I learned sad song lyrics are accurate predictors of how love will turn out in the end. I learned people are inherently good (except for assholes, who are everywhere). I learned that sometimes a job is a vocation and you do it despite the pain it causes you. And I learned where on the Internet to find photos of firemen putting oxygen masks on kittens, because sometimes you need to remember that good things happen every day. Every day.

DAVID SEARCY

El Camino Doloroso

FROM *The Paris Review*

I HAVE THIS STORY from the artist Tracy Hicks about his former father-in-law, who had a 1960s pickup he'd restored and cus-
tomized—spent years on the project, loved this truck like nothing
else—until one day he backed it over one of his kittens in the
driveway. Killed the kitten. Sold the pickup truck. Like that. *Well,
that sort of sums it up,* I thought. *That pretty much says it all,* it seemed
to me at the time. Is metaphor everywhere? Of course it is. Once
consciousness, once meaning gets a start, it keeps on going. You
get literacy and metaphor and God.

The thing about custom cars and hot rods—glancing through
a copy of *Rod & Custom* magazine, you can see they tend to grade
into each other—is the strangely counterintuitive sort of dream-
iness involved. I haven't checked to see if angel hair is still the
concours style, but it was when I was a kid. That ectoplasmic spun-
glass stuff they'd use sometimes in school plays to suggest a mist
or heavenly atmospherics. You would see these cars at shows—
again, in magazines; I never went to a show, but I was always fascinated—and they'd always have these cloudy mounds of angel hair
around them. Underneath and around the tires. Like they were
floating. Not entirely of this world. And yet so massively mechani-
cal and sculptural. The custom cars especially, which, although
they'd generally have these gorgeously chromed and souped-up
engines, seemed intended more as presence, pure idea. And the
idea, I think, was more or less that paradise is possible. That you
can actually get there in the proper frame of mind—which those
archetypal, chopped, and purple-painted '49 Mercurys sought to

represent. They'd hover just above the ground—no more than a couple of inches clearance, I would guess—sustained by angel hair, it seemed, and not much else, the wheels a concession, a politeness, ornamental and vestigial. I remember thinking how extraordinarily cool that looked. And how impractical. How could you drive that down an ordinary road? The road would have to be like a showroom floor. Where would you find a perfect road like that? Where would it lead? Yet here were the means for such a journey—as gloriously real and here-and-now as they could be. Which was the point. That they were not like "concept" cars—those empty visions of the future manufacturers like to roll out on occasion. These were ordinary cars transformed. Revealed, in a way, as what they ought to be. And *were*, essentially, we were allowed to feel. The marvelous implicit in the everyday. How striking and encouraging to discover that a '51 Ford pickup or whatever had a soul. Who would have thought? So, get behind the wheel of that and where do you go? Can you imagine?

Tracy's father-in-law, it seems, had had a pretty rough time in the war. He'd been in the infantry, in the thick of it. He'd tramped all over Italy, Tracy says, come home dispirited and worn-out, wanted safety and a wife and a little frame house in Marshall, Texas. All of which, by the time we're talking about, had settled into a fairly grim, habitual sort of life. His teenage bride had borne two daughters very early, lost her youth, and grown into a disagreeable, sharp-tongued woman Tracy remembers in the kitchen mostly, cooking and complaining at her husband, who was forbidden to smoke in the house and so would sit outside the kitchen in the carport, smoking and talking to the cats. He had a morning-to-early-afternoon job at the rail yard running a huge machine that straightened railcars damaged in collisions and derailings. It was quite a thing to witness, apparently—how this machine could grab a twisted boxcar, pick the whole thing up, and bend it back into shape. You tend to think of travel by rail as pretty safe—it's all laid out, after all; you can't get lost; there's really nowhere to go but where you're going, you would think—but maybe not. Among the people who would come by now and then to watch him run the operation was an auto-mechanic friend whose personal project was a wrecked but restorable El Camino pickup truck. Well, this guy seems to have died, and Tracy's father-in-law was able to buy the pickup truck and take the project on himself. It wasn't all that old. Not like some classic you could excuse yourself for spending too much money on. I'm sure he could have bought an unwrecked used one for far less than he eventually would spend. But you know how when something's wrecked, you kind of see it from a distance, see right past it toward what could have been and might be yet if you just take your time, don't try to rush it. In such circumstances one can glimpse perfection. So it was with Tracy's father-in-law, I guess. This truck became a thing of beauty. Not a full-blown chopped and channeled concours queen, of course, but given what was possible back then in Marshall, Texas, pretty nice. And better and better all the time. A fancy paint job—two-tone metal-flake gold and cream. Gold rolled-and-pleated leather seats with matching visors. Lots of little things as well, to keep him busy afternoons and on the weekends under the carport with the cats. He'd get it washed and checked out weekly. Once a month he'd change the oil. Sometimes, says Tracy, he'd just sit there under the carport with it. Cat in his lap, just sitting there and smoking and, I have to imagine, season after season, soft habitual sounds of cooking and complaining from the kitchen contrapuntal to the purring in his lap, just gazing off across the sadly less-than-prosperous little neighborhood and down the little street to God knows where, to who knows what subliminal paradise, not knowing really, consciously, I'm sure, but still, you'd think the heart must seek a destination.

It was early one winter morning when he backed it over the kitten. Tracy heard he never drove the truck again, and very quickly it was gone. And so, within a couple of years, was he—from cancer. Not much time to sit with nothing under the carport. But I bet that's what he did. Just let the air come through and sit out there and smoke. What would you do? You couldn't move. How could you not just sit right there and blink your eyes at having it all break down like that, a bump in the road—not even a bump; you hardly feel it, but you know. *That's it,* you think. *Right off the rails.* Can you believe it? Just like that. You have to wonder what to retain of a thing like that. Do you remember how it was? And maybe hold it in your thoughts? Or let it go and learn your lesson. How you can't get there from here. How love obliterates itself. How you should probably just keep still for a while and let the other things come back. The other cats, the less beloved ones. Their little water bowls and dishes here and there. The early morning sounds of movement in the kitchen.

STEVEN HARVEY

The Book of Knowledge

FROM *River Teeth*

IN 1952, WHEN I was three, my parents bought a set of *The Book of Knowledge,* ten hefty volumes bound in maroon leather, each filled with questions from the "Department of Wonder." Like sentinels posted at the gates of wisdom, the books stood proudly on a shelf between the glossy forelocks of equestrian bookends, each volume embossed with a golden torch. It was, my mother explained in one of the hundreds of letters she wrote to my grandmother, a purchase as much for her as for her boy: "I have really been enjoying it. I've been studying the subjects of music and art so far." Reading in *The Book of Knowledge* was one of the ways she fended off the depression that swept over her during these years, especially when my father traveled. "That is how I've been spending some of my evening while Max is away."

The Book of Knowledge evolved from *The Children's Encyclopædia,* the inspiration of Arthur Mee, born to a working-class family in Stapleford, England, whose formal education ended when he was fourteen. Questions posed by Mee's daughter, Marjorie, were the direct inspiration for the encyclopedia. In his letter "To Boys and Girls Everywhere," published in the first volume of *The Children's Encyclopædia,* Mee writes that Marjorie's mind was filled with "the great wonder of the Earth. What does the world mean? And why am I here? Where are all the people who have been and gone? Where does the rose come from? Who holds the stars up? What is it that seems to talk to me when the world is dark and still?" Mee's wife had "thought and thought" about these questions "and answered this and answered that until she could answer no more.

Oh for a book that will answer all the questions!" she complained. *The Children's Encyclopædia* was born.

What set his book apart, Mee explained, was the belief in children's eagerness for knowledge and their capacity for wonder. But he knew that his book also filled an important gap for adults. It "had the power to make plain to the average man, woman, and child the aspects and imports of the problems which the very men who had wrested them from nature could not make so plain." It offered up the mysteries of the few for the rest of us. By the time *The Children's Encyclopædia* had evolved into *The Book of Knowledge*, Mee had added the "Department of Wonder," and each volume contained sections devoted to "wonder questions" like the ones Marjorie posed to her perplexed parents.

For my mother, who had dropped out of nursing school when she was nineteen to marry my father, the gaps in her education were becoming an embarrassment. Born Roberta Maxine Reinhardt and called Bobbie, she had been the darling of her parents and of the small Kansas town of Glen Elder where she grew up. Pretty and bright, she made nearly perfect grades, but not without help. "As I remember I used to make A on every theme you wrote for me," she mentioned in one letter to my grandmother. A little unsure of herself when she entered nursing school in 1946, she created elaborate study schedules, but soon she found that she was good at school and liked her classes, which included American literature as well as courses in child guidance, microbiology, the history of nursing, nursing arts, physical education, home economics, and something called "the Home Project." As she pursued her studies she became more confident: "I'm so thrilled about my subjects. There is an awfully lot of reading to do, but it is interesting." Anxieties about how hard the classes would be proved unfounded, and she flourished in the program. "I've been wondering how I would like my nursing subjects—it is play to study them."

After she married, that confidence in her abilities slowly eroded, especially when my father joined the pharmaceutical company American Cyanamid as a managing director and our young family moved from Dodge City, Kansas, to Nanuet, New York, a suburb of the city. In the 1952 letter about buying *The Book of Knowledge*, she describes a lavish dinner party served by maids. "Of course the conversation got around to operas and plays," she complains, "as it always does here"; she did not feel comfortable again, she adds wryly, "until they all started talking about the pigs in Missouri." She admits that it was "an educational evening" and, after it was over, "a nice experience to have" but laments that she was caught off-guard: "Had I known beforehand I would have studied up." *The Book of Knowledge* was her way to "study up." "I've done very little brain work since I got out of school," she writes. "All you have to do is move around and meet new people to realize how dumb you really are." For my mother the gilded volumes of *The Book of Knowledge* served as a self-help textbook on culture.

For me they were simply wondrous. I liked to lie on my stomach on the floor in front of the bookcase, my feet kicked up behind me, just taking in the strange and glorious pictures: color illustrations in soft pastels from *The Book of the Dead,* which was left, the caption inaccurately tells us, "in the tombs of Egypt for the dead to read." A black-and-white cartoon of the globe in a ball cap, beaded in sweat and pulling down on a scale, to illustrate "Volume, Mass, and Weight." A four-page spread called "The Glory of the Grass" with detailed colored drawings of foxtail, rye, oat, timothy, manna, bearded darnel, broom, barley, reed, and wheat. Another four-page spread of "Beautiful Birds of the World," with a peacock in full array on the first page, surrounded by a blue-crowned motmot, a Leadbeater's cockatoo, and a Groove pygmy goose, along with nine other brightly colored birds. And in Volume Eighteen, the fourteen-page spread of butterflies and moths and beetles that begins with a peacock eye, an American species of butterfly, and concludes, 236 individual illuminated drawings later, with the European beetle called the great agrilus.

The famous frontispiece to the first edition of *The Children's Encyclopædia* shows a boy in knickers and girl in bloomers looking into a universe: a system of eight planets, alongside comets, stars, and galaxies, surrounding the sun, which sends a halo of sunbeams out into the darkness. But the inside cover illustration of each volume of *The Book of Knowledge* that I grew up with suggests a similar grandeur with a modern twist. In it, a boy in shorts and girl wearing a skirt stand alert and excited on a red book floating toward an island of worldly wonders, including a telescope, a pagoda, totem poles, a factory, the faces of Mount Rushmore, and a giraffe. Overhead soar a rocket, a dual-propeller commercial airliner, a helicopter, and some sort of futuristic V-shaped spacecraft. "Here is a gift to the nation," Arthur Mee wrote to the readers of

The Book of Knowledge. "It is a story that will never fail for children who will never tire; and it is the best of all stories, told in the simplest words, to the greatest of all ends."

And what is the end? On April 6, 1961, when I was twelve, my mother drove into a park near Deerfield, Illinois, where we lived at the time, and killed herself with a gun. Whatever knowledge she had gleaned from those books, as well as all that was left in her heart and mind of love, joy, sorrow, and agony, was swept away too. The obliteration ripples out from there. My father did not talk about the past, and the subject of my mother rarely came up after my father remarried and the family began anew. I remembered almost nothing of my life or her life before the suicide except a few vivid flashes—images, really—with the rest blown away by her death, and for years I was resigned to my ignorance, and perhaps even content with it. I grew up, raised by a caring stepmother who probably got more than she bargained for when she took on, along with my dad, my brother and me, and I acquired a wonderful older stepsister who socialized me, and we did not dwell on our history. I went to college and married, and when I was in my thirties, my grandmother gave me the letters of my mother, but by then I had a job and a family with four children. I worked hard and was not depressed or suicidal. Why would I want to read the letters of a mother who killed herself before I could even get to know her?

When I turned sixty, I was given a new office at work, and I used that change as an opportunity to discard files, magazines, and correspondence—the stuff that I had accumulated over the years. I threw away books that I thought I would never part with. My wife, Barbara, gave me a rule of thumb: if you feel the urge to sneeze when you open it, toss it out. In the end I threw away or recycled fourteen large plastic bags of junk, and I drove back from the transfer station feeling lighter. But when I got to the boxes of my mother's letters, I could not throw them away. I held them in my hand—they were dusty and definitely gave me the urge to sneeze—but I could not shove them in a plastic trash bag.

I made a vow that if I kept them, I would read them.

So, at the age of sixty-one, I bought a set of the 1952 edition of *The Book of Knowledge,* like the ones that I'd had as a child, and I read my mother's letters. Barbara raised an eyebrow when I mentioned *The Book of Knowledge*, a twenty-volume set bound in ten thick books, since she had been trying for several years to weed old books from our shelves at home, just as I had at the office.

"Are you going to *buy* them?" she asked. I think she was making soup or maybe spaghetti.

"They have a set for $350 at Amazon."

Barbara, poker-faced, just kept stirring the pot.

Eventually I found a complete set available at AbeBooks online for $150 and put in my order. Sheepishly, I promised Barbara that I would keep the box they came in and resell them online as soon as I had finished with them.

When they arrived they were as magnificent as I had remembered, each handsome volume feeling heavy in the hand. Substantial, I thought, cracking open the cover of Volume One. Quotations by the likes of Louis Bromfield, Eleanor Roosevelt, aviation pioneer Captain Harry F. Guggenheim, and Lou Little, the head football coach at Columbia University, added authority to weight.

"The poet Marlowe might have been thinking of *The Book of Knowledge* when he spoke of 'infinite riches in a little room,'" Mrs. James P. McGranery, a member of the National Executive Committee of the Girl Scouts of the USA, explained.

"There is only one good. That is knowledge," John S. Knight, the publisher of Knight Newspapers, announced, quoting Socrates while glowering at me from his photograph. He added a stern admonition:

"There is only one evil. That is ignorance."

We fanned the books out on the floor and began leafing through them, stopping at the colored spreads, Barbara running her fingers over the brightly illuminated pages. The books spoke of a time after the Second World War when knowledge and progress and hope were allies, a time that she and I remembered dimly now as we ended the first decade of the twenty-first century. Barbara found a page that asked, "Could We Ever Travel to the Moon?" and I cringed at the outdated question, but she smiled. "Listen to this," she said later, reading at random an article in Volume Thirteen called "Government and Taxes," which argued that simply taxing in proportion to income, as the Constitution says, is unfair. "Taxes should be levied in such a way as to establish equality of sacrifice between rich and poor."

"Equality of sacrifice," she repeated, "imagine that."

Before long she was eyeing the bookshelves we had been hoping to clear. "We'll make space right there."

"These books are pretty out-of-date," I said apologetically, opening a volume and resisting the urge to sneeze.

She was thinking about our new grandchildren.

"They could stand to read this."

She rapped the book with her knuckle. Decision made.

In retrospect I regret that I waited so long to read my mother's letters. There were 406 in all, carefully arranged by my grandmother in shoeboxes. Over time, as the family leafed through them, they had gotten out of order and had been placed in different areas of the house before most were carted off to the office. It was not until six months after I finally brought them home that I spread them out on a pool table and put them in order. I boxed them and marked off each of the years with strips of manila cardboard, tickets to the past extending back in time from 1960 to 1945, and one chilly morning in November 2010, some fifty years after my mother's death, I started to read the entire set through.

My mother's writing style is direct and friendly, and—since she saw my grandmother as a confidante, especially in the early years of her marriage—often candid. As she got older, and more troubled, she tried to hide her depression, but she had become so used to confiding in her mother that the truth comes out anyway in the letters. As I read about her life, my memories, lying like ashes in me, were sparked. The steady chronology of a letter or two each week allowed me to place the few vivid memories I had left in a context, so that I saw how they fit and understood why they, of all in my lost past, had remained as a glowing remnant. My dad, in that time before I remembered him, came back clearly as well. Most of all, I got to know my mother at last—not the stereotypical fifties mother forced to play an uncomfortable role, though she was that, but the real person with her achievements and flaws and hopes and many, many fears. As she married, left college, moved away from home, and had children of her own, I watched her change and grow, darken and retreat. The return addresses evolved from Bobbie Reinhardt, a young nursing student in 1942 at the University of Kansas Hospital in Kansas City, to Mrs. M. J. Harvey in Dodge City in 1947. By the time the family had moved to New York, she dropped the Mrs. altogether, and in Chicago in 1959 she retreated entirely by writing the return address using my father's name and title: Dr. M. J. Harvey.

Every letter stood alone—capturing a particular time and, more important, mood—and yet each danced in consort with the others. As my mother married and had children, the mobile of her life grew heavier and more complicated, with many moving parts, and by the time of her death the structure groaned under the weight of accumulated anxieties and regrets. Armed with letters and a children's encyclopedia, I was determined to know who this woman was and, with luck, claim a legacy of beauty and wonder from a devastating event.

Wonder Question: "Does the earth make a sound as it rotates?"

"No," *The Book of Knowledge* answers, the "earth spins silently in space. It spins all in one piece, and that means not only the solid earth and the waters but the blanket of air above us as well. All spins round, never pausing." Like some enormous carny ride, the globe rotates at a thousand miles per hour, and yet the mobile over my shoulder hangs motionless by a thread and going nowhere, expectant and watchful as an acrobat holding a pose. "If the air stood still we might hear the earth whooshing through it," but the "air is part of the earth and moves with it," creating the illusion of stillness.

Even if we could step off the earth—like the boy and girl in the illustration for *The Children's Encyclopædia*—and stand on some promontory separate from the planet and listen hard, we would not hear the earth spinning. The scene would unfold like a slow-motion silent film, the incredible rush of the whirling planet registering on our eyes like the imperceptible motion of the slow hand on a watch and on our ears as a held breath. The other celestial objects would lumber along in mute procession, with vast stretches of nothing at all between them. To hear any sound, "we must have vibrations, or waves, or trembling." But space is a nearly empty vacuum, and no matter how dark and gloomy and terrifying emptiness may be, trembling requires "something substantial" to be felt.

In space there is "no substance to be set trembling."

When she was five or six, Roberta trembled beside a toy tricycle that was built to look like a single-prop airplane. My grandparents took a Brownie photograph of her standing beside the new toy, with the shingled side of their house as the background. The front of the trike had a propeller with a circle of pistons behind it, and the tailpiece at the end had numbers stamped in it to make it look authentic. The cockpit swooped down so that the rider could sit down completely and pedal. The toy is large—longer than she is tall—and it is clearly made of metal, with dimples where bolts attach the wheels to the body. The wheels are inflatable rubber tires with shiny metal hubcaps. In the photograph my mother poses proudly, wearing Mary Janes, stockings, a pleated dress, a V-neck sweater, a beaded necklace, and a knit cap. She is dressed for cold weather, and since she was born in June, this is probably not a birthday gift but a Christmas present. A shadow of some sort, perhaps the shadow of a tree, rises like a thin stream of smoke from behind her shoulder and spreads across the shingles of the wall, the adumbration folding ominously, like the black contrail of a plane in trouble, and turning on her. Hurtling through space at a thousand miles an hour, my mother may be trembling a bit from the cold, but otherwise she does not feel the future rushing toward her. She cannot see the crash ahead. The air, after all, is moving too, at one with a planet of rocks and stones and trees and spinning silently in a universe largely without substance. The girl who is my mother leans casually with her open hand on the wing of the toy while a ribbon of black smoke billows across the shingles behind her. Unaware and smiling, she looks directly at me.

Wonder Question: "Why do faces in some pictures seem to follow us?"

"The rule is very simple," *The Book of Knowledge* says. "If the sitter is looking at the painter or at the camera, then wherever you stand, he will seem to be looking at you." I lift the photo of my mother beside her new toy and tilt it under the lamp, first to the right and then the left, and her eyes stay on me even though the nose of the airplane seems to bob away and return, the world of the photo turning on the axis of her eyes. And her smile—yes, it also seems to keep smiling at me, no matter which way I turn the stiff and fading image.

But this rule, as stated here, is not so simple as *The Book of Knowledge* likes our wonders to be. There is the word *seem* in the phrase "he will seem to be looking at you," which is never simple. It drains the ink out of the words around it, appropriating them subjunc-

tively. The little mood shift created by that one word invites suppo-
sition, hypothesis, possibility, and desire into the mix, leaving the
facts behind. It is the *seem* of what is not, the *seem* of absence and
longing and despair that these pictures in the end make me feel, a
magical *seem* bringing in its wake the black smoke of an apparent
accident that has not happened yet in the photo but has already
happened a long time ago in life. Nothing is looking at me in this
photograph, although it is smiling broadly into the camera and
trembling slightly in the cold, a trembling I can't feel because of
the nothing she is and the nothing between us, and this nothing
follows me no matter which way I turn.

Thirty years later, in November 1960, my grandmother "got word"
that my mother was in the hospital. I was eleven and we were living in Deerfield, Illinois. The phrase *got word,* taken from notes
that my grandmother wrote near the end of her life, is portentous.
It means that my mother was in no condition to write to her or
call her and that my father, whom my grandmother never trusted,
had to break the news. If I grow still and close my eyes, I can
imagine the sound of the conversation, him offering up the facts
through the mixture of sympathy and complaint he used to calm
anxious colleagues, and her, with her Kansas reticence, replying
in tight-lipped, staccato phrases. I cannot even begin to imagine
their words. She and my grandfather "left immediately by train for
Deerfield." They stayed with my brother and me until my mother
killed herself five months later. My grandmother never talked to
me about what happened when my mother was institutionalized
for depression, but she did talk to Barbara, who wrote letters to
her on a regular basis until my grandmother died in 1986, and
who was probably my grandmother's dearest confidante at the end
of her life. She told Barbara that when they released my mother
from the hospital, the doctors said that they "had done everything
that they could" and were still pessimistic. "When she left the hospital, your grandmother knew she would do it," Barbara said when
I asked her about it again this morning. She had told me about
the conversation before, but to make her point clear now she put
it this way: "When she left *that morning,*" on the day she killed herself, "your grandmother knew she would do it."

After I graduated from college, I asked my father about my
mother's death. We were riding in silence in his car early in the

morning. It was still dark outside, the only light the blue glow from his dashboard. I know he didn't want to talk about her suicide, but he wanted to answer my questions. Nothing made her happy, he told me, and the doctors could do nothing for her. "They tried everything," he said, an echo of my grandmother's words. He said that she bought a .44-caliber gun, which is a large bore. "She *meant* to do it—to end things." So she drove to the lake and killed herself. It pained him to say this, I could tell. I do not want to underestimate the difficulty of living with someone who is clinically depressed. I know now, from reading her letters. that he tried to make her happy, and he was very good at making others feel happy, but in the long run he could not work that charm on her. He took a long drag from his cigarette, squinted, and stuffed the butt in his ashtray, slowly exhaling the smoke as the car hurtled down the highway, waiting for my next question, but I did not ask any more. We rode silently into a predawn darkness illuminated by the blue light from the dash.

I turn to *The Book of Knowledge* for the answers to questions I didn't ask.

In its 7,606 pages, *The Book of Knowledge* has no entry for suicide. It has no entry for insomnia, alcoholism, or addiction, either. There is an entry for ragweed, but not for rage. In the age of anxiety, there is no entry for anxiety. No entry for depression without "Great" in front of it. The entry on sex is limited to plants and flowers. There is no entry for conformity or blandness or dullness or insipidity—and this was the 1950s! Sometimes I wonder about *The Book of Knowledge*. I find an entry for Peter Pan, of course, but none for Cyril Ritchard. No entry for either "Fever" *or* Peggy Lee. Nothing on the doldrums, the dumps, the mulligrubs, or the blues. No blue funk or the blahs. Nothing on grief—*grief!* No entry for funeral, burial, interment, last rites, cortege, mourners, pallbearers, or pall. No entry for self-murder, self-slaughter, self-destruction, and no entry for self. No entry for hara-kiri (which is a little surprising) or suttee (which is not). There are several entries under medicine, but no cure for despair, despondency, sadness, sorrow, unhappiness, melancholy, or gloom. Doom does not make the pages. Nor agony nor suffering nor woe. In *The Book of Knowledge*, no *woe!*

*

Wonder Question: "What is everything?"

In the late 1950s, after the doctors try everything else, they strap the patient to a gurney in a hospital room and tape the leads of a heart monitor to her chest. They do not inject her with an anesthetic for pain or use muscle relaxers to reduce the chance of bone fractures and other injuries when the arms, legs, and chest rise against the restraints, but they do place a block in her mouth so that she cannot bite her tongue while the procedure is performed. They attach electrodes on either side of her face at the temples after applying a conductive jelly so that an electrical current will pass into her head and brain more easily. Once she is ready, the doctor turns on a machine that sends a steady stream of electricity into her skull, the current running between the right and left lobe of her brain for twenty seconds, inducing a grand mal seizure and leaving her unconscious, usually for about a half-hour. No one knows for sure what happens in her brain as her eyes roll back and her body stiffens. The shock of electricity may slow overly agitated mental activity or dull the brain receptors altering her mood. It may release neuropeptides that ease depression. Or it may cause brain damage. Electroshock therapy helps many people, but, as one critic put it, the procedure is "like playing Russian roulette with your brain."

What is everything in the late 1950s?

It is a very sad figure of speech come true.

When I was a boy, I lay in bed at night listening to my parents fight downstairs. The arguments began as conversation mixed with the clinking sound of ice in glasses, the words spoken softly, clipped and brittle, dipping to inaudibility when whispered. The clicking of tree branches that is prelude to the storm. Eventually the voices rose until the two were shouting and finally screaming furiously, the sound coming through the walls in unarticulated growls. I don't think they ever hit each other, but sometimes they broke glasses and ashtrays. Dad may have caught her arms when she took drunken, limp, and futile swings at him. I think I saw that once.

I was too afraid when they fought to move and lay wrapped under a cocoon of sheets and blankets that felt like safety but acted like an echo chamber, amplifying and distorting the low rumble until the roar, punctuated now and then with a slam or a crash, spilled over me in torrents. I waited, understanding nothing, absorbing it all. It was only when the yelling was done that the silence after the curses brought me out of bed to the top of the stairs to be sure that they were all right. I usually walked down a few steps and leaned forward, peering between the balusters in order to see into the kitchen, blinking at the fluorescent glare. One night they caught me. I can picture the tableau even now. My dad, his sleeves rolled up, facing a wall, my mother sitting bent over in a kitchen chair with her back to him, crying in gasps, mascara running down her cheeks.

"Oh, no," she says when she turns and sees me running back upstairs.

The next day my father pulled me aside and asked what I had heard.

"You were fighting," I said.

He corrected me. They were not having a fight, but a "discussion."

"That's what adults do," he said.

The memory of the fight followed by the conversation with my dad glows like a lit match in the darkness that is my past. Here is another lit match. From my bedroom I see a light in the hall, soft this time like the glow of a candle. Drawing the twisted sheets up around my shoulders, I hear the clank of the changer and the long wavering whoosh and whir when the needle hits the disk. Clink of ice in a glass. Swoosh of a magazine dropped to the floor. My mother turns up the volume, and soon Peggy Lee's voice fills the house to the corners, beating back gathered silence. I slip out of bed and hide at the top of the stairs to watch. Snapping fingers, slapped cymbal, thud of a double bass and drum, and a lone, plaintive female voice. Mom's there, her back to me, her face partially visible, lit by the glow of the console. She sways, drink in hand, and sings, watching the record spin, holding the notes out for no one, trying to sound good.

"What a lovely way to burn," she croons. "What a lovely way to burn."

The fights and my mother singing "Fever" happened before my grandparents moved in with us in November 1960. Peggy Lee's new song, "Fever," was the rage, and my parents had the album in their record collection, and this record followed my family long after my mother died. I remember it because of the distinctive cover photograph of Peggy Lee in a black cocktail dress, her pale skin and platinum-blond hair set against a blue background. The album was released in May 1960. So the fights and the drinking alone while singing into the stereo console must have happened between May of 1960 and November 1960, in the time just before my mother was hospitalized for depression.

During 1959 and 1960 my dad was gone most of the time on business trips and to take courses in business management in St. Louis. My mother thought he was pushing himself too hard. He had developed an ulcer, and the doctor recommended that he cut back on his work. "Sometimes I think we are crazy," my mother wrote on June 24, 1959. "The men work at such a pace and under so much pressure." During that time she must have confronted him about the burden that the maddening pace and heavy responsibilities of his job placed on him and the family: "We discussed this when he was sick and I suggested a change, but he said he liked his work and seems to have the ability so we decided it would be a matter of adjusting our leisure time to make it workable."

I know what those "discussions" sounded like.

In the end my dad had his way. The trips continued. "Max has been in St. Louis," she writes on March 26, 1959, and on July 9 she mentions that "Max has been to St. Louis since Tues. will be back tomorrow." These business trips to St. Louis run like a refrain after 1959 until the letters come to an abrupt halt in June 1960, within a month of the release of the album that contained "Fever." The memory of that song may be the last message I have from my mother, since it probably came after the last letter.

My stepmother tells me that she met my father in St. Louis.

My mother seems unaware of infidelity during 1959 and early 1960. In the letters she appears to be genuinely concerned about the problems related to Dad's job. What upset her was the pressure that it put on their lives. It did damage to their friends, some of whom became alcoholics; made my father ill; and saddled my mother with social responsibilities she could not, given her tendency to depression, handle. I sense in all the letters from that time a desire to live in a way that reduced the strain on everyone, and I suspect that the conversation about leaving the company was real. Dad's ulcer and her exhaustion only reinforced the idea that their loveless marriage had to do with the demands of his career, not another woman, but sometime in June of 1960 she must have figured out that Dad had found love elsewhere, and the letters stopped.

The depression that perched on my mother's life and led to her suicide on April 6, 1961, had many sources, but here is one black wing: on April 29, three weeks and two days after my mother's death, Dad married my stepmother.

"What a lovely way to burn," Peggy Lee growls four times at the end of "Fever." "What a lovely way to burn." In the penultimate line her voice rises in desire on the first word — *What* — before it slides down *a lovely way* to the last note, *burn,* dying like the flicker of a heartache.

And the final line? It is a scorched whisper, a beckoning, and a come-on. It is a raised eyebrow. "What a lovely way to burn."

Wonder Question: "Who holds up the stars?"

The stars only appear to be nailed into fixed positions in the dome of the night sky, and no one really holds them up for us. According to *The Book of Knowledge,* "All the stars — in fact, everything in the universe, asteroids, stars, galaxies of stars — all are moving through space at unbelievable speeds of many miles a second." The "great force of gravitation" holds them in check. "Each bit of matter in the universe pulls upon every other particle of matter," and this mutual attraction can cause collisions. "If one body comes too close to another body, the lesser is drawn into the greater and destroyed." But when the velocity of the objects and the distance between them is right, they move in consort. In the end this apparently accidental dance of forces is "responsible for the balance and state of equilibrium in the universe."

On the day of my mother's death, I stared into trembling stars nailed into the night sky of my own making in the hope of achieving some equilibrium. I liked spinning in our newly renovated downstairs den, holding a *Jetfire* balsa-wood plane that I kept in my hiding place under the stairs. I usually got the planes at the five-and-dime when I visited my grandparents in Glen Elder, but they must have brought the plane to me, because this memory is in Illinois. I can still clearly picture these planes that I assembled myself and studied for hours. The wings were stamped with red designs marking the ailerons and flaps and labeled on one side with the name of the company, Guillow's, and on the other with the name of the plane, *Jetfire.* The cockpit was embossed on the fuselage, and inside a pilot with a red helmet leaned forward. Meant to ride breezes, the glider is light in my hand. It has a small piece of metal folded over the nose for protection when it crash-lands against the walls of the house or the concrete driveway, which is most of the time, but I'm not allowed to fly it indoors, so I hold it and spin, making airplane noises and getting dizzy. When I stop, the room seems to keep on spinning and I wobble a bit as if I have taken a blow. I'm almost twelve. Too old to be doing this sort of thing,

My mother died on the day that my father planned to leave the family for good. In retrospect I know that he intended to start a new life for himself in Kentucky without my mother or my brother and me. Was he anxious or exhilarated when he left the house that April morning, relieved or scared? Or some other emotion I cannot even imagine? If on that day my grandmother knew what my mother would do, he may have too, but I'm not sure, because unlike my shrewd grandmother, he was an optimist. After he left, my mother bought the gun, drove to the park by the lake, stepped out of her car, and pulled the trigger. My grandparents, who knew it would happen, were taking care of my brother and me. When Dad found out, he came back for us.

In memory I was alone downstairs in the newly renovated den, killing time with this spinning game, when my dad arrived and the house began to fill with neighbors and my parents' friends. I heard the ringing doorbell of each new arrival. The hushed greetings. The whispers. The shuffle of feet over carpet as adults overhead approached each other. I am pretty sure that no one had told me what had happened yet. Dad would do that when we were on the train going to Kentucky. But I knew *something*, because I hid under the stairs in my favorite hideaway, where I kept some toys like the balsa *Jetfire*, and sat there a long time before anyone noticed my absence. The points of the nails that had been used to secure the treads to the risers of the stairway protruded overhead. Like stars they glittered in the crawlspace, and I looked into them as I listened to the groan in the floorboards. Suddenly it grew silent, and I heard my father call for me. At first his voice was a question, but then, freighted with all the tension of that day, it became a barked command. Soon others joined in, their anxious voices a keening chorus on my name.

A shadow passed over the risers.

"Who holds the stars up?" Marjorie Mee asked her perplexed mother.

I covered my ears.

Last September, when Barbara and I visited my stepmother, Lou Harvey, in Kentucky, we spent a Saturday morning looking through pictures. Lou—who is nearly eighty—pulled them out of boxes one at a time with her arthritic fingers, stopping occasionally to talk, and the subject came around to my mother.

"No, honey," Lou said, when I asked if my mother bought the gun before that day. I'm sitting across from her at the kitchen table. Barbara, who is standing, stops flipping through pictures and listens. "She bought it that morning. She killed herself in the park. A policeman saw her and thought it unusual, so he watched. She stepped out of the car and then."

Lou puts her finger to her temple and lifts her eyebrows.

"Bam."

I look away. A cat waits in a crouch under the birdfeeder in her neighbor's yard.

"Neither of us had anybody," she says, explaining that her first husband was impossible to live with too. "I had nobody. Your dad had nobody."

Silenced for a moment by that story, we return to the pictures. Many of them show Lou with my dad through the years, but I pause over one in particular. In it, the two of them are preparing dinner. They both are young, in their thirties. My dad, heavyset in a dark shirt and white warmup pants, has turned, startled by the picture, and his face, picking up the full impact of the flash, wears a customary carefree and bold look. He's making a salad and is no doubt about to tell a joke. The flash explodes like a supernova on the sliding glass door behind him, turning the rest of the glass black.

It is the image of my stepmother that holds my attention, though. She stands in the wood-paneled room, looking young and very pretty in a striped sweater and tight slacks, her nose aquiline and her hair all dark curls. She leans toward my father from behind as if she has some secret to share, but the easygoing intimacy of the photograph keeps no secrets. He came to her in St. Louis for fun, happiness, love, and sex. He came to escape a home full of woe, some of it no doubt of his own making—some, but not all. He was leaving us for this, that was the secret, and when my mother figured it out, she gave my brother and me to him, to them, with a single gunshot.

Wonder Question: "What is the sound of everything happening at once?"

"When a gun goes off," *The Book of Knowledge* says, "the flash and the report of the gun occur in the same moment." If we stand at a distance, the flash appears first, as a silent flare in the darkness, and the muffled blow of the sound arrives later, in an echo of the flash. So if you stand at a safe distance half a mile away when the gun is fired, "you will not hear the sound for nearly half a minute.

"And yet," *The Book of Knowledge* adds, because it is also fond of "and yet," "if we are very near the gun, we see the flash and hear the noise at the same time." At that range, you miss nothing. If you hold the gun to your body, you feel everything happening at once, and it reverberates until the trembling stops somewhere at the edge of nothing.

Turning the self into a nothing is a moral conundrum too difficult for *The Book of Knowledge* to crack. A literal self-contradiction, the answer even eluded Jesus. The Catholic poet Dante may have planted the suicides with other violent sinners in a deep ring of Hell and tormented the poor souls with winged harpies, but the golden rule is about doing unto others, not doing the self in, and on suicide Jesus is silent. It wasn't until the nineteenth century that Immanuel Kant, whom some consider the wisest European philosopher, explained the immorality of suicide with his "categorical imperative." When faced with a moral dilemma, Kant argued, you should act so that your action becomes universal law. When you lift a gun to your temple to pull the trigger, you must imagine that the hands of all the people in the world are required by your version of the moral law to lift a gun to their temples too. No one escapes the bullet in this game of Russian roulette. "Do you like this vision of the world?" Kant asks.

I give it a try and see my mother in the hall of mirrors within her moral imagination, every hand in the world holding a .44 lifted at her command, and she pulls the . . . but no, that is not right.

Suicide is about the survivors.

Suicide is two boys and a father hurtled into darkness at the speed of a locomotive. The boys, sitting on the plush pile seat of a railroad car headed away from their home in Deerfield, Illinois, will never see their mother again, rarely speak of her again, rarely think about her again. Their father—a big man, bulging out of his suit—sits down on his haunches in front of them. Facing into the darkness ahead, he has been through hell and has been given one more impossible task, but he is a man who believes in taking charge and wants to fix things even when he can't, so he will do his job. The boys are headed backward into the night, the lights outside the window floating away from them, and I don't know if they are afraid or in shock or just tired. Who knows what the younger one remembers? He is eight years old and has penetrating blue eyes. The older one remembers his dad looking down, but only for a moment, and then, as he always did when he spoke to people, looking directly into his sons' eyes and saying the impossible. I remember him speaking, his voice a mesmerizing low rasp conveying confidentiality this time as well as command, and I remember him reaching out with his arms to kind of hem us in as he spoke, his large arms coming out of the sleeves of his suit a bit as he extended them. I remember—or I think I do—the maroon plush of the seats in the Pullman and the windows black as we rode into the open fields of Illinois at night.

But I have no idea what he said.

Someone took pictures at my mother's funeral. I found them in a wicker basket with other photos and memorabilia. Several show the graveside service conducted on the open prairie of Kansas, the land that my mother wrote of "going back to" in her memory while living in New York. The photographs are mixed in with a nearly identical set of pictures from my grandfather's funeral, which came three weeks after hers, including a particularly sad one of my mother's and grandfather's graves side by side, her blossoms windblown and slightly wilted beside his new batch of greenery and white.

But the hardest pictures for me show my mother's open casket surrounded by a shower of flowers, a mound of red and white carnations, daisies, and pink mums. The coffin is draped in a spray of red roses, and my mother's body lies in a bed of satin, the opening of the casket draped in a transparent mesh. The picture of her face is very small, but I can see that her hair is pulled back from her forehead in tight curls. She wears a suit with a silk scarf at the neck, exposing the base of her throat. I find a magnifying glass that I keep with my dictionary and examine the picture up close. The cotton and plaster of Paris that the morticians used to reconstruct the face make her cheeks look puffy, and the dermal wax and restorative cosmetics hide her wounds and bruises under a shiny pastiness betraying the illusion of life. There is something wrong with the mouth, which has been stretched wide into a smile after the mortician pulled together the scalp, and the eyebrows are heartbreaking, dark and perfectly arched like wings, as if, after all, death took her by surprise, and maybe—who knows?—it did.

My gaze settles at last on her eyes. Leaning forward into the lens to see more clearly, I tilt the page this way and that for a better look before slumping back into my chair.

Faces in photos don't follow us if their eyes are closed.

Until I read her letters, those closed eyes were my mother's story, an image that I carried until I became a sixty-year-old man. And yet—because there is always this "and yet"—there is more, much more, and it is in the letters, not the photographs.

"We took our first drive yesterday," my mother writes on Monday, November 20, 1950, from a brick bungalow in Monsey, New York, when she and Dad first moved away from Kansas to live in the Northeast. "The scenery around here is gorgeous. We took the Hudson River Drive on the way up." She explains that she is sending pictures, and I find the colored postcards in my wicker box, stiff and pretty colorized photographs of West Point and the river, but her words say more than the pictures. "The river is very large, calm, and beautiful," she writes. Having lived on the prairie all her life, she is unaccustomed to seeing large bodies of water and is filled with wonder. "Saw the ships and were quite thrilled—first large ones I've ever seen. We took Bear Mountain Drive home. We were sorry we didn't get to see all of this because it got dark before we got home. It is completely dark by five here."

My mother weathered the mental cyclone of depression much of her adult life, but there are moments in the letters when she paints, in words, another self—whole and wonder-struck—and the whirlwind stops. These moments often happen outdoors, or while looking outdoors, and record a joyous embrace of a wide and open sky that may have evoked feelings of the family farm in Kansas where she and my grandparents picnicked while she was growing up. They are sublime glimpses of grandeur, often bounded by darkness—the blackness that finally claimed her, creeping in at the edges—but they are also marked by a brilliance of light and an expansive vista that is exhilarating. The sights transported her, lifted her momentarily out of the troubles of life; they helped her to be her best self and reengage with family.

In one letter she describes a flight back from Kansas in prose reminiscent of her descriptions of seeing the Hudson River for the first time. "Had such a smooth flight from K.C. to N.Y. Slept part of the way. The plane was very crowded when we boarded so I had to sit on the inside seat of the three[-seat] row which was fine except I couldn't see out too well but thought the view of K.C. and Chicago were gorgeous. Looked like a huge Christmas display." She explains that she arrived early at LaGuardia and took the time to freshen up before meeting us. "When I walked out I saw Max & boys—called to them. The boys were so surprised for a second—I squatted on my knees—Ronnie said, 'Mommy' and gave me a big hug. I hugged Steve with my other arm. He put his arms around my neck and said 'Hello, Mommy.'"

After my mother died, I forgot the sensation of her touch and the sound of her voice. I could not hug a shadow. I could not fill her silence with my words.

Who is suicide? She was suicide.

She became her death.

And the pictures, hundreds of curled shavings of the past in a basket, did not bring her back. Even when my mother gazed directly into the camera, I knew that she was looking into a future that was already over, with shadows like gun smoke folded into the glossy black-and-white. I needed a voice speaking in her present, not one whispering to posterity, a voice animated by the desire to capture the present for someone alive. *That* is the voice I heard in the letters. When I read them, I got to know her—for the first time, really—know her and miss her. Miss *her,* not some made-up idea of her. The pain, which had been nothing more than a dull throb, changed in character, becoming softer, more diffuse, and ardent like heartache.

"They each held on to my hands," my mother wrote, describing our triumphal exit from the airport at LaGuardia. "They kept talking to me about how happy they were that I was home — and sorta beamed."

Wonder Question: "Could we ever travel to the moon?"

"We know everything we need to know for the planning of such a trip," *The Book of Knowledge* claimed optimistically in 1952. Its writers argue that the first real problem will be creating a rocket with enough thrust to allow a "space-ship" to reach "escape velocity," the speed required to lift the ship beyond the gravity of the earth and let it float, unimpeded, toward the moon. The formula for determining this velocity is too complicated for *The Book of Knowledge* to make clear, so it asks that we accept on faith that by means "of a computation belonging to the realm of higher mathematics," the velocity required for a rocket to rise into space and escape the gravitational pull of the spinning earth is "7 miles per second." Once a rocket can attain that speed, the "earth's gravity is powerless" to pull it down and the rocket can drift into the vast emptiness of silent space, leaving the weight of its earthly burdens behind.

Five years later, the Soviets rocketed a satellite into orbit.

At midnight on the last day of January in 1957, my mother and father woke me to watch *Sputnik 2* cross the dome of the sky, and I don't remember it happening at all. I do remember *Sputnik 1*. We were still living in our house on Caravella Lane in Nanuet, New York, and many from the neighborhood, including my mother and me, had lined up on the dead-end street in front of our houses to see the first satellite propelled into orbit, but the memory of the second satellite is gone.

It was an anxious time internationally, causing Americans, like my mother, to have mixed feelings about the space race. "It is a shame," she wrote, that "the great event of launching a satellite into space has to be overshadowed with the fear that the Russians are a great deal ahead of us scientifically." At the dawn of the nuclear age, she lamented that the Soviets had "perfected the intercontinental missile" and wondered about the ability of America to prevail. "It makes us all realize we have been complacent." Despite these anxieties, she wrote that we were all "very excited" and that *Sputnik 1* was a "spectacular sight."

Sputnik 2 caused a stir because it carried Laika, the dog, but by this time our family had a new set of anxieties to deal with. After seven years of living in New York, we had moved out of our house in Nanuet and were living somewhere near our new house on Warrington Road in Deerfield, Illinois. Construction had been delayed and my parents had not yet moved in, but they were checking on it daily. "This is the finishing work that makes a house a home," my mother wrote. I am sure, with the move, the delay, and the new house, that this was a busy and exhausting time for my father and mother, but I must have pestered my parents to let me see *Sputnik* 2, and they relented. "Steve has been so interested in the satellite that we promised him we would wake him if it did orbit."

In my imagination they both wake me, my mother nudging me quietly while shushing me so as not to wake my brother, my father standing behind her holding my coat. I rub my eyes awake and see their faces glowing in the half-light of the room, my dad waving us toward the bedroom door. Outside it is cold—this is February, north of Chicago—but it must have been clear. The three of us walk into a grassy clearing away from trees and train our eyes on the evening sky.

Dad lights a cigarette for my mother and then for himself, the glow from the match illuminating their faces against the night sky for a moment like two crescent moons. He shakes out the match and takes a long draw, letting the smoke out slowly. My mother fiddles with her cigarette before taking a quick puff, pulling her coat around her. We wait in the cold briefly, me standing between them, my mother pulling me toward her for warmth.

Suddenly it appears. "Over there," my dad says, squinting from the smoke, and we turn to face east. The treeline forms a black horizon, and above it the Milky Way shimmers in the chilly air.

Dad kneels down, pointing up for me to see. The cigarette at the tips of his fingers traces the arc against the sky. My mother sees it too, and putting an arm on my shoulder, she leans forward to be sure that I have found it. I follow my dad's arm to the spot among the stars and locate it at last, not the satellite itself, which is too small, but the casing, a tiny oblong of light, tumbling silently across the constellations nailed into the night sky. It flip-flops in a regular rhythm, like a heartbeat, without glittering, and, despite its size, glows with a white-bright incandescence. In her letters my mother calls this satellite "Muttnik"—a phrase in the press at the time—because of the dog inside, but it is hard to think of a dog now, or anything else, living in this slug of pure light.

I cannot imagine that night sky now without creating metaphors from the time three years later that I hid under the stairs and looked at the nails driven into the treads overhead, that coffin lid of stars that still haunts me as one of the few vivid memories of that time. Thinking of it now, the other memories come flooding back as well. Of me at the top of the stairs watching my mother crying at the kitchen table while my dad stands off to the side. Of me stepping out of my bedroom to see my mother sing "Fever" into the record console with a drink in her hand. No, those thoughts —those precious and horrible clues—don't go away, but they also don't erase that night, lost to memory but captured in a letter that I almost didn't read, when my parents and I, somewhere in Illinois, stood in a darkened field together and looked into the heavens. I picture the tableau now like some illustration out of *The Book of Knowledge,* with me standing in my coat and flanked by my parents, my dad pointing and my mother with an arm around me, while the three of us gaze into the night sky with wonder.

"This is," my mother wrote, "a fabulous age."

Contributors' Notes

MARCIA ALDRICH is the author of the free memoir *Girl Rearing*, part of the Barnes & Noble Discover New Writers Series. She has been the editor of *Fourth Genre: Explorations in Nonfiction*. In 2010 she was the recipient of the Distinguished Professor of the Year Award for the state of Michigan. *Companion to an Untold Story* won the AWP Award in creative nonfiction. She is at work on *Haze,* a narrative of marriage and divorce during her college years.

POE BALLANTINE is getting taller and younger. He plans to one day be a professional skater. He lives on the Howling Plains of Nowhere with his wife, Cristina, and his son, Tom. His latest book is *Love and Terror on the Howling Plains of Nowhere* (2013). As always he wishes to thank the editors of the *Sun* for making him presentable.

CHARLES BAXTER is the author of twelve books of fiction and nonfiction. His most recent collection, *Gryphon: New and Selected Stories,* was published in 2011. His novel *First Light,* from 1987, has just been reissued. He lives in Minneapolis and teaches at the University of Minnesota.

J. D. DANIELS has written for the *Paris Review, n + 1, Oxford American, Agni,* and other magazines. He is the 2013 recipient of the *Paris Review*'s Terry Southern Prize.

BRIAN DOYLE is the author of many books of essays, nonfiction (*The Grail,* about a year in an Oregon vineyard, and *The Wet Engine,* about the "muddles & musics of the heart"), "proems," and fiction, notably the sprawling Oregon novel *Mink River*. His essay collections *Reading in Bed,* about books and writers, and *The Thorny Grace of It* (spiritual matters and conundrums) will be published in the fall of 2013, and his Big Whopping Sea Novel, *The Plover*, will be published in the spring of 2014. He is the editor of *Portland Magazine* at the University of Portland, in Oregon.

DAGOBERTO GILB is the author of *Before the End, After the Beginning* (2011). His previous books include *The Flowers, Gritos, Woodcuts of Women, The Last Known Residence of Mickey Acuña*, and *The Magic of Blood*. His fiction and nonfiction have appeared in a range of magazines, including *The New Yorker, Harper's Magazine, ZYZZYVA*, and *Texas Monthly*, and are reprinted widely. Gilb makes his home in Austin. He is the executive director of CentroVictoria, a center for Mexican American literature and culture at the University of Houston, Victoria, where he is also writer in residence and the founding editor of the new literary magazine *Huizache*.

TOD GOLDBERG is the author of several books of fiction, including the novel *Living Dead Girl*, a finalist for the *Los Angeles Times* Book Prize; the story collection *Other Resort Cities;* and the popular *Burn Notice* series. His essays, journalism, and criticism have appeared in the *Los Angeles Times*, the *Wall Street Journal*, and *Las Vegas CityLife*, among many others, and have earned five Nevada Press Association awards for excellence. He holds an MFA in creative writing and literature from Bennington College and directs the low-residency MFA in creative writing and writing for the performing arts at the University of California, Riverside.

STEVEN HARVEY is the author of three books of personal essays: *A Geometry of Lilies, Lost in Translation*, and *Bound for Shady Grove*. He has also edited an anthology of essays on middle age, written by men, called *In a Dark Wood*. He is a professor of English and creative writing at Young Harris College as well as a founding member of the nonfiction faculty in the Ashland University MFA program in creative writing. He lives in the north Georgia mountains.

WILLIAM MELVIN KELLEY is the author of three novels—the award-winning *A Different Drummer, A Drop of Patience*, and *Dunfords Travels Everywheres*—and a short story collection, *Dancers on the Shore*. In 2008 he won the Anisfield-Wolf Book Award for Lifetime Achievement. He has taught creative writing at Sarah Lawrence College since 1989. He lives with his family in Harlem and has recently completed his fourth novel, *Dis/Integration*.

JON KERSTETTER completed three combat tours in Iraq as an army physician and flight surgeon. He earned an MD degree at the Mayo Medical School, an MS in business from the University of Utah, and an MFA in

creative nonfiction from Ashland University. Dr. Kerstetter's medical career included practice in emergency and military medicine, disaster relief,
and education in emergency medicine in Rwanda, Bosnia, Kosovo, and
Honduras. He was the in-country director of the Johns Hopkins training
program in emergency medicine at the University of Phristina in Kosovo.
He retired from medical practice and the military in 2009 and resides in
Iowa City with his wife.

WALTER KIRN is the national correspondent for the *New Republic*. He is
the author of several novels, including *Thumbsucker* and *Up in the Air*, which
were made into feature films. His most recent book is a memoir of his education, *Lost in the Meritocracy*. He lives in Montana and California.

MICHELLE MIRSKY lives and writes in Austin, Texas, where she also works
an earnest nine-to-five job, kind of like a superhero with a secret identity.
Only not super. Or secret. She was the winner of the grand prize in the
2011 *McSweeney's* column contest. Her essays have appeared in *McSweeney's*
and in print.

ANDER MONSON is the author of, most recently, *Letter to a Future Lover*
(forthcoming in 2015), short essays on six-by-nine-inch cards written in
and on libraries and things found in libraries and thereafter published
back into the spaces where they originated, and eventually collected, un-
ordered, into a box, which he supposes is a book, since it is after all bound
and collected there.

ANGELA MORALES'S most recent essays have appeared in the *Harvard
Review*, the *Baltimore Review*, the *Southern Review*, and *River Teeth*. She holds
an MFA in nonfiction writing from the University of Iowa. Currently she
teaches English at Glendale Community College and is working on a collection of autobiographical essays.

ALICE MUNRO is the author of *Dear Life: Stories*. Her recent collections
include *The View from Castle Rock* and *Too Much Happiness*. In 2009 she was
awarded the Man Booker International Prize.

EILEEN POLLACK'S most recent novel, *Breaking and Entering*, was awarded
the 2012 Grub Street National Book Prize and named a *New York Times*
Editors' Choice selection. She is also the author of *Paradise, New York* (a
novel) and two collections of short fiction, *In the Mouth* and *The Rabbi in the
Attic*, as well as a work of creative nonfiction called *Woman Walking Ahead:
In Search of Catherine Weldon and Sitting Bull* and two innovative textbooks,
Creative Nonfiction and *Creative Composition*. "Pigeons" is an excerpt from

her memoir in progress, *Approaching Infinity*. She teaches in the MFA program at the University of Michigan.

KEVIN SAMPSELL is the author of the memoir *A Common Pornography* (2010) and the novel *This Is Between Us* (2013). His essays and fiction have appeared in *Nerve, Hobart,* the *Good Men Project,* the *Rumpus,* the *Fairy Tale Review, NANO Fiction,* the Associated Press, and elsewhere. He lives in Portland, Oregon, with his wife and son.

RICHARD SCHMITT is the author of *The Aerialist,* a novel (2001), and has published in the *Cimarron Review,* the *Gettysburg Review, Gulf Coast, Puerto del Sol,* and other places. His story "Leaving Venice, Florida," won first prize in the *Mississippi Review* short story contest and was anthologized in *New Stories of the South: The Year's Best 1999.* Schmitt has been nominated for multiple Pushcart Prizes and was the recipient of a National Endowment for the Arts grant in 2002.

DAVID SEARCY lives in Dallas, Texas. His first collection of essays, *Shame and Wonder,* will be published in 2014.

ZADIE SMITH is the author of four novels, *White Teeth* (2000), *The Autograph Man* (2002), *On Beauty* (2005), which won the Orange Prize for Fiction, and *NW* (2012). She is also the author of *Changing My Mind: Occasional Essays* (2009) and the editor of a story collection, *The Book of Other People* (2007). She has taught creative writing at New York University since 2010.

MEGAN STIELSTRA is the literary director of 2nd Story, a personal narrative performance series dedicated to bringing people together through story. She has told stories for all sorts of theaters, festivals, and bars, including the Goodman, Steppenwolf, Museum of Contemporary Art, Chicago Poetry Center, Story Week, Wordstock, Neo-Futurarium, and Chicago Public Radio. Her story collection, *Everyone Remain Calm,* was a *Chicago Tribune* Favorite of 2011, and her writing has appeared in the *Rumpus, Pank, Other Voices, f Magazine, Make Magazine,* the *Nervous Breakdown, Swink,* and elsewhere. She teaches creative writing and performance at Columbia College Chicago and the University of Chicago, and her debut essay collection is forthcoming in spring 2014.

JOHN JEREMIAH SULLIVAN is a contributing writer for the *New York Times Magazine* and the southern editor of the *Paris Review.* He writes for *GQ, Harper's Magazine,* and *Oxford American* and is the author of *Blood Horses* and *Pulphead*, a 2011 National Book Critics Circle Award nominee. Sullivan lives in Wilmington, North Carolina.

VANESSA VESELKA is the author of the novel *Zazen*, which won the 2012 PEN/Robert W. Bingham Prize for fiction. Her short stories have appeared in *Tin House* and *ZYZZYVA*, and her nonfiction is found in *GQ*, the *Atlantic*, the *American Reader*, and *Salon.com*. She has also been, at times, a teenage runaway, a union organizer, a student of paleontology, a train-hopper, a waitress, and a mother.

MATTHEW VOLLMER is the author of *Future Missionaries of America*, a collection of stories, and *Inscriptions for Headstones*, a collection of essays, each crafted as an epitaph and each unfolding in a single sentence. With David Shields, he is coeditor of *Fakes: An Anthology of Pseudo-Interviews, Faux-Lectures, Quasi-Letters, "Found" Texts, and Other Fraudulent Artifacts*. His work has appeared in a variety of literary magazines, including the *Paris Review*, *Glimmer Train*, *Tin House*, *Virginia Quarterly Review*, *Epoch*, *Ecotone*, *New England Review*, *elimae*, *DIAGRAM*, the *Normal School*, the *Carolina Quarterly*, *Oxford American*, and the *Sun*. A recent winner of an NEA fellowship, he is an assistant professor at Virginia Tech, where he directs the undergraduate creative writing program.

Although she is "originally from" Shanghai, VICKI WEIQI YANG currently resides in Chicago's Hyde Park neighborhood, where she studies political science at the University of Chicago. Her research interests include structures of governance, political theory, and security in East Asia. She has yet to muster the mettle required to call herself a writer, so she prefers the term *student*.

MAKO YOSHIKAWA is currently at work on a memoir about her father. She is the author of the novels *One Hundred and One Ways* and *Once Removed*. Her work has been translated into six languages; awards for her writing include a Radcliffe Fellowship. As a literary critic she has published articles that explore the relationship between incest and race in twentieth-century American fiction. Her essays have appeared in the *Missouri Review* and the *Southern Indiana Review*. She is a professor of creative writing at Emerson College, Boston.

Notable Essays of 2012

Selected by Robert Atwan

MAUREEN McCoy
Brother Joseph, *Wapsipinicon Almanac*, no. 19.

THOMAS McGONIGLE
Then, *Notre Dame Review*, Summer/Fall.

MICHAEL McGREGOR
A Gyroscope on the Island of Love, *Image*, no. 70.

JOHN McPHEE
Editors & Publisher, *The New Yorker*, July 2.

DANIEL MENDELSOHN
Unsinkable, *The New Yorker*, April 16.

DAPHNE MERKIN
We're All Helmut Newton Now, *Elle*, October.

CLAIRE MESSUD
The Road to Damascus, *Granta*, Winter.

KIMBERLY MEYER
Demeter and Persephone in the Heartland, *Kenyon Review*, Fall.

CAROLYN MILLER
Arts and Science, *Missouri Review*, Fall.

DAVID MILLER
The Four Seasons Mini Almanac, *Wapsipinicon Almanac*, no. 19.

SAM J. MILLER
The Luke Letters, *Upstreet*, no. 8.

TONI MIROSEVICH
This Once Bright Thing, *Hayden's Ferry Review*, no. 51.

DEBRA MONROE
Gray Area, *Guernica*, April 1.

AMY MONTICELLO
The Other Woman, *Iron Horse Literary Review*, vol. 14, no. 3.

DINTY W. MOORE
Buried Alive, *Zone 3*, Fall.

COREY MORRIS
Carp River, *Crab Orchard Review*, Summer/Fall.

SANDELL MORSE
Hiding, *Ascent*, August 12.

SCOTT NADELSON
I'm Your Man, *Iron Horse Literary Review*, vol. 14, no. 1.

ALEXIS NELSON
On Love and Memory, *Normal School*, Spring.

JACOB NEWBERRY
French Suite, *Hunger Mountain*, no. 17.
Summer, *Granta*, Winter.

ROB NIXON
Baboon, *Sycamore Review*, Winter/Spring.

NANCY NORDENSON
Prelude, *Lake Effect*, Spring.

MARK O'CONNOR
Holy Ghosts, *Massachusetts Review*, Winter.

SARAH A. ODISHOO
Eat Me: Instructions from the Unseen, *Zone 3*, Spring.

ARIKA OKRENT
Body Language, *Lapham's Quarterly*, Spring.

BRIAN OLIU
Friday the 13th, *Los Angeles Review*, Fall.

W. SCOTT OLSEN
Tag, *Tampa Review*, nos. 43 & 44.

RICHARD O'MARA
Brothers, *Sewanee Review*, Summer.

MARK OPPENHEIMER
Who Needs Poetry?, *New York Times Magazine*, September 16.

PETER ORNER
Renters, *Fifth Wednesday*, Spring.

LAUREN C. OSTBERG
On Hair, *So to Speak*, Spring.

DAVID OWEN
Scars, *The New Yorker*, March 19.

ADRIANA PARAMO
Oil Spills Remind Me of Him, *Compass Rose*, vol. 12.

JESSICA WILBANKS
Father of Disorder, *Ruminate,*
no. 24, Summer.
JOE WILKINS
Eleven Kinds of Sky, *Orion,*
January/February.
BROOKE WILLIAMS
Moving Stones, *High Desert
Journal,* Fall.
C. K. WILLIAMS
On Being Old, *American Poetry
Review,* July/August.
FRANK WILSON
Time Crystals, *Boulevard,* Fall.
JASON WILSON
Food for Thought, *Washington
Post Magazine,* September 16.
CHRISTIAN WIMAN
Mortify Our Wolves, *American
Scholar,* Autumn.
SHERRY WONG
Dandelion, *Prism,* Fall.
ERIN WOOD
We Scar, We Heal, We Rise,
Anderbo, n.d.

STEPHANIE WORTMAN
Greens, *Southwest Review,* vol. 97,
no. 3.

ROLF ALBERT YNGVE
Three Tips for Those Returning
from Deployments: A Memoir,
War, Literature, and the Arts,
no. 24.
NINA YUN
Kimchee, *Fourth Genre,* Fall.

VICTOR ZAPANA
Shaken, *The New Yorker,*
November 26.
ARIANNE ZWARTJES
This Suturing of Wounds or
Words, *Gulf Coast,* Winter/
Spring.
JESSE ZWICK
Up in the Air, *New Republic,*
July 12.

Notable Special Issues of 2012

American Letters & Commentary,
The Future of the Book, eds.
Catherine Kasper and David Ray
Vance, no. 23.
Antioch Review, Intimate Memoirs, ed.
Robert S. Fogarty, Winter.
Atrium, Graphic, guest eds.
Catherine Belling and MK
Czerwiec, Spring.
The Baffler, The High, the Low, the
Vibrant!, ed. John Summers,
no. 20.
Chattahoochee Review, Ireland, ed.
Anna Schachner, Fall/Winter.
Chautauqua, War & Peace, ed. Diana
Hume George, no. 9.
Conjunctions, Riveted: The Obsession
Issue, ed. Brad Morrow, no. 58.
Georgia Review, Georgia Writers Hall
of Fame, ed. Stephen Corey,
Summer.

Hobart, Luck, ed. Aaron Burch,
no. 13.
Hunger Mountain, Labyrinths, ed.
Miciah Bay Gault, no. 17.
Image, The Word-Soaked World, ed.
Gregory Wolfe, no. 75.
Lapham's Quarterly, Magic Shows, ed.
Lewis Lapham, Summer.
Mamalode, Capacity, ed. Elke
Govertsen, Winter.
Manoa, Almost Heaven, ed. Frank
Stewart, vol. 23, no. 2.
New Criterion, Hilton Kramer, 1928–
2012, ed. Roger Kimball, May.
New Letters, Resilience and Art, ed.
Robert Stewart, vol. 78, nos. 3
& 4.
Normal School, Film and Music
Spectacular, eds. Sophie Beck,
Steven Church, and Matt
Roberts, Fall.

Notre Dame Review, Memes and
  Memories, ed. William O'Rourke,
  Summer/Fall.
Pen America, Teachers, ed. M Mark,
  no. 16.
Ploughshares, Truth: All-Essay Issue,
  ed. Patricia Hampl, Fall.
River Styx, End of the World, ed.
  Richard Newman, no. 88.
Sewanee Review, Bound by the Cause
  of Words, ed. George Core, Fall.

Slice, Growing Up, ed. Elizabeth
  Blachman, Spring/Summer.
Texas Monthly, How to Raise a Texan,
  ed. Jake Silverstein, September.
Tin House, Science Fair, ed. Rob
  Spillman, no. 51.
Witness, Special Issue: Disaster, ed.
  Amber Withycombe, vol. 25,
  no. 1, Spring.